Baron Harvest

Peter Lind

JD Publishing
A Jensen Development Company

BARON HARVEST
Published by JD Publishing

© 2004 by Peter Lind
International Standard Book Number 0-9760617-0-8

Cover Image and Design by William Bushell

Printed in the United States of America
ALL RIGHTS RESERVED

For information:
JD PUBLISHING • PO BOX 20095 KEIZER, OR 97303

Library of Congress Cataloging-in-Publication Data:

Lind, Peter
    Baron Harvest/by Peter Lind
    ISBN: 0-9760617-0-8

Library of Congress Control Number: 2004111617

DO NOT PLANT TWO KINDS OF
SEED IN YOUR VINEYARD; IF YOU
DO, NOT ONLY THE CROPS YOU
PLANT BUT ALSO THE FRUIT OF
THE VINEYARD WILL BE DEFILED

DEUTERONOMY 22:9

CHAPTER 1

Elliott Chapman sat in President David Whitman's waiting room pulling leaves off the ficus tree. He tossed them on the floor as he stared at the bell-shaped graph for the hundredth time. He dropped the last leaf of the branch onto the small pile of flora at his feet, and slid his green finger along plotline D, the only line that continued rising above the curve. His finger moved off the graph and made a green smudge on his khakis as the page slid off his lap and floated to the floor. He sat back in the chair, tipped his heavy head against the wall, and looked across the room at the painting of snow-covered Mount Hood. He had assured his friends that he could dash his senior project out in a short weekend. Now it was due in two weeks or he would not graduate.

Every day for the past four years at Royce University, Elliott had had thoughts and ideas that strayed through his mind, and they had nothing to do with being on task at school. He should have been focusing on his courses like everyone else, but he passed them all happily unconscious. All he really aspired to do was raise the eyebrows of Dr. Quinton Kingsley, the illustrious biochemistry professor—an overwhelming challenge and feat he finally admitted he could not achieve. The fact was now firmly established that Dr. Kingsley's eyebrows would not be raised for anyone, even if God Almighty commanded it.

But for the past three weeks, Elliott's senior project had driven away any delusions he'd had about Dr. Kingsley, and he became so focused and determined to conquer his project that now the problem seemed almost incapable of having a mortal solution. And since he could not quite accept this reality yet, he turned the project into an obsessive pursuit.

According to his friends the problem was simple, simple. All he had to do was look at data that came across the Internet and plot the points on a graph. Once the entire project was plotted, he had to write up a discussion, sign it, and turn it in to Dr. Kingsley. It was a biostatistics problem that amounted to determining how certain genetically altered foods affect groups of people. Magalto, the bioengineering company sponsoring the project, wanted to know what food crops caused health problems, so they could fix the engineered seeds before they were mass-produced.

Elliott knew the variables only by alphabet. Daily, he trekked to the lab, pulled up the data, and made correlations based on the groups of people, type of food ingested, and the therapeutic approaches taken. The results came in as expected. All except D. The line for variable D continued rising exponentially on the Y-axis. This deviation consumed his waking thoughts.

Across the waiting room, inside President Whitman's private office, sat Dr. Kingsley. For the past twenty minutes he had spouted his grievances to President Whitman about Elliott Chapman and the project he held hostage. As President Whitman took his slow and careful time to look over the latest graph, Dr. Kingsley had a few moments to ponder why he ever had chosen Elliott to perform the time-intensive genetic project in the first place. The most annoying thing about Elliott was that he expressed the most absurd ideas out loud in class so they seemed normal and ordinary, when in fact Elliott himself, knew they weren't. Then, right on cue, a back row classmate would enter into the argument, and in no time the entire class was involved in a lively discussion—about nothing. These shenanigans were a complete waste of valuable classroom time, and worse, a testament to the professor's lack of intellectual control in his upper level classes.

A project like this would give the kid busywork, and enough stress to keep him occupied for an entire semester. But what Dr. Kingsley found most advantageous was that Elliott's natural laziness would keep him from digging too deep into the underpinnings of the project. No one needed to know the details. Dr. Kingsley would handle the details himself, just as soon as Elliott handed it over to him. Then, the magnificent data and statistics would be exchanged for everything an esteemed professor at Royce University could imagine: millions of dollars from Magalto, the sponsor of the study, Federal scholarship money from the National Scientific Merit Scholarship Foundation, and most importantly for Dr. Kingsley, a cover article and complete outlay in the prestigious *Cambridge Science Review*. The more he thought about it the giddier he became, as he fantasized over the completed project even before he had seen the results. Most recently, he fancied himself standing at the podium of the World Science Federation, accepting accolades and being crowned a hero in front of thousands of jealous academic colleagues. He found ample room in his humble self to fill with visions of prestige and respect that worldwide scholars would certainly shower on him. But today, all notorieties were far from his mind because of the complete neglect of that delinquent student, Elliott Chapman.

President David Whitman listened from across his desk to Dr. Kingsley continue on and on with his grievances about the kid. Although he appeared somewhat academically interested, nodding at a point or two Dr. Kingsley made, his own dream was about all the places at Royce University he was going to spend the money. Somehow Dr. Kingsley would get the project finished. He always did. All President Whitman had to do was get the two of them through graduation ceremonies in two weeks, before they were at each other's throats, and the matter of the tardy project would naturally be resolved. He was the president, and good presidents found peace at all levels of inter-personal conflicts. His faculty and students always got their work done somehow, and in this particular case, he would personally see to it that they would.

Dr. Kingsley took off his square-framed glasses and finger-combed his dark eyebrows a few strokes. He laid his glasses on the corner of the desk and looked up at President Whitman, who seemed to be somewhere else.

"Did you hear what I just said, David? I said he's supposed to have the latest numbers plotted"—Kingsley leaned forward, looked at the graph lying on the desk and jabbed his finger on it two times—"right here. This is not difficult." He sat back but held his finger on the page.

Whitman rolled his eyes and pulled the graph out from under Kingsley's finger. "Yes, I heard what you said. But all we need is for line D to merge into the bell with the others, right Quinton? You can't ask him to turn it in before he's finished. He told me last time that the new data should lower the graph height. Then he'll write it up. It's just a matter of time."

Kingsley narrowed his eyes and tried to smile. "But that's what I'm telling you. I don't have the time. I should never have chosen Elliott to do this. He's had all year and now here it is, two weeks before graduation, and I don't have a thing ready to submit." He moved forward in his chair and said, "I can't wait for him any longer, David. I'm going to have to find someone who can write a few words about engineering and be willing to sign their name to it. I can do the final going-over late tonight."

Whitman sat back in his tall chair. He leisurely took the glasses from his thick face and pointed them at Kingsley. "We can't do that now. Elliott's too far along to let anyone else sign it for completion. Now I don't know if he's stalling until the final hour, or if he really is waiting for the numbers, but it seems to me that you're pushing him too hard. If he senses that, he won't do it at all. He has two weeks."

Kingsley bolted upright. "No, he doesn't! This is due today! He's supposed to have all the numbers in and signed—today. I only have ten days to submit it to the journal. If that doesn't happen, the report won't be published, and Magalto won't pay us a dime. I'm working on a deadline here, David!"

"Elliott is fixed on this, and you better believe he'll make it perfect for you before he turns it in, you should know that. He just needs a little more time—or help. Why don't you help him? Have you even con*sidered* that?"

"I don't have time to help him. I teach class, you know, and I have a few hundred other projects and papers to evaluate."

"Yes, but you're his advisor. You could give him a hand."

"He doesn't need a hand."

"So—what? What are you going to do?" Whitman put his glasses back on and looked directly at Kingsley. He knew that if Kingsley was pushed too far, he would become as stubborn as Elliott, and might go on to do something they both would regret. The professor and student were too much alike. Whitman couldn't suggest an obvious solution for Kingsley, but he couldn't let him handle this on his own, either, without a little presidential involvement. Whitman had to make it appear that the resolution to this delayed project was the brainchild of each of them. That was his goal, however dull it might appear to anyone else.

"I need the numbers and at this point, I don't care how I get them." Kingsley turned to the wall and looked at Whitman's elaborate bookshelf for a moment. It was tidy. There were biographies and history books, philosophy texts and business books. There were even a few books written by alumni. And between the rows of these rarely opened books, perched the trophies won by the science students, the tangible rewards for making smart scientists. This was Dr. Kingsley's passion to a fault: creating protégée's in his own image, and watching them breed his ideas about science and biology. He turned back with a rare, forced grin on his elegant, scholarly face. "Actually, all I need is his signature on his report for publication. *I'll* get the figures myself."

"Now you're being irrational, Quinton. That is not how we're going to do it this time."

President Whitman looked down at the graph lying on his desk. It was wrinkled and had Kingsley's coffee stains on it. This graph, along with the report, would certainly put Royce University on the highbrow in Portland, Oregon. The abstract had already been accepted for publication in the prestigious *Cambridge Science Review*, and that made Kingsley proud beyond normal. But the money, the glorious money, was coming from Magalto, the biotechnology company that had chosen Royce to do independent research for its global products. This time, it was millions.

Whitman rolled the paper into a tube and tapped it on his desk. "Well, tell him to come in and let's the three of us get this figured out"—Kingsley stood before he was finished and Whitman followed him with his eyes—"but I want you to go easy on him this time, Quinton. He'll get the numbers and sign it, just like he's supposed to. I'll make sure of it. You can spare a few more days."

Kingsley did pad the projects with extra time, because someone, usually someone irresponsible, would come up with an astonishing story about their project being stolen by aliens from a friendly planet who were going to 'borrow' it for a few days, and finally get it back minus the references. He'd heard all the excuses, and still thought he could change the juvenile trend by being strict with time constraints. But with Elliott Chapman it was useless. The kid could always come up with a plausible explanation and someone to verify it, even if it meant that an alien did show up in class, and give riveting testimony to the fact that a certain assignment was indeed missing.

Kingsley reached the door. He opened it and looked at Elliott asleep in the chair: the most willing student to do this project for him, and now the only one who so suddenly became self-absorbed enough to try to find meaning in it. Why this time?

"What the hell are those leaves doing all over the floor?" Kingsley walked toward the stripped tree and looked down at the spoilage with his hands planted on his hips.

Elliott opened his eyes, bolted forward in the chair, and grabbed the graph off the floor. "Quinton! Quinton, I was going to tell you! I got the greatest rejection letter today. It was the practice application I filled out in September, the one with your name on it and my recommendation of you. You won't believe it—you were rejected from Johns Hopkins!"

"It's *Dr. Kingsley*," he said raising his voice, "and I told you not to send that mock application. It was for you to practice on."

"Yeah, but Dr. Kingsley, I mailed it to them and you know what happened? You were right. The only difference between this application and all the others was the name and recommendation. Everything else was the same—the same! You said so, and I didn't believe it. It was your recommendation that got me in. I've been accepted to four med schools, and you haven't been to any of 'em—all because of your recommendation."

"I don't have to go to med school. I don't need another degree. But you don't have one and you won't until you graduate. Don't get ahead of yourself, Chapman." Kingsley reached for the paper Elliott held. "Is that it? Is that the letter? Let me see it."

Elliott pulled it back. "No, this isn't it. It's hanging up in my room, right next to your picture."

"My picture? I told you to take that down."

"I can't take it down, Dr. Kingsley. It inspires me."

Kingsley shook his head.

"I can show you your rejection letter Monday, if you want to see it."

Kingsley straightened. "No. I don't want to see it. Is that the new graph?"

Elliott looked down at the paper. "Yeah, the graph."

"Well bring it in. Let's see what kind of improvements you have." Kingsley turned partway and stopped. "What *are* those leaves doing on the floor?"

Elliott stood with stooped shoulders and looked down at them. "I dunno. Plant's probably dying of psychological terrorism here in this place."

"Plants don't have feelings!" Kingsley whipped around and went into Whitman's office.

Elliott scooped up the leaves with the paper, slid them into the planter, and followed Kingsley into Whitman's office one more time. This was becoming a habit. If he didn't have to sit in all these offices all the time, he might be able to get some work done.

"Hello, Elliott," Whitman said gently, looking up at him with a smile. He pointed to the chair next to Kingsley. "Come in and have a seat. Thanks for waiting."

"Hello, Dr. Whitman. No problem." Elliott smiled at him and brushed a few blond strands of hair off his forehead with green fingers. "I was just on my way to the lab. I'll probably be there all evening. Again." He flashed a smile at Kingsley.

Kingsley rolled his eyes and shook his head at him.

Whitman bore an angry look into Kingsley and turned to Elliott with a smile. "Well, we've been going over and over this thing, Elliott."

"Oh, that's great." Elliott sat in the chair, looking up at Whitman. "I think I'm getting closer. It seems to me that there's some kind of contaminate in D. I don't know what else it could be. And if that's the case, then there's something seriously wrong with that crop yield. You can't get numbers like this without some kind of contamination somewhere." He spread his wrinkled, green-smudged paper across his lap and looked down at the graph.

"Well, when can we expect you to finish it?" Whitman asked.

Elliott looked up at him. "It's not due for another two weeks. I think I can have the analysis and discussion finished by then. It really depends on the numbers that come in . . . "

"That is totally unacceptable!" Kingsley said quickly, furrowing his brow. "Your job is to plot the damn data, not make one of your theoretical opinions about it. That's all I want you to do. You spend too much time trying to figure out things you shouldn't. And, you're supposed to have it finished two weeks *before* graduation. That's today!"

"You never said that. All you said was that it needs to be in before graduation."

"Oh, no I didn't. I never said that. How do you think you're going to be graded? Everyone else is finished, and most have gone through critique. You know, critique—it's required." Kingsley took off his glasses and rubbed his eyes with his fingertips. "You know Chapman, you've given me more stress this year than everyone else put together over the last four years."

"Well, I'm sorry. You're my advisor. You've either given me too much advice, or not enough."

"Oh, come on," Kingsley snapped. "You've never once listened to my advice."

"I've told you more than once not to waste it on me."

"Look, Elliott," Whitman began softly. "I know you've been working hard on your project, but you're just going to have to sign off on it." He looked at Kingsley, nodded, and asked, "Isn't that what you want, Dr. Kingsley, for him to finish it where he is?"

"That's exactly what I want." Kingsley turned to Elliott. "You're waiting for the perfect numbers to come in so you can be a hero. Well, you're laboratory prowess isn't going to help you this time. If you don't get this finished, you're going to fail the project."

"Fail the project?" Elliott hesitated and looked at Whitman.

"Yes!" Kingsley bleated. "That's what this is all about. Your senior project has to be finished or you don't graduate from this university."

Elliott turned back to Kingsley. "Then I have a question about that. What if I skip my classes and work in the lab until I'm done?"

"You can't do that," Kingsley said, shaking his head.

"Why not?"

"Because you're supposed to be in class!"

"Most of my classes are a waste of time, including yours. I mean, what I mean is, I just read the class notes at the end of the week, anyways. You should be happy I'm keeping up."

The groove in Kingsley's brow deepened and he spoke loudly, "Any classes you skip from here on out you *fail*, I'll make sure of it, whether it's mine or anyone else's. Don't mess with me, Chapman."

Elliott looked to Whitman for help. Whitman shook his head gently and said in a grandfatherly way, "I'm sorry Elliott. You need to cut your losses on this project."

"But, Dr. Whitman! You can't expect me to turn this in when line D is so high. It doesn't make any sense. It isn't anything like the abstract we submitted. I'm hoping it will come down next week, and when it does, I'm going to write an accurate summary. I don't want this published just on Dr. Kingsley's recommendation this time."

Kingsley shook his head. "My recommendation has nothing to do with this. This submission is to the *Cambridge Review* and will win the National Scientific Merit Scholarship. It has to be completed by a student. And let me remind you, the money funds yours and half of your classmates' scholarships."

"Well then, I want to be accurate."

"Your accuracy has nothing to do with this. If you'd been in my class, you'd know that very few, if any, articles published in the journals are scientifically sound anyway. I'm not asking you to be accurate. I just want it finished."

"*British Medical Journal*, 1991, page 798."

"What?"

Elliott shrugged his shoulders. "That statistic was a question on your second test. Not only that, but less than fifteen percent of all medical interventions are supported by any scientific evidence. You assigned some extra credit. Some point of yours about ancient history still being relevant."

"Well, you barely passed."

"I got an 'A.'"

Kingsley glanced at a smiling Whitman, who gave him a nod. He said to Elliott, "All right then, here's the deal: I want your senior report on my desk, signed, in three days. That will give you enough time to put a short summary together, if you must. And you don't have to worry about the critique. As soon as it reaches my desk, you pass. I'm doing you a favor I hope you realize."

Elliott looked down at the desk and picked up a photograph of President Whitman playing catch with his grandson. It reminded him of the only picture taken of him as a child, rolling a ball to his father, but left the dull memory that no one rolled it back. He fingered it like he could bring it to life, or at least rub it for a little advice in the midst of his elders.

Whitman took the picture from him, placed it facedown on his desk, and said, "If Dr. Kingsley doesn't get your entire report in three days, you won't be graduating. And if you break our contract, you *will* repay your scholarships. That's the agreement you made with the university. No projects, no scholarships. I don't believe your parents are in any position to repay even a fraction of your tuition."

"Grandparents."

"Oh, I'm sorry. Yes, your grandparents." Whitman slid the paper across the desk. "Now, I suggest you take this and finish it up as we have suggested."

"I have my own copy." Elliott took his green-stained graph and walked out of the room.

Elliott picked up his pace as he walked to the Rothman Science Center. Up ahead, in the middle of the sidewalk, Kelly Landis stood in the center of a group of students, engaging them in some vaguely recognizable discussion he tried to ignore as he slipped by.

Kelly Landis. Everything about her made a statement. Loose T-shirts hung heavy on her thin frame, broadcasting social messages on both sides. Her baggy pants had big pockets that held any tidbit she might need during the day: organic carrots, bottled spring water, at least one bag of dried tofu. Her sandy blond hair was straight, when it was combed. No make up, no fuss. She was quick to get ready in the morning and didn't worry about her appearance during the day. She could be pretty.

From the beginning, Kelly fought for a cause. She hugged trees in the forest, returned stranded starfish to the ocean, and every month slapped another *FREE TIBET* sticker on her old Volkswagen. She was an Environmental Science major and after graduating, she was going to Willamette University to complete a law degree. She called herself an enviropolitician, and was determined to put the right back into righteous, whatever that happened to be at the moment.

"Hey, Chap. Where you going?" a male voice called out as he passed, disrupting the lecture of the day.

"Rothman," Elliott said, looking over at the group.

The guy poked his head around Kelly. "Jeez, man, you even know where it is?"

"Yeah, very funny, know where it is. I live there. It's my new home."

"What—it's your project, isn't it? You're not finished!"

"Close. An hour. Maybe two."

"Want me to write it up for you? Hey, I can add a tight reference page I found a month ago. Did I tell you about it? It's a killer. I use it on all my papers now."

Elliott stopped. Any time someone came up with a new angle, Elliott had to find out about it. Not that he would use it necessarily, but a student at Royce could never know when something as valuable as a reference page, the likes of a term paper or leaked final exam, would come in handy.

"What's it about?"

The guy stood tall with his hands in his pockets and beamed. "General relativity, materialism of ethers, and polymerization of organic compounds, mostly."

Elliott looked hard at him. "What does that have to do with anything?"

"That's just the point"—he let out a howl—"absolutely nothing or absolutely everything! There's not a professor anywhere who'd ever figure it out."

"Kingsley would. Forget it. You'd probably spell my name wrong, anyways." The two females snickered.

"No, really. I promise I'll spell your name right."

"Nah, don't think so."

"Is Dr. Kingsley still giving you a hard time about it?" Kelly abruptly ended her lecture to the group, leaving them helpless to discuss their own issues, which she would have liked, or free to leave, which they did quickly, and walked up to Elliott. "What are you wearing that for? You never wear a shirt you have to button." She looked him up and down and said with a smile, "You're trying to dress up, aren't you?"

Elliott looked down at his wrinkled, white long-sleeved shirt that hung outside of his khakis. "Yes, as a matter of fact, I dressed up for a meeting with Whitman. I thought he was going to ask me to teach this summer."

"Well"—she slapped him with an open hand on his chest—"you can't be dressing like someone you're not. It wouldn't be like you. Besides, do you really think he'd let you do that?"

"Why not? I've been teaching for Old Furrowed Brow most of the year."

"You should stop calling him that, Elliott. Dr. Kingsley does the best he can and you give him such a hard time every chance you get." Kelly planted her hands on her hips as she stopped her train of thought. She stared at his head. "Did you loose your brush? Your hair looks like you lost your brush."

"No. I don't even have a brush. I have a comb."

"Well, you didn't use it, did you? You went into Whitman's office and didn't even use your comb."

"I never use my comb. It just sits on the dresser, waiting until I need to look good some day."

"Someday." Kelly shook her head. "Your days with all your messy hair are gone, and you don't even know it. Comb your hair, Elliott, and you might find what you're looking for.

As it is, you're going through life and all you have is messy hair to show for it."

"Don't lecture me, Kelly. I've had enough for one day."

She dropped a hand from her hip. "Why, what's wrong *now*?"

"He wants me to finish my project in three days."

"Whitman? Why's he involved in your project?"

"I don't know. But now they're both on my back. Kingsley *and* Whitman." Elliott began walking. "Kingsley was in there yelling at me again."

Kelly walked beside him. "Kingsley was there too?"

"Yeah. He assigns me this project and he's never once checked with me about it. He doesn't even care if it comes out right. All he wants is the data."

"Kingsley? Of course he cares. He probably thinks you'll sail right through it. He likes you, Elliott. It's just difficult for him to show it. Feelings are difficult to show for people like him."

"Reptiles don't have feelings. No, he doesn't like me. All he cares about is this dumb project and his place behind the lectern."

"Well, then, just finish it. Why do you have to put it off like this?"

Elliott stopped in front of the Rothman doors and turned to her. "It's my *project*! I've been working hard on it, whether you believe me or not, and I'm not going to write it up when I don't understand what's causing this problem."

"So you're going to wait for one of your green alien friends to show up in class again and hand over your data on a silver platter? Ah, Elliott, just get it over with." Kelly shook her head.

"I'm waiting for my last plot line to come down. Is that so difficult? It'll probably come in next week sometime. Maybe even this weekend."

"Well don't wait until Whitman's mad at you, too."

"He won't get mad at me. I'm like his grandson he never knew."

"Did Kingsley threaten you?"

Elliott looked at her. "They both said I wouldn't graduate."

Kelly's mouth dropped open. "That's ridiculous, Elliott. Why are you even fighting with them? Is this another one of your stupid jokes?"

"No. This is all I've been doing for the last three weeks."

She stepped right in front of him and pointed her finger at him. "They can fail you. And if your senior project isn't completed by graduation, you're going to have to repay your scholarships. No one else made the deal of the century like you did. Do you really think your grandparents can pay it back? I don't understand you."

"You don't have to. Now, if you'll excuse me, I'm going to the lab." He pulled the door open.

"Well, I'm coming with you." She followed him inside.

CHAPTER 2

Whatever was needed to promote science, education, and research, Royce University bought it. And most of it went into the Rothman Science Center. Electron and confocal microscopes, chromatography units, ultrasounds, and lasers lined each laboratory room and stimulated exciting projects that caused great chatter throughout the academic world. Whether Royce graduates went into medicine, atomic energy, or genetic research, each was trained in the most compelling scientific theories, with the latest equipment, and by the best professors in the country.

This Friday afternoon, Rothman was vacant. Classes were over, and all but a few professors were on the golf course or at a meeting in the administration building. Most of the students were in their dorm rooms or the library, with their heads in books and notes, studying for final exams.

Elliott and Kelly walked down the hall, passing the largest lecture auditorium. This was where they had sat in comfortable seats as unsuspecting freshmen science majors, and got their first jolt of the educational requirements at Royce. Before the first semester had ended their freshman year, a quarter of the class changed their majors to something they really wanted to pursue. Science wasn't their thing after all. Their decision, they would say, had nothing to do with what happened in the auditorium, and certainly had nothing to do with Dr. Quinton Kingsley and his flagrant teaching antics.

The room that the two seniors were most interested in was beyond the auditorium. It was a small research lab where they worked on their projects in secrecy. The room was dark, but the door unlocked. Elliott pushed it open and flipped on the lights. He walked a few steps to the computer station, sat at the chair, and logged on to his account. Several pages scrolled down and the graph appeared.

"Look at this," he said to Kelly.

She leaned over his shoulder, her chin next to his ear.

He moved his head forward, away from her, and pointed to line D on the graph. "It's even higher today! I just don't get it."

Kelly stood up straight and said, "You just have to write it up and call it an anomaly in your summary. You don't have to know why it happened. It's a statistical deviation outside the normal range. Big deal."

"Yeah, but look at this," he said, looking at the monitor. "Three weeks ago, line C went up way above the bell curve, then almost overnight it fell right back inside normal range." He looked up at her. "Why did it go down, and why won't D go down with it?"

"Do you know what D is?"

"No, they're all crops of some sort."

"You don't know what kind?"

"No. It's a blind study. No one's supposed to know."

Kelly smiled at him again. "Then just write it up. You don't have to analyze it to death. You're spending a lot of time getting nowhere."

"Apparently that's all I do these days." Elliott moved forward and looked at the graph. All he could do now was wait helplessly and hope that any new data coming through in the next three days would miraculously put an end to the misery of his senior project. The write-up would take ten minutes and he'd be done with the thing. But as he sat looking at the same skewed data points, he began to think that this entire event was a figment of his imagination. All the voices in his head were asking the same question: was it really possible to complete the project the way he once thought? He began to fear that he had stumbled on to the beginnings of a new psychosis, one that had completely mutated from all conventional illnesses, and it was going to drive him mad because of his own self-indulgent determination. It was only a matter of time before anyone noticed, but the inevitable crack-up was happening.

Kelly had been talking about his delinquencies; he could hear her in the periphery, but it was nothing that required him to respond. He sat, gently tracing the line on the screen with his finger, trying to make it conform.

Kelly said something about her project being a shiny star in the annals of Royce, he heard that much. Then she said something else and with a shake of her head she walked toward a door leading to a small laboratory darkroom. "Have you *seen* mine, I said?" she said forcefully over her shoulder.

"Your project?" Elliott broke from the fog and looked up at her from the screen.

"Yeah," she called back. "Come here and have a look. It'll take your mind off your problems for awhile."

"I thought you were finished." Elliott stood and walked toward her. Anything to change the scenery.

Kelly unlocked the door and slowly pushed it open. He reached inside behind her and flipped on the light switch.

"*Nooo!*" Kelly grabbed at his hand, but instead hit a flask that crashed to the floor. About thirty multicolored worms wriggled in all directions.

"They're different colors!" He bent down and looked closer.

Kelly quickly reached for an empty flask on the countertop and dropped to the floor. She began carefully scooping up the runaway worms and dropping them into the flask. "They're getting away. Give me a hand, will you? Chase that one down over there." She pointed to one darting towards Elliott.

He didn't move.

She looked up at him then hurried to the worm, grabbing it by an end. It wriggled between her fingers and fell to the floor. She picked it up again and made a fist around it. She dropped it in with the others, swiped a stray cork from the tabletop, and pushed it into the neck of the flask.

Elliott looked around the room at the bins of earthworms on the counter.

Kelly stood. "I didn't want you to turn on the ceiling light. I have to use red light now or they get scared. It's too late now." She bent down and rolled the flask gently on its edge, looking with affection at the worms sliding around each other. She rubbed at them on the side of the glass with her index finger.

"Scared? They get scared?" He let out a laugh.

"Well, yeah."

"Sorry, I can't see in red light." Elliott leaned closer and looked at them. "What're you doing now?"

"I've been trying to change their metabolic rates. I should be finished by Tuesday." She turned on the faucet in the sink, uncorked the flask, and ran cold water into the flask. They squirmed and wriggled, floating to the top as the water soaked their dry bodies. She whirled the flask clockwise in an ellipse and the ball of worms converged in the whirlpool. She held her hand over the spinning worms and tipped the flask over, letting the water run out. Two large bright red worms slithered between her fingers. Quickly, she reached into the sink and rescued them before they slid down the pipes to become another urban legend.

"Why are you still working with these? I thought you were finished with your project."

"I was. Apparently one batch of multi-colored insects isn't enough for Old Furrowed Brow. He wouldn't let me turn it in to the critique board, and then he tells me that I have to expand my report by twenty pages or I have to add a few more experiments to verify my premise. Verify my premise. I'll verify my premise. I'm going to give him more worms than he's seen in his life. Next week I'm going to dump them all over his desk and stick my report into one of them. Once I get these figured out. I'm so close."

"Then you're not finished, either."

"Just as well." She shrugged her shoulders.

Elliott leaned down and looked closer. "How did you color them?"

"Color pigments. All the colors are found in similar locations on the chromosome, no matter what the species: tomato, squash, grass. I just cut the gene out and inserted them into these little guys, and they developed into real beauties. Here, look at this one." She pointed to one in the flask.

"It's green *and* red."

"Yeah, that was tricky. The ring around its belly separates the worm into top and bottom halves. It's the natural division for color separation. The green color comes from a grass gene, the red from a tomato."

Elliott shook his head.

Kelly capped the flask, pulled a paper towel from the dispenser, and wiped the worm slime off her hands. It slopped onto the towel as she pulled the strings of gunk off her fingers. She tossed the saturated towel in the garbage, wiped her hands on her pants twice, and picked up the flask. She dangled it in Elliott's face. Elliott backed away.

"Kingsley's really interested in this one, the red one." She pointed to one in the flask. "He wanted this done three weeks ago. He had me tinker with the carbohydrate, protein balance. So finally, after weeks of going to the worm cemetery, I finally adjusted these guys so they are genetically engineered to operate at a high protein metabolic rate. I'll tell ya what, I'm about fed up with worms."

"Yeah, me too."

She looked at him with concern. "Are you bored already?"

"I'm never bored with you around."

She smiled and turned to the counter. "Actually, drosophilae are a little more exciting," she said, pointing to a flask.

"Fruit flies?" he laughed. "Why are you wasting your time with fruit flies?"

"I'm not wasting my time. And you know—time flies like an arrow; fruit flies like bananas."

"Ha, ha."

She smiled, craned her head to look at her brood, and picked up the flask of flies. They flew around inside, some crawling up the glass trying to get out the top. "Yes, you little darlings are doing well today. These are nice because they multiply so fast. The momma has about 400 babies, so every ten days or so, I get more little ones. I can make a modification and see it pass down through its offspring, just like that," she said, snapping her fingers.

"Well, yeah. We did that our first year. Had compound eyeballs all over the place."

She turned again and looked at her colony. "We didn't use this type of fly our first year. These can't reproduce."

"What'd you do, neuter them?"

"No. I've been working with *superoxide dismutase* and getting it pumped into their cells. You know, the enzyme. It seems to add some time to their life cycle, but they become sterilized as a result. These are ancient, in fruit fly terms, but someday I think they will outlive humans." She turned and watched them jump around.

Elliott nodded and leaned forward to watch them fly around, his eyes darting in all directions.

"They're not even geriatric," she said, staring at them. "But there's more promise by extending the telomeres on the ends of their chromosomes. If the telomeres can stay on instead of breaking off all the time, these little guys will live indefinitely."

"You're getting the telomeres to stay on longer?"

"Yeah. The secret is telomerase. It's the enzyme that keeps the telomere growing on the chromosome. As long as telomerase is producing its enzyme, the cells will never stop dividing. I'm very close to coding it into cells of more evolved insects." Kelly rinsed her hands in the sink. "But what I'd really like to do is insert chloroplast into an animal host."

"Chloroplast?"

"Plants make their own energy from the sun by photosynthesis, right? The chloroplast converts sunlight into energy."

"Yeah, but chloroplast is only found in plant cells."

"So why not take it out and insert it into an animal cell?"

"It'd be green."

"So? The animal would be able to make its own energy by photosynthesis. Any extra energy it makes can be transferred into fat cells and used during the wintertime when the sun doesn't shine. The host would never have to eat again. This would solve world hunger."

Elliott looked around the room, pondered a moment, and turned to Kelly. "Very interesting. So you think you can fix the problems of nature and humanity, you and all your animals?"

"Insects. Sure, I'm improving their lives, as well as improving nature around us."

"No you're not. You're going way beyond the bounds of nature. What happens when your guinea pig hosts revolt against the new genes? What happens when your little green animals shut down their cholesterol production? Either cell walls defend gravity, or cholesterol does. You can't have both. How much of what you've already done is irreversible? You're venturing into new territory, Kelly, and destroying the trail you've left behind."

She stopped what she was doing and looked hard at him. "I'm doing *science*. I'm doing things that can't be done in nature. That's what this is all about, in case you decide to work on a real project. You're just upset because you're not finished."

"My project doesn't replace nature."

"I'm not replacing it, Elliott. I'm lending a hand to things that nature can't do."

"Well, things have been going just fine without you."

Kelly shook her head. "You're so delusional." She whipped around and went to confide in her worms.

The sights and explanations broke Elliott's spirit even further. He leaned down to the flask and looked closer at the fruit flies buzzing around inside their glass cage. Around and around they flew. Some inexperienced youngsters still bumped their heads on the cork as they tried to escape. Their life's only destiny was to be trapped inside this prison, waiting to be sacrificed, leaving behind tiny translucent wings, oversized bodies, and huge compound eyes. In the end, their chromosomes would be sucked up through a pipette, squirted onto a glass slide, and squished by a cover slip. The glob would sit under the hot light of some scientist's microscope, completely exposed to the whole world. And to know that these tiny flies share most of the human genetic blueprint was just about enough for him to give up altogether and look for a different major to pursue.

Elliott straightened up and looked around, shaking his head at all the creatures in the room. He turned, and walked mutely out of the darkroom toward the computer station. He plopped down in front of the screen and looked again at the graph.

"You have the easiest project in the entire senior class," Kelly said, walking up behind him. "So what if your data stinks? Just write it up like Kingsley's been harping at you to do. You're not getting on his good side by waiting until the last minute—as if you thought you ever could. But through some twist of fate, he's made this very easy for you. Just get it over with, Elliott, and get on with your life." Kelly walked toward the door. "We're meeting at Leo's in an hour," she said over her shoulder. "You *ob*viously don't have anything in here to do."

Elliott sat staring at the screen, thinking of a comeback to what she had said, and decided a comeback wasn't even worth the energy.

CHAPTER 3

Steven Sloan sat with his hand holding his head off the table. He stared down from the third story conference room window of Magalto, watching with glazed eyes the Friday afternoon crew load boxes of seeds and vegetation into the company truck. The produce was transported from Brownsville, Texas, to an obscure compound outside Matamoros, Mexico. He formed a lazy smile watching them scurry below, thinking how far the company had come, and dreaming how far he was going to take it. Even his menial workers were experts now; they answered the border patrol easily and passed through surprise inspections quickly. More importantly, they could provide any document of the North American Free Trade Act to anyone who so demanded. Sloan had worked tirelessly to degrees no one imagined.

He had just returned from New York from yet another meeting with a famed marketing group who had promised to occupy the feeble minds of American consumers. This group had dispelled the fears of ignorant citizens in the United States for decades. Nuclear disasters in the heartland. Chemical explosions in the cities. Oil spills in the ocean. In almost every corporate disaster attracting violent public outrage, the consulting firm of Bard and Hegel, Esq. was called in to battle weak opinions and avoid multi-million dollar indictments.

They had already performed a miracle or two for Sloan. Years ago, Magalto was caught in the tangle of the Agent

Orange backlash. In a clear demonstration by the prosecutors during the seven-year trial, Magalto was found guilty of manufacturing the prime herbicide responsible for massive sickness and the deaths of veterans after the Vietnam War. However, not only did Bard and Hegel, Esq. receive full acquittal, they pushed the courts to allow the same active ingredient to be used in common weed killers sprayed in every backyard across America. They positioned the product as biodegradable. That one word made all the difference.

But this time, Sloan wanted to skirt problems before a major public calamity occurred. Because Magalto trended from chemicals to the new science of genetically engineered biology, he entertained the ideas of Bard and Hegel, Esq. to soften the image of new products before another serious problem surfaced. Large green activist groups were organizing and learning how to play the game of social faultfinding with remarkable effectiveness. Worrying about them kept Sloan up at night. What would happen if a green radical torched a Magalto building, or called for a national public demonstration three stories below? They routinely pulled similar stunts on other company presidents: tossed harpooned whale hearts on their lawns, splattered oiled ducks on their automobiles, sent baked seal pup pies to company parties.

The greens had virtually shut down the genetic engineering business in Europe, and now they were rapidly infiltrating America. The greens had to be stopped. Bard and Hegel, Esq. had an agenda that Sloan liked, and he bought into their ideas now more than ever. They planned to feed the minds of Americans with Magalto's own research and use legislation and the media to exhort the Greenwash message: *food biotechnology will feed and improve a starving world. And as the population explodes and land shrinks, genetically modified organisms will be more important than ever before.* Now who's going to argue with that? Greenwash was the answer to the greens, and all it amounted to was using stockholder dollars to blitz the media with the company's own research and interpretations. These campaigns promised to silence the radicals who were threatening to mount unnecessary battles. All this, from the firm that saves companies from the public.

But Sloan had had to leave the inspirational meetings and fly back to Brownsville to meet with a customer. He would do his business, then return for more soothsaying. He would rather have stayed, but the importance of this customer weighed stronger than usual.

Jorge Martino and his assistant sat across the large table from Sloan, watching the drama unfold on the whiteboard from Dr. John Barringer, the eccentric lab man, in the front of the room. The men were dressed in green-patched military fatigues as usual, when they met with Sloan at Magalto. Martino wore his black hair gelled with comb tracks running across his head so stiff that if they were ever measured, would not be displaced by more than one millimeter from morning to night. His mustache draped just over his lip, glistening, as always, on the edges. This small man, sitting with his gold-ringed fingers interlaced over his knee, had become more courageous each meeting. It was impressive, really, that he had such epic goals.

Martino was the undisputed leader of the Revolutionary Armed Forces of Colombia, the Fuerzas Armadas Revolucionarios de Columbia, the FARC. Forty years ago, this group had established itself as the military wing of the Communist Party, when the world still allowed the equal distribution of poverty. They called it Marxist economics. The FARC were now the most capable insurgency in Columbia and becoming so throughout South America. But since the fall of communism, the group began a dedicated effort to move into peace negotiations with the recognized Columbian Government. Who would have thought? The FARC made several concessions in order to advance the peace process with the Briceno Administration. They established a demilitarized zone, a neutral zone where there would be no bombings, kidnappings, extortions, hijackings, or murders. Crime lessened considerably. Then the government wanted more, and made the FARC move their operations from urban fronts to rural compounds; get the criminals out of the city. The FARC lambasted this and carried heavy resentment at first, but the move began to offer unexpected benefits for them, not realized until years later. The group befriended thousands of farmers throughout the vast countryside and established a mutual partnership. Providing heavy protection to the farmers, the FARC processed and trafficked the crops the people grew. It was a huge business and over the years, the world looked to Columbia for certain mind-expanding exports.

For several years, the relationship between Magalto and the FARC was symbiotic. Under Sloan's direction, Magalto produced an assortment of exclusive crops and Martino bought tons of it. No other company created these products and no other customer paid as good of price. Martino used the opportunity to develop an even stronger following of Columbian farmers. The people and communities held under bondage during the communist regime were timidly coming out of their collective cocoons, testing their hand at the new economy. Thousands of people were coming to the FARC for their chance at the economic hope of bringing life from the earth, to be turned into cash in hand and food on the table. In return, the people gave their allegiance. Until now, the FARC hadn't asked for it. The group was too busy supplying the demand and plotting stages of their long-standing desire to overturn the Columbian Government, their eyes on the rest of the Americas.

However, Martino was up to something unusual. Sloan knew it, but he couldn't figure out exactly what. Business between them lately was strained, and Sloan had to be here in the boardroom every time Martino asked one of his foolish questions. No one else in the company was capable of making the final deal with him, or pacifying any ulterior motives he tried to articulate. Martino, with his assistant Antonio who barely spoke a word of English, visited Magalto almost every month now, and had to sit and courteously tolerate the ramblings from the laboratory director, Dr. John Barringer, before he could ask a question that Sloan would answer. It was Magalto policy, and Martino respected it.

After two hours of listening to the ramblings from the eccentric lab man, and with a big jet lag hangover, Sloan's senses dulled considerably. His view out the window had turned into a blur. His fifty-six-year-old head bobbed up and down every few minutes as his hand slid off his stubbly face. It was only noticeable to him until the last bob whipped his head back so hard his glasses fell onto the table with a bang. The two guests in the room turned to look as Sloan picked them up. He tapped them on the table a second and third time. Without looking up, he took his pen and jotted down a few lines on the back page of the report, like he suddenly had a flash of insight and had to write it down before the thought escaped. It was impressive comeback, really, and the two other men in the room found no reason to stare. They followed the explanations on the whiteboard, or tried to.

Dr. Barringer absentmindedly looked across the mess he created on the board and turned to his jumbled notes on the podium. He dropped his marker down the side of his ever-present tie-dyed lab jacket, along the same blue swath he had made on it a few minutes earlier. He flipped a few pages, let out a grunt, then returned to the board and continued writing more equations, making a ruckus as he explained the process to himself.

In a brilliant scheme he developed over the years, Sloan had Barringer speak for a 'distillation period' which was anywhere from one to three hours at the beginning of every meeting, unless of course the audience didn't need to be confused prior to a haggard round of negotiations. The longer Barringer spoke, the more eager the guests were to hear oracles from Sloan. It never failed, and no one seemed to be offended by the complete disdain they were shown by the lab man. He was as pompous as the guests were clueless.

But Dr. Barringer was supposed to be prepared for this part of the meeting. Prepared? He had never prepared a day in his life, for anything outside the laboratory. His diagrams and explanations, which were not the least bit related, popped from his current fleeting thought. If anyone could follow Barringer's discourse they would have to be a certified genius. He was all over the place; transgenic plant technology in one sentence, and the molecular structure of a bad experience in the very next. He had equations of what looked to be neuropeptide sequences on one side of the board, connected by arrows to diagrams of spliced genes on the other side.

Sloan looked up for a moment at the commotion Barringer was making, shook his head at him, and returned to his own doodles. Shocking blue lines streaked across the entire page, as an image of a cityscape began to emerge. The buildings, drawn tall and narrow, cast shadows on the surface below. Large evergreen trees—blue in this case—were inappropriately placed in the Texas desert, surrounding a transplanted plot of land in which Sloan had drawn a garden with tiny flags labeling each row. In the middle, he sketched one large bush, from which came a surreal assortment of produce. A sizeable apple shared a drooping branch with a banana, as did a pear with an ear of corn, detailed with its bustling kernels. Another stick emerged from the top of the opulent bush and spiraled upwards. At the crown, he drew several sprigs that sprouted in all directions. Sloan tapped the pen against his chin. He broke into a quick smile, leaned forward, and whisked his pen on the paper several more strokes as his artistic inspiration guided him. He leaned back a second time and admired the piece. A large sprig of wheat projected from the middle of the omni-fruit-bearing bush. On either side, two spindly arms wielding large swords, had struck into the tallest building, having destroyed every other piece of growth as evidenced by the darkened pen strokes all over the page.

"Steve? Isn't that right, Steve?" Barringer looked at him with his arms folded over his brightly colored lab jacket. His head was cocked to the side, waiting for an answer he couldn't give. Wasn't supposed to give. He loved to offer his opinion on everything from politics to religion, but it was agreed that he wouldn't speak his mind during any more meetings. The last freewheeling opinion he proffered was very costly. So now any time a political question came up, it was automatically deferred to Sloan.

Barringer's tie-dyed jacket, and his ideas, came from the 70's, when he was caught in the euphoria of the drug experiments he had done at Berkley. He always said he had to try 'em out on himself before he would let anyone else risk the embarrassment or trauma of a bad trip. So he experienced them all. Some worked okay, some didn't work at all, and some performed so strangely that he quietly filed the data away for future reference. The seventies ended in a puff from his last admitted toke, but Barringer clung to the tie-dyed jacket, the long silver hair he kept up in a ponytail, and the handlebar mustache.

"*Steve*—Mr. Martino here wants to know." He was now drumming his fingers along his sleeve.

Sloan put his pen down, slid his masterpiece under the pages of the uninspired report, and looked at Martino. "No, there aren't any new regulations," Sloan said with a Texas drawl, looking from the report to Martino, already up to their level of conversation. "If there were, I'd surely know about them."

"Mr. Sloan," Martino said with a slight Spanish accent, as he brushed his glistening mustache with his finger and thumb. "The World Trade Organization makes it very difficult for me to sell these products."

"What have they done? You've never let their trivial regulations bother you before."

"I am charged higher tariffs. I cannot keep paying the government this money to cross the border."

"Well, we all have the same problems then, don't we? Raise your prices."

"I have, but my farmers become upset. Their prices are very high already."

Sloan looked at him then at Barringer, who had already turned and begun another indecipherable set of equations and diagrams. They looked so foreign to his small audience—or for that matter, to anyone else but this particular biochemist who scribbled them. For all reasonable assumptions, Barringer could have written the engineering sequences of cocaine insertion into a simple garden plant in large letters and numbers, and no one would have the foggiest idea. Martino pretended to scribble notes on everything Barringer wrote, but what did the little gelled-hair rebel know about biochemistry? Sloan never knew what Barringer scrawled on the board these days, and really could not have cared less. Cooking up chemical formulas was a job for the biochemists, organic chemists, and cell biologists at Magalto, not the CEO or any of his international customers.

"It's part of the deal, Jorge," Sloan retorted. "When you play by the rules of the Organization, you do as they ask."

"That is why we place a delegate."

"A *delegate*?" Sloan laughed and looked at Barringer.

"A delegate," Barringer repeated as he turned, shrugging his shoulders in concert. He searched for and found a page on the podium, turned around to the white board, and continued scripting.

"You can't send a delegate," Sloan said. "You're not a recognized government. You're a rebel group from Columbia."

Martino's expression didn't change. "Regardless, I am going to buy a seat in the Organization."

"To do *what*?" Sloan barked. "There a hundred and forty six seats on the board, and they're all filled. Besides, even if you could buy a seat, what the hell do you think you would accomplish?"

"The World Trade Organization dictates our food distribution. We suffer direct consequences from any of their decisions. I wish to establish negotiations with other members."

"To do what . . . change the rules?"

"Yes, that is my intention."

"Change the rules," Sloan repeated. "Everybody wants to change the rules."

Sloan's expression quickly changed as his grogginess disappeared. None of Martino's recent questions had anything to do with the drought in Columbia or the upheaval of farmers and their rights to sell at a fair price. Martino was digging to find out about the most powerful organization in the world, The World Trade Organization, and how he could become a player as his rebel group continued punching inroads into the Columbian government.

"Mr. Sloan," Martino began quietly, "I have enough support from my country to be elected President. We have taken enough polls to know our bid will be successful."

Sloan looked at him stoically.

"I don't mean to play a game of politics. I mean to win the presidency. Our rebel group, as you say, has established itself as the new power in our country. We now supply most of the jobs. We control the exports—and the income. We have strong relations with many of the countries you do business with."

Sloan shifted in his chair. He tapped his glasses on the table a few times. For him and Magalto, this might be a good deal. Having another delegate pawn on the World Trade Organization would help in the company's supreme goal of advancing their products into every corner of the world. In fact, this new operative couldn't be better, especially if the FARC could overturn and control the government of a sizable country.

"What do you want from me?"

For the first time in two hours, Martino broke a smile. No teeth showed, but it was a smile nonetheless. Antonio sat just as stone-faced as he always did in the presence of his boss, the President-to-be of Columbia. Martino shifted upright in his chair.

"Please, could you sit, Dr. Barringer?" Martino said with authority.

Shocked at the request, Barringer stopped mid-cartoon. He backed away and looked at his stick dude standing on a chemical equation. It had one foot on each side of the equal sign, and both of its hands held a rainbow he had colored in a fit of silliness. Barringer dropped his hand with the marker down the side of his jacket, making a red streak this time. He capped the pen and sank into the chair next to Sloan.

"I want to know how you direct the World Trade Organization," Martino said to Sloan, focusing on him with complete attention.

"Yes, and I'm happy to oblige you, but"—Sloan glanced at his watch—"it's late in the day, and I'm tired. Let's do this tomorrow morning. It can wait until then."

Martino nodded. "Tomorrow."

CHAPTER 4

Leo's Pub was the closest eatery to Royce University. It sat on a corner of a slow scenic street in the posh district of Old Town Portland, and had become a haven for students. On Friday evening, it bustled with the college crowd: the overachievers who always studied, the partiers who never studied, and those on a cheap date trying to make conversation. They were scattered throughout the place. Waitresses with short aprons moved quickly between the tables, trying to memorize simple orders and fight off obvious moves of the male gawkers. The cooks busily slapped food together and tried to keep patron orders similar to the items listed on the menu.

Leo stood perched in position with his hands on his hips, barking commands to both waitresses and cooks. His T-shirt sleeves were rolled up, exposing tattoos inked in the late sixties. Every so often he ran a hand over the bristles of his crew cut and wiped his palm across his stained white apron.

"What'ta hell d'ya call that?" he snapped at an innocent freshman, as the wiry boy slunk between the tables.

"What?" The boy recoiled like a scared cat.

"That friggin' bone in your throat. Where d'ya think ya are, Africa?" Leo turned to a group of guys at the table nearby. "Look at this crazy-ass. He's got a bone stickin' in his throat."

The wide-eyed freshman dropped his head and scurried away to his group of odd-looking friends, who were deep in conversation, unaware of the commotion their clan member had caused. The table of guys sitting beside Leo erupted into laughter, having been in a similar position at least once before. Leo shook his bristled head and walked away.

In a booth near the back of the pub, Kelly and Rina were trading food back and forth, trying to straighten out their orders.

Rina Das held a double major. She began with Public Policy, and added Molecular Biology her second year. She spoke fluent Spanish, French, and last year added conversational Japanese. She came to study in the United States from a volatile South American country, where her parents had been killed in a civil war. Her dream was to graduate from Royce and return home to help less fortunate people in society.

She was taller than Kelly and filled her clothes out better. No T-shirts or baggy pants, ever. She wore a tinge of makeup that brought out her olive skin, large dark eyes and black hair. She was elegant enough to carry the most expensive lipstick in her upscale purse, but primal enough to carry pepper spray and a high-decibel alarm along side it. Most of the males on campus pursued her and repeatedly tried to convince her of their worthiness or their desperation. From day one, Elliott had offered Rina his. She never accepted and he never gave up.

"I don't know where Elliott is," Kelly said, looking at her watch and glancing around the pub. "He was really upset this afternoon when I left Rothman. He's determined to wait for these magical numbers to drop out of the sky and land on his graph."

"He's a bum, Kelly," Rina said, picking off a small piece of garnish and dropping it on the table. "I knew he would wait until the last minute to begin his project. He always thinks he can get away with things like that."

"But he's working on it. That's all he's been doing for the past month."

"No, he's deceiving you. He wants everyone to think he has a difficult project so you'll feel sorry for him. He does it all the time."

Kelly forked a small wad of alfalfa sprouts from her plate and nibbled them. "Whitman and Kingsley both threatened him. If he doesn't finish his project by next week, he's not going to graduate, and he'll have to pay back his scholarships. They just told him."

Rina's eyes narrowed. "And you feel sorry for him. He doesn't do a thing all year and you feel sorry for him."

Kelly chewed, then, "Yeah. I do." She pushed the fork with sprouts through the middle of her cold slab of tofu. "Elliott is afraid of responsibilities. He doesn't want to move on. Yeah, he put off his project just like he puts off everything else. But sooner or later he'll come through, just like he always does."

Rina shook her head at Kelly. "We're about to graduate. He's supposed to have everything finished by now."

"He works better under pressure." Kelly worked her fork in the tofu, broke off a piece, and mashed the sprouts into it. "It's all part of his low self-esteem problem and his missing identity."

"No, it's a lot more than that."

"It's because his parents were killed," Kelly said, then immediately looked down.

Rina shot her a scowl. "Don't use that excuse with me."

"I'm sorry. I didn't mean to say that."

"Do you want to compare our miseries? The death of my parents has done nothing but inspire a purpose in my life, one, I'll remind you again, that Elliott is oblivious to. Our problems don't grant us excuses. He's using his twisted tactics to pull you and everyone else into his pathetic little world. Don't fall into his trap, Kelly."

Kelly saw Leo meandering toward their table. Her look of dejection changed into distress. "Oh no. Here comes Leo," she said, fidgeting in her seat. She gave Rina a weak smile.

"What's wrong witha food?" he barked at them. He put his hands on the table and leaned his hulky body over their plates.

"It's not what we ordered," Rina said. "And it would take longer for you to fix it than we want to be here today." She moved her plate out from under him.

"But really, this is the closest food to what we've ever ordered," Kelly said, smiling at him.

"Well," he said, swaying his prickly head a couple of times, "are we hav'n a little PMS here today? Don't believe that was on the menu." He straightened and crossed his hairy arms over his barrel chest.

"Should be," Rina said. "That's what we've been served here for four years now."

"And besides, it would go well with the testosterone trash you serve Monday nights," Kelly said and both girls laughed.

"Well, well, well, looks like we have a comic duo. And to think your boyfriends aren't even here listenin' to you spout it out. Where are your boys, by the way?" He glanced toward the door, looking for a way out of this match. The girls were too tough today.

"We don't have boyfriends," Rina said. "Gave them up a long time ago."

"Boys get in the way of social progress." Kelly picked up her fork with the mashed tofu and sprouts and waved it in the air. "The only way to improve our society is by allowing the extinction of the species that is least important for survival. That would be the male, the foragers, who are destroying the world to make a buck. They're all a bunch of righteous capitalists. Who needs 'em?"

"Well, well, looky there," Leo said, wiping his bristles as Elliott walked toward them. "I think one of your righteous capitalists just saved my arss. Apparently, I owe him a buck."

"Elliott? He's not a threat to the species," Rina said as Elliott approached. "He's too busy trying to *find* himself."

"They giving you trouble again, Leo?" Elliott slid in next to Rina, flashing her a scowl.

"Yeah," Leo said. "Would you mind taking over here for me? I just served these two the last PMS specials and it seems to be takin' a *power*ful effect." He laughed.

"Very funny, Leo," Rina said. "You should try it. You might make a fortune on it and prove our point."

"Let me think about it," he said, composing himself. He caught sight of another happening that involved one of his people. A waitress was in a tangle, and he was off to the rescue without a salutation to the group.

"What was that righteous capitalist stuff all about?" Elliott asked Rina.

"Just part of the conversation," she said.

"Yeah," Kelly began. "We were talking about school. You know, what they're teaching us here. It's overt capitalism, and I think you are a prime specimen."

"So what's wrong with that?"

"Well, it's not that it's wrong, it's that I didn't come here to learn that kind of stuff."

"Then you should've taken the Mother Jones Home Study course, and stayed away from Royce for the past four years," Elliott said.

"They have a course? I haven't seen it." Kelly looked with wide eyes at him.

"Yeah. They have a program for getting your diploma without books or notes, or doing anything but talking about creating social change. The more people you convert to your cause, the more points you get, until you rack up enough to graduate."

"That's not funny, Elliott," Kelly said. "Every brand of media is under control of capitalistic giants. There are only a few publications that come from the free press. Mother Jones is just one of them."

"Well it looks like the capitalists have gotten a grip on you," Elliott said.

"No they haven't." She wrinkled her brow. "Why do you say that?"

"'*Pave the earth and enjoy the great outdoors. Jensen Concrete Company*'," he read off her T-shirt. He burst out laughing.

She looked down at her faded and wrinkled shirt, which displayed a sleek car with fat tires smoking the road underneath, and the slogan written across the top. She snapped her head up and wisped her hair back. "I'm doing laundry."

Rina smiled at Kelly. "So much for your economic theory."

A waitress approached, clicking her pencil on her pad. "So whad'ya want?" she asked, cracking her gum, looking at Elliott.

Elliott looked at the plates then pointed to Kelly's. "What's that?"

"Tofu with bean sprouts, avocado, and cream cheese," Kelly said, picking through it with her fork. "But I'm not really that hungry."

"Do you have anything from the great outdoors?" Elliott asked the waitress.

"I can get'cha a club sandwich. I'll have a cook drop some exotic game in it for you. How's thaaat?"

"Sure, that'll work."

"Okay, I'll be right back wit' yer order." She whipped around and hurried away without writing a thing on her pad.

"Speaking of capitalism, Kelly," Elliott said with a laugh, "why don't you sell your little wormies to the fishing industry? They'd probably bite hook, line and sinker."

"Very funny. At least I *have* a project."

"But, worms?" Rina asked, with a putrid look on her face.

"I guess it's better than your first project." Elliott rolled his eyes. "Your brilliant theory of why butterflies swarm around the world in the jet stream, or something like that."

"Kingsley wouldn't let me do it. He said the subject was too elementary. Can you believe that? The Monarch butterfly's migratory genetics are influenced by the four equinoxes and weather patterns, that's what I wanted to prove. Besides it is *so beautiful* how they fly together in patterns, searching for food and a home. We could all benefit from using those wonderful insects as prime examples of social behavior. But Kingsley made me do another project—worms."

"That's not important either, Kelly," Elliott said. "Neither one have anything to do with helping society."

Rina looked at him with her big brown eyes. "What? Since when do you know anything about helping society? All I hear anymore from you is how your little project isn't coming out the way you want it to. Your hopeless project certainly isn't helping society."

"When I finish my graph and write my summary, I'll know how genetically altered foods affect groups of people, and what kind of treatment they can get to help them. I'll have answers for the betterment of society."

"No. You're not finished with it," Rina said with a grin as her eyes narrowed. "What good is that? Everyone else is finished with their projects, and here it is, almost graduation, and you don't have a thing to show for it. A half-done genetics project is not helping anyone."

"Well, you're working on the politics of third world countries or something dumb like that. What's *your* point? How can a project about a bunch of wealthy politicians complaining about their country's problems do anyone any good?"

"That's exactly what I'm talking about!" Rina said. "My project has validity. The needs of the people are a lot different than the needs of the rulers. I'm proposing a hierarchy of communal power that is already in high demand throughout many third-world countries. I'm creating a surge of hope for thousands of people in the form of policy . . . a constitution like the United States began with, but from which it has moved miles away."

"Oh, come on," Elliott said. "Your project won't change a thing. Theoretical policy doesn't change society anymore—the direct application of information does. We're living in a new century, in case you haven't noticed, and my project is at the forefront. It will impact people worldwide. When I finish, mine will have far more important implications than either of yours."

"Elliott," Kelly began. "Right now, it has nothing to do with being important—which it's not, by the way. It's a matter of getting it finished, getting a grade on it, and graduating. You don't seem to understand that."

"You know, none of them matter anyway," Elliott said, looking down at Kelly's messy plate. "None of our projects will be used by anyone outside of Royce. We're a bunch of undergrads, under the allusion that someone's going to listen to what we have to say. It's a diversion and it's perfect. Royce says you need a big-ass, time-wasting project before you graduate with a science degree. They do it to keep you from studying and learning things, like how to think and apply yourself in the world."

"Studying?" Rina's mouth fell open as she looked at him. "Since when do you study?"

"I study all the time," Elliott said. "Well, I used to. But now I'm spending all my time on this senior project. I've had to skip most of my classes for the last three weeks to work on it."

"Like your philosophy classes. Now those are real important, *sheeze!*" Kelly whooped.

"I take philosophy to clear my head and to understand the mechanism of thought," Elliott protested. "Besides, I'll get more out of my philosophy courses than you'll even dream about getting with your stupid forest degree."

"En-vi-ron-mental," Kelly spelled out.

"Oh, it's mental all right."

"You're such a smoke blower," Rina said to Elliott. "That's all you do anymore, is complain how you can't get your work finished. Kingsley's on your case and now so is Whitman. What's it going to take, Elliott?"

"You both don't get it, do you? Nobody gets it. I'm not lazy. I spend my time doing work you can't see. What, you have to see something before you believe it? This is a racket and you've fallen for it. The education here forces the stupid and represses the bright, so we all conform to the same dull, dead level of mediocrity. Our society fits people into the same preconceived mold, usually what they're least capable of. This philosophy is rampant here at Royce, and our senior projects are the biggest testament to that. Maybe I won't do it, just to prove my point."

Rina laughed. "You have to do it Elliott—but you can't, and you're running out of excuses."

"They'll kick you out, Elliott," Kelly said, leaning forward on her interlaced hands. "Your grandparents will both have heart attacks."

Elliott raised his eyebrows. "This isn't about me anymore. This is about Procrustes."

"Procrustes?" Kelly asked. "What's that?"

"It's one of his mythology lessons again," Rina said, rolling her eyes.

Elliott ignored her and spoke to Kelly. "Procrustes kept a house by the side of the road and offered hospitality to passing strangers. He invited them in for a pleasant meal and a night's rest in his bed. A bed, he said, that was standard length, but would fit his guest exactly. But he didn't tell them how he'd do it. As soon as they lay down, he went to work on them. If the person was too short, Procrustes stretched them until they fit. And if the person was too long, Procrustes cut their legs off until the person was the right length. He made everyone identical, so they all fit his standard. It's forced conformity and you're all falling for it."

"Then what happened?" Kelly asked with her eyes wide open staring at him.

"Some other dude cut his head off," Elliott said.

"That's not true." Kelly said loudly.

Rina smiled at her. "It's a myth, Kelly."

"It's a parable about forced conformity," Elliott said. "We're all in his bed. That's what we're doing here, getting our heads lopped off to fit preconceived standards someone else has for us."

"You're here for the very same reason we are, Elliott," Rina said. "But I'm not getting my head lopped off."

"Why *are* you here," Elliott asked, looking at Rina. "Could you re*mind* me again? You seem to have it all figured out."

Rina lifted her dark hair off her shoulders and looked at him with her brown eyes opened wide. "I'm here to learn who Procrustes is, so I can stay away from him. If you watch and learn, you don't have to go to his house and lay on his bed. What you're talking about is just like how the United States cripples my country and all the other small countries in the world. The United States is like Procrustes and they use Procrustean methods to force conformity, to use your example."

"How?" Kelly asked, staring at her.

"How, what?"

"How is the United States like Procrustes?"

"It's called altruistic domination. America barges into countries and offers their intervention to prevent wrongs that they see. Then, they subtly move into a moral right, so they can dictate decisions and control events wherever they run counter to the wishes of these governments. So, this moral responsibility and moral right is used to justify the demand by the United States that it is the world's only superpower. And I'm going to change that. I'm here at Royce to learn how to use information and technology so my people and I can make our own way, without the infamous American intrusions."

"Your people?" Elliott asked.

Rina turned to him. "Yes, my people. But right now, we're all American displacements trying to retain our heritage. I want to give them structure and support their ingenuity so they can implement their own ideas again. The United States' form of altruism has taken it all away. It is domination taken to the extreme."

"Oh, that's beautiful Rina," Kelly said. She turned to Elliott. "Now she has something important she's doing with her life. Maybe that's what you need Elliott, a cause to work for."

"I don't need a cause," Elliott said.

"They *why are* you here?" Rina asked, turning to him. "You're two weeks away from graduating and you're crying like a baby about our education. I bet if your project was completed, you'd be harping about something completely different."

"He would." Kelly said. "I just know he would."

Rina continued, "Your problem is that you can't make this Procrustes thing apply to anything real. You're blaming your project on Royce because you think they're forcing you to do things that you don't want to do. When all along, you don't understand the bigger reasons, like why our projects might be important. You think they're going to cut your head off. They're not going to cut your head off if you don't get into their bed, Elliott."

He smiled. They all smiled and laughed.

"You know what I mean," Rina said.

"Maybe you're too proud to admit your failure to Kingsley," Kelly said. "Is that what it is? You're upset because you can't finish your project and turn it over to him."

Rina looked from Kelly to Elliott. "You'll just have to write it up like Kingsley wants you to."

"That sounds reasonable," Kelly replied, then turned to Elliott. "You did your best under the circumstances. Just turn it in. Kingsley and Whitman are threatening you. Unless, of course, you can whip up something else before it's due."

"I could, easy."

Rina laughed. "What would you do?"

"I could come up with something in ten minutes."

"Like what?" Kelly asked.

"I could go into Leo's kitchen right now, and squeeze out the DNA from some lame organ meat. It would take me ten minutes to write it up."

"Ewww!" Kelly squealed. "That's repulsive! I'd never eat here again."

"Are you serious?" Rina asked. "Could you really extract DNA in a kitchen?"

"Oh, yeah. Easy. I can prove to you right now that I can do a stinkin' project." Elliott scooted to the edge of the bench and stood.

"Are you going to do it right now?" Rina asked.

He raised his eyebrows twice, turned, and before they both realized it, he was off to Leo's kitchen.

"This I've got to see," Rina said, pushing herself along the bench. "Dr. Ethereal makes The Creature."

They got up from the table and followed Elliott. Just as they left, the waitress returned through the side door with Elliott's food. She looked up and saw he was gone, spun on her heals, and stormed back into the kitchen.

"What the hell are you all doin' in my kitchen?" Leo boomed. "Your food just went out. Ya hav'ta come lookin' for it?"

"No," Elliott said looking around. "I need to check something out in your kitchen."

"You're not goin'ta inspect anything, are ya? Cause I went through that last month and I'm not changin' another gosh darn guard, blade, or nothin'. They said it'd be a surprise next time and it'd be big trouble."

"He's not qualified to do an inspection, Leo," Rina said, holding the door for Kelly.

Elliott looked at Rina. "I just might want to be an inspector some day."

"No," Kelly said walking closer. "He wants to get some DNA."

"*TA EAT?*"

"No, not to eat," Elliott said, wandering to the countertop. "I want to show them how to extract DNA from something in your kitchen. You served any liver and onions today? How about chicken gizzard? Even split peas will work."

Leo crossed his arms and raised an eyebrow, looking like he should expect trouble. "What're you gonna do?"

"Nothing that hasn't happened before in this kitchen, I'm sure," Elliott said. "I just want to show them something." He winked at Leo.

The waitress burst through the door holding Elliott's plate of food. "Well I tell ya. Sometimes you oughta just kick out a few of your customers, Leo." She turned and saw Elliott. "Well, there you are!" She set his plate down and slapped her hands on her hips. "You gonna make your own chow? Go right ahead, and then you can just clean up your own mess."

"No. He'll eat what he ordered," Kelly said. "He just got sidetracked. We'll be out there in a few minutes."

The waitress rolled her eyes and picked up his plate. She glared at Leo then whipped back through the door.

"She's hav'n a tough day. Must've found the women's special we're serving now." He smiled, winking at Kelly.

"Very funny Leo," Kelly said. "I don't have to eat here, you know. You know that, don't you? I oughta write you up for that inspection right now. We just might get some better food around here."

"Nah. You don't hav'ta do that." He turned to Elliott. "Well now, liver you say?" He walked to the large refrigerator and opened the door. He reached a container labeled 'ORGAN MEAT'. "Here we go." He lifted the lid.

"Eww, yuk." Kelly moved back.

"Came from a cow. Well, I think it was a cow. That's what they tell me. It's hard to know these days." With a pair of tongs he poked inside the container and lifted out a piece of meat. "This whatcha need?" He held up the dripping meat for Elliott to see. Blood trickled down the tongs.

Elliott smiled and raised his eyebrows. "Yes. That's beautiful."

"Well, here ya go." Leo plunked it down on the counter and reached for a large, sharp cleaver. "How much do ya need?" He dropped the blade down with a thud, slicing off a small hunk. "Ya can have as much as ya'd like. The rest of this'll last all next week yet. Liver's good for ya." He held up the dripping cleaver and had a mischievous look on his face, like he enjoyed the wallop.

"No, that's enough." Elliott said, then with a smile, "Get this stuff real cheap, huh, Leo?"

Leo just beamed from ear to ear. The girls each made a horrific face.

Elliott capitalized on the moment by asking Leo for a list of ingredients and utensils. He dropped the liver in the industrial blender while Leo poured a teaspoon of salt into a glass of warm water. Elliott took the glass and poured the warm salt water on top of the liver. It splattered on the organ and sprayed the sides of the blender. He put the lid on and covered the top with his hand. A curious crowd of waitresses and cooks joined the audience. The people in back strained to see over the heads of people standing in front. Leo enjoyed the best view. Elliott waited as a few more waitresses jockeyed for a position. He raised his eyebrows a few times and ceremoniously turned on the blender. The bloody mixture spun and spattered against the glass. It gurgled and babbled, gyrating up and down as the blades puréed the mixture. A few bystanders turned their heads and left the crowd. Rina and Kelly grimaced at each other. Leo wore a huge yellow-toothed grin.

"Gawd, this looks like something my psycho brother would do," Leo said loudly above the noise of the blender.

"What?" Elliott asked, turning in his direction while keeping an eye on the action. "What did you say?"

He smiled. "Nothin'."

Elliott shut off the switch. "There, that should do it." He carried the pitcher to the sink, oblivious to the crowd. "Now I need a strainer." He turned to Leo. "Cheesecloth would do. Have anything like that?"

Leo scrounged through another drawer. He pulled out several old, stained cloths and held them up. "Here, any of these work?" he asked, looking through a hole at Elliott. "This one's pretty thin."

"Yes, that'll work. And I need another glass." Elliott took the cheesecloth from Leo and put it over the top of a glass a waitress offered, and said to her, "You hold this on top. I'll pour."

The waitress made a face but held out the glass for him. Elliott swirled the pitcher around a little. The bloody liquid sloshed up the sides and streamed back down. He held the cheesecloth in place and carefully poured the mixture through it. Liver chunks collected on the top as the finer liquid drained through.

"There, just about half full." He put the pitcher and cheesecloth on the counter, and took the collected liquid from his new assistant. "Here," he offered it to her. "Served chilled, it makes a tasty appetizer."

"Ewww!" she squealed, clasping both hands to her face.

"You're gettin' a little too close to home, there bud," Leo said.

"Oh, gross," Rina said making a move toward the door. "I'm getting out of here."

"No, wait," Elliott said to her. "The worst part is over." He gave the glass back to the waitress and looked at Leo. "Now we need some dish soap. You ever wash dishes?"

Leo squinted at him. "My kitchen's spotless. Ya have to ask?" He walked to the sink and reached for the detergent.

"It has to be clear liquid," Elliott called after him.

"Well, this is all I got." Leo held up a bottle of soap.

"That'll work." Elliott took the bottle from him and popped the top open. Slowly, he poured a stream into the glass the waitress held. "Just a teaspoon or so." He gently stirred the mixture with a spoon. He took the glass from the waitress and held it up in front of the spectators. "Stir very gently. Very, very gently."

"You're such a dork," Kelly said shaking her head.

Elliott watched the red liquid whirlpool. He looked up at Leo. "Got any rubbing alcohol? You know, the kind you mix with your microbrews occasionally."

"Hey watch it, young man. That last batch had lazy yeast. It wasn't my fault. Besides, I gave all of ya free drinks the next round." There were muffled laughs. "Hey, I'm serious," he said looking around at the crowd. He rummaged through the first aid kit under the sink. He pulled out broken scissors, stained tape, and opened bandages. He picked up a half full bottle of rubbing alcohol. "Who's been in here?" He closed the lid and looked up. "We been havin' some accidents that I don't know 'bout?" No one spoke.

Elliott slowly poured the alcohol down the side of the glass, filling it nearly to the rim. The alcohol formed a separate layer on top of the soapy mixture. "Now watch." The crowd, as a group, leaned over for a closer look. "In just a minute, the DNA will slowly rise from the bloody layer, up into the alcohol layer. DNA doesn't dissolve in alcohol. It precipitates out . . . look." Elliott pointed.

"I don't see anything," Kelly said.

"Got a toothpick?" Elliott turned to Leo flipping his hand open.

Leo dug around in his front pocket. "Here, this work? I been pickin' with it a coupla days now. Use the side that's not been chewed." He flipped it end to end. "Well, looks like both of 'em are."

"Yeah, that will do," Elliott said, rolling his eyes. He slowly reached for the toothpick, keeping an eye on Leo. He dabbed the toothpick into the top of the liquid a few times, then twisted it around and pulled out a stringy glob.

"It looks like snot." Kelly said as she leaned forward and squinted. She turned to Elliott. "That's DNA?"

"Yes. Well, you'll need a microscope to see all the chromosomes, but this is it. DNA, the essence of life." Elliott straightened and cleared his throat. He held up the glob for his audience to see. "What we have here is the basic blueprint of life. You can choose to ignore it, or embrace the very idea of . . ."

"Oh pa-*lease*," Kelly interrupted. "Enough of your philosophical manifesto already."

Some of the crowd began to leave. "All right. Everybody— back to work," Leo barked, looking around at his crew. "Food class is over for today." Some stayed and ogled, the rest scattered. Leo followed the last waitress out of the kitchen, turned to Elliott with a big grin, and said with a wave over the room, "This is how my little brother got started—in mom's kitchen."

Rina walked by Elliott and said with a smirk, "Ten minute project. Ten minute write up. What are you waiting for?"

Elliott watched her pass through the swinging door and said after her, "I'm not doing this for my project, you know."

Kelly followed Rina to the door, looking at Elliott, shaking her head. "Noble try."

"Why is it," Elliott began as his audience walked away and he was left standing as a lonely orator from an enlightened era long gone, "that I must do things that have serious consequences to prove myself?"

Kelly heard what he said and stopped, slowly turning around to look at him.

Elliott stood with his arms outstretched. "Or that I do nothing and watch myself, like the masses, fall off the flat part of the earth and be called a fool."

Kelly looked hauntingly at him and stretched out her arms. "What are you *tal*king about? The earth is round."

"I will be a leader of fools, then, because I understand we are all characters in a great play, interrupted by the whim of a master for an evening of pleasure. Sure, I can learn how to live without thinking, and I'll learn to understand that I will never be happy until I am gone."

She looked at him and shook her head.

"I do things that you think amusing, but I find no other option. How can I convince you or anyone of my intentions, not in a hundred years, but in my lifetime?"

Kelly turned squarely toward him. "It's just a stupid project. Get over it. Why do you always try to find meaning with things that aren't even there?"

"I'm talking about my life here." He dropped his arms down to his side.

Kelly said angrily, "You know what your problem is? You wanna know? Well I'll tell ya. The problem with you is that you go from one extreme to another, and you gotta know both of 'em and what's in between. You gotta figure everything out, so you end up doing nothing. Nothing! Why do you make things so difficult all the time?"

"Then I'll search for a new meaning in my life—I can do that. I have no more faith in the one I have."

"Your life is working out just fine without you. And it would work even better without you messing with it. Now, are you coming, or you gonna stand there until Leo kicks you out?" Kelly turned and walked back to their table.

Elliott, suddenly realizing that he was in kitchen traffic and that no one cared or understood if they heard what he had been uttering, started for the door. He had tried for four years to talk about ideas and meaning-of-life kinds of things, but no one caught on. Everyone else was busy living their own life to care what he had to say.

He left his DNA mess in the kitchen and returned to the table. He slid in next to Kelly and began eating his dry food without a word to either one of them. They stopped their conversation, and Kelly turned to him and said, "You know how to do a real project, Elliott. The genetic experiment is done. All you have to do is log the data and write it up. You write your conclusions whether it succeeds or flops."

"You're waiting until it's just right, so you can hand it over to Kingsley," Rina said. "Ultimately, you don't really care what your project is. All you want is for Kingsley to pat your head."

He stopped eating and said, "That's not true. I couldn't care less what Kingsley says about it. I'm doing this because I found some things in the data that don't add up, and I think they're important. I'm having my own moral issue here. It has nothing to do with anyone, especially Kingsley."

"Moral issue?" Rina shook her head. "How can you turn this into a moral issue now? If anything is a moral issue, it's my project. I'm doing the moral thing. You're performing an introspective-waste-of-time moral tirade, if anything."

"Don't confuse morals with ethics, Rina. Your project is ethical, and I appreciate your sincerity. But what you don't understand, is that ethics are based on moral principles,

principles that you should have previously decided on and worked through. Like what I'm doing now. If your morals aren't in line, you will never have a positive ethical outcome. If you think you've reached a higher capacity of knowledge, then you can make ethical decisions, ones that affect all these people you keep talking about. But don't make them pay for your morality. Morals are personal. Ethics are based on moral principles and affect a broader society."

"My morals are just fine, thank you. I don't have time to waste, trying to detail every one of them like you do all the time. If what you say is true, that ethics are about society, then I'm going straight to the heart of ethics. My dreams are larger than yours and affect more people than you can even imagine. When you've found your moral approval from a certain professor, who shall remain anonymous, then apparently you can move on with your life."

"I will. And I'll be able to live with myself, while you screw up the lives of your people because you don't have a moral backbone to base your ethics on."

"Well, Elliott," Kelly said, "I think you've just advanced to being a slacktivist. I'm impressed. Instead of thriving on ambiguity like I always thought you did, you really do care about something."

"A what?" Rina asked.

"A slacktivist. You know, someone who's a little more than apathetic about issues. He really is concerned about things, but he still won't do anything about them. It's not in him." Kelly smiled at Elliott.

"I'm not one of your slacktivists." Elliott answered. "I'm working things out that you two can't comprehend."

"We're not insulting you, Elliott," Kelly said.

"And besides," Rina said, "according to your morals, you probably don't let our insults bother you anyways."

"That's right, I don't. I always forget about your insults. Immediately—I forget about them. Like the time you called me a jerk last semester, on Monday, right before Valentine's Day, when we were sitting in Kingsley's class together."

"Aww, Elliott," Rina said. "You're always looking for something. You're waiting for your life to show up. And even when you find everything you're looking for, you still won't be happy because there will still be *some*thing. You have to get outside of yourself. Your morals are just fine. Now it's time to apply them to the ethical issues you always talk about. And don't go having another one of your envy attacks about this discussion tonight, because I know you'll go and ponder this to death."

"No. I won't tonight."

Elliott finished his food and the three left Leo's just as the place was getting exciting. Rina and Kelly went back to their apartment. Elliott drove his old car back home to his grandparents' house. He unlocked the side door, walked into the kitchen, and threw his backpack on the table. He continued through the small living room and found his grandmother reading by the soft lamp, waiting for him. She looked up and smiled at him, and the light sparkled off her cataracts, reflecting a glow of warmth about her: the closest person he would ever have to a mother. Her movements were slow and deliberate as she closed her book and switched off the lamp. She asked him to go please and wake his grandfather, sleeping in his easy chair. Elliott went to the den, roused grandfather enough to help him to his bedroom, and settled him in. He said goodnight to them both, went back into the kitchen, and took out his project. He spread the latest graph over the kitchen table and looked at it. Three lines still remained comfortably low on the Y-axis, but line D was plotted even higher today.

The easiest thing in the world would be to write up the conclusion and explain that variable D had deviated from normal for unknown reasons. He could sign his name and turn the report in to Dr. Kingsley, and he would get an A on the project. Then all Elliott would need to do would be to pull an A on the final, and more scholarship money anyone ever imagined would be his. Everyone else would be happy.

CHAPTER 5

At eight o'clock Saturday morning, Steven Sloan sat alone in his conference room, quietly enjoying a cup of coffee. Since Jorge Martino wasn't due until 9:00, he had a rare moment to contemplate this meeting. He set the mug down on the table, looked up at the whiteboard, and read the outline he had just completed. Seven United States government organizations and three international associations were listed on the left side of the board. Seven industrialized countries and their corresponding leaders were listed on the right. At the top of the board he had written in large letters, 'THE WORLD TRADE ORGANIZATION', and this he had connected with lines to the two groups below.

But something was bothering him. A militant doesn't care about an organizational process like this. Jorge Martino was only concerned about his produce. He always had a question about a crop that had not grown to his satisfaction, or some kind of seed that had not germinated. True, there were often problems with Barringer's seeds in the early stages. Sometimes they grew and produced, sometimes they didn't. To rectify these minor problems, Sloan established a primitive laboratory at Martino's compound in Mexico where the Columbians grew and harvested the produce. The lab had been used over the years to complete the faulty stages of engineering. When one of Martino's men called Magalto to report a problem, a researcher was sent from Brownsville to the compound to diagnose and correct it. A fixer was usually added to the fertilizer, or an acidic reagent was triturated into the herbicide for the crop duster to spray over the fields. Sometimes it took a few days to get the correct chemistry solutions; sometimes it took several weeks. Then, after two or three generations of trial without harmful effects, the crops were transported and grown in Columbia.

So if this new World Trade Organization question was only academic curiosity, Sloan would placate him and be back to the New York convention in a day. And if he could pacify the man's requests for a few more months, he wouldn't need the little Columbian again.

He sipped his coffee and mustered the patience to wait.

At 8:55, Barringer waltzed into the room with his bright lab jacket flapping and a few long hairs loose from the rest of his flowing ponytail. He was told to be in his seat at 8:30, so this was not a bad show for the lab man, this early in the morning. He went directly to the breakfast table in the back and loaded his plate, mumbling to himself.

At exactly 9:00, Martino and his assistant walked in to the room and straight to their seats.

"Go get some food," Barringer said to Martino as he walked past the men. "We have a food stockpile going on right now, here in Texas." He plopped his plate down in front of an empty seat. A few pieces fell to the table, some to the floor.

"Yes," said Sloan smiling at them. He held up his coffee mug and pointed to the spread. "Help yourself to the food. It won't do any good uneaten. Then, let's get on with this little chat."

Both Martino and his assistant went to the table and each filled a plate, the total less than Barringer's, sat quietly, and focused on Sloan.

"Mr. Martino," Sloan said as he stood and turned toward his most important customer, "you want to know about the World Trade Organization."

"Yes, that is correct."

"What I'm about to tell you will help you in your efforts to secure a delegate, if that's what you want. That person, however, will need to be educated and versed in the workings of government and science, I hope you know. But that's your problem. What I have to say may not surprise you, but I will tell you what you need to do to play their game."

Martino nodded.

Sloan continued, "This worldwide organization has nothing to with a sovereign body convincing others that they help people across the globe. It has everything to do with how multinational companies control the world's food growth and distribution. When it comes right down to it, the WTO is continually removing decisions regarding health, food, and safety from national governments, and making resolutions behind closed doors. A third world country, like your Columbia, has no say in any matter related to the American rules promulgated through the WTO. The Organization dictates everything to minor countries like yours, and if you have a membership with them, you obey. As a matter of fact, all members are obligated to adopt and implement United States protection, because the U.S. has the largest contingencies of corporations—the muscle. Only governments that have powerful corporate backing are given any rights, and they are enforced by trade sanctions. In other words, Mr. Martino, if you, as a small potato country, disagree with the WTO, you are heavily sanctioned. That's why you are paying stiff trade tariffs now. Your country doesn't cooperate with our corporations. And the corporations ultimately make the decisions, and in fact, appoint delegates."

Sloan paused. "But you need to understand something here: you're not asking Magalto to place a delegate for you, because as I have told you before, you have practices that we cannot participate in, nor can we condone them openly."

Martino looked at him without blinking.

Sloan continued, "And besides, even if you could find a corporation to place a delegate for you, it won't do you any good, because you can't change a damn thing for many years.

They're not going to let you barge in and bark commands at them, like you think." He looked at Martino who stared back, completely absorbed in the message. Not a morsel was eaten from his plate.

Martino spoke calmly. "You always think short range, Mr. Sloan. We are working on agricultural procedures that the WTO will find very valuable in a few years. Something that will secure our position in the Americas. Time is relative. I do not need Magalto to appoint a delegate for us. What I do need is a friendly recommendation. I have the delegate."

Sloan paused and rocked on his heals. He turned to Barringer, who was just stuffing the end of a bear claw into his mouth. Turning back to Martino, he wrote one word in big block letters as he continued, "All right then, if you must do so, there is another way. You can have just as much say without belonging to a powerful government or any other organized affiliation. All you need is—*money*. This is how you can get a seat. A large donation of money to the Organization gets noticed, but it takes a lot of it. An individual investor can be allowed virtually unqualified access to international enforcements. You can even invoke sanctions directly against other nations. That's right. You can be a foreign investor. Screw the government—it's the age of the corporation and the billionaire."

Martino smiled slyly and nodded. "Yes, money always seems to encourage certain politics."

Sloan put his hands on the table, leaned toward Martino, and smiled with him. He said softly, "If you want to play this game, I will make certain your money gets into the right hands."

Martino narrowed his eyes. "Are you asking me for a bribe?"

"That is how this game works, and I know exactly where your money will buy you the most influence." Sloan held his smile.

"Oh, Mr. Sloan, I am sure that you do. But the kind of money you are asking for will divert my efforts, and you will ask far more than I can afford at this time."

"Then you doubt me!" Sloan took his hands off the table and stood upright.

"As any good businessman should." Martino pushed his chair back and stood. "This offer that you have so brilliantly proposed will not be necessary. No, I thought that you would ask for a bribe, and I had hoped you would not. I choose not to participate with you. I have taken into account everything you have said for these two days"—he began walking toward Sloan—"and I have decided that we will pursue my original plan to achieve our goals." Antonio stood and followed his boss.

"That's it?" Sloan bellowed. "I have just offered you your only chance of having any kind of influence in the Organization, and you balk. Here I am, giving you an open invitation into the largest, most powerful organization in the world so you can exert power where you see fit . . . and you refuse!" He shook his head and turned to the board. He grabbed the towel and quickly wiped a clean swath across what he had written.

Martino stood tall in his stiff green fatigues behind Sloan. "I don't want to merely influence this Organization. I plan to control it."

Sloan whipped around with the towel in his hand and faced him. "*Control it?*"

"You do not understand covert power, Mr. Sloan. That is why there is such aggression against this Organization. There are protests wherever world leaders meet. It will not be long until it is deposed of altogether. Money may influence the greedy leaders, but the hearts of people they control cannot be purchased. My plan is to feed their souls."

Sloan laughed, shaking his head. "Your plans are amusing . . . foolish . . . "

Martino held his hand up to silence him. "My foolishness, as you say, will soon become a powerful force to deal with, of such large proportions, Mr. Sloan, that even you will shake your head in wonder. It will happen in due time. But today you have an immediate problem. The squash. We are still having difficulty with your squash. The gourds are soft and collapsing, and we leave millions rotting in the fields at the Matamoros compound."

Sloan poked his head around Martino and looked at Barringer who looked back with a mouthful of food, shrugging his shoulders.

Sloan turned back to Martino. "We had someone down there just three weeks ago when you called, and they didn't see any problems. No one's said anything to me."

"My men could not transport them."

"The squash?" Sloan said with concern.

"It is serious problems like this that your company has been overlooking for far too long," Martino said.

Sloan stepped to the side and asked Barringer, "John, do you know anything about this?"

"Mmm," Barringer tried speaking with his mouth full.

"Can you explain this collapse to him in a reasonable way?" Sloan stood waiting.

Barringer shoved the last of a cream puff into his mouth, wiped the corners, and knocked off the chunks that clung to his mustache during the feeding. He stood chewing vigorously, and moved to the board.

"Now don't get into a long drawn-out explanation, John. Mr. Martino has more important things to do, like controlling world trade. He doesn't have time to keep up with any of your confusion." Sloan emphasized the last word and tipped his head, scolding him before he even began.

The head tilt and the emphasis was Sloan's signal that a long drawn-out confusing explanation would indeed be in order; it would buy some time. Any problem with one of the products had to be discussed in private, not in front of a customer. Barringer would have no problem with this little exercise.

Barringer nodded back, took the towel from Sloan, and reached for a marker on the podium. Martino promptly took a seat. Sloan sat two chairs away.

"Well, we did have a problem with an earlier batch. You said the gourd is rotting?" Barringer asked Martino.

"Yes. That is what I say."

Barringer spun back to an empty part of the board, and in a matter of seconds covered it with his formulas as he carried on his own conversation, " . . . the *Agrobacterium Tumefaciens* was used in the last batch. That's the one you got. It's an organism that delivers specific DNA sequences during its life cycle. It's a great gene transfer system. I don't know why the cortex of the squash should be weak, because it was a normal transfer. Why would that be?" He turned around with his index finger on his chin and looked up to the ceiling to find an answer. Then he quickly turned to Martino. "Were there any bugs on the squash?"

"None at all, a very good effect, Dr. Barringer, but the produce is no use to us if these gourds collapse."

"Well that's it!" Barringer whipped around again and wrote a few more sequences. And in short time, the board was a mess of genetic sequences on the left side diagrammed by Barringer and political graffiti on the right written by Sloan. Now none of it made any kind of sense, but Martino nodded, pretending to understand.

"You had the parasite-free squash," Barringer said to the board. "We had to take out the synergistic gene so we could get it to cross the geographic barrier." He turned back and looked at Martino.

"The *what*?" Sloan sat upright in his chair. "The geographic barrier?"

"Oh, yeah! Now, it's all coming back to me," Barringer said with a big smile. "The squash you have is from the Northern Hemisphere. This is the very first time we've used it south of the border. The cortex of the gourd must not be handling the change in geography very well, but it sure does keep the bugs away, doesn't it, Jorge?" His smile continued for an uncomfortable moment as Martino glared back.

"We are here to purchase your seeds and plants. If we cannot harvest them, we cannot sell. We don't pay."

Sloan looked from Martino to Barringer. "Do you have any seedlings ready now that will work for Mr. Martino?"

Barringer smiled as he fumbled with the marker. "Ah, nah . . . don't think we do. We converted the transfer bacteria using the North American gene. It will take a month or more to harvest enough of the Southern breed. Well, what you could do, Mr. Martino, is let the squash run its course for a coupla weeks. Maybe then it will evolve in its new habitat." His smile turned feeble.

"I don't have a few weeks," Martino said. "Again, gentlemen, as I have told you for months now, the problem is with the *tomatoes*." He turned to Barringer. "Dr. Barringer, they are affecting the crops."

"No, they're not!" Sloan said quickly and bolted forward. "We've had this problem before with other crops. It's the geographic barrier, just as Dr. Barringer has told you. We'll fix the squash, just like we've fixed all the seedlings before. We'll send you a researcher within a week."

"I don't have the luxury for that kind of time."

Sloan glared at Barringer. "John. Can we send someone down?" He didn't wait for the answer. He turned back to Martino. "All right. Give me a few days. I'll get someone down there as soon as I can."

"Very well. We will expect a researcher. But I do not pay you until problem is corrected. Our agreement." Martino stood and shook their hands, and the Columbians left the room.

Sloan turned and accosted Barringer. "Tell me what just happened here, John! You don't have *any* seedlings ready?"

"Well, no." Barringer's voice faltered. "We changed sequences. They're not going to be ready for several weeks now."

"You said it was completed!"

"I guess we didn't put the synergistic gene back in. I haven't exactly had the time."

"Haven't had the time! *Dammit*, John, Martino is the largest contract we have. We need their payment for six more months, at least until we get our data to the Patent Office. I have everyone in the labs working to secure these patents. Why is this so hard for you to understand?" He paused but continued his glare. "Are you still working on that hedonistic shit?"

"Yes," he replied, forcing a smile.

"Barringer! You're not to be working on that!" Sloan slapped his hand down hard on the table.

"I'm almost there," Barringer said excitedly. "The pleasure pathways have been mapped. I'm ready for the gene insertion."

Sloan stood for a moment and contained himself. "Martino's squash are rotting. I want you to stop your pet projects until we get this squash fixed and get our patents through." Sloan shook his head and paused. "But now, I don't see how in the hell you're going to do that, if you have to get the synergist back into the sequence. How long will that take?"

"Three, maybe four weeks."

"Well, there's no way he's going to get any new squash harvested this year. We're going to have to get someone down there again and find out what the problem is. In the meantime, maybe we can get some seedlings started for him as a backup. We've got to stop these contaminants from happening. Every time he has a problem, he brings attention to the tomatoes. Your pretty patch of tomatoes. Somehow he's still trying to get them to Columbia."

Barringer pulled his hair back and refastened his ponytail. He smiled wide and snickered. "You're forgetting about the Terminator. The suicide sequence is locked in the tomatoes. Even if he steals them, the plants will self-destruct. The seeds are sterile, so he can't grow 'em."

"No, I didn't forget about the Terminator. Martino's too smart to try to steal the plants, but not smart enough to decode the Terminator even if he did. It'd take him and his men thirty years to decode it." Sloan turned around and began wiping the board. He stopped and turned to Barringer again. "We've got to get him focused on this squash problem. If we make a concerted effort and get it fixed, he'll be pacified a little longer."

"It shouldn't take much to fix it, just a little time."

"So then, who can you send?"

"I don't have anyone," Barringer said, looking at Sloan helplessly. "I don't have any researchers to spare. Why don't you send someone from administration? He'd never know."

Sloan narrowed his eyebrows. "I'm not crossing Martino. Not this time."

"Well, everyone I have is buried. His project isn't the only one we have, you know."

"He's paying our bills, John. When the patents come through, we'll be finished with him. Everything about Magalto is riding on these patents coming through." Sloan held up the towel he used to wipe the board. "Until then, we send someone to Matamoros every time he calls."

"For a week, or two? I don't have anyone that can be down there for that long. Everyone's working overtime as it is."

Sloan looked at his watch then dropped his arm to his side. "Look, I have to meet with the accountants right now, and I'm sure that'll blow the rest of my day. In the meantime, see what you can do . . . you might even give Quinton a call and see what he says. You're going to have to light a fire under your people, John. I want everyone stuck on the patents, but we're going to have to get someone on the squash. Before I fly back to New York, I want this problem worked out."

"I'll do my best."

Sloan squinted across the large table. "What *is* that little rebel up to?"

CHAPTER 6

It was three o'clock on Saturday afternoon, and Sloan could not take the droning any longer. For the past three hours, the accounting team had detailed a dreary financial forecast for Magalto. Sloan excused all five before they were finished, and sat alone in the boardroom, holding his head in his hands.

The telephone rang and he reached over to push the speaker button.

"Can't find nobody," Barringer said. "No one can leave their stations for even a day or two, if we're going to stay on schedule."

"Oh, that's great!" Sloan roared into the phone. "Martino's little crop problem is going to be our nemesis. What the hell are we going to do? The accountants say we're way behind schedule with the statistics, so we can't get anyone from the stats lab to go. Hell, if you don't have anyone, then I'm going to have to call Quinton. Did you call him? Forget it, I'll call him. He'll have to send one of his kids."

Barringer laughed. "He won't let any of 'em out of his sight."

"Well, it's going to have to work this time. I don't know what else to do." Sloan hung up on Barringer and dialed Dr. Quinton Kingsley, waiting impatiently in his comfortable leather chair, bouncing his leg. He looked at the report from yesterday. On one side was his artwork; on the opposite page was the chart the accountants were interested in. It related to the production and output of the latest products grown by the

Columbians. Martino, Sloan had been reminded by the accountants again, was becoming an important customer not only in South America, but rivaling the business across Europe and Asia.

"Quinton. Sorry to bother you."

"What's going on? I'm busy grading papers."

"It's Martino. His damn squash are collapsing."

"What? You're kidding me. The cortex?"

"He says the gourds are caving, and they're all rotting in the fields. He can't sell them, so we might be out a minor fortune on this one."

"John didn't put the new sequences in, *did* he?"

"Yeah, that's what he said."

"I specifically told him to put in the Southern gene so it would handle the geographic barrier. The strains in Mexico can't handle the gulf climate without the synergist gene. And I'll bet they're parasite-free, aren't they? He had to leave that in so we could spray more herbicide on the crop. That'll destroy them for sure. They're not ready for all that spray."

"Well, we have to find out what's wrong, get it corrected, and get some seedlings to him in time for his next harvest. He's expecting a researcher in the Matamoros compound in a few days."

"A *researcher*! There's no way anyone can re-sequence the seed he has. They're finished."

"Well, he wants someone down there."

"So send someone from theoretical analysis—they do nothing all day."

"Can't. Every one of 'em is working overtime on the patents. I don't like any of this, but I see no other option. We need someone to go down."

"Dammit, Steve, then why are you calling me?"

"I need *you* to send someone down, Quinton."

"No way. I don't have anyone to send."

"You're going to have to. We don't have another choice."

"I have classes to teach. I don't have time to be searching around another lab. What about John? Why doesn't he go? It's his screw-up, again."

"He has to be in the lab, Quinton."

Steve paused and let the problem sink in. They were all in the same hole: Sloan, Barringer, and Kingsley. Their responsibilities were tiered, as were their payoffs, but they were all in this together. It usually happened this way. Barringer would screw up some kind of lab project. Sloan would hear about it secondhand and try to pacify the problem as long as he could. But sooner or later, he would have to call on Quinton, their academic consultant, to bail them both out. It didn't help that he was located two thousand miles away.

"Get some kid to work this up as their project. A cross-cultural experience," Sloan offered into the silence.

"This is extortion, Steve."

"So we pay a little ransom. We've done it every time we have a crop failure. This is no different."

"I don't like this. John's had too much liberty in the lab. Here I go, paying his bond once again."

"I'm counting on you, Quinton. After this squash problem is corrected, I'm putting you in complete charge of the lab. Help me out one more time."

"When do you need someone?"

"Tomorrow. We'll need to give a quick lab orientation before we send him down."

"Tomorrow? You want someone tomorrow?"

"I want this person updated quickly. You don't have some kid that can finagle their way around a primitive lab, do you?"

"Not that I want to send. Aww, Steve . . . you put me in a real bind. Finals are in a week." He paused and thought for a moment, then said slowly, "Yeah, as a matter of fact I do have someone I want to send."

"Thanks, Quinton. I owe you."

"Yeah, I know."

Kingsley put down the phone and smiled as he leafed through the report on his desk. The abstract explained the intentions of the experiment well enough, and with enough excitement to send to any science journal. The methodology was listed and approved by the company supporting this important study. The data gathered over the last six months was compiled and analyzed through several different spreadsheets. On the graph, three plot lines formed a bell curve; one line extended up the Y-axis—not a huge deal. But there was no signature on this report. Without a student signature, this project would not be accepted in the *Cambridge Science Review* for the purpose of awarding the next National Scientific Merit Scholarship. This was the most important article Kingsley had ever submitted to the journal. It was this kind of work that brought prestige and money to Royce University, and pure esteem to the professor who advised the project. He had fantasized about it enough that it was almost real.

Kingsley flipped the report to the front page and scrawled a big red 'F' beside Elliott's name. And on that Saturday afternoon, two weeks from graduation, he picked up the telephone and called the university president, Dr. David Whitman, at his home, to explain this unexpected turn of events.

CHAPTER 7

Elliott sat in President Whitman's reception room the first thing Monday morning. It was unusual that a university president called a student over the weekend. But Whitman was the caring type, always interested in his students and their welfare at Royce.

Elliott looked at the branches on the ficus tree that he stripped on Friday. He reached up and tugged on a leaf attached to a new twig, but it would not let go.

"Dr. Whitman will see you now." The secretary rested the telephone on the cradle and said, "What is happening to that tree? Is there something eating it?"

Elliott released the leaf and it snapped back. "Looks like a shock virus of some sort. Probably devour the thing by the end of the week." He stood, walked past the wide-eyed secretary to Whitman's door, and pushed it open.

"Sit down, Elliott." Whitman smiled. He always smiled in the first few minutes of a personal meeting. It was a reassuring kind of smile that made Elliott feel at ease. Elliott sat on the chair in front of the large desk and brushed his hair out of his eyes. "Dr. Kingsley called me over the weekend. Sounded like he was in his office going over projects. Can't keep that guy out of Rothman." He chuckled, shaking his head at Elliott.

Whitman lost the smile. "He failed you, Elliott."

"He what?" Elliott bolted out of the chair.

Whitman held his hand up. "Now, wait. He failed you—but I made him reconsider. I'm buying you a little more time."

Elliott eased back into the chair. "But how can he do that? He said I could turn in my final copy this week."

"Yes, I know he did."

"I've been working on it all weekend. I'll have it finished just like I said."

Whitman twisted his glasses off his face and tapped them on his desk a few times. "You don't understand, Elliott, what kind of stir this report of yours is generating. The reputation of our university, not to mention the number of students the scholarships will fund next year, are riding on the hopes of your completed report."

"But it's just a simple project."

"Yes, maybe in your eyes it is simple. Some of the most important breakthroughs in science are simple. But yours won't be worth anything unless we get it published in the *Cambridge Science Review*. Dr. Kingsley needs it signed by Wednesday, and that's what I reminded him. If it's not in, he's going to have to wait until next fall when the journal will accept new submissions again. By that time, it will be too late for the results of the study to be realized."

"Too late? What results?"

Whitman placed his glasses down and looked directly at Elliott. "Let me be very clear, Elliott. Dr. Kingsley gave you this project and the entire year to complete it. Now he's asking you to sign it over to him and be finished with it. Your project needs to be completed, so we can have another article for the school's record."

"Well, it's not right. The data still isn't correct."

Whitman formed a smile. "You're going to learn, Elliott, that sometimes you have to be told what is right and what is correct. You don't realize it, but I just saved you from failing altogether. Now, I suggest that you reconsider your decision. You have two more short weeks. That's it for you at Royce. You can make this right for all of us and end on a good note. I told him to hold off on your grade until Wednesday, just like we'd agreed. That should give you time to put your final thoughts in it and sign it over." Whitman paused and looked at Elliott with concern. "Look, I know Dr. Kingsley gets on your nerves. He's got a lot on his plate this year."

"Well, he always takes it out on me."

"Oh, no. I wouldn't say that. He takes it out on everyone." Whitman smiled and lightened his tone. "He gives me grief most of the time. You just have to put up with him for another two weeks. I have many more years with him."

Elliott smiled. "That's too bad, Dr. Whitman."

"Don't feel sorry for me. I just don't want you to cause any more problems for him." Whitman's smile faded. He pushed himself away from his desk and stood. "Now you better get to class. I told him that you weren't going to miss it."

Elliott left and quickly walked to the Rothman Science Center, on the way trying to understand what had just happened. Kingsley failed him but Whitman vetoed the decision. So really, nothing had changed. No problem. What else was new?

CHAPTER 8

Elliott slipped into Dr. Kingsley's senior Bioethics class at 7:59, one full minute before the professor began a rampage through another novel version of science. He walked down an aisle and settled himself in a soft lecture seat near the back of the room. He opened his notebook, looked up, and watched the man in his expensive slacks, pressed shirt, and snappy tie scribble the outline on the board.

Dr. Quinton Kingsley taught most of the higher science courses at Royce University. His Ph.D was in molecular biology. He held several consulting jobs during the year and did research in laboratories around the country, about which he often boasted to his class. He bragged that his research was in demand across the country, from leading institutions and businesses in the bioengineering field. But like he said many times before, his clear choice was Royce U, performing in front of starry-eyed, impressionable undergrads. Some seniors were still cautious in his classes. And that was exactly what he liked, the reverence of someone who didn't know as much as he did. In front of crowded student auditoriums his flamboyance was impressive. He spoke in sharp tones about the marvels of biology and modern science, and how fortunate they were to be in school at Royce, at this time in history, and still more fortunate to be one of his pupils. For most freshmen, his Introduction to Biology class was required, so of course his 101 lectures were filled to capacity. But the upper

classmen were in his classes because he was the only one to
teach the specialized subjects. Why else were they there?

Kingsley had a theory about teaching this particular class:
begin with basic elements of the subject in the first few weeks
of the year and confuse the hell out of everyone with brilliant
facts that had some vague historical significance. Then with a
few weeks to go, he would tie the facts together with his own
opinions and call it Bioethics. But who really cared? It was
just another course required in the fourth year, for the heavy
science majors. The students were too busy trying to get
through their other important courses, to challenge a point in
this class.

At exactly eight o'clock, when everyone should have been
seated and waiting in suspense with pencils sharpened and
ears tuned to listen to the seer, several students were still
staggering into the classroom, half asleep. This behavior
would not have been accepted earlier in the year; they would
have been told to go somewhere else. But now they were
allowed to stumble between the rows, trying to find a seat near
the back, hoping to catch a few winks behind the person in
front. The back two rows were almost filled. Those most
awake and anxious to impress for a grade, sat in front. The
very front. The middle of the auditorium was sparsely
populated. Kingsley's classes usually had this kind of
polarized seating arrangement in the early hours. Made no
difference to him. All he really cared about was catching their
sleepy minds early in the morning, before some inferior
colleague tainted them.

The scholars in front kept peeking at the clock on the wall,
hoping he would notice how punctual they were, in dire
contrast to the noisy interruptions of those tardy. They looked
up at him in admiration all year, hoping he'd call on them, but
not really willing or able to give an answer. He ignored them
as usual. Those in the back busied themselves with their notes
or anything else they could find, to hide from his opening
questions.

But at 8:01, he was still writing on the board. Very unusual. The class settled and the chatter promptly stopped, all without being told. Kingsley finished his outline on the board, capped the marker, and confidently pivoted to face his congregation.

"Good morning, fledgling scientists," he said with a wide smile. "You in the back may want to come forward for once this year. We are going to have a discussion review." No one moved. No one spoke. Most pairs of eyes were focused on him. The ones that weren't open rolled under their eyelids. Elliott did that and shook his head.

"Fine." He shrugged his shoulders. "Doesn't matter to me. If you have questions, today is the day you'd better ask." He turned and looked at his scrawl, then up towards the back of the class. "Can you all see this? Because if you can't see this, you'll be in big trouble." Five or six students in the back took the second hint, and resettled themselves way down front, in the atmosphere of high intellect. "I'll wait, if there's any more of you who want a good seat." Several more, with confidence shaken, took the opportunity to relocate themselves. Elliott didn't move.

"All right. Let's get started. This is Bioethics for those of you who are lost and happened to wander in. And if that's the case it's too late to refund your tuition." He smiled again. He never smiled in class. "Wednesday is the pre-test. If you don't score well on it, you may as well forget about taking the final next week. I set it up like this so you can see what you need to work on. Is everyone with me? Some of you look like you just rolled out of bed." He scanned the room, then turned to the board. "Okay, here we go. Take a look at this. You are responsible for the material from the very beginning of the term. You need to know everything about the history of genetics, how it began, and the progress that has been made up to the present. Names and dates are important. We have to start at the beginning of the Scientific Revolution and the mission of Modern Science, first proposed by Francis Bacon in 1543. If you remember, he said the purpose of science is to control and dominate nature. You should understand how science today has maintained a very close relation to his statement. You need to know about Charles Darwin and his monumental work, *The Origin of Species*, published in 1859. I hope you remember his contribution. His theory stated that natural variations occur in each generation of a species and natural selection preserves the good while dooming the bad. Natural selection is like the grim reaper holding a scythe, saving the strong and shredding the weak. Questions about Darwin will populate your exam. Get it—populate? His sub-thesis was population control, just remember that.

"You have to know about the monk, Gregor Mendel, and his work published in 1865. Let me stop there a minute. Here's a monk who planted pea seeds in his garden for seven years and counted over ten thousand of them. Counted them by hand—without a computer! He counted every one of them and wrote down his findings. If I could just get half of you to be that meticulous, I would die a happy man. He's one of the first experimenters who took real data and came up with his theory of heredity. If you don't remember what it was, here's a hint: the male and female parents contribute equally to the offspring. His ideas were different than Darwin's. Mendel said the traits of two parents don't blend but remain distinct. You should know that. You will be asked about his observations of the superdominance of unusual plant length, and what importance it had in his theories. Mendel's work will be planted all over your exam." He laughed aloud at his joke, as did his followers in the front rows. They snickered quietly as a group, their shoulders wobbled together as their hands covered their mouths.

"Question," Elliott said, breaking the communion.

Kingsley looked up at him, still smiling. "Yes, what is it?"

"If we do well on the pre-test Wednesday, why do we even have to take the final next week?"

Aghast, several intellectuals in the front turned around with wrinkled foreheads, not to look at Elliott necessarily, but to show their disapproval of another dreadful remark coming from the back of the room.

"Your question is not relevant to our discussion. We're reviewing the course material for the pre-test."

"That's what I mean, what's the point of taking the pre-test?"

"You take my pre-test to see how you fare. If you don't do well on it, then you have some time, though not a lot, to get yourself ready for the final."

"But that's a waste of time," Elliott said louder. "I have other things to do than to take two of your exams."

Kingsley glared at Elliott. "I'm not discussing this now."

"So pick one."

"Pick what?"

"One of your exams. I'm only going to take one of them, because I have things in the lab that I have to finish. You should know that."

Kingsley looked around the classroom. Every eye was on him, waiting for a response to this intrusion into the lecture. "All right, I'll make you a deal. If you get an 'A' on the pre-test, you don't have to take the final. But, if you get below 95 percent, you fail the class. And, *your* entire exam will be essay."

"Essay? That's hardly fair."

"If it's too much for you, please don't bother. You can take both the pre-test and the final just like everyone else."

"But you won't grade my essay objectively." Elliott stared down at him. A personally prepared exam wasn't about the material covered in class. It wasn't even about bioethics. It was about whom was going to win: the frustrated senior who was without a project, or the illustrious professor who could sneeze and have most of his students suspended for hosting some kind of airborne virus.

"No tricks?"

"No tricks. In fact, we'll spend some time today going over the majority of your questions. If that's all right with the rest of the class." He turned to look around the room. They all nodded. What were they going to do? Several broke out in quiet chatter.

"Then I'll do it."

Kingsley shook his head and spoke to the class. "Look— for the rest of you reasonable people—I give you ample time and instruction so that you can perform well on my difficult exams. That's why I give you two. Elliott, here, seems to think he can second-guess my teaching strategies." He stared at Elliott and turned around, muttering, "We'll just see how well you do."

Kingsley looked up at the board, trying to find his place in the review outline. "Now, we have to keep moving. We were talking about Darwin and Mendel and their contributions to science, before we got sidetracked. See, the difference between the two is this: Darwin came up with a theory he tried to prove, whereas Mendel planted and counted. He began with an experiment, *then* formulated his theory. No one had performed such a large experiment before. This issue is critical.

"In 1883, along came Francis Galton, Darwin's cousin. He took Darwin's theory of evolution and mixed it with his own ideas, and set down the principles for a new field called eugenics. Notice the root of the word is gene. But everyone slept through his lecture and nothing happened until 1900, when De Vries woke the sleeping scientists and said there was something important about all these numbers that the monk had come up with.

"Then, Darwin and Mendel came to America by way of the famous Scopes Trial. Remember, that happened in the summer of 1925. You know the story: John Scopes, a high school football coach, was paid by the ACLU to be the defendant in a lawsuit to test the anti-evolution law of Tennessee. Of course, scientists won, and were given the right to put these new theories into every biology textbook in the country.

"Then, in 1953, Crick and Watson discovered DNA and woke everyone else up. Regular people suddenly got interested in science. There, in the laboratory, they showed the blueprint of life twisting on the frame of a ladder. It was the culmination of everything that had only been postulated all the years before. And for you women, don't loose heart. It was Rosalind Franklin who discovered that DNA is a double helix, so you shouldn't feel left out. She took X-rays of it, but Crick and Watson got all the credit. That's the politics of gender.

"Now, I don't take issue with a lot of things—you may have noticed how objective I have been all year—but there was a transient idea proposed in the late 1990's that has taken issue with the Primacy of the DNA. It is called the Primacy of the Environment. It's not important, but I want to bring it to your attention in case it pops up in your education somewhere. You should at least be aware of it.

"There was a simple paper written, "On the Origin of Mutants" by John Cairns, that has tried to change the thinking of mainstream science. Now, there are people who actually subscribe to the notion that the environment stimulates genetic expression rather than genes being endowed with their own self-regulatory elements. Don't get hung up on this, people. Science has proved again and again that the gene itself governs structure, function, health, behavior, and even the fate of an organism. Everything is predetermined by heredity. If we let these Primacy of the Environment people push this view, we are vulnerable to think that nature cannot be influenced. This belief runs completely counter to the purpose of science, which is to dominate and control nature. Are we going to believe that everything happens at will, and that we have no control? I don't think so. This won't be on your exam."

"Question," Elliott said with his hand up.

"No, we're not going to talk about this anymore. I said it wasn't important." Kingsley turned back to the board to check his outline.

"Question," Elliott said again.

Kingsley spun around and looked up at Elliott. "No, I'm not taking your question."

"You brought it up, so why can't I ask a question?"

"Because that subject is not on the exam. This is supposed to be a review for your exam."

"Then why did you bring it up?"

"Because I want you think about what's going on in the science underworld. There are some second-rate ideas floating around, just like this one, and they try to sneak into the ranks of science. Just because you write a paper about some wild-ass idea doesn't mean you think you can uproot an establishment. That's what these people are trying to do."

"Well, I read Cairn's paper."

"Good for you. I didn't assign it."

"I read it in one of your lectures." Elliott shifted forward in his chair. "What he said was that organisms can actively induce genetic mutations in response to environmental stresses in order to survive."

"No—they can't. Genes control function. I just went through that."

"So what do you do with this environmental stress theory?"

"Ignore it like a passing fantasy." Kingsley looked out across his class and interlaced his fingers together. "Look, people. I've called you fledgling scientists before every class begins for a reason—I want you to feel inadequate. You'll never know everything, but I want you to be aware of what's out there. The clear lesson in that example is this: you have to think and apply things in context. This environmental whimper is clearly out of phase with science. It has no place. Think in context, people. You have to think about the gaps in time and understand what they mean. It's the time between events that allow history to happen. You have to be ready to defend science against some of these cavalier ideas. Sometimes people sleep while others advance their own agendas. You have to be ready for them."

Elliott slowly lowered his hand.

"Now, let's bring ethics into our discussion." Kingsley stopped a moment and gazed over his captive audience. He turned back and looked at the outline. He had a long way to go. He turned around and faced the class with his arms folded across his chest.

"Look people, I've said from the very beginning, this is a class about biology, not ethics. There is a difference whether you believe it or not. But since we're required to call this class 'Bioethics' we have to talk about ethics a little. So let's talk about it for a moment."

Kingsley cleared his throat and continued. "Much of our society is a lying contest. We reward dishonesty. And you don't have to look very far. It happens in politics, religion, even in education. The courts are full of it, and the lawyers are trained how to do it. But the practice of ethics is a feeble exercise for a scientific mind. There are only two pure disciplines as far as I'm concerned: mathematics and chemistry. There are no others. This course of Bioethics is required for your majors. It has nothing to do with science or your chosen professions. So when we approach our so-called ethical debates, as we have from time to time all year, I don't want any of you to blow a sphincter over them. When you deal with science problems like we do, it's not whether something is right or wrong. That's not the issue at all. I hope you understand. It's whether something is possible. The application of science is the art of possibilities. Let the politicians and clergy figure out what is ethical. In practical terms, you're going to graduate and get a job in a laboratory creating new kinds of life forms or work in a hospital as a physician some day. If you don't feel comfortable doing a particular procedure, you don't have to do it. That's your right. But rest assured—someone will do it if you can't handle the pressure. So get used to making the difficult decisions early on, and you won't have to lie awake all night thinking about your problems. If you don't get this point now, the bulk of our discussion today won't do you any good, and neither will taking the exam."

No one moved. No one said a word. Kingsley uncrossed his arms and waited for someone to ask a stupid question. "All right then, we understand each other. Let's move on."

He walked to the edge of the platform and stood with both hands touching at the fingertips. "I'm going to give you questions on your exam that deal with heredity and genetics. Let's try an example. Say you live in Europe in the 1930's, and work at a public health clinic. A young, blue-eyed, blonde girl, with a touch of Mediterranean pigment, walks in and wants care. Under state law, you must administer an intelligence test before you examine her. She's nervous and upset because she has to take the test before the clinic can do anything for her. But she knows exactly what it is. She's rude to the staff and throws the papers on the floor and the pencil across the room, hitting another young girl who's obediently taking the same test. She swears at you, the doctor, and calls you names you've never heard before. She's not from a respectable home and hasn't even finished school. She lives off handouts from a state agency that feed her and her two bastard children. In spite of her poor social status and education, she takes the test and manages to score an IQ of 75, which is quite respectable for her. But at the bottom of her test results is a box with the statement: '*applicant has no qualities required for responsible motherhood. She has antisocial tendencies that necessitate sterilization.*' You are encouraged by the administration to put a mark in the box. *Do you?*"

"What kind of a test is it?" Rina Das asked. "An IQ test?" Rina sat towards the middle of the room, not in the very front, not in the back, but near the middle, surrounded by a few admirers.

"Yes, an intelligence test. You've heard about it," Kingsley shrugged. "Just like I said, they were required."

"But what does that have to do with a clinic exam?" she asked.

Kingsley laughed. "Nothing. The test had nothing to do with a clinic exam. The state agencies used the test parameters to "clean up" society. If you had a low IQ and social status, you were sterilized."

"From taking a test?" Elliott asked.

"Yes. Come on. Why does that surprise you? Every one of you took a test just like it when you were in high school. It was called the Student Aptitude Test, the SAT. Most colleges and universities still use it. Think about it, will you? An IQ test was used decades ago to justify sterilization. The SAT is used today to gather all kinds of information about you: social status, religious affinity, sexual preference, economics, race. It's far more advanced than it used to be, because it's all word coded. All your answers are cross-referenced. And you had no idea, did you? Most people in Europe *knew* what they were taking. You took the damn thing and thought it had to do with getting into college."

"But nothing like that happens here," Elliott said

"Then why do you take it? Because some university requires it? See, this is the context that I want you to think about. Something like an SAT is quantifiable, mathematical. You are given a number. That number is placed against all the others and ranked top to bottom. You've had four years of high school education. Do you really think you can be evaluated fairly by a one-day test? What if, like our Mediterranean blonde, you don't feel so well and maybe you don't score so well? Your manners are a little better because you don't throw your pencil at someone, but say your score is lower than it should be. On the bottom of *your* results is a little box with the statement: *'Applicant is of African descent and lower economic status. This subject has tendencies toward homosexuality. This subject has anti-social skills and has scored in the lower percentile. A D2 defect in the allele gene links the applicant to addictions of cocaine and alcohol. Recommend genetic counseling, require genetic testing, and reject financial aid.'* You want someone to put a mark in the box? Come on, let's wake up. This is applied biology, and these are examples you're going to face when you graduate. Eugenics is one application of biology, genetics another. It will be on your test."

Elliott shook his head and stared at Kingsley like he had never heard this before. Actually, he hadn't. He'd skipped more than his fair share of the term, and these discussions weren't in his class notes.

Kingsley scanned his congregation as he slowly turned around. He looked at the board and read the outline. He stopped at Adolf Hitler. There were other characters below, but Hitler would probably take the rest of the period. Class time would end before another hot debate whipped up. He turned around to his silent class.

"Now let's talk about Hitler's contribution. Adolf Hitler was neither the first nor the last person to use genetic traits to remove social undesirables and save money or, for that matter, help with population problems. He read Darwin and Galton and knew basic hierarchical hereditary principles. What he did was a little like your first problem about the blonde. He tried to control the genetic spread of what he thought were bad genes. He didn't want certain segments of society to procreate."

"How can you say Hitler contributed to science?" Elliott said loudly. "I don't remember him as someone to credit with anything like that."

"Now, just wait a minute. Don't take offense," Kingsley said calmly with a smile. "Adolf Hitler was very significant in the course of human evolution. He was very cultured; he was an amateur artist and he liked the music of Cole Porter. I bet you didn't know that. He was married. I'm not even married. No, what he did was apply the principles of these new sciences. I'm not suggesting he was a scientist who—"

"He murdered millions of people! That's no contribution to society." Elliott sat rigid in his chair.

"That depends on how you look at it. Again, ethics is opinion based on principles. His ethics carried out what had already been known. It wasn't new, and what he did will certainly happen again. There will always be another Hitler. It's like this, and I'll keep the discussion focused on genetics. A young couple visits a genetic counselor. This counselor offers them an extensive genetic test on their unborn child. The couple is of high social and economic status, and they want to produce a child in the best interests of the community and of humanity in general. Why shouldn't they have the right to do so? On top of that, say the child does have a serious health condition. Why wouldn't they end the misery before anyone else has to suffer? Wouldn't it be unethical if they *didn't* abort the thing? How different is that than what Hitler did?"

Elliott sat on the edge of his chair. "So you're saying people like Hitler and genetic counselors are the ones responsible to decide the fate of other humans? That Hitler's application of scientific principles is okay, because of what some other scientist came up with a hundred years earlier, and we should follow that example?"

"Well, Darwin came up with the first part of the hereditary ideas, really, but I'm not agreeing or disagreeing with them."

"Then you *have* no opinion?"

"Well, yes I have an opinion. Not one that's appropriate to offer in this kind of setting."

"This is *your* Bioethics class," Elliott said, enunciating each word. "You haven't had difficulty offering your opinions so far this year."

No one moved or made a sound.

Kingsley stared at Elliott.

"You've been talking about eugenics and how that's part of the science of genetics," Elliott said quickly. "What is your opinion?"

Everyone looked back at Elliott then down to the front.

Kingsley took off his square-framed glasses and wiped his brow. "No, what I mean to say is that for the period, at that time, it may have been appropriate. Sterilization was a cheap and simple means to exterminate the undesirables, and even reduce welfare spending in a time of global economic depression. The older, sicker, and less potential people were given death. It was their great relief. The others were left to survive. It's the same thing as genetic counseling. You create a moral issue for society when you *don't* abort a diseased fetus. Too many diseases put a drain on society. Too many undesirable traits interfere with the human genetic potential. "

"*THAT'S BULLSHIT!*" Elliott yelled as he stood. "You've taken an ethical issue and turned it into a moral one! You've made it your own moral opinion. You left the principles of ethics! You see no difference between the two, do you?"

"In this course, morals and ethics are the same thing. They're both grounded in what the majority decides them to be."

"*THAT'S BULLSHIT AGAIN!* There's a *significant* difference between the two. Morals are personal principles. Ethics are formed from moral principles—they're based on a set of moral principles that govern society. And there's no majority opinion that decides *anything*. The majority compromises on inferior ideas like your morals you are trying to shove down our throats! Your logic is flawed and your argument is invalid!"

"This is *my* class and I'll teach bioethics any damn way I want to. It's based on ethical principles that have been—"

"*NO! You did it again!* You turned it into a moral issue again. *You can't do that!* You're calling *your* morals *our* ethics. They're not because I don't agree with them."

"There is no difference between the two."

"Oh *really*?" Elliott said. "Then based on my morals and not your ethics, I refuse to take your imbecilic test Wednesday and the final next week, or whenever the hell you try to give it to me."

"Fine with me. You'll fail the class." Kingsley rocked his head and put his glasses back on his face.

"No I won't. I'll go to President Whitman right now and demand immunity."

"You can't do that. He has nothing to do with this." Kingsley walked slowly to the edge of the platform and looked hard up at Elliott.

"I sure will. There are enough witnesses in this room who will testify that you use information from test questions to derive racial, sexual, and genetic information that have been used against me without my knowledge or my consent." Elliott stared down at him.

"I said no such thing. You're making this all up."

The heads turned to Elliott's volley. "You just said it with all that word-coding SAT shit. You're bringing up Hitler as a scientific hero. You're talking about eugenics as if it's a branch of genetics. That's all part of *your* moral code. Don't call it ethics, because it affects everyone in this room who has to believe you to pass your tests. I'm not buying it and you can't keep teaching the shit that just falls out of your head. I'll give Whitman the last reason to fire your sorry ass." He grabbed his notebook and took a step toward the aisle.

"Look Elliott, I don't want to argue about this right now," Kingsley said sharply, glancing at the clock on the wall. "We have a pre-test that the rest of the class is trying to get ready for. I don't want to use any more class time discussing this with you."

"Fail me!" Elliott yelled as he walked up the row of knees that swiveled clearly out of his way. He continued to the main aisle.

Kingsley watched him carefully as he reached the last seat in the row.

"Fail me," Elliott repeated as he stood at the top of the aisle looking down. "I dare you."

CHAPTER 9

Elliott's attempt to demand immunity for taking a biased examination was based on the well-known fact that President Whitman had had just about enough of Dr. Kingsley's questionable conduct. Rumor was that Whitman was looking for a way to get rid of him. The only reason Whitman hadn't fired him was because of the money the professor brought into Royce every year. It was more money than all the other contributions put together. And Whitman never refused money, no matter where it came from.

But the most pressing issue for Whitman was the consulting Kingsley was doing for Magalto. It was supposed to have ended this year, but Kingsley told him that Magalto had pleaded and begged, and asked him to stay longer and take on more work. The company, he'd said, wouldn't consider his resignation. They needed his expertise in formulating the academic portion of their marketing plan. Kingsley told Whitman that the company was matching his university salary and had given him work the government required; there was one else to do it. Many times Kingsley had flown to Brownsville, to the company headquarters. Sometimes he traveled to Europe. That irked Whitman to no end; the traveling, the courting, the stealing of his time away from the university. Kingsley hadn't brought many new ideas to Royce lately, and this company was taking him further away.

Finally, at the beginning of the year, Whitman had demanded that he terminate the relationship. Kingsley agreed to do so, right after Thanksgiving. It never happened. Whitman had come unglued at a faculty meeting during the Christmas Holiday when he found this out, and made another demand that Kingsley quit at semester break, this time adding that if any student suffered under his tutelage, Whitman would personally bypass all normal channels of terminating a faculty member and fire him himself. Kingsley didn't end the relationship and it was then that the rumors stirred.

There were about ten minutes left in class; not enough time to finish this discussion, nor begin another. Everyone waited, either looking up at Elliott standing in the back of the room, or down at Kingsley, poised on the stage. Finally, Elliott turned to the back door and took a step toward it.

"Stop. I want to see you—*right now!*"

Elliott stopped and turned around.

"This class is *dismissed!*" Kingsley slammed his notebook closed. Several loose papers floated to the floor.

It was the quietest dismissal all year. Elliott stood at the top of the stairs, waiting for his classmates to file out. His buddies smiled an oh-my-gosh-I-can't-believe-you-did-this smile at him as they walked by. He nodded back without the smile. The front row intellectuals didn't even look at him as they scurried by. It took forever for everyone to leave. Elliott slowly made his way down the aisle. He reached the platform and stood with his hands in his pockets, holding the thin notebook by his elbow.

Kingsley reached for the papers that had fallen on the floor, then jammed them inside his briefcase. He turned and folded his arms across his chest. His eyebrows were deeply furrowed.

"Don't you *ever* take issue with me like that again! That was the most contemptible exhibition I have ever seen in my life. You know better than to argue with me in front of class."

"Is it the argument, or the scene in front of class that you're so mad about?"

"Both."

"Both? So you're okay if I disagree with you outside of class?"

"You're not smart enough to disagree with me, inside or outside of class. If you had any sense at all, you would've figured that out four years ago. But it's way too late for that. You *fail!* Your project is history, and if you have another outburst like that in front of my class again, I'll have you expelled in nothing flat."

"Fail?"

"I gave your project an 'F'—you fail!"

"You said I had until Wednesday to finish it. Whitman just told me."

"I changed my mind."

"You can't fail me for what happened in here this morning. That's hardly fair."

Kingsley dropped his arms and pointed his chin at him while he spoke. "There is no such thing as fair. Don't be so naïve, Chapman. You think everything is about what's fair and right—it's not. One sad day, you'll wake up and realize the happy dream you've been living is over. You'll have to forage like everyone else. Everything in this life is based on a hierarchy. Domination and submission. And some day you will understand where your place is. You have no special gifts or talents that allow you to move up the ranks."

The door at the top of the auditorium creaked opened and Rina Das walked inside. She stopped when she saw Kingsley standing over Elliott.

"What do you want?" Kingsley snapped at her.

"I'm sorry. I left my notebook. May I . . . "

"Yes, come and get it." Kingsley motioned to her with a quick move of his hand. He turned back to Elliott. "And you can just forget about the little deal we just made."

"I'm not afraid of taking your test."

Kingsley shook his head at him. "I'm not letting you take it."

"What? Why?"

"Because. But I'll tell you what I am going to do. I'm going to give you one more chance to turn things around for your sorry self. I'm giving you an opportunity to call a truce. If you don't accept, I'll go right now and turn your failed project in to the board, and I'll fail you in my class. Then, I'll call every med school you've been accepted to and tell them you committed a serious school violation. Do I make myself clear?"

For a moment, Elliott shook his head and just stared at him. Then he looked up and watched Rina walk slowly down the stairs. He turned to Kingsley. "What's your offer?"

"Actually, it's too good. I shouldn't even be giving it to you."

"What is it?"

"It's a little project that will improve your résumé quite significantly. If you take it, I'll pass it as your project. Hell, I'll even give you an 'A' in this class just because I'm such a nice guy."

Elliott stood straight and looked at him with intensity, his eyes riveted on his professor. "Just like that?"

Kingsley nodded. "Just like that."

"What is it?"

"It's a project in Texas for a company I work with. They're doing some agricultural engineering for a South American client, and they're pushed for time. They need assistance in one of their labs."

"Texas?" Elliott said loudly.

Rina turned to look at them as she shuffled into the row she sat in. She moved slowly as she reached under the seat for her notebook.

"Yes. They want to fly you out tomorrow."

"*Tomorrow*?"

"Yes, I know it's short notice."

"Yeah it's short." Elliott looked up towards Rina who seemed to be having difficulty finding her notebook.

The top of her head bobbed up and down in the row. She finally popped up and looked directly at Elliott. She smiled at him and waved her notebook as if it had been lost for weeks. "Got it!" She stood and walked down the aisle. "Do it, Elliott."

Elliott looked back at Kingsley. "How long will I be there? Coupla days?"

"No. More like a week."

"A week? What about my other finals? How am I supposed to take them?"

"I will make arrangements with your other professors. I'll take care of them for you."

"I don't know if I can be gone from home for that long."

"Well," Kingsley said, snapping his briefcase shut. "This is your last shot. I have to get to my next class. If you're going to do this, I need to know before noon. I'm your advisor, Elliott, and I'm assigning you this new project. I'm giving you one last chance. Don't let me down." He turned and walked up the aisle, brushing Rina as she walked down.

She reached the bottom step. "Sounds like a no-brainer, Elliott."

"Yeah, a real no-brainer coming from Old Furrowed Brow." He watched Kingsley walk away.

CHAPTER 10

It was rare that Rina carted anyone around in her car, but she quickly volunteered to take Elliott to the airport. It took her a long thirty minutes to drive, Tuesday morning. Thirty minutes of captivity. She pelted him with questions about the company and what he knew about it. She asked him about the laboratory. She asked him about the products, and if he knew where they were destined. On and on she queried. He told her all he knew: that because of his brilliance in finally cornering Kingsley and making a mockery of him in front of his class, he was being sacrificed to the genetic gods. That he only had to pay a small penance for his actions and return to graduate in two weeks, without having to take one final examination. That was about all he knew.

Elliott woke up in time to watch the brown ground of Texas approach as the airplane landed. He walked through the Brownsville terminal within minutes of the time stated on the ticket stub and into the crowded lobby. He looked through the mob and saw his name, minus an 'L' and a 'T', written in large block letters on white cardboard, held up by a squatty man in crumpled blue pants and a filthy white short-sleeved shirt.

"I'm Elliott," he said to the man.

"*You're* Elliott?" the man asked gruffly, looking at him from head to toe.

Elliott sized him up. The man's body poured out of his clothes. His pants hung high enough on his legs to expose sagging white socks. A short, wide tie draped to the side and covered a small portion of his mustard-stained shirt that overhung his beltline. His black plastic-framed glasses sat crooked on his face. His hair was mussed as if it hadn't been combed all day. A shiny silver badge hung at an angle above his left pocket.

"Yeah—Elliott Chapman. Just came from Portland."

"Where?"

"Oregon."

"In that case, let's go get your bags," the man said.

"All I have is this carry-on." Elliott held up his bag and smiled. "My grandfather used to write Accidental Tourist travel brochures. You know, pack light. Only take one carry-on. You must've read the book, as old as you are. It was quite the best-seller."

The man looked at him, shook his head, and turned to walk away.

Elliott followed the man outside to the short term parking deck. The man took the bag and threw it into the trunk, lit a cigarette, and got into the car. Elliott waited.

"Are ya coming?" the man said to him through the opened window.

"I was going to wait until you finished."

"Finished what?"

"Smoking."

"Nah, come on. I'll leave the window down."

Elliott slowly lowered himself into the seat.

The man started the car and exited the parking deck.

"Thanks for the ride," Elliott said as he buckled his seatbelt and settled himself. "My name's Elliott," he said extending his hand.

"I know, I held up the sign." He shook his hand. "Name's Murdoch. It's my job," he grumbled. He spoke through his partially closed lips as the cigarette dangled between them. The cigarette was a fast burner; a half-inch ash skeleton quickly formed on the end. He flicked his cigarette to the opened window. The ash blew back and flittered in his face. "Gosh durnit." He quickly put the window up, as if it would help, and dusted off his blue pants.

"You work for this company?" Elliott asked.

"Magalto? Yeah."

"What do you do?"

"Work in security."

"Security? Like what?"

"It's security." Murdoch looked at him. "I can't tell you. If I did, it wouldn't be security, now, would it?" He turned his shaking head back to the road.

"I was just wondering. I'll be working here for the next week or so, and I don't know much about it."

The man took his eyes off the road and turned slowly to Elliott. "Really," he said as if he could not have cared less.

"Yes, I was asked to help out with a project. It's probably easier than the one I was working on in school."

Murdoch turned back to the road. "You're a student?"

"Yeah. I'm about ready to graduate. I'm doing this as a senior project."

"Uh-huh. That's nice." Murdoch took another long drag from his cigarette.

"How long have you been working with this company?" Elliott asked.

"Long time."

"How long have you been working in security?"

Murdoch didn't speak. He opened the ashtray and crushed the butt of his cigarette in with a pile of the others. He took out another cigarette, dangled it between his lips, and lit it. He blew a cloud of smoke against the closed window. It billowed back into his face and he coughed it away. "Damn." He put the window down. "Don't mind if I smoke, do ya?"

"Yes, actually I do."

"I've been working this job for twelve years, ever since the company moved to Brownsville. I'm sixty-two years old, and now all I do is drive this damn car." He turned and looked at Elliott.

Elliott looked around. "It's a nice car. It's very comfortable."

"I used to be in security. I used to be in charge of the whole department, hiring and firing, purchasing equipment, developing and training." He turned back and watched the road. "Now this is my life. Driving you punks around."

"What happened?"

Murdoch blinked hard a few times. "I knew every inch of the company: who came, who went, and who wasn't supposed to be there." His lips closed around the dangling cigarette and he took a long drag. "Now all they let me do is drive."

Elliott watched the road.

Murdoch stared straight ahead. "My wife got a cancer in her throat. It changed everything."

Elliott turned to the scenery as they drove in silence. Murdoch mumbled over the next few minutes and every so often he broke out in a laugh. The ash broke off each time, falling on his pants. He didn't notice. "Now that sounds crazy, doesn't it?" He rolled his eyes upward as he turned his head and looked at Elliott.

"What's that? I missed what you said."

"Here, let me put this out." He took the cigarette off his lip and flicked it out the window.

"Thank you."

"If you do it, they wouldn't blame me."

"Do what?"

Murdoch turned and looked at Elliott. "No, I hafta do it myself."

"Do what?"

Murdoch turned back and looked at the road. "They killed her. You know that? They killed her."

"Who killed her?"

"Security is an issue nobody takes seriously."

Murdoch pulled the car up to the security gate at Magalto and flashed his badge to the attendant.

"Good afternoon, Murdoch."

"Afternoon, Mike. This here's Elliott." He pointed to him. "He's supposed to be cleared for a coupla days."

"'Ellow," said the security officer, leaning down and looking through the window. Elliott nodded. The officer pushed a button and the security bar swung open, allowing the car to pass.

Murdoch drove to the front of the building and pulled into a stall marked for the company taxi. He turned to Elliott. "Your guest pass and all the other information is waitin' for you at the front desk, right inside."

"Great. Thanks, Murdoch." Elliott reached out his hand and Murdoch shook it. He got out of the car, went to the trunk, and picked up his own bag. He stepped to the sidewalk and watched the smoke billow inside as the car backed up. Murdoch gave a nod and maneuvered the car through the complex.

Elliott turned and looked at the large building—seven stories tall and at least three times as wide. At the entrance, white marble columns separated huge glass panes. A large bronze fountain bubbled in the center of the manicured courtyard. Several groundskeepers worked, clipping square hedges and pruning ornamental trees. He walked toward the building and the sensors tripped and two large glass doors opened into a beautiful foyer. The busyness of the place stopped him. People were coming and going. School children on tour huddled in groups were given the company spiel by old ladies in blue blazers. Employees in suits scurried to their workplaces, carrying briefcases or stacks of documents. Laboratory personnel in white jackets punched buttons on hand-held instruments or read papers held close to their noses. Security guards dutifully inspected people and personal items as they clustered around the checkpoint, just ahead. Elliott stepped forward, placed his bag on the conveyor, and walked through the electronic sensor. He picked up his bag without incident and continued to the large circular desk arranged squarely in the middle of the lobby.

"Yes, may I help you?" the receptionist asked as he approached.

"I'm Elliott Chapman. I'm here . . . "

"Oh yes," she sang with a Texas accent. "We've been expecting you." She reached for a plastic card and a notebook. "Here, these are for you. This pass will get you into most of the rooms in the building and the notebook is about company policy. There you go." She slid them across the countertop. "Now I need to get your fingerprints." She took out an ink stamp pad and placed his right index finger in it, dabbed it on to a clear plastic sheet, then handed him a towel. "That's all we need right now. When you are finished for today, please return here. A driver will take you to the hotel where you will be staying."

She motioned with her left and said, "Mr. Sloan is waiting for you in his office on the third floor. Now, see that elevator"—she pointed with her torrid red fingernails and bobbled them as she spoke—"you take that straight to the third floor. There's a receptionist, Becky is her name—very nice lady. Well, she'll be expecting you. I'm going to buzz her now and let her know you'll be right up. We hope you have a nice visit with us." She flashed him a company smile.

Elliott smiled back as he wiped his inky finger in vain. He picked up his bag and walked in the direction she pointed, looking around the lobby. What a lobby. Flags from foreign countries were suspended from the open-beamed ceiling. South American tapestries hung high on the white marble walls, depicting early life of the natives. Below these, at eye level, large, beautiful imitations from any number of well-known impressionists were secured by elaborate golden frames. Each had its own spotlight, and it was daytime.

Elliott took the elevator to the third floor, and stepped out into another Magalto lobby: smaller but highly decorative and teaming with employees. Becky, at the reception desk, welcomed him and told him to wait in a black leather chair near Mr. Sloan's office. Elliott walked with his bag to the far side of the lobby and stopped to listen to the yelling he could hear coming from inside the room.

"Are you saying you just began recombining? Today? I told you to put that on hold until next week. What t'hell's the matter with you, John? Now I suppose you want to work on it until you're finished. Is that your intention?"

"It should replicate within two days, three tops. When it's finished, I'm gonna incubate it all next week. Then I'll have time to get on with Martino's squash."

"Well, I'm leaving for New York tomorrow, and I'd like you to have things in some kind of order before I go."

"I will, Steve. I will."

"That kid from Royce hasn't shown up yet. As soon as he does, I want you to take him to the lab and brief him on Martino's project. Get him familiar with some of the equipment and techniques you're using. Martino doesn't know who he is. Make sure he's part of the company, for a week or two, anyway. He should have every kind of clearance necessary. I want him to fit right in."

"Okay, Steve. I'll get him to fit in. I'll go wait in my office for him."

Elliott quickly dropped his bag, bolted to the closest chair, and plopped down. The door burst open and out flew a man who took one step, tripped all over the bag, and fell hard to the floor. Elliott peeked at him through half-closed eyes.

"What the hell!" The man picked himself up and brushed off his brightly colored lab jacket. He looked over at Elliott, who had slid down and rested his head against the back of the chair. His eyes were closed and his mouth hung open. "Damn janitors," said the man as he picked up the bag and tossed it to the side. It hit the wall with a thud.

Elliott peeked again and watched the man with the ponytail and tie-dyed lab jacket whisk into the lobby and down the hall. He got up, reclaimed his bag, and raised a hand to knock.

"Door's open."

Elliott pushed it open a little further and stepped inside. "Hello?"

"Yes?" Sloan drawled as he looked up from his desk.

"Is he all right?" Elliott asked.

"Dr. Barringer? Of course he's all right." He stood from his desk and took his glasses off. "You are . . . ?"

"My name's Elliott Chapman. Dr. Quinton Kingsley sent me from Portland to work on a project for you."

"Oh yes, Elliott." Sloan smiled as he walked around his desk for the greeting. He wore a snow-white shirt with puffy sleeves. It had no wrinkles. Around his collar hung a gorgeous pastel tie, which just touched the top of his shiny rhinestone belt. Dark cuffed slacks brushed the top of his patent leather Gucci's. "Come in," he said extending his hand. "My name's Steven Sloan and I run this place. Impressive, isn't it?"

"Yeah."

"We're happy to have you with us. Come in and sit a minute." Sloan poked his head out the door and looked out across the lobby.

Elliott dropped his bag against the wall, out of the way of foot traffic, and walked to the chair in front of the desk. From the looks of his office, it wasn't difficult to tell that Steven Sloan commanded a multi-billion dollar global conglomerate. Above his desk hung a large metal replica of the world; the top half spun slowly with earth axis rotation, the lower half spun opposite. Two side walls were covered with plaques and awards. On the back wall were photos: Sloan with the past three United States Presidents and other dignitaries from around the world, pictures of kids or grandkids, and a very friendly younger woman hanging on Sloan's arm. His large, black desk was sleek and spotless. The only items on it were a lamp, a telephone, and a marble plaque that read: 'Science Explores, Technology Executes, Man Conforms.'

Sloan shut the door and walked to his chair. "Well, I'm glad you could give us a hand."

"Happy to." Elliott settled into the chair in front of his desk. He picked up the plaque and looked up at Sloan. "Your commitment to the Scientific Revolution?"

Sloan reached for the plaque and took it from Elliott. "Ah, someone gave it to me. It was the World Fair's motto a few years back." He looked at it, placed it on his desk away from Elliott, then sat back with his hands behind his head. "So, I hear you're one of the top in your class."

"Is that what Dr. Kingsley said?"

"That's what he said. One of his best, that right?"

"Really? He told you that?"

"Oh, don't be modest, boy. You're in Texas." Sloan let out a big laugh.

"Well then word's finally getting beyond him."

"Of course it is. That's why Quinton recommended you. He wouldn't talk that way about just anyone. I do know that." He winked at him.

"I guess. Nice office you have here," Elliott said looking around.

Sloan took the opportunity to explain each plaque and photo, about where he'd traveled and who he knew. He talked about the connections his company had with American governmental agencies and how they influenced third-world countries, then he parleyed into discourse about the amount of power they were harvesting in agriculture. Sloan talked nonstop, occasionally asking Elliott a question. But before Elliott could ever get a word into the Texan monologue, Sloan stampeded on to another topic.

"So, are you ready to orientate?" Sloan paused for a moment, then leaned forward. Elliott waited. "It's not a big deal, but we want to give you a little heads up before we let you go. We have a project for a client in Bogotá that we need you to help with, but before you leave, we want to orientate you here in our lab. Dr. Barringer will go over Magalto protocol and give you a manual that I want you to go over very carefully. I know you understand most of the lab shit from your training with Quinton, but we're going to give you some very important details that will help you with your work down there."

"In the lab."

"Yes," he drawled. "We've come up with some pioneering methods in the field that you'll be privy to. We have a lot of chemical patents, and we have some agriculture patents pending. I think Dr. Barringer will talk to you about them."

"Dr. Barringer?"

"Dr. John Barringer. The guy who just fell out the door. Ha. You'll get used to him." He smiled.

Elliott smiled back.

"You're going to be leaving tomorrow, so we hafta send you through our four-week training program in a coupla hours here today. Sounds like you can handle that."

"Sure."

"Then you can relax the rest of the evening. There are a lot of sights to see here in Brownsville. You know that big ol' river. Natives call it the Rio Grande. We'll get you out there, if you'd like. Otherwise there's the city. I never really get out there much, but I can hook you up with a good restaurant and a show. Come to think, I believe someone's already made all the arrangements for you. You'll have to check at the desk. Tomorrow morning we'll ride to the airport together."

"Airport?"

"Yes. I'll be going to New York, to the biggest biotech conference in North America, and you're flying down to the lab in Mexico. We're leaving at the same time."

"Mexico?" Elliott shifted forward in his chair.

"Well, yes. The lab at our compound in Matamoros." He looked at him with concern. "You understand, the lab is in Mexico. Aren't you clear about this?"

"Not really," Elliott said quickly. "Dr. Kingsley said that I was to help in a lab in Texas. Nothing about Mexico." He smiled and shook his head. "You're kidding me."

"It's right across the border." Sloan laughed. "No, I'm not kidding. We're working with some Columbian businessmen. They grow crops for us on our compound outside of Matamoros, Mexico, just across the border. When our new crops can grow there without any problems, we sell the whole batch to 'em. But, we have a small problem with the new squash crop. We need you to figure out the titration levels so the dusters can spray the fields. We might be able to save the second planting. You need to do this in the lab. It's no big deal for us, we do it all the time. But we're in a time crunch with some other products, and we don't have a researcher to spare on this project. Dr. Barringer is going to go over some important laboratory things with you. You didn't know *anything* about this?"

"No."

"Well, this is a big deal for a smart kid like you. This is an opportunity not many in the field get, to help with a foreign laboratory. Kingsley spoke highly of you, and he said you'd be more than willing to help us out."

Elliott smiled and nodded at him. "I probably didn't hear him correctly. We've been having some difficulty communicating lately."

"Well son, don't let your hearing interfere with your education. We'll have your passport and some legal papers you'll need to carry. Everything's ready, except your photo. They'll do that today. You're going to have a great experience and it won't hurt you at all to log the trip on your résumé. I apologize about the misinformation."

"That's all right. Actually, this'll be great. Finally, I get to do something important outside of Royce. Does he know what I'll be doing? I'd like to tell him exactly what I'm doing, if I could."

Sloan shook his head with a crooked smile on his face. "Quinton? Well, sure, kid. If you'd like to tell Quinton what you're doing, you go right ahead. I'm sure he'd like to hear. Well . . . " Sloan stood and moved to the side of his desk. Elliott stood in response. "I have some work to do around here, and you need to get up to the laboratory. You go out there in the lobby and wait for Dr. Barringer; he'll take you to the lab." Sloan reached his hand and shook Elliott's forcefully. "It's a pleasure to meet you, boy. I'll have a driver pick you up at your hotel in the morning."

"Thank you. I do appreciate this, Mr. Sloan." Elliott took his bag, walked to his new favorite chair in the lobby, and sat.

Elliott pushed himself farther into the comfortable chair and crossed his legs, waiting for Dr. Barringer. All ten digits drummed the leather armrests. He looked around again. What a place. He looked down at his old Rockports with their tattered laces. One more pull and they'd probably break. He brushed his hair out of his eyes and sat up straight.

Several people in suits and lab jackets walked by and asked for whom he was waiting, and if he needed anything. No, just waiting for Dr. John Barringer. Then, twenty minutes later, just as he was about to close his heavy eyes, Elliott looked down the hallway and spotted the man in the brilliantly colored tie-dyed lab jacket, waltzing side to side, greeting everyone he met with a salute or a vigorous handshake. The man walked by the reception desk. Becky and two other employees timidly waved to him and he responded with a salute and a great big smile. The tails of his lab jacket flapped behind him and loose strands of hair that had escaped from his ponytail floated in every direction around his head. A bushy handlebar mustache rested neatly on his face, and glasses hung around his neck from a black croakie. His white pocket protector was stuffed full of writing utensils, crumpled papers, and sprigs of wire probably attached to hidden electronic devices. Birkenstocks covered most of his yellow sock-covered feet. Right—on.

"Hallow. You're Elliott," he said with the same big grin, reaching out his hand.

Elliott stood with a matching smile and shook it. "Yes I am. You're Dr. Barringer?"

"Me?" He stopped and looked up. "Oh, yeah. But you can call me *Easy*. Or *Barring*. I like things easy. Only my mother calls me *Dr. Barringer*, so whenever I hear it I hafta look around. Sometimes she sneaks up on me. She does that a coupla times a year. Done it for years and it just drives me *crazy*."

"You're the lab director?"

"Well, *yeah*." He plopped into the chair beside Elliott and smiled at him. "And you're here for the project, right? If you are, then I'm the lab director. Have a seat a minute."

Elliott lowered himself into the chair.

Easy leaned in close to him. "And, uh, which project would that be?"

"The one for Quinton," Elliott said. "Some kind of titration in the lab."

"You know about the lab?"

Elliott wrinkled his face at him.

"I'm kidding ya," Easy said, winking at him. "I'm supposed to go over some things we're doing here. Kinda run down the highlights. Then you get to go to the lab in Mexico, tomorrow."

"I guess that's the one. Why do you have labs in Mexico?"

Easy's eyes bulged. "It's just *one* of our labs. We have 'em all over the place. And you've been chosen to help figure out some simple titrations. I'd consider it an honor, son."

"Yeah, I do. But you'd think I'd get a little more notice, going to Mexico and all."

"That's the way things work in this field. Fast as an electrical spark across a nerve synapse." Easy settled into the chair. "You do a good job there, and you might even get an offer from us. We're always lookin' for someone who can find his way around a lab." Easy stopped and peered at him for a moment. "You look very familiar. Have we met before?"

"No, don't think so."

"You sure? You're not that crazy bronco rider from Colorado that interviewed here a coupla months ago?"

"No. Never been to Texas."

"Well gall darn. Now I'll be up all night thinking about this, and a few other things I've stumbled over today." He slapped his leg and gave a laugh, then settled again. "Whew-*y*! You'd think I was a comedian or sompthin' if I weren't wearing this lab jacket"—he reached the lapels of the jacket and looked at them shaking his head—"but this doesn't make

me look any more serious, now does it? Well, what the hell."
He let go of the lapels and looked hard at Elliott. "I'm going
to be needin' a good researcher, real soon. I have this little
project I'm working on, and I'm gonna tell you about it today.
Then we'll go over a few simple things you'll need to do in
Mexico." He stopped for a moment and peered at Elliott. "You
pretty good in the lab?"

Elliott shifted in his seat. "Yeah, I do okay."

"Well that's what I like to hear. I've been working on a
project and it's taking me all year. I gotta get it finished,
because it's just drivin' me crazy."

"All year?"

"Oh yeah, man, at least all year. It's a little complicated,
but I think you'll enjoy the results when we get 'em."

"But I'm only staying until this project is finished. I
haven't even graduated."

"That's all right. What are you gonna do when you
graduate?"

"I'm going to med school this fall. I just can't decide
where."

"Do'ya wanna work here during the summers?" he asked
with a big smile.

"I don't know. I haven't really thought about it."

"Well, think about it. I'll have a job for you."

"You do? You'll hire me, just like that?"

"Yeah. We don't waste any time around here." He winked
at him.

"I'm not sure. It just seems a little . . . "

"Fast? No matter. You're hired," he said with a laugh.
"You'll get top pay, benefits, and time off for good behavior."

"Just like that?"

"Sure. You accept?"

"I have to decide right now?"

"Well, yeah. Then we can go have a looky around." He
leaned forward towards Elliott, covered his mouth, and said
with a low whisper, "We're going to make some heads spin

with this one, let me tell ya." He slapped Elliott's knee and sat back into the chair, laughing.

Elliott glanced at his shoelaces. They would break right now. Maybe one or two more pulls, but they would definitely break. Who really even needs shoelaces, working in this place? Or shoes, for that matter? This is what Kingsley was always promising. A job with a good company, working the summers between school. Magalto money would be hard to beat. The salary would pay for living expenses at school, and then some. A tie-dyed lab jacket would be cool, but the pocket protector and yellow socks would most certainly have to go.

"I can't consult with anyone else about this? It seems pretty quick to decide. And I am still in school, technically."

"Sure you can. Who would you like to talk to?"

"Well . . . I . . . ."

"Your mother?" Easy chuckled and winked. "Yeah, that's what I did too. She was sittin' at the home watching, I think it was one of those cotton pickin' soap operas she always watches, when I gave her a jingle on the ringy-dingy . . . "

"No wait, on second thought, I'll do it. This is what Dr. Kingsley's always been talking about. And how fortunate, I'll be working for the same company. Yeah, this sounds great."

"Outta sight, man. Welcome aboard. It'll be just great havin' ya here." Easy shook Elliott's hand vigorously. He hopped to his feet and motioned him to follow. "Let's move out, but you're going to have to loose the bag. Here, let me take it over to the desk. They'll keep it safe for you." He reached down and grabbed the bag.

"Sure."

Elliott watched as the man handed the bag to Becky, who put it down at her feet. Easy shook her hand vigorously, then whipped around and moved quickly through the lobby and down the hall, his words out of earshot, but his hands expressing everything. Elliott made an attempt to catch him. Up ahead, Easy was carrying on a conversation with himself, oblivious to the serious people in suits who passed by. They, in turn, paid no attention to him. Elliott politely nodded or said hello to them, even if they didn't look up. He quickened his step to catch Easy.

" . . . hidden things . . . top secret . . . never tell anyone . . . take over the world . . . " Easy stopped. He looked to his right and left, then spun around and threw his hands up. "Oh man, I'm sorry," he said to Elliott, who was almost running to catch up. "I thought you were right next to me."

"I am now," Elliott said, breathing fast.

Easy held the elevator door open for Elliott. He followed him inside and pushed the seventh floor button.

"There I go again," Easy said. "Did you follow what I was saying? I was talking as if you were listening. Now I'll have to repeat myself, and whenever I do that, I never know if I'll say the same thing. It always comes out different the third or fourth time."

"I heard bits and pieces."

"Oh. Well, I was talking about how nice it is to live here. It's so beautiful. No one in the country knows how great it is to live here, in this part of Texas. It's a real secret. There are so many things to see, so many things to do. It's the best dern part of the world."

"Yeah, it looks like it. I saw a little on the way over from the airport. Your courteous driver pointed out a few things in between cigarettes. It looks like a nice, brown place." Elliott looked his host up and down.

Easy didn't speak, but stood with his head cocked, intently watching and mouthing the numbers that lit up as they rode the elevator. The bell rang and the doors opened.

"Yeah, you're going to really like it here." Easy looked at Elliott then charged out. "Come on, let's giddy-up. And I'll try to slow down for you a little," he said over his shoulder. "I get so excited, you know. We're on a mission, young man—a mission from the gods."

"Where are we going?" Elliott walked quickly.

Easy stopped in his tracks, turned around, and looked at him, wild-eyed. His face morphed into a stone cold gargoyle's, then immediately softened. He broke into a toothy grin. "To the lab, man! My most favorite place in the world. Where new worlds are made. Where the crucible of time collides with the energy of intelligence. Hell, I'm like a cow in a candy store in there."

"Kid. You mean kid in a candy store."

"Kid? Kid in a candy store?" Easy looked up to the ceiling scratching his head then burst out laughing. "Yeah! Yeah, now *that* makes more sense. I never understood what a cow was doing in a candy store. Hey, hey. A kid in a candy store. Now, that's a whole bunch better." He continued walking, talking, laughing at himself, and waving his hands all at the same time. Elliott stood gawking at the man. The man in the tie-dyed lab jacket.

" . . . make you rich . . . from the dungeon . . . climb out . . . Elliott?" Easy stopped up ahead. His head arched to the right, then left.

"Yeah?" Elliott responded, hurrying up beside him. "I'm right here."

"I'm sorry. There I go again, and I leave you behind. What I was saying was that you park your new car in the dungeon. Well, I call it a dungeon, the commoners call it the basement. Then you climb out of this elevator and the door to your office and lab is right here." He pointed to the door he was about to enter.

"Car?"

"Well, yeah. You get a car while you're here. Didn't nobody tell you that? Gosh darn." He smiled and twisted the edge of his mustache, and said with a wink, "Management is falling apart, Elliott. They'll tell you sooner or later. Yeah, and if things go as well as I expect, you'll be getting a place to park your car—a house. Well, Magalto owns it, really. You'll just get to live in it rent-free while you're here. I call it a halfway house . . . you know, halfway between your three month probation and a long-term position with the company. That is, if you wanna bag med school and work here full time." He stepped up to the door entrance.

"Bag med school?"

He turned to Elliott. "Well sure. Medical school is highly overrated. Medicine's going downhill, I tell ya. Once we get our little treats finished in the lab, it'll all be over. We'll be singing with the fat ladies. I sing tenor, someone told me. But I don't know why she said that, because the only time I sing is in my shower. Unless . . . hmmm . . . " Easy looked him up and down. "Are you all right? You don't look so well. Like you're a little woozy."

Elliott held his hand across his forehead. "Nah, I'm okay. A little jet-lag breakfast combo. I don't fly very often."

"Okay. So once you get into the house, I'll be over a *whole lot*. Visiting, you know. I won't at first. I'll let you settle, and then I can come over and help you decorate. I'm a really good decorator. I helped pick out the décor around here, the wall hangings and statues and the furniture. I do some pottery myself, late at night in my basement. It helps me unwind after a long day in the lab, squeezing bacteria into their little suits. Well, we can talk about all that later." He turned around to the door and waited.

Easy widened his eyes in front of the retina scanner. A light beamed crossed his face and a lock clicked inside the door. He put five fingers up to a scanner on the wall. A light flashed upward across his fingertips, and another lock clicked. Several loud bangs followed, and the door swung open. "Here we go." Easy motioned for him to follow.

The first room was a holding cell and containment area. Sanitary suits with headgear lined one wall. Clothing lockers lined the opposite. There were emergency showers overhead, and a few washbasins.

"Here, put this on." Easy handed a suit to Elliott, who was looking around the walls admiring the safety equipment. "We'll just be a minute in here. Put it on over your clothes. You'll be assigned your own in a day or two."

They began suiting up. Easy took the glasses from his neck, folded them into one of his more vacant lab pockets, and re-banded his ponytail. They moved to the next room, which had only a retinal scanner, and the door unlocked to allow them in. The sterile room was filled with laboratory equipment: some that Elliott had worked with at Royce, and some he had never seen before. Several technicians were crouched over their workstations, using pipettes to drop little beasties into petri dishes. Others were peering into their microscopes.

"Hey, Gail. Mike. This here's Elliott. He's going to be working with us. He's like a cow in a candy store." Easy let out a loud laugh and looked at Elliott. "Was it cow or kid?"

"Oh, no. Not another one," Gail said. "I can't handle two of you around here, Easy." She looked up from her work. "I'll quit, I tell you. I'll quit right now."

Mike looked up at Elliott. "Hi Elliott, nice to meet you. Don't believe a word this guy says." He pointed to Easy with a smile. "Actually, most of it *is* true."

"They always do that," Easy said to Elliott with a chuckle, poking him in the ribs.

"Nice to meet both of you." Elliot smiled and nodded to them.

They continued on their tour and walked into another room. It was vacant. "Over there's where you'll work when you get back from your little job in Mexico. It has a computer station, coupla microscopes, and just about anything you'll ever need in a lab." Easy walked ahead, then stopped. "You went to Royce, that right?"

"Yeah, still do, technically."

"Any of this equipment look familiar?" He smiled.

"Yeah." Elliott looked around. "I worked on a lot of the same stuff."

Easy cupped his hand to his mouth and lowered his voice. "We give a lot of money to Royce." He stood up straight and looked around. "Why do I do that? I don't have to whisper in here. There's no one else around"—he leaned toward Elliott and cupped his hand over his mouth again—"but you never know who's listening, and sometimes when the wrong person hears something important, it causes problems for everyone."

Elliott let out a nervous laugh. He looked around the room. "So, what will I be doing? Now that I'm a laboratory technician and all."

"Come on, let's strip out of this get-up, and I'll tell you." Easy turned and walked back towards the first room. Elliott followed, looking around the place.

"Hope you find the cure this time, Mike," Easy said. "We can't be having any more wild viruses orbiting around here, like we did last month."

Mike looked up without a smile.

"Come on, Elliott, let's let these kids work on their viruses, or patents, or whatever they're doing."

Elliott walked slowly, peering over their shoulders to see what the technicians were doing under their microscopes. Then he quickly followed Easy out of the room by the same process they entered. Easy didn't talk, and his movements were flaccid as they continued walking down the hall. He turned the corner, approached another door, and put his eyes up to the retinal scanner. The door opened automatically.

"This is my office," Easy said. "You'll get one when you work here permanently. Here, sit down." He motioned for Elliott to sit in the chair across from his desk.

"Nice office. It's very homey," Elliott said, admiring the décor. A huge polished desk half the size of Sloan's filled most of the room. Several high-backed leather chairs stood in front of the desk, and a large leather captain's chair stood behind. Three Texas cow skull paintings hung on the walls. Easy closed the door behind him.

Elliott sat slowly.

Easy walked around to his chair and sat. "Thank you. You'll get to decorate yours any way you'd like. Unless, of course, you want my help."

Suddenly his smile vanished and his entire face changed shape. His eyes drew closer together and bore into Elliott. "What we're doing in this laboratory is so incredible, so magnificent, that we cannot let any information leave the premises. I think we've had this talk before."

"Well, no, actually—we haven't."

"Then we're having it right now. You'll need to sign confidentiality agreements and a contract to work here this summer." Easy cleared his throat, leaned back in his chair, and looked at Elliott intensely. "Now we need to have crystal clear understanding about a few things. Any information you receive from here is to be held in strict confidence. I hope you understand the gravity of what I'm saying. You can't talk to anyone about your work at Magalto. Nobody. You'll be visiting universities and companies around the country, exchanging a few ideas. Other than that, you don't speak to anyone, you don't browse, and you don't write down *anything* during your probation period. Am I being clear about this?"

"Yes," Elliott gulped.

"First of all: the squash problem in Mexico. You'll need to titrate out a coupla hydrochloride solutions. There should be some HCl in the laboratory to do it. Titrate it into some of the herbicide, until you get an acidic pH. When you get between 5.4 and 5.6, take the solution out to the field and pour it on the roots of one of them squash plants. In one or two days, the stem should firm up. When it does, you'll need to add more fixer to it, or it won't hold the hydrogen. Someone there will show you what the fixer is. Just ask one of the lab hands, that's about all they'll know. When you get the mixture at the right pH, tell them to mix the entire herbicide with that ratio. It'll probably be around twelve milliliters of herbicide to one liter of HCl. Whatever it is, have them mix it, then have the crop duster spray the fields. Only the squash. Exactly sixteen hours later, have the duster spray one hundred percent fixer on it. Now, some of the squash will be lost. That's okay, the majority will be salvaged. And you gotta be sure about the pH. If it isn't right, this ain't gonna work. You'll get a color change, a dark yellow. That's how I can always tell. If you have any questions I want you to call me. All righty?"

"Yeah, all right. I think I did something similar at Royce a while back." Elliott laughed nervously.

"It's pretty straightforward, son, but a little time-consuming. We just can't spare anyone for this long. I think you can handle it, but I'll get you some of my notes. They're around here somewhere." Easy sat back and smiled broadly. "Now. Let me tell you what I'm working on, and in just a short time, you'll be helping me with it—my project. I call it the Seventh Day Ecstasy. You just sit back now and listen to me."

CHAPTER 11

Easy sat with his hands folded on his desk, his smile gone. He peered at Elliott and began: "I had a difficult time growin' up; I'd rather not go into that right now. And I vowed that when I got older, I'd go and make some changes that'd help out a few people. Help 'em get through life a little better than I did. Well, I got through school—no thanks to any of my teachers—and learnt a few things that I'm proud to rank as some of the best this world has ever seen."

Elliott nodded.

Easy smiled. "Remember Darwin? Well, he just didn't get it. You know, his goofy theories of evolution and all his other hallucinations he pontificated? Only the fittest survive? It's all bullshit, man. He makes the world of evolution unfair for the weaklings and the moral morons. It's twisted thinking and them damn schools keep teaching that trash. I want you to stop yourself right now from falling into that mindless evolutionary tar pit. Lemme tell ya, this is post-Darwinism, dude. It's freakin' twenty-first century!

"Know what that means? It's time to create, man. And I mean, let's get serious about it. You ask me what I'm talking about. Let me ask you right back—what is there too much of in this world? Do you know? Well I'll tell ya. It's negativity, man. It's everything that causes pain and suffering. I'm going to eliminate every damn negative molecule from the living world. Every bad thing that can possibly happen will be programmed out through genetic engineering and the biological sciences. What am I talking about, you ask again? I'm talkin' emotions, man! I'm talkin' nerve responses at the synaptic level. Pain. Suffering. That's what's holding us back—holding you back. The biological molecules of these useless connections will be completely disposed of. That's what they are anyways, just molecules. Why not wipe'm out? Every damn emotion is a molecule. So, any kind of pain that we helpless humans experience from these molecules, will be wiped out. Gone, goodbye, and don't come back no more. Even the not-so-good days will be programmed out. Who the hell even wants a not-so-good day? Are you with me on this? I'm talkin' and you're just lookin' at me."

Elliott blinked his eyes a few times and refocused. Easy didn't wait for an answer.

" . . . so the post-human race will live in a chronic, constant state of euphoria. Peace, love, and happiness will be the only kinds of emotions we will experience, and they'll be turned on *all the time*! The post-human mind won't even work the way we know it today. It will be a super consciousness, living in *total* bliss. Revolting thoughts and bad actions will only appear in your old history books. You'll find them to be pathological, but *how would you even know*? You won't even *recognize* them—the negativity."

Dr. Easy Barringer let out a belly laugh that continued for a few moments. Elliott sat with glazed eyes, looking at the man who had just hired him for a summer job in the lab. Easy wiped his brow with his hand and composed himself.

"*Whew-y!* This gets me *so excited!*" Easy shook his head forward, then looked up at Elliott.

"It's like the color 'buefie', Elliott. Do you know what color buefie is? Of course you don't. You have no idea because the word doesn't even exist. That's what'll happen to sadness, pain, and suffering. You'll have no idea what they are. They'll only be words written in boring novels of the past. And who wants to read a boring novel that goes on and on about things that sure as hell don't make any sense? I won't read 'em, let me tell ya that right now. The words won't even register. How pathetic.

"You're not gonna need drugs, sex, money, or power. Why would you? They won't do you any good. There won't be any neurotransmitters in post-human neurology that will recognize these distracting stimulants. Good feelings will be automatic. Bliss will be constant. Happiness will pervade all post-human beings. What more do you want? This is the moment in time the entire world has been waiting for! And we get to deliver it to 'em. Yeah, Darwin was the father of genetics, and Hitler carried out some of his ideas, the crazy bastard. But we—*we* are the administrators. It will be effortless and no one will care to argue with us. Why would they argue against eliminating all the bad, when we'll give 'em all the good? We are on the verge of changing the history of the world and, in fact, creating beings in our own image but without our bad traits. It will be all good, all peace and love, or whatever the hell emotions we decide to program.

"Elliott, you're going to help us. We are getting closer to determining the precise molecular structure of bad experiences and the genetics that make them happen. After a few more years, the very last unpleasant human experience will occur. Then, it will be gone—*poof*!—passed into oblivion. Just as some bad diseases have been eliminated and are now sad memories that an occasional psychopath wants to revive, so too will adverse human experiences be banished. It will happen in my lifetime, and your generation will get to live in the ambiance of absolute euphoria.

"After this has happened, our sophisticated bioengineering will combine with supercomputers to produce rapid evolutionary changes within the post-human genome. Hell, of *course* evolution of the species never happened as Darwin hallucinated. He was looking to nature to make mutant species and their phylogeny. And it's *never happened*! *Never*—until now! Today, new evolutionary species are created in our labs every day of the week. Soon, these species will be self-replicating and they will eventually create the next beings.

These beings will be much more cerebral, have more consciousness, and be supremely moral. And talk about morality. Who the hell knows what morality is? Is morality the right and wrong ideas some politicians and preachers try to inflict on their subjects? They've told us that they have the highest morals, and that we should let them decide what's good and bad. Yeah, like *they're* moral? Isn't it usually the immoral morons making decisions for society? Hell no, not anymore. Now it will be the biologists who'll decide what's right and wrong. *What* am I *saying*? There won't *be* any wrong! It's just like buefie; it doesn't even register. You won't think 'bad' because it won't even exist.

"These outdated ideas have come from our present educational systems. Yeah, like Royce. And every one of their philosophical and biological theories are delusional, Elliott. They're based on the strong overcoming the weak. It's all bullshit. It's a despicable system; one that began a coupla hundred years ago. Why would you choose to live an inferior life, be miserably unhappy, and then be obliterated by a painful, uncertain death—*when you don't have to*? That's what they teach in our society. Look at all the retirement homes where we lock up the old people. My mom watching her cotton pickin' soap operas on satellite telly, thinking she's retired. Now *that's* a good one. No, soon you'll have the choice. Is that what you'll choose—to slowly fade away into oblivion? Nah, don't think so.

"If you even had the *possibility* of a negative thought, you would be an amoral, narcissistic creature yourself, not to choose to purge the world of suffering through biological technology and cerebral computations. Generations later, no one will be able to conceptualize our pain and misery, just as we can't comprehend buefie. Buefie, Elliott. Never forget that word—it has no meaning.

"Ya think I'm kidding? I'm not kidding. This is not a figment of science fantasy. This is not fiction, Elliott. We have found exactly where these changes are being made, and how they evolutionize. They're deep inside the human limbic system, the command center of pleasure in the existing human. You should know this from basic biology. The neurotransmitters, neuropeptides, opiates, and their receptors in the dopamine cascade reward system, are what make this possible right now, but it's *so damn primitive!* Today we can improve the pleasure synapses, and eventually we'll abolish the pathways for pain and unpleasantness, all through genetic sequencing. Why do you think this country is so damn drug-induced? People want to feel good now, to hell with the future. Well, we're going to obliterate the instant gratification receptors. Post-humans will be euphoric every damn second of their new lives. Let's *get it on!*

"Can you imagine if every thought was a beautiful flower? If every color danced in your head, leading you to the next undiscovered one? If powerful new emotions that you had never experienced become part of your daily life, and new ones flooded your nervous system with pleasantries, twenty-four hours a day? Cerebral concepts will bubble exotic sensations throughout your being all the time, and will continue evolving into the next level of consciousness, until levels of these higher consciousnesses become completely obsolete. They'll all be one. *One wavelength!* How difficult can that be?

"True, there are obstacles to overcome. They'll be people bitchin' and moanin' about our approach, but they don't have answers either. They'll be countries to convince and leaders to persuade, but that'll be easy when we show 'em what we can do. We'll put on a horse and doggy show about a little nerve regeneration over here, and a demonstration about nerve receptor enhancements over there. Elliott, do you realize what I just said? If we can multiply nerve tissue, we will soon be able to increase and enhance consciousness. That means that post-humans will have no limit on development whatsoever. To be sure, their limbic systems and pleasure metabolic pathways will be very highly developed—a hundred times as large as ours. Almost makes you jealous, huh? Buefie, Elliott. Buefie.

"It all comes down to molecules and chemicals. And we can make both of 'em. Chemicals have always ruled the world. Those damn physicists think they have the corner on science and technology. What they have is too much gravity—it's weighin' 'em down.

"They don't understand. Every thought or action, every discovery or invention, everything is the result of chemicals. Your feelings right now are being made by neuropeptides jumpin' through your nervous system, attaching to specific receptors in your brain and spinal cord. It's all excitation or inhibition. You feel good or bad based on binary switches. It's that simple. The future will be better than you can ever imagine . . . "

Elliott was catatonic, close to being comatose. His eyelids were droopy and he was slouched way down into the comfortable chair. Someone had been jabbering.

" . . . the big lake? Elliott? Are you with me?" Easy sat with his fingers interlaced on top of his head, and a big smile.

"Yeah." Elliott jerked upright, almost falling out of the chair. He repositioned himself. "I think I missed that last part."

"What I was sayin' was, we should get out on the lake, the Mexican Sea. It's so beautiful outside today, and I haven't had my boat out in a coupla weeks now. What do you think? Besides, the day's almost over and I can't do much with my stuff until incubation's done. That won't be until tomorrow, anyway."

"You know," Elliott fidgeted in his seat, "I really don't feel so very well."

"Aw, you don't get seasick, do you? We're going to be doin' a lot of fishing once you're back. There's a whole bunch of catfish out in that lake. Well, I call 'em sea catfish. They'll be jumpin' into the boat this summer. Someday I'm gonna run a charter down there, I swear it. You fish, don't you?"

"No, it's not that. I mean, I'd like to go fishing and boating and whatever, but I really don't feel well right now."

Easy Barring transformed in front of Elliott. His face lost all signs of his nickname. His eyes angled midline and the lines in his skin deepened. His cheeks flushed bright red. The man changed into another person, one terribly different than his name suggested.

"You don't want to go out on my boat?" Dr. Barringer said through his clenched jaw.

"Well, I just don't feel very well," Elliott said in his most Kingsley-pleasing voice. "Maybe we can do it some other time."

Dr. Barringer slammed his open hand down on his desk, and the sound made Elliott jump. "*Everyone likes to go out on my boat!*"

"You know I'd really like to sometime, but not today." Elliott shifted again.

Dr. Barringer stood and pushed his chair back. It smacked the wall and fell to the floor. "*Well then, I suppose we'll have to do it some other time, now, won't we?*"

"Yeah, that'd be great. How about when I get back?"

Elliott followed the cue to stand and as he did, he doubled over. He clutched his stomach and almost fell back down. He stood up as straight as he could. Slowly, he turned and followed Dr. Barringer, who stood already holding the door open for him. The lab man looked completely different. His eyes were wide open and the facial lines had relaxed back into their normal grooves. A big toothy grin reappeared on his face, and his handlebar mustache lifted on the edges. His name took on meaning again.

"You look a little pale," Easy said.

Elliott held his stomach and shifted his eyes to the floor.

"I guess I wouldn't want you pukin' all over my deck. Why don't you go back to your hotel and rest awhile. You're going to have a big day tomorrow. We'll do this some other time, I promise." He gave him a wink and patted him on the shoulder.

"Yeah, okay." Elliott kept his eye on Easy all the way through the door. "Thanks. I hope you don't mind. I just need a little rest. Actually, a lot of rest."

"You go get it, son. Do ya think you can find your way downstairs to the information desk? There's an elevator down the hall to your left. It's the one we came up. Take it all the way to the first floor."

"Great. Yeah, I'll find it."

"Well, I guess I'll see you in a few days. It was nice talkin' with you, El. You don't mind me callin' you 'El,' do you? It means 'the' in Spanish, like 'the El.'" He let out a big laugh.

"Sure. That'd be all right."

Easy slapped him on his shoulder and gave the muscle a squeeze. "Just remember what we talked about," he said with a big grin. "Everything in these rooms is on the hush-hush train. We'll go over it some more when you return." He smiled, gave Elliott a gentle nudge moving him into the hall, then quickly shut the door.

Elliott stepped shakily into the hall. He really wasn't well. Maybe it was the jet lag, or the bowl of buefie potpourri Easy dished out. He looked down the hall. No restroom in sight. He began walking the opposite direction Easy told him, running and now covering his mouth. No place to go. He turned down the hall and came upon another elevator. He quickly pushed the 'down' button. The door opened slowly. Just as it cracked enough for him to get his head inside, he let it hurl. And out it came. It splattered all over the back metal wall and over the carpeted floor in a soupy mess. He wiped the dribbles from his mouth with the back of his hand and looked to the side to see a pair of very polished black wing tips partially covered with chunks of digestive matter. Elliott stood up straight and stepped into the elevator, feeling much better and quite relieved.

"Going down?" Elliott asked.

The man looked down at the expelled muddle then at Elliott. "Are you okay?"

"Yeah, I'm all right now." Elliott reached up and wiped his forehead with his hand.

"You don't look well."

"Sorry about that,"—Elliott pointed to the floor—"some of it's on your pants."

"Awww," the man said, lifting his leg. "Now I have to get these cleaned tonight."

The doors closed, locking them into the airtight vesicle without ventilation. Worse than being in an elevator alone with a stranger is experiencing the pungent aroma of another's vomit. The man quickly pushed the button to open the doors but it was too late. The elevator began moving. He stared at his assailant.

"What are you doing here?"

Elliott stood with his hands in his pockets. "I just met with Dr. Barringer about a project I'll be working on."

"Oh, not another one," the man said to the puke, shaking his head.

"Who, Dr. Barringer?"

"They call him Easy. He's not easy."

"Really?"

"If you only knew."

"I know a little."

"He does what he wants, when he wants to do it. Everyone sees him as a happy-go-lucky kind of guy. He's easy unless you cross him, or try to get an answer from him, like I've been trying to do for the last nine months. He's the most unorganized, incompetent lab director. I don't understand half of what he tells me in our meetings. He's always bringing the wrong notes about something completely unrelated to what we're supposed to talk about, and he always says whatever comes off the top of his head. Then he rants and raves about something new his department just came up with. I think he makes up things up as he goes, just to please Sloan. I'm tired of it." He stopped, shook his head, and smiled at Elliott. "Man, I'm sorry. I didn't mean to crab all over you. I just met with the financial team, and his name kept coming up the entire time." He reached out his hand. "My name's Martin Cole. I'm in accounting."

"Hi," Elliott shook his hand. "I'm Elliott Chapman. Sorry about the puke job."

"It's cleanable." He let Elliott's hand go and backed away from the smell that was getting heady.

Elliott nodded.

"So you're working with Easy?"

"Looks like it. Just for the summers between med school. I'm graduating in a week from a college in Portland, Oregon."

"Great." Martin nodded then looked Elliott up and down. "Summers, huh? That's good. We need someone with a little sanity. When do you start?"

"Coupla weeks, officially. I'm going to Mexico tomorrow, to work on a small project."

"Doing what?" Martin wrinkled his forehead at Elliott.

"I'm supposed to figure out a simple titration in their lab. I'll figure it out when I get there."

"Anyone going with you?"

"No, not that I know of."

Martin slowly shook his head. He brought his hand up to his chin and stared at the vomit. "That's strange. You must know someone around here."

"Dr. Kingsley sort of sent me down here."

"Quinton? You know Quinton Kingsley?"

"He's my advisor, who hooked me up with this. It's a long story."

"Yes, of course," Martin said slapping his forehead. "Quinton Kingsley, from Royce University. He's probably told you everything about their laboratory down there. I think he helped set it up a few years ago."

"No, we didn't have time. I had to leave my classes early, and actually, I'm skipping my finals next week to do this job for you guys. I kinda fell into this. Why?"

The elevator sounded its ding and stopped on the first floor. The doors opened. Elliott almost hurled again after the floor rebounded. What made this jolt worse, was the stench that had grown inside the enclosure. The accountant was apparently too focused on the conversation to notice the doors open and the fresh air. Elliott didn't move. The doors closed with a ping.

The accountant stood with one foot ahead of the other, his hand stroking his chin. He stopped, lifted his glasses off his face, and stared coldly at Elliott. "The lab you're going to in Mexico is run by the Armed Forces of Columbia, the FARC. They're growing all of our agriculture now. They know how to grow and deliver the produce much better than the Mexicans ever did. And they own hundreds of acres right across the border. The only things Magalto runs are the laboratory and the clinic. Everything else is done by the FARC."

"Why would they do that for you?"

"Because we sell most of our seed to them. The compound in Mexico was our first genetic test plot. We tested everything there: plants, animals, and effects on people. Our products have increased the impoverished farmers' yield a hundred times. Now their crops are insect resistant, weed resistant, they don't freeze, they don't get sunburned, they don't need much water, and they produce five times the yield of traditional crops. The farmers actually made money. Before the FARC came along, we found the right Mexican officials to sell our products to, and they helped implement the sale of the harvests throughout the world. But then they got a little too independent and began to separate themselves from the family-run line of government. Thousands of Mexicans learned how to become capitalists. It was the newly independent Mexican farmer who voted for the new government. Political heads turned when they replaced over seventy years of control. We don't need that kind of exposure right now. Seems ironic, doesn't it? After the new government took control, we took the opportunity to turn things over to the FARC. Now that's what the FARC want to do in Columbia— take over the government. That is why they want to run our agriculture compound. They pay us very well and have been very helpful to us, up to this point."

"So why am *I* going?"

"You? I don't know why. It used to be that someone from the lab would go down at least once a week to fix something. There's always some kind of emergency. But it's been awhile, come to think of it. I haven't written a check for that trip for a month or two now. Must be something new Easy's cooking up. I know he's supposed to get their laboratory in better shape. He was supposed to do it months ago; we had the money for it. But now everyone's working on another project. You're probably going because he's screwed things up again, and there's no one else to go. Can you handle the job?"

"It's a simple titration. Sounds like it'll take a few days."

The elevator pinged again and the doors opened. They both stopped talking and looked out to see two dark suits, waiting for a ride. The odor could no longer be contained in the small space, and the air whooshed out like a popped balloon.

"Ohhh, God," said the first man, wafting his hand across his face.

"What the hell died in there, Marty?" the second man said, pinching his nose.

The two newcomers backed away fast and turned toward the next elevator. Elliott and Martin stepped out as the doors closed behind them.

"So that's the experiment . . . " Elliott said. The two men looked at him. " . . . to see how quickly the mixture can grow in an enclosed space like an elevator. I think it worked superbly."

"Yes, I would agree," Martin said.

The other set of elevator doors opened for the two lightweights, and they rushed inside.

"I hope you feel better," Martin said as he walked toward the foyer.

"Thanks. I do."

Martin walked down the hall and Elliott watched pieces flake off his pants and shoes. Elliott turned and walked toward the front desk.

"Mr. Chapman," said the receptionist. "Your ride is waiting outside. But here, I have something for you." She reached under the counter, pulled out a passport and folder, and slid them towards him. "This is your passport and papers."

He opened it then looked up at her quickly. "How'd you get my picture?"

"Oh, one of the optical sensors picked it up. When we found an image we liked, we copied it." She frowned. "I hope you like it." She spun the passport around and looked at it.

"Yeah, it'll be okay."

"Good." She reached down again, and set his bag on the counter.

"How'd you get my bag?"

"Had it sent down from upstairs. No one ever remembers their own luggage—don't forget it. I have a funny feeling about you. Now, you'll be flying down in one of the company jets, and the pilots usually like to get off pretty early in the morning. So, I'd say be ready to leave around six-thirty. Someone will pick you up at the hotel and take you to right to the terminal. Then you'll be off to wherever you're going."

He smiled back courteously, picked up his belongings, and walked out front to Murdoch's car.

CHAPTER 12

At six-fifteen in the morning, Elliott stepped into the gracious hotel lobby. Two well-dressed businessmen crowded around the breakfast buffet table, discussing some kind of sporting event that had happened last evening. The louder one speared the last sweet roll with his fork and shook it onto his plate, already piled high with other pastries. He said something to the other man, laughed, and turned to sit in a nearby chair. The second man glanced at Elliott and joined his friend as they continued their discussion.

Elliott dropped his bag on a bench against the wall and walked to the table. The only pastries left were prepackaged; the ones with the jelly middle squished inside the plastic. Elliott turned to the overflowing fruit bowl, picked out a banana, and sat beside his bag. He peeled the banana, took a bite, and leaned his head against the wall. For a few moments he chewed with his eyes closed.

"Time to go, Elliott Chapman."

Elliott slowly blinked his eyes, looked up, and saw Murdoch. The man looked about the same as yesterday except, maybe, his eyes were a little puffier. His shirt was wrinkled as ever. His pants were still much too short and his socks flopped over. His hair didn't look like it had been combed since his last hair cut.

"You can sleep in the car." Murdoch kicked his foot.

Elliott opened his eyes a second time. "All right, I'm coming."

Murdoch picked up his bag and shuffled across the marble floor of the lobby to the car waiting outside. Elliott followed.

"Good morning, Elliott," Steven Sloan said from the front seat. Elliott tucked his head down and slid into the back. Sloan turned around and smiled at him. "I hope you rested well."

"It was all right. Short. You know, I'm still on Pacific Time and recovering from jet lag."

"You'll get used to it. I do this flying bit all the time. It's a mental thing." Sloan turned around and went about his business.

"Flying is mental?" Elliott dropped his head against the headrest and closed his eyes. "Then we should be flying TranceWorld airlines, huh?"

"No, no. I mean the jet lag. You just tell yourself what time zone you're in, and bingo, you're in it." Sloan turned around again.

"Let me sleep on it. I'll tell you in an hour." Elliott closed his eyes.

"Good. You sleep on it, but we'll be at the airport in fifteen minutes. The pilots are ready and waiting for you. It'll be a short flight to Matamoros. You'll arrive at the airport and then be escorted to the laboratory. Did Dr. Barringer go over everything with you? Do you understand what you'll be doing?"

"Yeah. He told me a few things." Elliott opened his eyes and, with an annoyed look, turned around to watch Murdoch, who was making all kinds of noise outside in the back of the car. Finally Murdoch slammed the trunk, walked along the side of the car, got in the driver's seat, and slammed the door shut. Maybe it wasn't a slam, but it was loud and deliberate. He pulled the seatbelt across his belly four or five times then finally managed to buckle it.

"Everybody ready?" Murdoch grinned at Sloan.

"*Yes* Murdoch." Sloan didn't look at him.

Murdoch jammed the car into gear and drove.

"Dr. Barringer scribbled a few things down for you," Sloan busily rummaged through some papers in his lap, "but I can't seem to find the paper."

"What's that?" Murdoch asked. "The secret recipe?"

"No, it's not for you. For Elliott."

"Yeah, he said he had something about the lab specs to give me. That would be helpful," Elliott said with his eyes closed. "But I think I understand the titration."

"Well, he told me he changed a step in the procedure." Sloan continued the paper shuffling. "I just saw the thing this morning. Maybe I left it at the office. There are a few things I want to go over with you, that you won't be prepared for. I wrote 'em on a page." For the next several minutes, he dug through the papers in his briefcase, trying to find the updated protocol.

Elliott slid under his eyelids. And Murdoch, just as soon as he drove the car onto the highway, babbled nonstop about his difficult work, about the company, about the latest problems with the governor of Texas, about his brilliant solutions to the economy. Sloan was too busy rummaging through his briefcase to notice the droning.

" . . . so you're making a trade," Murdoch said in a monotone voice. "Elliot is your free agent in this big drama, huh, Mr. Sloan? He's going to Matamoros to consummate the marriage."

Elliott cracked open his sleepy eyes and looked at the back of Murdoch's wispy head.

"No," Sloan said sharply, looking up from his papers to the road ahead. "They need some academic assistance in the laboratory. I consider it an honor that Mr. Chapman go and offer his services." He turned back at Elliott with a nod and forced smile.

"Well, he's not going to help with those plants they're harvesting in Mexico and movin' across the border, is he?"

Sloan turned sharply. "Magalto is the premier developer of produce worldwide. The Columbians are experts at growing and harvesting. They have developed some very important farming techniques that allow our agricultural products to be grown in many different kinds of terrain. And as it is, the compound in Mexico is a strategic site for distribution throughout the world."

"What a deal. That's what I say." Murdoch nodded his beady head.

"We have been working on these outreaches for a long time." Sloan turned around again and spoke to Elliott, "One of our challenges is to feed the hungry throughout the world, beginning with our neighbors to the South." He glared at Murdoch.

"Magalto tests on pawns and sells to kings." Murdoch turned and looked at Elliott and said to him, "That's how she died, if you want to know."

"How?" Elliott said quickly. He leaned forward and looked at Murdoch.

"Well *now* they use the clinic to test the grub," Murdoch said loosening his collar button and straightening his clip-on tie. "Isn't that right, Mr. Sloan? You find out if people get sick on it. Then what you do is—"

"*THAT'S ENOUGH, MURDOCK!*" Sloan slammed his briefcase, closing it on a few papers that didn't quite get inside. "That's *completely* uncalled for!"

"Clinic? What kind of clinic is it?" Elliott asked. "I heard about it yesterday."

"We're not doing the clinic," Sloan shot. "That ended years ago. Everything is tested in the laboratory in Brownsville."

Murdoch turned around and looked at Elliott. "That's what they tell ya. We used to get their free food. The company still makes trips down . . . "

"MURDOCH! Stop this car!"

"Well, Mr. Sloan, I'm right in the middle of the highway here."

"Pull over to the side of the road—*NOW*!"

Murdoch steered the car to the side and eased it on to the shoulder. He was not visibly moved, as though he took this abuse every day on the job. Elliott looked back and forth between him and Sloan, waiting for the next strike. Sloan unbuckled his seatbelt and threw the door open before the car came to a complete stop. He jumped out and marched around to the driver's side.

"Get out!" Sloan yelled as he reached for the door handle.

"What?"

"*Get the hell out of the car!*"

Murdoch unbuckled his seatbelt and slowly unlocked the door. As soon as it was unlocked, Sloan yanked it wide open. The door sprang backwards and slammed shut. Sloan opened it a second time and held it. Murdoch slowly shifted his legs to the side and hoisted himself up.

"Get out of the car!" Sloan took a fist of Murdoch's short tie, pulled it from the clip, and threw it to the ground. "You're *finished*! Get back to the building, pack your things and get out—*today*!" He pushed him out of his way and dropped into the drivers' seat.

"Hey . . . what? You're just going to leave me here?" Murdoch held both hands up in the air.

Sloan turned and looked up at him. "You were removed from security because you always stick your damn nose in business that doesn't concern you. Now you can't even drive to the airport without getting into trouble. Find your own way back." He jammed the car into gear and stomped on the accelerator. The back tires threw out two arcs of dirt and gravel, pelting Murdoch. The tires finally grabbed and left skid marks, before the car straightened out and barreled down the road.

Murdoch stood alone on the shoulder of the highway. He reached down and picked up the clip-on tie. He straightened it out as best he could and reattached it to his stained collar. He ran his hands down both sides of his wrinkled shirt, dusting it off, and did the same to his short, dirty blue pants. He took out a cigarette and ignited it with a match. He took a long drag and watched the car drive down the road, then turned and began walking the other way.

The man lumbering down the road had given twelve years of his life to a very ungrateful company. Over those years, he had become more vocal in his opinions as the head security guard, telling others how things were and how they ought to be. They needed to know, he would say. But his wife would tell him to not get wrapped up in things, that he should mind his own business and take up a hobby like most men do at his age. Someday he would take up politics, or bowling, he'd tell her. Then, soon after she passed, he became even more absorbed in his attitudes towards the company and his fellow employees. His comments weren't threatening, just very pointed, coming from a security officer. That's what got him demoted to driver. Murdoch the company driver. He settled with the idea, for a while. But his anger festered. Now, as he continued down the road, he began making plans from the ideas that had been percolating in his wound-up brain over the past several years. It was time to plot revenge against the man who had owned his soul for so long.

"Thanks for the ride," Murdoch said to the driver as he opened the pickup truck door.

"Sure thaaang," said the straw-chewing stranger who had picked him up. "Well you have a real inter—restin' story there, partner, I must say."

"Yes, it is. I got it all planned out." He slammed the door shut.

Murdoch turned and faced the Magalto building. His greasy hair looked as if a gust of wind had taken one side of balding locks, whipped it across his head as far as it would reach, and plastered it against an uninhabited part of his skull. His fat face was flushed and showed signs of drainage from all orifices. His shirt had armpit stains and sweat marks down the front, and his clip-on tie hung crooked from the left collar. His shirttails were out and his pant legs rolled up. His shoes were untied and barely able to hold in his fat feet.

He took out a cigarette, his last, and lit the dangling stick. He took a long drag and blew it out the side of his mouth. He rolled the cigarette between his fingers and watched the people coming and going. No one noticed him. He took another drag, flicked the cigarette on the sidewalk and smashed it under his foot. He hitched up his pants and moved toward the building.

The doors opened and he walked through the first sensor. Two security guards quickly approached him. "I'm sorry Murdoch," the smaller guard said rushing up to him. "Mr. Sloan called and told us you no longer work here."

"*Oh he did, did he?*"

"Yes, you are to be escorted to your locker, get all your things, then leave the premises."

"He stole my damn *car*! Did he happen to mention *that*? He left me on the side of the road for *dead*!" Murdoch stomped forward two steps as he shouted.

The larger guard grabbed his flailing arms and forced them behind his back. "Hold it right there, Murdoch. Those are our orders. You need to cooperate with us." He walked Murdoch out of sight of the public. The smaller guard walked behind.

"You can't do this to me! I have my rights, you know."

"Yes you do, but right now you have to cooperate," said the guard twisting his arm tighter. He moved him against a wall then let his arms go. Murdoch grabbed his wrist and massaged where the man had held him. He looked like he had been beaten and robbed, and now was being accused of a crime he was only just premeditating.

"I just want to drive, that's all. Now he's taken that from me." He brought his dirty fat hand up and covered his eyes, and out came the sobs. His shoulders bobbed up and down as he leaned against the wall. The two men looked at each other, then at the grown man crying. "He's destroyed my life . . . it's gone . . . I have nothing . . . " Murdoch blabbered in between breaths as the sobs grew even louder.

"Hey, Murdoch, it's okay," said the short guard, reaching up awkwardly and touching his shoulder. It bounced up and down in rhythm. The larger guard looked around, embarrassed, to see if anyone was watching the show. He whispered something to his partner then quickly walked back to his station.

Murdoch continued sobbing. His hands were over his face as he slowly rocked back and forth. Finally, he wiped his eyes with the backs of both hands. He coughed violently, cleared his throat loudly several times, and lifted his head up.

"What t'hell *you* lookin' at?" he said to the smaller guard, who turned away quickly.

"I'm going to take you up to get your things, Murdoch. Then you'll need to leave all your keys at the front desk. Those are the orders."

The guard escorted Murdoch through the lobby to the small locker closet, and waited outside. Murdoch didn't waste time. He gathered all his things and dumped them into two boxes. Two boxes. Everything that he had at the company fit inside two boxes. Ten minutes later, he opened the door and walked ahead of the guard back to the lobby. The large guard left his duties when he saw him coming and walked up to him, reaching out to shake his hand.

"I'm sorry, Murdoch. Thanks for all you've done for us here."

Murdoch dropped the boxes on the floor, reached to his belt clip, and took off his batch of keys. "How'm I gettin' home?" He pushed the keys into the guard's hand.

"There's a taxi out front," said the short guard.

Murdoch stooped down, picked up his two boxes, and exited the building. He took the paid ride back to his apartment.

CHAPTER 13

He was leaning against a wall, his head listing to the side. The blindfold was wrapped tightly around his head, pressing into his eyes. His hands were tied behind his back; the fibers from the twine cut into his wrists, and every time he moved, the tiny string razors made the gash deeper across his thin skin. A drop of blood pooled on his middle finger and fell to the small puddle on the floor. Mucous crusted around his mouth and his stomach growled. He sat at such an angle on the rickety chair that his back couldn't help but hurt. This was not supposed to be part of the deal. The noise of the door opening roused Elliott. Several footsteps echoed in the room and moved quickly toward him. He shifted in pain and slowly sat upright.

"Untie him. *Rapido!*"

The footsteps clamored closer on the hard floor.

"Has he had food? Drink?"

The twine was cut from his wrists, and the bandana stripped off his head. Immediately, Elliott looked away from the brightness of the room, then reached up and rubbed both eyes with the back of his bloody hands. He grabbed his wrist and massaged it lightly, slowly looking around. The room was filled with pieces of furniture: a table and chairs, several cabinets and bureaus. There were windows on both sides of the room. Two men stood on either side of him, and another directly in front.

"Señor Chapman, I am Jorge Martino," said the man with glistening black hair, offering his hand. Elliott didn't take it; he sat and stared at him. "I apologize for the inconvenience." Martino pulled his hand back, turned to both men, and barked, "Get him some food and drink!"

The men walked quickly through the room. The two guards standing at the door let them pass. Elliott squinted as he watched.

"You are in the guest house," Martino said with a smile. He reached inside a cabinet, took out a towel, and tossed it to Elliott.

"Thanks for the hospitality," Elliott returned sharply. He wiped his face and dabbed his wrists with the towel.

"You are the researcher from Texas?"

"Yes."

"You did not supply my men with correct papers this morning, when you arrived."

"They didn't ask to see any papers. They pushed me into their car and blindfolded me, brought me here, tied me up, and left me to die."

"Why do you make things so difficult?"

"Difficult?"

"You are not a typical researcher." Martino stood over him and looked closely.

Elliott looked away, rubbing his wrists.

"You are too young and inexperienced to be here. Who sent you?"

"Steven Sloan, the president of Magalto. I'm here to do a job in a laboratory—if there is one."

Martino nodded slowly. "There is."

"I was told that I'd be picked up and escorted to a laboratory on a compound. Not kidnapped and roughed up by a bunch of goons. You know, that's a serious charge in America."

"How do we know you are not a spy for another organization? You have no proof."

Elliott turned his head down and looked around the chair. "My bag! Where's my bag? Everything's in my bag. I have all the documents for the job."

"Your bag is safe." Martino smiled. He turned and walked to the window with his hands held behind his back. "I know who you are." He spun around and looked at Elliott.

"Yeah, well I'm here to help, and as soon as I'm finished, I'm leaving. I've got more important things to do than be held captive. Where's your lab? Do you even have one?"

"Oh, yes. We have laboratory, not far from here."

"Well then, what am I doing here?"

"First, I have questions to ask you, about your work." Martino looked out the window again and said, "You are angry. I understand."

Elliott slowly pushed himself upright, walking his hands up his thighs. Standing straight was too much for his back. He lurched forward in pain. He stood and walked away from Martino, to the window on the other side of the room. Just as he reached it, the door opened and two men walked inside. One carried a large platter of food, and the other a golden goblet. They placed both on a small table closest to Martino and spread out the utensils. Martino gave an order to them in Spanish and they quickly left the room.

Martino turned to Elliott. "Please, come sit and eat. You are hungry." He pointed to a chair at the table.

Elliott walked to the table and slowly lowered himself into the chair. In the center of the platter was a wild game hen glazed with brown mushroom sauce, and garnished with plump raisins and herbs. Around the meat lay clusters of brightly colored vegetables in cream sauce. Elliott did not delay. He quickly took the silver fork and began shoveling in the mouth-watering morsels. After several bites, he reached for the goblet, which had condensed sweaty droplets running down the sides. He tested it with a sniff. He sipped a mouthful, rolled it around in his mouth, and let it trickle down his throat. He sipped again, and set the goblet down on the small table. Martino watched with amusement.

"What do you want with me?" Elliott took the fork and gripped it tight.

"You are our guest for a short while."

"You tie and blindfold all your guests?"

"No. It was a precaution my men are trained to do. We cannot be too careful. Please, there will be no more. Señor Chapman, we want you to be happy during your stay."

"Happy? How long will that be?"

"A short time." Martino walked closer to the table and sat in the chair across from Elliott. He crossed his leg and interlaced his ringed fingers over his knee. The gold and diamonds sparkled. "I am from Columbia."

Elliott slowly chewed the mouthful, and glanced at the two guards standing in front of the door. "You are the Columbian businessman!"

"You are fortunate that I am."

Elliott put his fork down and reached for the goblet, keeping his eyes on Martino.

Martino looked at Elliott. "We are here at this compound in Matamoros for a few more months only. That is our concession for the time. To the rest of the world, we are fools. But let me tell you something. I live on a green plateau, 7,000 kilometers above sea level. The great Andes Mountains are the backdrop to my beautiful city of Bogotá. The temperature stays 70 degrees, all year. The sun sets at six o'clock and rises at six o'clock, every day. We have no seasons, no change. We have food of all kinds, and the resources are abundant. My people are happy. I am happy. But you—you are not happy. No one in America is happy."

"I'm happy," Elliott said with a scowl.

Martino smiled at him. "No, you are not. That is why you are here working for me."

"I came here to do a job in the laboratory. The squash titration."

Martino laughed as he leaned back in his chair. "Oh, Señor Chapman, we have already finished that little problem. Do you think I wait for someone from your company to come and help? When I heard it was you who was coming, I knew it was time for the special project. I have had in mind for some time now. It is a simple one, but one only you can do."

"What is it? Tell me what it is, I'll do it, then—I'm out of here."

"You are so quick to make a decision. You are like the country you come from, always acting without thought."

Elliott shrugged his shoulders and looked at the loot on Martino's fingers.

Martino watched Elliott, rolling the jewels as he spoke. "I govern thousands, soon millions, of people in my home of Bogotá. I know what makes people happy. Your little project will help all of us." Martino stood, picked up a newspaper from a bureau, and returned to the table. He lifted up a section for Elliott to see. "I want you to hear something. This will help you understand what people think about me. Then I will tell you the truth. Truth you need to hear. I will read to you while you eat."

Elliott took another bite and listened while Martino read:

"United States drug agents cheered victory when reputed drug boss Manny Ortega was extradited three years ago. He was the leading member of the Zamarippa cocaine cartel in Columbia. For years, this group waged terrorism against the Columbian government to stop extraditions to the United States. It advanced simple drug smuggling to the professional leagues, delivering tons of cocaine into the U.S. through pioneering avenues."

Martino looked up from the paper. Elliott slowed his chewing.

He continued: "The Zamarripa cartel receives its help from The Revolutionary Armed Forces of Colombia, the FARC. They are the major liaison between the government and drug traffickers, the mother of all cartels in South America. They control the production and export of cocaine and other illegal drugs that reach the United States every year. Ortega faced trial in Texas, was convicted of international drug trafficking, and sentenced to a maximum prison sentence. Not only had the Zamarripa cartel lost a strong leader, but the FARC took deep monetary hits.

"By making popular connections, Jorge Martino progressed through the ranks during this time, and has become the new leader of the FARC. Three years ago, he helped orchestrate a new alliance with an American company in Texas, a brilliant move that has established him as indispensable to the cartels and major player in business worldwide."

Martino lowered the paper and peered over at Elliott. Elliott stopped chewing.

"This came from the Associated Press. Your American journalists wrote. I don't have much use for your news writers, they always make things up." Martino threw the newspaper on the table and continued to stare at Elliott.

Elliott wiped the corners of his mouth. He sat back into the chair and cleared his throat. "You're a freakin' drug pimp. You harvest and smuggle drugs out of Columbia into the U.S., through your own damn government."

Martino smiled. "It sounds like it, doesn't it? No. Our reputation precedes us. Now we work with more productive, let me say, activities."

"I'm right, aren't I? I'm sitting here, the hostage of an international drug smuggler. You're going to skin me and wrap your drugs in my corpse. You're going to smuggle millions of dollars across the border in my dead body."

Martino smiled. "Señor Chapman, I am not interested in your corpse, although you do propose an exciting idea. No, you are far more valuable to us than that."

"That's comforting," Elliott said, sinking deeper into the chair.

Martino fixed his eyes on his tired guest and continued. "Let me ask you, Señor Chapman, why do we deliver drugs— for money? Is that what you think? You are partly correct. Our farmers grow coca plants and dry them. They grind them into fine powder and we pay them for it. Easy for them, easy for us. We sell on high demand to your country. Simple economics. Your country has big demand, and we supply.

American happiness does not need much encouragement. Yes, it is big business, but not big enough."

"Big enough for what? What else do you want?"

"My Armed Forces is a governing power much like your military in United States. Some do not share this view. Is all right. Your newspaper writer is uninformed. Your country is uninformed. You see, Mr. Chapman, the FARC is good for our country. Colombia is a republic and we have a large middle class. Like your country, we value free speech and the right to print materials. We are fiercely independent. No different than you. We have a candidate who will be the next president of Columbia. It will be me. We have learned from the Mexican people how to overthrow a seventy-year reign. The National Action Party in Mexico is same as Armed Forces in Columbia. Is same. They have new President and soon, I will be. Our farmers, you Americans call peasants, number in the millions and are very productive, because of what we have done for them. We have brought them dignity. We have compensated them handsomely. Much more than they have been paid for drug harvests of years past. What we have done is of importance to you."

Elliott ran his fingers through his hair. It was dirty. His eyes were bloodshot. His clothes were stained and he stunk of body odor. He glanced up at Martino. "What do you want from me, Mr. Martino? I have no money. I have no connections. I am a poor college student just hoping to graduate."

Martino leaned forward and looked at him with piercing eyes. "You are working on a doomed project. Your research data is faulty and you cannot complete it for your arrogant professor. Now you have been asked to help with our agriculture project, one that we have finished a long time ago."

"How do you know this?" Elliott raised his eyebrows.

"Magalto is desperate because they have not completed their statistics for the patents they seek, and we threaten them because soon we will not need the company. They know this. But now we are paying them far too much money."

"But how do you *know*?"

"It is my job to know these things. This is how I become president."

"Well, you're wrong. I'm working on a biostatistical exercise for my senior project. I receive data from a health clinic. I log and plot the data."

"No. You are working on a problem for Dr. Kingsley and Magalto. You are helping with secret engineering projects. It is very convenient for them."

"My project is for Dr. Kingsley's research," Elliott shot. "It's a stupid project that I've been working on all year. All I do is plot data and make graphs."

"Kingsley, Magalto. They are same." Martino lowered his eyebrows as he spoke. "He does not need you—*I* need you, and you will help me."

Elliott looked up at the guarded door and became silent. After a moment, he asked in a soft voice, "So what is your little project?"

Martino smiled. "Your project is a statistic problem, that is true, but a very tiny part of what will be in store for you. You have no idea. You will work for me on this project, then you will be free to go and pursue whatever may be in your interest. But, you will not be working for Magalto. That is what I do not want you to do."

"Who said anything about working for Magalto?"

"Soon they will ask you to work for them."

"Well they already have, and I've already accepted."

"You will not. You will do something for me that I have been long anticipating."

"What?"

Martino turned his glossy head to glance out the window, and the light sparkled off his oil-slicked hair. He turned back to Elliott and spoke, "Tell me, what is something that everyone in the world is in demand for?"

Elliott shifted his eyes back and forth. "Tobacco."

"No. That is small. Bigger, much bigger."

"Drugs?"

"Food!" Martino wrinkled his forehead as he said this. "Food will get me into the presidency, and it will make every other country in the world depend on us."

"Food?" Elliott snorted. "You're going to make enchiladas and sell them from taco trucks. Yeah, that'll get you elected."

"Nice to see you in good spirits." Martino smiled. "No, no taco trucks."

Elliott repositioned himself in the chair and cracked half a smile.

"Señor Chapman, we make food in our laboratory in Columbia, just like your American company taught us."

"Magalto? Magalto isn't my company."

"They pay money to your university."

"I'm doing a little project for a requirement, so I can graduate."

"Whatever you say. But let me tell you, we are making biology in our laboratories as well. Because of engineering, we can make foods as pleasant and addictive as our cocaine. We can make new species of plants and improve the old. We do this now. Do you know how? Mr. Sloan knows we do. You see, Señor Chapman, we needed the American company years ago, but not now. Now we are very close to ending our relationship. The little projects they are working on for us— foolishness. Is all rabbit chases. The company is busy; they lose their mind over projects. Do you know what they are working so hard to do? They want to patent their life forms. Patent life forms. Let them try, their silly patents. We keep them busy. Busy enough for us to finish our work."

"Patents?"

"Of course, patents. They believe whoever owns the patents will rule the world. Let them believe. Mr. Sloan wants nothing more than to think the world will eat from his table."

"How close are they with the patents?"

Martino smiled. He cleared his throat then raised his dark eyebrows as he spoke. "Mr. Sloan and his men think they are close. Does not matter. Is all for nothing. You see, we are writing new law, because there is no established international law on engineered organisms. We have multinational legal experts, biology experts, and government insiders working on these issues day and night. We write new global laws on this, and your government will protect them. Soon we will have delegate to the World Trade Organization and play the dumb American game of international politics."

"You're writing international law on bioengineering?"

"Of course, we write law." He laughed.

"You have experts on these subjects?"

"Of course." Martino smiled. "What do you take me for—chopped liver, as you Americans say?"

"Yeah, well, I happen to like chopped liver."

"A disability with your taste."

"I don't *eat* it."

"Yes. You make joke and I laugh. Is all right." Martino smiled and continued, "We have many experts. We have many countries involved with our work. This isn't being done alone, you realize. When one of our laboratories make a new plant, we submit it for international protection, and control its manufacture and sale. Right now we make seeds and give them to our farmers to grow—the millions of farmers who will vote for me. But soon, farmers in other countries will learn to grow and harvest these plants. It will be a short time when we collect tax and royalties. If they don't pay, they will be violating international law and sanctioned by governing bodies—you Americans!"

"And you're going to use The World Trade Organization to do this."

"Of course! Soon we have a delegate on the counsel and play the same game as everyone else, all following the American rules."

"From your bandits, the FARC?"

"Yes, does that surprise you? You shouldn't be surprised. This is not your problem. Your problem is something that will make our years of toil worthwhile, and make your education useful."

"What is it? You want me to do something illegal. Is that right?"

"No. Not illegal. It is called the Terminator."

"The Terminator?"

"Yes. I believe your movie stars made a picture show. This is much different, much different. It is the largest, the most important project in the world today."

"I'm going to help you build a terminator?"

"No. It is already built."

"What is it?"

"It does just what it says. Terminates."

"Terminates what?"

"Your company has made the Terminator process. They did it in one of our laboratories to escape government inspections. Then they took it to one of their laboratories, and I know which one. But, Señor Chapman, it belongs to me."

"What is it?" Elliott's eyes widened.

"Forgive my improper biology. The Terminator is a process that is applied to seeds in their genetic structure. It is a seed that only sprouts once. After that, it dies. Its offspring are sterile, no longer able to, how would you say, have children. The seed has to be replaced by a new one. There is no way to replant any part of it. Do you know what that means, Señor Chapman? It means every farmer in the world and every manufacturer of agriculture will have to buy the seed every year. They will buy it from whoever owns the process. And that will be us. Then, after a number of years, everyone will eat our seed, our plants. We will own the genetic makeup and the legal rights. It means a considerable income, but more importantly it means—"

"You will control genetic consumption," Elliott cut in. "You will control the freakin' genetic structure of everything edible!"

"Only whatever has the Terminator genes in it," said Martino quickly. "But yes, eventually. And it will all be protected by the laws we ourselves have written." He paused and looked down at the plate, then back up to Elliott. "This is for my people. For the first time in our history, we will have independence. I am able to create a future for my people. I am the liberator."

"Liberator? Liberator of what?"

"See, you do not understand—is difficult for you. My people want to be happy. Do you know how I will make them happy? I will liberate them from your country's oppression. I give them freedom."

"No. It sounds like you'll have them do what *you* want."

"Please, Señor Chapman, do not misunderstand my intention. I only want what is fair."

"How can you decide what's fair, when you make the rules?"

"People beg me to make rules. The rules—they make people happy. My people trust me and trust my form of government to solve the problems your country has created for us. We have come far, but still, a long way to go. We are moving very quickly, but this final problem is one only you can help us with. That is why you are here with me now, no?"

"No. I am here to complete a task for a school assignment. Then, I'm going home."

Martino shook his head. "No. Again, you do not understand. You want to be happy, but you cannot be. You will not find happiness if the things you believe are different from the things you do."

"Oh really? Now you're my spiritual adviser?"

"What is even worse—you do not know what you want."

"How do you know what I want?"

"I watch people. I talk to people. I listen."

"*Who*'ve you been talking to?"

"There are people, does not matter. You still lack happiness, so you get into trouble with others. But it will get worse when you do not seek what is worth seeking—that is torture on your soul. Why are you here, Elliott Chapman, because you want to, or because someone else wanted you to? This was not your idea."

"I made a deal with Dr. Kingsley, and he tried to weasel out of it."

"I see. The company educator likes to make deals." Martino nodded.

"So he sent me to Brownsville to work on this project."

"And that was your idea?"

"Well, it was either that, or fail my senior project."

"So you thought his idea was better than yours?"

"Yeah."

"Then, you lose." Martino shook his glistening head. "Is that your procedure? You have never learned to think for yourself, to find meaning for yourself. You look to others to find it for you. Well then, you will search your lifetime and be tortured. You will always be unhappy, because happiness and unhappiness cannot live in you at the same time, you do not realize. Now, I am giving you an opportunity to help me and my country be happy. If you cannot decide for yourself, then you will help us in our endeavor. For you Americans, money always seems to make you happy. What kind of money would interest you?"

Elliott raised his eyebrows. "Money? You're going to pay me money to be happy?"

"Of course. How much would you consider fair for your part of the project?"

"A million dollars."

Martino laughed. "A million dollars? What would you do with a million dollars? See, you make decisions without thinking. You do not know even what the project is."

"So what is it? What am I supposed to do?"

"All right then, I will tell you. Then you decide how much it is worth. I am sending you to a health clinic in the city. It is Magalto's. The Terminator protocol is located in their computers. You are to go as a United States Food and Drug Administration agent and spend a day searching, making threats about this and that. You are to copy the plans for the

Terminator and give it to Antonio, my assistant, who will be traveling with you. Then, you are free to go. Back to Brownsville, or Portland, wherever you wish that makes you happy. However, if you leave the country without getting me the plans I ask for, I will let Steven Sloan and Quinton Kingsley know that you haven't followed through with your end of the deal. Then, it will become my business to make every one of your short days, miserable days. I believe you had a preview of this when you arrived. For this, I am willing to pay you fifty thousand American dollars today. You will carry a briefcase with the bills. When I receive the legitimate copy of the Terminator, you will receive another fifty thousand American dollars."

Elliott sat with blank eyes staring out the window for a moment then back to Martino. "A hundred thousand dollars?"

"It is fair."

"The FDA? They have no jurisdiction in Mexico."

"Oh, they do. They have been threatening Mr. Sloan for some time now. A surprise visit to their Mexican clinic is overdue."

"So you're saying you want me to go into this clinic posing as an American FDA agent, and confiscate all data related to the engineering projects?"

"Only the Terminator data."

"And if I can't get it?"

Martino smiled. "Oh you will. I have calculated this plan for months. For them it is routine, they have been through this before. You will lock down the clinic for a few hours, and everyone inside will be evacuated. The data is stored in a computer inside one of the rooms. You will copy the data onto small discs. It should not take long. You clean up your mess, and reopen when you are completed. You will issue a fine of a few thousand dollars for faulty equipment, or improper storage, anything you find. It will be over. We will have our data, and Mr. Sloan will be relieved that an inspection has been made without closing the clinic for good. You will warn the medical director that if in the future the same problems exist, the clinic will be shut down and reported to Washington. There will be no problems, I assure you. When Antonio gets the data, I will call Mr. Sloan and tell him that you have fixed the titration chemistry, which of course is why you are here. As I see it, you have no choice, Señor Chapman."

Elliott took the last bite and placed the fork on the table. He had eaten all the food on the platter. He turned and looked past Martino out the window and thought for a moment.

"Why do you think now?" Martino asked. "You have no decision to make."

CHAPTER 14

Murdoch kicked the taxi door shut then turned and walked up the sidewalk to his apartment. He dropped his two boxes to the side of the entry. He stuck his fat hand into his pocket and fished out his one remaining key. He unlocked the deadbolt and the door creaked open. He picked up the boxes, tossed them through the doorway, and followed them inside. There were no messages on his answering machine or mail in the slot. No one bothered to call, and no salespeople were interested.

He walked into his bedroom, kicked his shoes off, then stripped off his dirty uniform right down to his discolored underwear. He kicked his clothing into a rumpled heap against the wall. In the closet, a week's worth of wrinkled, white short-sleeved shirts and their coordinating blue pants hung together. Murdoch swooped them, hangers and all, off the rack and threw them on the pile. The man and the uniform were parting ways. Farther inside the closet, in perfect form, hung a stiff set of green army fatigues. He took the pants and slipped them on, laced the wide black belt through the loops, and buckled it tight. He put on the iron-pressed shirt. It fell outside of his pants, and that was the way he was going to wear it. Next, he pulled out the shiny black boots that had never been worn. They were rigid and clomped on the thin carpet as he walked. He glanced in the full-length mirror, and looked upon the new man he had become. He gave himself a salute and walked down the hall into his project room.

Murdoch walked through the room to the magnificent gun cabinet and opened both large doors. He stood for a moment, looking at his display. Finally, he reached for a semi-automatic handgun. He brought it out and held it carefully, fingering the details on his favorite instrument. With a grim smile he turned, plopped down on the easy chair, and switched on the cheap lamp. The light illuminated survival and wilderness training magazines that lay open from long nights past. Titles like "How to Defend Yourself in the Wild" and "Shoot to Kill First" lay opened, their pages dog-eared, and many of the words heavily underlined.

He looked at his weapon, curled his fingers around the handle, and held it tight. The little nodules gripped the skin of his sweaty palm. His index finger moved to the trigger. Lightly, he tugged on it a few times. It had never been used; the trigger had never released a bullet and he could hardly wait. He brought the gun up and looked down the barrel. It was as clean as the day he bought it.

With great urgency, he pushed himself forward, mustering enough energy to stand on his squat, shaky legs. His booted feet clomped around, searching to support his portly body. Upright he parked himself, swaying to and fro as a smile grew on his grumpy, stubbly face. He shoved the gun under his wide belt, swaggered to the gun cabinet again, and lifted another out of the case. This he put into the holster sewn under the left arm of his shirt. He opened the drawer underneath the cabinet. An array of knives spread out like the wings of a large bird. There were long ones, serrated ones, and ones with appendages sprouting out in all directions. He took out one of the longest blades—it must have been a foot long, sheathed it, and stuffed the weapon in the largest pocket on the side of his fatigues. He lifted out another long blade and ran his hand down its steely edge. Just as quickly, it sliced a deep wedge of flesh in his clumsy thumb. The knife clattered to the floor as he grabbed the gash and squeezed the sides of the wound together. Blood trickled between his fingers and dripped onto the carpet. He quickly ripped a strand of cloth tape, wrapped his thumb tight, and stuffed the roll into his pocket. He picked up the knife from the floor, wiped the red on his green pants, sheathed it, then put it into another large pocket. From out of the ammunition cabinet, he took out a green musset bag and opened it on the floor. He put as much ammunition as would fit in one side. Finally, with dainty hands, he lifted out the canisters of explosives and placed them inside the bag.

He turned around and faced himself in his crooked mirror: a human arsenal in the making. He reached for a tin of brown face paint inside the cabinet and smeared a dab under each eye, and a little down his face. The excess he wiped into his wispy hair. He glanced up into the mirror again. A troubled sight, but he smiled all the more as he bent down and grabbed his bag.

He shuffled stiffly at first, but after a few steps, no one could tell if he was packing heat or constipated, which he was most of the time. With an unsettling grin, he walked through his apartment and stepped outside into the night.

CHAPTER 15

The night guard looked up from his booth as the cab approached the shipping entrance of Magalto. The car stopped and Murdoch got out, threw some bills through the window, then turned and approached the gate.

"Hello Murdoch," said the guard. He looked at the message posted inside the booth.

"Hello." Murdoch kept walking, carrying his bag close beside.

"Got a note here. Something about this being your last day."

"I won't be long. Just pickin' up a few last things."

"It's too bad. I'll miss seeing ya around here."

Murdoch stopped and waited for the gate to swing open. "You'll get used to it."

The parking lot was mostly deserted. A large tractor-trailer drove past him and the driver waved. Murdoch followed it around to the back of the building, then paused to watch the activity under the bright floodlights. A driver stood next to his truck, signing a paper. He handed the clipboard to another man, jumped inside the cab, and inched the semi forward. The company truck lugged and rocked as it pulled the weight, moving through several more gears, crawling toward the shipping exit.

Murdoch watched an empty truck back up to the dock. He walked closer into the loading zone. "Hello, amigos."

Murdoch waved at the men who were busy packing cargo. They stopped as Murdoch marched stiffly toward them.

"Hello, Señor Murdoch," said one of the men.

"Where's Carlos?" Murdoch asked the closest dockworker.

"Inside, getting ready for his run."

"Thank you." He slapped the worker on the back and walked inside. A man driving a forklift honked for him to get out of the way. He tipped his head and continued walking. "Carlos. Where's Carlos?" He asked several workers standing outside a room.

"He's in here." The man pointed to the room where several others were taking a break.

Murdoch stuck his head inside and bobbed it around. "Carlos. Carlos, you leaving soon?"

"Murdoch, how are you, amigo? Come in, sit down," Carlos said with a big grin.

"You ready to go?" Murdoch stood in the doorway looking at him.

"Truck isn't loaded yet. Come. Have a seat." He patted the chair next to him. Then he stopped and looked intently at him. "What is all over your face?"

"Dust from the parking lot. When we leaving?"

"Just a few minutes, amigo. Would you like some coffee?"

Murdoch didn't answer, but never refused the dockworker's strong coffee. Carlos got up and poured him a cup.

Careful to move without exposing his gear or letting it dig further into his flesh, Murdoch lumbered across the room and slowly lowered himself into the empty chair next to Carlos, where the coffee was waiting for him.

"Hey Murdoch, you're here pretty late at night," said the man across the table.

"Yeah, more action than at home."

"You look stiff. Your back okay?" asked another.

"Yeah. Been a long day."

"Murdoch's going on my route tonight," Carlos said excitedly.

"Really," the foreman said as-a-matter-of-factly.

"You going on delivery to the compound?" asked the first man.

Murdoch shrugged his shoulders. "Dunno."

"Better do it before the new regulations are put in place," said the foreman. "After that, it'll be pretty difficult to get in. If you want to go in to the compound you'll have to wait until the office opens in the morning. You need a permit before they'll let you in."

"I'm not going that far," Murdoch said, taking a sip of the coffee.

"Where you want to go?" asked Carlos. "You can't stay in the truck."

"Ah, I'll go to the city."

"Where?"

"I'll tell ya when we get there."

"You're crazy. You're just going for the ride?" The foreman stood. "Whatever floats your boat. Come on boys, back to work." He turned to Carlos. "Your truck should be loaded by now."

"Okay," Carlos said.

"I'll see you back here in a coupla days," the foreman said and shooed the rest of the workers out of the room.

"Okay," Carlos said with a smile. He turned to Murdoch and said with a nod, "Let's hit the road. Mí amigo with a dirty face."

Murdoch took one last swallow of hot coffee and plunked the mug down on the table. He pushed himself to an upright position and rearranged his equipment under his clothes. Carlos was too busy packing food for the trip to notice his awkward movements.

Two men stood on the deck. One closed the truck doors, the other barked commands.

"Miguel, Murdoch's here," Carlos said, abruptly ending the one-sided conversation. The man giving Manuel instructions in locking the door looked Murdoch up and down. Miguel snapped the lock shut, turned with a smile, and said,

"Hello, amigo. It is good to have you go along with us tonight." He put his arm around Murdoch and slapped his back.

"Are we ready?" Carlos asked.

"Sí."

"Well, *vamos*," Carlos said walking up to the driver's side.

Murdoch hoisted himself up into the cab of the truck and sat in the middle with his bag between his legs. Miguel followed, and Carlos jumped up to the driver's seat. Two of them buckled, and they all prepared for the hour drive down into Mexico. Carlos slogged the truck with its cargo and passengers through the Magalto exit and barreled down the highway, south.

"You look for *muchacha*?" Miguel asked Murdoch.

"Yup."

"She live in Matamoros?"

"Close."

"Hey, Carlos. Our friend finally get a woman," Miguel said, giggling as he leaned forward to look at Carlos.

"Very good," Carlos said.

"You one lucky hombre," Miguel said nudging Murdoch in the ribs. "The best in Matamoros. They good."

"I know. I been waitin' a long time." He flinched from the pain of the firearms digging into his side.

"I bet you have," Carlos said, laughing.

Carlos and Miguel continued pestering Murdoch. The man was venturing into Mexico late in the evening, not sure of his destination, looking for a foreign bride. *Loco gringo.*

They approached the first border containment. It was routine for Carlos and Miguel to pass through the checkpoint without incident. But Murdoch was having difficulties. He became fidgety, moving his hands into his lower shirt pockets, taking them out and folding his arms across his chest, putting them back down again. He crossed his legs, left over right, right over left. Every so often he scratched his ribs. He was a nervous wreck and began sweating beads across his forehead, and his pits wet his new fatigues.

Carlos pulled the truck into the commercial lane, the one with the shortest line. A new company Certificate of Admission was fixed to the windshield, in the corner above the driver. It was issued with a seal designating the truck to be in compliance with the North American Free Trade Act. Magalto had played a large role in this new arrangement. The certificate meant that any vehicle displaying it should cross the border without question or search. It meant the owners and drivers of the vehicle were in absolute compliance with the requirements of NAFTA. No more hassles of inspection. No more half-day waits in line. International freedom came at a high price, which Magalto always paid. The assurance of crossing didn't stop Murdoch from becoming more uncomfortable.

"Señor, don't be nervous," Miguel said. "Your new woman won't like you all sweaty."

"I do this all the time when someone else is driving."

"I understand. Carlos is bad driver many times."

The truck stopped. The border officer approached Carlos's lowered window. Carlos pulled down the certificate of passage and held it out the window. The officer took the page, read through it, and looked up at Carlos.

"What is your destination?"

"Matamoros, Señor."

"What is your cargo?"

"Domestic vegetation," he said without hesitation.

"Who are your passengers?"

"They work at Magalto."

"Both of them?"

"Sí."

The officer stepped up on the running board and stuck his face inside the truck. He looked at Murdoch who had his arms crossed over his chest. Murdoch couldn't sit still. He shifted from side to side trying to pry the pieces out of his ribs. "I really don't feel so well, sir. I've been sick all day."

"Officer," Carlos interrupted. "We are cleared for passage. The papers are here." He pointed to the certificate the officer held.

"He's taking me to a clinic!" Murdoch blurted.

The officer pulled his head back out of the window, handed the certificate back to Carlos, and stepped to the ground. He motioned them with his hand. "You are free to pass."

Carlos put the certificate back in place, geared the truck, and drove past the detainment area. Murdoch breathed a deep sigh of relief and took the dirty rag Miguel handed him. He wiped his brow and tossed it on the floorboard. He took out a cigarette and a pack of matches from his pocket, lit it, and began puffing furiously.

"That was easy," Carlos said as he drove down the Mexican road. "Pretty soon we drive right through without stopping."

"Then I get to drive," Miguel said.

"Oh, no you don't. Never."

"How 'bout you?" Miguel said to Murdoch, nudging him again. "You want to drive?"

"Hey, will ya quit hitting me there?" He rubbed his hand over his side. "That hurts. No. I don't want to drive." He took a long drag and exhaled past Miguel, toward the window.

"What is that? Is hard." Miguel felt Murdoch's side.

"It's my luggage. I pack inside my shirt."

"You are funny man," Miguel said with a smile.

"I'm hilarious."

"Where you want to go in Matamoros?" Carlos asked.

"To the clinic."

"What clinic?"

"The one Magalto owns."

"Ohhh, *that* clinic."

"The *muchacha* work at clinic?" Miguel asked.

"Yeah, she does."

"All *right*." Miguel smiled.

"Are you working there?" Carlos asked.

"Yeah, I'm doing a little touchin' up work. Been meaning to do it for years."

"That's nice." Carlos nodded.

"These are my tools." He padded both of his sides. "And in my bag. It's full, so I had to put things inside my shirt."

"You doing carpentry work?" Carlos asked.

"Yeah, they don't have the tools I'm going to need this time."

"You a very smart man." Miguel smiled at him.

"Sometimes things fall into place. Doesn't take much to do the job, if you have enough sense about it all." He took another long drag on his cigarette. The ash dropped off onto Miguel's pant leg and Miguel brushed it off. For the next several kilometers, they drove and spoke of unimportant matters. Most of the conversation was the two of them poking fun at Murdoch. They slipped into Spanish, and every now and then, looked at Murdoch and laughed. Murdoch just smiled back and patted his sides.

After a time, they approached the city and Carlos slowed the truck. "Señor Murdoch, the clinic is closed, I am sure," he said.

"Yeah?"

"You want to go with us to the compound?" Miguel asked. "You can help unload."

"No," he said quickly.

"Well, you're going to have to get off soon," Carlos said. "We have to turn back onto the highway. You want to find a motel?"

"No. Where's the clinic?"

"A few blocks from here," Carlos said. He glanced at his watch. "But amigo, I am sure it is closed at this hour."

"Well, just drop me off here, then."

"No, wait. There's a park up ahead."

"Fine. Drop me off at the park."

"You stay at the park?" Miguel asked, smiling at him, shaking his head.

"Yeah. I stay at the park."

Carlos drove a few more blocks. The dirt road was virtually empty, except for a few nocturnally-challenged chickens walking down the middle, bobbing their heads about, making dares with each other about crossing to either side. A few adults were still out on their porches, enjoying their brew. Carlos slowed the truck and turned into a large open lot, fenced with a waist-high concrete wall. He pulled up close to a large lamppost and banged against it. All three heads lurched forward.

"Sorry, amigos."

"Sheeze, now I got a whiplash," Murdoch said, rubbing his neck.

"Here you go, Señor," Carlos said, ignoring the injuries of the moment. "This is where you get off."

"All right," Murdoch mumbled. He pushed against Miguel.

"The clinic is about two blocks in that direction," Carlos said, pointing.

Miguel opened the door and hopped down. Murdoch followed, though not as gracefully. As he stepped, his long bootlace caught in the door. He spiraled to the ground face first, his hands hit and wrists sprung backwards. His arms gave way to the next barrier that really did break his fall: the artillery. He landed with a thud and a puff of dust. All the metal he packed smacked heavily against his ribs, forcing the air out of his lungs. He lay face down for a moment, motionless.

"Señor Murdoch!" Miguel rushed to him and kneeled down. "You okay, amigo?"

Murdoch lay still.

"*Murdoch*!" Miguel shook his shoulder then looked up at Carlos in the truck. "He's dead!"

"Roll him over so he can breath," Carlos called down.

Miguel tried with both hands but couldn't budge him. He shook him again.

"Ohhh, God . . . " Murdoch finally breathed.

"No, no, he's awake!" Miguel said, smiling up at Carlos.

Carlos jumped down from the truck and they both helped Murdoch to his feet. He staggered for a moment, trying to gain his balance. "Ohhh . . . " he bellyached.

"Señor," Miguel said with his hand on his shoulder. "You be okay?"

"Ohhh, God . . . "

"Come, sit here," Miguel said, leading him to the concrete wall. He helped him to the ground and propped him up.

Carlos went back up into the truck and reached behind the passenger seat. He pulled out a paper bag, reached inside, and took out a brick-sized package wrapped in brown paper. He untied the string, and the pack of leaves splayed in all directions. With his thumb and index finger, he pinched a small amount and handed it to Murdoch, who was still writhing in pain.

"Here, Señor. Chew this."

Murdoch lifted his head and inspected it, then put it into his mouth. His teeth clamped down into the soft, tender leaves and the molecules of pleasure gave him the rare delight of a smile without the compulsion to look over his shoulder. "Ohhh, God . . . "

Carlos took a small pinch and gave it to Miguel, who promptly began chewing. Carlos himself took another wad and found a seat on the bumpy ground, next to Murdoch. The three sat masticating the leaves into tiny fragments in silence for several minutes. Finally, Carlos took out his wad of leaves and tossed it on the ground. He re-wrapped the brick of leaves back up in the brown paper.

"Hey, amigo." Carlos nudged Murdoch.

Murdoch sat rocking with his eyes closed and a wide grin on his face.

"Amigo," Carlos said again, pushing his shoulder.

Murdoch slowly opened his eyes and turned his head. "Whaaat...?"

"Here, you take this." He handed the package to him.

Murdoch reached for it in slow motion, closed his eyes and chewed leisurely.

Carlos stood and walked back to the truck. Miguel followed.

"Tomato leaves are good for you," Miguel called over his shoulder. "But don't eat too many." He cackled, walking back to the truck.

"Yeah," Murdoch said.

"Do you need a ride back to Brownsville later, amigo?" Carlos called as he climbed back into the truck.

"No. I'm not going back."

"Ahh, the *muchacha*," Miguel said laughing. "You in big trouble now, Señor Murdoch." He hoisted himself inside, grabbed Murdoch's bag, and tossed it down to him.

"Hey watch it, there," Murdoch said with a scowl. "I have some important things in that bag."

"Oh, sorry." Miguel slammed the door. "Invite us to the wedding, eh, amigo? We'll be there," he cackled.

"Yeah, sure." Murdoch threw a wave at them. "I'll letcha know."

Carlos bumped the truck forward into the lamppost again, then backed up and turned it down the road. Murdoch watched them drive away. He tucked the package inside his shirt, then staggered to his feet and shuffled to the nearest park bench.

A lacerated thumb, whiplash, bruised ribs, and two sprained wrists; he no longer felt the pain. He eased himself down onto the bench. He sat in darkness for a few minutes until he could no longer keep his eyelids open. His head tipped to the side. His body tilted. He leaned farther until he had sprawled completely onto the park bench. He reached for his bag and stuffed it under his head as a pillow, then promptly fell into a deep sleep. It had been a long day.

The morning sun warmed a day-old newspaper that covered Murdoch's face, as he lay on the park bench. It rose and fell in timing with his shallow respiration. He certainly did not want to oversleep. Not today, the most cathartic day of his life. Every humiliation, every setback, and every defeat was wrapped up in a tight ball of emotional tension, ready to explode. The countdown had begun—and he was *sleeping*.

Mass had ended at the church next to the park, and children were congregating with whoops and hollers in the dusty playground. They played tag and kicked cans. They laughed and yelled to each other.

Murdoch was roused by the noise of the kids, whose simple games became a squealing irritation. He lifted the paper off his face and threw it to the ground. He looked around groggily, slowly lifted his head, and gradually pushed himself up onto his side. The kids stopped and noticed him for the first time: the bum in the park with a very messy face. He yelled some English profanities at them, which they understood to mean *get the hell out of here and back to church*, and scattered as quickly as they had come.

Sitting straight up was as difficult as it had been lying on a hard wooden bench all night. Murdoch stretched his arms above his head, popping a few vertebral joints on the way. He reached inside his shirt and checked his heat. It was still there, as it had been all night, digging into his sides. It had prevented him from rolling off the bench.

Slowly he pushed himself to a standing position and repositioned his gear. He glanced at his multi-functional watch he had bought for just this occasion. All it told him was that he had overslept. He had only walked a few steps when his right foot caught the edge of a hole the children knew to avoid.

His leg buckled, and he came crashing down with his left arm fully extended to break the fall. He landed with a loud *pop*! His wrist snapped backward and he immediately grabbed his arm. Both white bones in his forearm were splintered and had jammed through the skin about an inch. Blood trickled from the puncture. He screamed loud vulgarities as he writhed in agony on the ground. Back and forth he rolled, holding the broken, deformed arm. After a moment he tried to raise it, but all it did was flop; his hand dangled backward, the muscles were strained beyond their limits.

Without thinking, he attempted to push the bones back into the skin. He stopped immediately and screamed, as his whole body contorted in agony. For a few moments, he lay still on the ground. Then he slowly picked his head up and looked around, seeing no one. He had chased everyone away. He dropped his head back down and breathed a few deep breaths. Perspiration soaked every inch of his squat, fat body. His dirty face was smeared with paint and debris that he picked up from his night on the bench. He reached inside his bulky, green camouflaged shirt, pulled out the bag Carlos had given him, and unwrapped it. The first wad went under his lower lip, and immediately began to take effect. The second and third wads were larger, and he packed them inside each cheek. Three was all he needed. He folded the bag tenderly, and put it back in his shirt for safekeeping. Then he lay still and felt the rush: the miraculous transformation from pain to pleasure.

Before he got too comfortable, Murdoch felt the side of his leg for the pocket that held the knives. He reached inside and took out the two long survival blades. From another pocket, he pulled out a roll of white tape. He put one of the knives along the side of his arm and held it in place with his knee. He set the other knife on top of the open wound. Then he ripped off a two-foot section of tape, stuck it on the knife, and wound it around his arm. Just before he covered the exposed, splintered bones, he poked them into his skin. With a slurp, the bones disappeared inside. Quickly, he finished wrapping the makeshift splint and fell back flat on the ground. He was all but unconscious, in a visceral cacophony of pain and pleasure, and stayed in that position for the rest of the day.

CHAPTER 16

Elliott Chapman, FDA imposter, was dressed for his first day on the job. His navy blue suit was much too small. His arms extended well past the coat sleeves, and the shoulder seams puckered. The pants barely fastened around his waist and hung just above his ankles. He wore dark socks rolled down below his high pant legs. Shining leather Ciardins adorned his feet, but they were close to splitting in the sides. A counterfeit badge hung around his neck, indicating a feeble association with the United States Food and Drug Administration. It looked official enough.

Antonio's clothes fit better—they were his own. He carried a large stainless-steel briefcase. Except for the butt of a gun that stuck out from a chest holster when he reached up to comb his black oily hair for the millionth time, he looked very businesslike.

Martino walked up to Elliott and pulled on his lapels, then brushed them with the back of his hand. "You look good. An important job to do."

"I don't know anything about inspecting a clinic." Elliott lifted the badge and looked at it.

"You will do fine. Antonio will help. He has been on these missions many times."

"Well, I'm not familiar with sneaking into a building and stealing information."

"You are not stealing. You are making copies that are rightfully ours."

"Same thing."

"That is all you have to do." Martino stepped directly in front of Elliott, shoe-to-shoe, and looked up at him. "You are the only one who knows what this information is and how to get it. Don't make this difficult. You finish your work, and give Antonio the Terminator protocol. Then, you are free to go." Martino reached down and picked up a black briefcase. He popped open the fasteners and turned it around to show Elliott. "Your money is here." He loosened a corner of a flap and held it open with two fingers. "Fifty thousand dollars. All hundreds."

Elliott craned his neck to peek inside. "Can I see it?"

"It is all here." Martino closed it quickly and opened a small pocket inside the lid of the briefcase for Elliott to see. "These are for your transmission."

"Discs. Those are discs."

"To copy Terminator. When I get these back, I will finish payment." He fastened the pocket, snapped the briefcase shut, and handed it to Elliott. "It is time. The drive to the clinic will take twenty minutes. The driver will drop you off two blocks away. Now, you go." Martino rattled off something in Spanish to Antonio, turned and opened the door of the building and motioned with his hand down the rock path. He nodded to Elliott.

Elliott picked up the briefcase and his bag, and followed Antonio. The car was an old Cadillac, not beaten up enough to be a low rider with fuzzy dice hanging from the rearview mirror, but not nice enough to transport important money people around southern Texas, as it had done a few years ago. The driver standing beside the car lifted the trunk lid, took Elliott's bag, and tossed it inside. He motioned for him to get into the backseat. Elliott settled himself next to Antonio, his new partner.

Elliott and Antonio walked the two blocks from the park where they were dropped off. The clinic was situated near a poor rural area. The outside of the building had not been kept up well. A shoulder-high rock-mortared fence topped with broken glass protected it, and a large iron gate secured the only entrance. Broken windows were framed with crossed bars. The walls were dirty, having had neither paint nor a wash in years.

Elliott checked his badge one more time, picked up his bag and briefcase with one hand, and pushed the gate open with the other. Antonio followed closely up the path. The front door wasn't shut completely, so he pushed it open. Inside, every chair was taken and as many people were standing or sitting on the broken floor, mostly women and their children. Elliott walked through the crowd to a large lady, the head nurse, sitting at a plywood desk in front of a curtain that led to the back. Her name, 'Juanita', was stitched across the upper pocket of her smock. She kept a list of names on a clipboard, marking them off as they came from the bowels of the clinic. Elliott stood for a moment as she called another name. She looked up at him, holding herself as the one in charge.

"*¿Como se llama?*" she asked flatly.

"*Hola,*" he tried in his best junior high Spanish. "My name is Dr. Friedman." He flashed his badge. "I'm with the United States Food and Drug Administration."

"Oh, *Señor!* This is *not* a good time." She looked down at her pages of names and thumbed through them. "We very busy today. Please, *mañana.*" She held up the pages and stared at him with cold eyes.

Elliott looked weakly at his assistant who slowly nodded, adding a frown. Against the rules of the operation, the man rattled off a sharp discourse in Spanish to the lady. He was quick and firm, and his voice grew into a crescendo. At this, Juanita threw up both hands, plopped them on the table, and lofted herself upwards, putting a sizable bow in the plywood. She turned to the curtain behind and disappeared. Elliott turned to Antonio with a look, as an explanation was in order. He didn't respond.

In a moment, a man in a white clinic jacket and Juanita in tow, flung open the curtain. Juanita promptly sat back down at her quarters.

"Hello, I'm Dr. Duane Rice. I run the clinic." Dr. Rice had wavy red hair and a matching goatee. Underneath his jacket, he wore old blue jeans and a faded buttoned-down shirt. He stuck out his hand and shook Elliott's. "Does there seem to be a problem, sir?"

Sir? Elliott was lost for words. The man in white was at least ten years older than he, and had just called him sir. Sir? That title belongs to an older, respectable man, someone more deserving than a kidnapped imposter, posing as a United States government official in a foreign country, trying to steal a genetic protocol so he could finish his senior project. He looked at his badge and lifted it.

"Uh, yes, we're with the FDA and we're here to inspect your equipment, per our last conversation. You were in violation of U.S. code 362, with regard to faulty equipment."

"Well, yes," Dr. Rice said shaking his head. "But we have another six months before the final inspection. I'll tell you right now, we're not ready. We can't get the damn service people down here from Comtex. I've been on them for weeks now, and they try to instruct me over the phone. *That* sure as hell doesn't work."

"Regardless, we need to have a look around to see your improvements."

"We haven't *made* any improvements. That's what I'm telling you."

"Please, Dr. Rice," Elliott said, gaining authority. "We must inspect today or we will have to impose a fine."

The doctor looked at him. "All right, all right," he snapped as he turned around. He flapped open the curtain and led the United States inspectors inside the clinic. Elliott winked at the lady in charge as he passed.

The noise level increased sharply as they walked down the long hallway. The small treatment rooms were filled, and some overflowed with people into the hall. They were yapping or yelping, depending on whether a family member was consoling, or the patient was receiving care. Two clinic assistants tried to manage the triage. The three continued through the hall to the data rooms, located in the back of the clinic.

"They're right here." Dr. Rice stopped and pointed to two rooms. He turned to Elliott. "Have you been here before? You don't look familiar."

"No. Those guys were from D.C."

"One. There was one here last time." Dr. Rice squinted and looked carefully at him.

"Yeah, you're right. I get the clinics and inspectors mixed up," Elliott said, turning to the door.

"What other clinics?"

"Oh, all kinds."

Dr. Rice looked Elliott up and down. "How long have you been doing this? You look a little young to be inspecting for the FDA."

"I just graduated from the institute. This is my first mission south of the border."

Dr. Rice nodded slowly. "Do you have *any* experience?"

"Oh yeah. I just came from a job a few kilometers from here. They had a problem with a produce tincture. I've been all over two countries in the last forty-eight hours. After this, I'm heading up to the Pacific Northwest. Inspecting's pretty easy if you know what to look for. Believe it or not, a lot of inspectors don't know what the hell they're doing. That's why I was called in on this one."

Dr. Rice just stood and stared a moment at Elliott. The badge looked real. The suit looked seriously too small. But the shoes; way out of style for an FDA inspector. The second man stood without saying a word. He had no expression and made no gestures. Now that was typical behavior of one who could lower the boom on a noncompliant foreign clinic.

The last inspector was strictly business. He had been rude, obnoxious, and threatened Dr. Rice with an impossible fine and the likelihood of a shut down, unless they cooperated with his petty requests. He jumped all over the overcrowding, the understaffing, and lack of record keeping. He said nothing about the clinic equipment or computers. Wasn't interested. He *said* he'd be back in four weeks. He wanted to see the changes first hand. Dr. Rice made a quick call to Steven Sloan and told him there was no way to meet this idiot's demands. For crying out loud, they were only a nonprofit clinic set up by Magalto to help the poor and unfortunate in the area. What jurisdiction did the FDA have there anyway? That was nine months ago. Not a peep from the FDA since then: no letters, no calls, no visits.

"Here," Dr. Rice snapped as he pointed with his head. "The equipment is in these two rooms. The problem in question was this old centrifuge unit. But we're not using it now. Everything else is working fine."

"Well, we're going to have to take a look around."

"How long will you be?" Duane blocked the door with his arms crossed.

"Depends on what we find. We don't want any more problems with your clinic."

Dr. Rice turned and unlocked the door. He opened his mouth for a pithy remark, but stopped short.

"What was that?" Elliott asked.

"Nothing." Dr. Rice turned and walked to the second door and unlocked it. "You'll probably want in here, too. I wish you guys would let us know when you're coming." He pushed the door open and stood to the side. "Just let me know when you're finished."

"Sure thing."

Elliott and his assistant entered the room and shut the door. He dropped his bag on the floor and kicked it to the side, then put down his briefcase on the counter. There were banks of computers on one side of the room, and printers and storage cabinets on the opposite. He opened the briefcase and took out the discs fastened inside the front pocket. The money was underneath, wrapped tightly in brown paper, he checked again. He looked up at the monitors and approached the first. Coyly, he sat and typed a few keys at the keyboard. It whirled several pages and the Terminator protocol appeared, just as Martino predicted. Quickly, he loaded a blank disc and began copying. Antonio sat, put the briefcase on his lap, and watched.

Instead of returning down the noisy hallway, Dr. Rice continued around the horseshoe-shaped hall and slunk into his private office a few doors down. He closed the door, grabbed the telephone, and dialed Steven Sloan's direct number.

The telephone rang three times and was answered by a female voice.

"This is Dr. Duane Rice. I need to speak with Mr. Sloan."

"I'm sorry. Mr. Sloan is in New York at the moment. I will give him your message if you—"

"No. I need to speak with him."

"I am sorry, there is no way you can do that. If you leave me a message for him—"

"I need to speak with him, *right now*! He must have another number where I can reach him."

"No. It would be impossible for me to connect you."

"Look! I have two FDA agents in my clinic doing an inspection and they're *not supposed to be here*!"

She paused. "What department are you with?"

"I'm in the Matamoros clinic!"

"One moment, please."

Dr. Rice sat impatiently for a second or two, then clicked on the speakerphone button, dropped the headset in the cradle, and started for the door. Slowly he opened it and looked down the hall. The noise of the clinic gushed but the door to the equipment room remained shut.

"Dr. Rice," Sloan's voice cackled.

Dr. Rice ran back to the desk. "Yes." He picked up the telephone. "Mr. Sloan."

"You have FDA there? *Right now?*"

"Two of 'em."

"What's the name? Did you get a name?"

"A Dr. Friedman. I didn't get the other one."

"Friedman," he repeated. "Never heard of him. What did he say they're doing?"

"Some kind of equipment inspection."

"*Equipment*?"

"Something about a violation from the last inspection."

"Aw, for chrissakes!"

"I can't have a couple of feds barging in, upsetting this clinic. We can't handle it right now. You said there'd be no more inspections."

"Just hold tight. I'm right in the middle of a meeting."

"So what am I supposed to do in the meantime?"

"Give me thirty minutes, just keep them busy. I'll have to make a few calls. Did they ask for an evacuation?"

"No. They're in the computer rooms."

"Computers?"

"They haven't gone through the treatment rooms. Don't think they will. Something about a violation of 362."

"Hell, that was nine months ago. They were supposed to let that go."

"Well, they're here right now!"

"All right, just keep an eye on 'em. I'll call you back in thirty minutes."

The copying was almost complete. Elliott showed Antonio how to load the data on the last disc, then got up and wandered around the room, looking at the other monitors. He peered at one, and did a double take. He walked to it and looked at it intently. A graph displayed several lines plotted along an X and Y-axis. It was the same graph he had been working on at Royce. The same—exactly! He touched a few keys and the graph moved backward, showing the past timeline. Just as he had noticed for months, one line moved well above the others. Couldn't be!

"Señor," Antonio said. "There is blink now."

Elliott turned, still looking at the monitor. "Yeah, all right." He got up, walked to the computer, and took out the last disc. He labeled all three and placed them into the briefcase.

Antonio reached over and closed the lid. He pulled it away from Elliott, snapped the fasteners, and stood. "Now, we go."

Elliott stepped towards him. "Give me the briefcase."

"No. I take it."

"No. Mr. Martino wanted me to take it. Give it to me."

Antonio smiled. "Unfortunately, Señor Chapman, you lost the briefcase during your careless inspection, and I have found it. Mr. Martino will be pleased that I have recovered the Terminator."

"You can't take it. That's my money!"

"The money—has been lost. But fortunately for you, the information has been found."

The door opened and Dr. Rice walked in. "Is everything satisfactory?" He scanned the room.

Elliott looked at Antonio. Antonio nodded back slowly, his eyes piercing.

"Yes," Elliott said.

"Are you finished here?"

"Yes." Elliott turned to Antonio and said to him, "Go check the next room, but leave the briefcase. I'll just be a moment with the doctor."

Antonio took both briefcases, and went through the doorway, brushing against Dr. Rice. Elliott watched him leave, then turned to Dr. Rice and pointed to the graph. "Tell me, Dr. Rice, what is this graph?"

"Oh that," he said, walking over to it. "That is one of our research projects. I should have turned off the monitor. It's a failed project."

"Why is it failed?" Elliott asked looking back at the monitor. "What is it?"

Dr. Rice looked at Elliott with a wary eye. "I don't think this is part of your jurisdiction. Your concern is with the violation of code 362. You said it deals with faulty laboratory equipment, not computer systems."

"Yes, that is correct, but now I'm interested in the data on the screen."

Dr. Rice waited.

Elliott waited. He looked down at his badge. It was still there, but didn't offer much influence at the moment. "Look," he said finally. "I've seen the same graph. I would like to know about it."

"You have? Where?"

"Portland, Oregon."

"Oregon?"

"I was involved in a case at Royce University."

Dr. Rice stepped towards Elliott. "The FDA has no jurisdiction at an educational laboratory! You are way out of line as an inspector. Who the hell are you?"

Elliott didn't move. His clothes felt even tighter as he began to perspire. He was told that if something unexpected should happen, his assistant would take care of it. His job was to retrieve the copies of the Terminator, not try to be a hero. Martino made the point over and over.

"This." Elliott pointed to the highest line on the graph. "Right here. This is the faulty data. Yes?"

"Yes," Dr. Rice said elevating his voice. "It's been like that for months. Why? What do you know about this?"

"Because I've been receiving it for months. I collect this data through the Internet."

"Impossible! There are only two places this is transmitted: to a lab in Brownsville, and one in Portland. It doesn't go anywhere else." He stepped closer to Elliott. "Who are you and what the hell are you doing here?"

Elliott moped his brow. His suit sleeve pulled up almost to his elbow. "Have a seat, Dr. Rice. There's something I need to tell you."

CHAPTER 17

Steven Sloan sat on the edge of his chair at the New York Biotechnology Conference, listening to the brilliant speaker from Bard and Hegel, Esq. This firm, Europe's leading public relations agency, made their case disturbingly evident that the radical Greens fighting the biotech corporations were now raising the stakes. No longer could a rogue biotech company continue engineering without this, a new powerful weapon in biotech publicity: Greenwash.

"Here's how we're going to do it: Green-wash the public, public interest groups, and the highest offices of government by painting the wonders of biotech green with complicated data, and make all the mistakes and blemishes disappear. It's done through science, anecdotes, and skewing current information. And to no one's surprise, only the smart, sophisticated public relations firms have influence over the masses and those who make public policy—that's us. We've lifted the Greenwash message from the Greens and we feed it right back, filtered of course, through mainstream media.

"Profiling. That's how we know so much. We've been to rallies in Seattle and abstract university towns in Oregon, like Eugene. We've been to underground lectures given by defunct college professors. We've taken notes and interviewed the messed-up garlic-eating misfits wearing body art and bold, misguided messages on their clothing. The revelation to this generation of biotech companies is this: partner up with us, or you'll be green food. And don't think for a second that a biotech company can battle with a three-person-budget public relations department. Not today.

"We're bringing it to the major media, and fast, before the Greens get there first. The Greens are coming! And they're coming with a vengeance, to wage war against the conglomerates, with their impish ideals and their reckless actions. The radicals always find something to protest. They're all young punks looking for trouble. They used to be disorientated, drugged-out, and not know a thing about the environment or what was good for people on spaceship Earth.

"But this generation of protesters is a different breed. They are educated, sophisticated, and informed, and they are getting on the front pages through unconventional ways. They know that MTV news, CNN, and the Posts are always pushing to grab higher ratings, and will allow any attention-hungry east coast reporter, hell-bent on getting a story, stoop to acceptable levels of lowbrow copywriting. Some newsmakers are even willing to sacrifice their careers to bend the rules of journalism for fifteen minutes of fame. This new *tour de force* has to be stopped before they take a foothold in American Media. And of course, all this was going to cost—big time."

Sloan got the message loud and clear, and was preparing to negotiate with Bard and Hegel, Esq., the equivalent of a full-time position with Magalto. No company in the business had their own public relations of this proportion. With Bard and Hegel, Esq., Magalto could forcibly position any image of biotech they wanted into every corner of the world. And all the people watching television or reading a newspaper would slowly nod their heads in agreement—spellbound.

Right in the middle of the speaker's conclusion, Sloan's phone began vibrating on his rhinestone belt. It was the expected call from Washington. He excused himself from those sitting next to him as politely as he could, exited the large auditorium, and stepped into the foyer.

"Stuart," Sloan said quickly. "Thanks for getting back to me right away."

"Nah, forget about it. What's going on, Steve?" Stuart Bainsworth asked.

Bainsworth worked at the Food and Drug Administrative building in Washington, DC. He was a high-ranking FDA official who dealt with international drugs, the illegal ones. He had worked the private sector for years as an analytical chemist, and even did a stint at Magalto years ago. Sloan had known him since college, and they had crisscrossed paths throughout their careers. For his friends in the business of food or drugs, a phone call to Stuart Bainsworth would squelch almost any problem they faced in the land of FDA persecution. That's what Sloan had done nine months ago about the FDA inspection at the Matamoros clinic. "Of course they don't have jurisdiction," Bainsworth had blasted. "There is no evidence, case closed." But the inspector did issue a 362 violation to Dr. Rice and reported it to Washington. Bainsworth told Sloan to forget about it, and it was never discussed again. That inspector, the joke went, was demoted to monitoring bovine growth hormone levels in dairy farms, up in Northern Alaska.

"Got another 'spector, Stu."

"What? Where?"

"Matamoros."

"Oh God, you're kidding."

"Two of 'em. They're on the equipment again. Computers, too."

Bainsworth paused and breathed heavily into the phone.

"I can't have them snooping around there anymore, Stu."

"Well, I know we cleared all the damn inspectors out of your area. Must be from a new division somewhere. Names? Order numbers? Did you get a division?"

"A Dr. Friedman. Sounds like he works for your outfit in D.C."

"Never heard of him. You say they're on the equipment again?"

"That's what the director said. Just got the call."

"I can tell you they're in a hell of a lot of trouble, if they're from my unit." He sighed and paused a moment. "Well, let me make a few calls, and I'll get back right back to you."

"Appreciate it, Stu."

No one paid much attention to the bum lying on the ground. He had been sleeping near the bench all day. He was just another bum in the park, sleeping until noon.

But Murdoch finally awoke. He lifted his filthy head off the ground, grimaced, then quickly dropped it back down. With all the strength he could muster, he slowly pushed himself up with his right arm, until he sat fully upright. For a moment, he looked at his knife-splinted, bloodstained appendage, and picked a few pieces of dirt from the wound. He brushed his hand through his oily hair, and wiped it on his pants. He began rocking back and forth, until finally, with one great push, he threw himself to his feet, staggered, and mustered up every ounce of energy to put some life back into his flaccid leg muscles. He managed to remain standing. Moving one foot hesitantly in front of the other, he began walking in the direction he had originally intended to move the day before. A severely shattered left forearm and accompanying makeshift splint were his new accessories, and they slowed him considerably.

Murdoch, the crippled potential terrorist, hobbled through the park on the way to his first assignment. No one bothered him. No one knew his purpose or intention.

"You're *not* an inspector with the FDA?" Dr. Rice cracked a crooked smile as he looked at Elliott. It was the kind of smile that accompanies an unbelievable joke.

"No. I'm a student at Royce University. I'm supposed to be working on this project." Elliott pointed to the monitor.

Dr. Rice dropped his jaw and stared at him. "I knew you were an imposter. You don't look FDA." He looked at him as he nodded. "You're a student at Royce."

"Yeah."

"What's your name?"

"Elliott . . . um, Chapman."

"So you're getting this?"

"The data?"

"This, right here." Dr. Rice pointed to the graph.

"Yeah, the same. Exactly."

Dr. Rice looked back at the graph.

"So you're the one messin' with my project?" Elliott asked.

Dr. Rice turned toward him. "Messin' with it? Your project will never turn out. It's completely skewed. It's the most abysmal piece of crap data you can put on a graph. The X-Y coordinates are entirely wrong, because I'm trying to squeeze all the numbers on."

"Then why are you sending it?"

"You don't know anything about this, do you?"

Elliott shook his head. "No. I don't and I'd sure like to find out. My senior project is riding on it."

"Well let me tell you, you'd better get up to speed real quick." Dr. Rice sat down in front of the monitor beside Elliott and pointed. "We have to plot the effects of genetic food ingestion with the type of food grown in the fields around the area. I've been measuring these effects on the people in the area for years. At first, people were getting sick from toxins and allergens. Intestinal symptoms were common. Then it got worse. Heavy dysentery and virulent infections showed up. The patients coming in had thyroid and spleen panels off the charts. Sometimes we get a real immune-compromised patient, one that we couldn't trace to anything else but the toxins in the foods. No other patients come here except the ones fed from the food grown in the fields owned by Magalto. It's free and so is the medical care."

"Also from Magalto."

"Yes. A few years ago, Magalto bought this old building and converted it into a clinic to deal with the health problems and to hide their own. They made an agreement with the city of Matamoros and the government of Mexico, that they would offer care to the public and provide it for free. Magalto continued planting. See, years ago, there used to be fields of genetic crops planted in this entire region. The seeds were free to all the farmers, but after a couple of years, some of the farmers began to notice that their original crops were becoming contaminated. The plants were crossing genetic lines and producing phylogenies that were completely foreign. They turned out to be transgenic mutations and they all died after one season. Of course, the farmers had never seen anything like it before. Species of plants that had been in their families for hundreds of years were disappearing. That's when the outrage began. The promise of something free turned into something money could never buy back."

"So why can't they just engineer the old species back?"

"You can't do that. The code has been cracked, and it will never be the same. Nature's secrets have been exploited. It's now in the hands of the conglomerates, companies like Magalto. Some people think they're smarter than God."

"But why can't they put in the original sequences?"

"They are, and selling it right back to them. But it's still engineered. So now the farmers have to buy their own seed that they used to germinate themselves. The ones that have become mutants. Damn mutants that no one knows anything about. Some of them get out of control and skew all the other data. Then it takes months for the researchers to tinker with it, to bring it within a normal range again."

"So that's what this data is for," Elliott pointed to the monitor, "isn't it? The testing is for the health effects."

"Yes. But the data is for the patents and becomes a record of any type of health problems that show up. The numbers have to come out right for the patent applications. That's what's in these storage units and computers."

"How are they tested?"

"Every crop is marked with a radioactive isotope; when it's ingested, the type of clinical symptom is recorded. Then they're compared and graphed. Up until two weeks ago, we were having a big problem with the squash. They were ripening just fine, and then the lab guys ran some routine tests on them just before they were to be harvested. They found a problem with cellular respiration. The gourds were giving off very harmful toxins, then a day or so later the cell wall collapsed. Thousands of them were left to rot in the fields. Then, *poof!*, two weeks ago, the graph line comes back to normal and the rest of the squash turns out all right. Sometimes it happens like that, but most of the time they have to send someone down to the lab on the farm to fix the problem. I guess we'll chalk the squash up to another spontaneous recovery."

"Are all the crops tested like this?"

"Yeah."

"What about this here, on the graph?" Elliott pointed to the line on the graph that went high on the Y-axis.

"That has been the problem." Dr. Rice turned from the graph to Elliott. "That is our infamous tomato crop. These Y-axis plot points have never been anywhere near normal."

"What do you know about it?"

"Well, I think I know what's going on and I hope to get it cleared up soon, or there'll be some real, irreversible problems. If it doesn't come down, it will become a very sad problem, like some of the previous crops."

"Like what?"

"Years ago, we had gender changes."

"Sex changes?"

"Yeah. Girls not older than six or seven beginning menstruation. Their mamas bring them into the clinic because they think they're hemorrhaging—and they're menstruating! Then I began to look around. Did you notice anything strange in the waiting room? There's a hell of a lot more girls than boys out there, about four to one. But the worst part is, half of those girls started out as boys. They have the Y chromosome, but they're not boys anymore."

"No way."

"Yeah. So I began snooping around and had the lab run some tests on the soil at the compound. They found toxic levels of estridiols in the soil composition and the plant spoilage. That means either toxic levels of estrogen are being ingested, or the adrenal cortex and gonads are growing like pumpkins. Or both. Pregnant women are exposed to these large amounts of hormones during the embryonic stage, and then they pop out females left and right."

"What'd you do about it?"

"What am I supposed to do? I called Magalto and reported it. There was no response, for about a year. Then they got the definitive word back to me: keep my nose out of it. They don't like anybody doing things outside of their job descriptions."

"They didn't do anything?"

"Of course they didn't. So I reported the soil tests to Washington and said people were getting sick at my clinic. Haven't heard a word. In the meantime, Magalto keeps buying up hundreds of acres around here and growing tons of food. That way they can bypass most of the FDA inspections. They're working hard to get these statistics right, so Sloan can get the patents issued. The squash was his latest problem. But it's the tomatoes that are screwing up all the statistics." Dr. Rice looked intently at Elliott. "That's why I was suspicious when you and your assistant walked in."

"Antonio," Elliott mumbled.

"All this information goes to Magalto and they don't even bother with it. Then it goes on to Royce, where it's supposed to be compiled, by you. You're supposed to compile it, aren't you? For your project?"

"Yeah. The project that has never worked out."

"And now you know why. It'll never work out. Not as long as the tomatoes stay up so high on the Y-axis. Another one of Kingsley's projects going down the drain."

"Kingsley? How do you know Kingsley?

Dr. Rice smiled and said, "I was a student there ten years ago, one of the many to get kicked out of his class."

"You went to Royce?"

"Yeah, and got into the same mess it looks like you're in right now. They busted me my senior year."

"Busted?"

"They planted drugs in my dorm room."

"You're kidding."

"Two campus security officers came out with a bag of cocaine and waved it in front of Whitman and Kingsley. So they sat me down and offered me a deal before they threatened to take it to the police."

"A deal? With Kingsley?"

"Yup. He told me that if I went to work for Magalto in a privileged laboratory, they wouldn't press charges. They needed someone they could blackmail. That was ten years ago, and I've been working for them ever since. Five years in the lab, and five here at the clinic."

"Then you never finished school."

"Not even a real doctor. They trained me. Sent me to a few clinics to prep and learn some basic procedures. After a few years, you learn what to do around here, to treat the kinds of problems that walk through the door. I use about nine different medications—the pharmaceutical reps keep me updated."

"Ten years with Magalto. Why don't you leave?"

"I can't leave. They can still press charges."

"No they can't. The statute of limitation has expired."

"Not for federal drug charges. Plus, I'm in a foreign country. "

"You're screwed."

"No—I got out alive."

Elliott shook his head, looking at him.

Dr. Rice continued, "This goes on every year at Royce. Some sorry-ass student gets in a little trouble and becomes the target, then a deal is made between him and Kingsley. Just like you. He finally backed you into a corner, didn't he?"

"Yeah, actually, I've been trying all year to get on his human side. At least get a little rise out of him."

"He doesn't have a human side."

"He tries. So I made a bet with him, that if I did well on the pretest then I wouldn't have to take his final."

"No. He made the deal and you fell for it. He acts like he wants to be nice to you—it'll never happen."

"Whatever. It was an easy bet; I would've aced both tests."

"No," Dr. Rice laughed. "Bet or no bet, you were this year's victim. It always happens right before graduation, so no one can follow up. It's a perfect scam."

"What do you mean?"

"You'll do whatever they say. And it will probably be working for Magalto."

"Dr. Barringer already offered me a job. I just won't take it."

"He did, huh? Oh yeah, you're already in too deep."

Elliott looked at him carefully. "No. I'll just walk away."

Dr. Rice smiled at him, shaking his head. "There's nothing you can do without Magalto knowing about it now. They have connections all over the world. They have businesses and liaisons you wouldn't believe if I told you."

"Like the Columbians."

"Sure. Their largest customer and most antagonizing friend. They've been here many times."

"Like today."

Dr. Rice's eyes popped wide open. "You were sent by the Columbians!"

"Yeah," Elliott said softly.

Dr. Rice leaned back in the chair and clasped his hands across his forehead. He jumped up and ran to the door.

"Where're you going?" Elliott asked as he stood and followed after him.

"Gotta call off Sloan."

"What?"

"Follow me." Dr. Rice ran out of the data room, down the hall, and into his office. Elliott followed and closed the door behind them. Dr. Rice dialed Steven Sloan and waited; Sloan was unavailable, so he left an urgent message that it wasn't really the FDA, it was an old buddy pulling a prank and everything was okay.

Dr. Rice dropped the phone on the cradle. "God, I hope he gets that before he calls Washington," he said, letting out a sigh. He sat back in his chair and rubbed his hands over his face. "This place is a time bomb."

"Sorry. This wasn't my idea."

"So." Dr. Rice lifted his head and looked at Elliott with narrowed eyes. "Martino sent you here. Isn't that right?"

"Yup."

He shook his head at Elliott. "You came for the Terminator protocol."

"Yeah."

"Dammit! You were trying to copy the records, weren't you?"

"Already did. Took three discs. They're in the briefcase."

"Before you get too cozy with Martino, let me tell you a few things about the company you keep. The FARC. Do you know anything about them?"

"Just what Martino told me."

"Well let me give you the other side of the story. The FARC is a rebel group. Martino tried to tell you they were part of the government, yeah? Well, far from it. They're extortionists and murderers. They smuggle drugs. They want to take over the Columbian government and with the help of Magalto, they're getting close. Magalto has been supplying them with genetic research for years: seeds, plants, even crude laboratory equipment and some protocols. The Columbians have been the second mass experiment, right behind Matamoros. And things haven't been going so well with them, either. They've been able to supply tons of seed for farmers, and tons of food to sell. But they're having the same kinds of problems with secondary attrition like we are around here. The crops keep dying on 'em. You just can't take age out of the DNA, no matter what you're engineering. Martino is working fast and furious to get elected before the entrails hit the fan. If he can get the Terminator protocols, the FARC will be unstoppable."

Elliott stared at him. "And if they get the Terminator and get it into the genetic structures, all the farmers will be completely dependant on them. Martino brought me up to date on the issue."

"He said that? What else did he say?"

"That they're working to get a delegate to the World Trade Organization. They want to write international patent law. On the Terminator, huh?"

"Totally makes sense." Dr. Rice slapped his forehead. "I should have seen this coming. This has been building for years. All the meetings. All the exports. Even some strange people who've been showing up here the last couple of months." Dr. Rice sat back into his chair and spoke to the ceiling. "Sloan would call about a new gene that they'd been putting in some kind of crop, and he'd want to know if anything unusual showed up in the clinic. What will it take, an epidemic?"

"Sloan called you often?"

Dr. Rice looked at him. "Oh, yeah. A couple times a week someone from Magalto calls me. But I'd get the weirdest calls from Dr. Barringer. He's always engineering something. I helped him design several research projects years ago, and used to help him in the lab up there when I had the time. But I couldn't deal with him after awhile."

Elliott's eyes widened and he smiled. "Did he get into the neuropeptides and pleasure pathways?"

"Yeah, did he tell you?"

"Oh yeah, all kinds of bizarre things."

"That man is a few genes short of a full deck."

Elliott laughed. "Gene pool. He's been playing too many games of gene pool."

"What?"

"Nothing. A joke we had in class."

"Well, I told him to find another place to experiment, that I'm busy enough just dealing with the locals around here. So he doesn't call anymore. He's a crazy-ass, Elliott. He just might come up with something."

"It's certainly fascinating, the part I heard."

"It's all fascinating. That's the problem. Somehow this is all fitting together. It won't be long; the plants, the food, the neuropeptides. Magalto is in cahoots with the FARC. Steve Sloan is close to committing murder to get these statistics right, so he can get his patents approved. Martino is gaining support for the presidency of Columbia, then he'll write international law on genetic organisms, patents, and whatever else he comes up with. He'll blow right past Sloan. Especially if the World Trade Organization gets involved with him."

"So what are you going to do?"

"*Me*? There's nothing I'm going to do. I've learned not to stick my nose in their business."

"There must be something."

"Well for one thing, you're not giving Martino the copies you made."

"I understand." Elliott nodded.

"You'll have to give him something else. I'll put together another Terminator protocol, but I'll skip several steps in the sequences. He'll never know. You're going to have to play along until you find a chance to get away."

"Why can't you go to the authorities?"

Dr. Rice shook his red head. "And what authorities would that be? Why do you think they have the lab, compound, and clinic here in Mexico? There are no authorities."

"What about Martino?"

"Martino has done his homework. He's carefully planned this political move for years. He'll probably get elected, but his ideas on engineering are very weak and he can't influence anyone in the scientific world without a fully operational lab. I know he doesn't have one, yet. But once he does, there will be real trouble. That's when he'll go global. Magalto is the one to stop. If Magalto collapses, Martino and the FARC will die a quick death. But Sloan will never let that happen."

"So . . . " Elliott eyed him.

"*Me*? Don't look at me like that. I'm not doing anything about it. I'm planning on dying of a heart attack right here in one of these rooms. Maybe today, the way it's going around here."

"Someone needs to do something."

"Well, not me. I've done enough." Dr. Rice stood and walked toward the door. "Now if you'll excuse me, I've got to get back to work. There are people waiting in the street by now. You just wait here. I'll be back in a few minutes, then we'll figure out how to get you out of here." He looked back at Elliott. "Your guy, Antonio. Is he okay for awhile?"

Elliott shook his head. "He has the Terminator."

"He has the Terminator?"

"He took it from me."

Dr. Rice reached the door then turned. "I'll get it from him. You just wait here."

"Thanks, Dr. Rice, for all your help."

"I'm not a doctor. Call me Duane."

Chapter 18

He walked with a limp. The handgun jabbed into his side. His legs chaffed as they rubbed against the inside of his fatigues. His right ankle, badly sprained from the fall, had swollen so large it pushed against the sides of his boots, cutting off circulation and entrapping the major nerves in his foot. He limped higher now, as he fought harder to swing the swollen foot forward. His left arm jutted out from his portly belly, like he was signaling a left hand turn with his prosthesis. Back and forth it oscillated, balanced by the swing of his other arm carrying the bag of artillery. He gimped another block.

It certainly seemed farther to the clinic than his friends had told him. His round head beaded with sweat and he had fresh stains circling under his pits, down the front and back of his shirt, and around his crotch where his legs were rubbing. He stopped to dab his forehead and to look for any kind of new terrain. Yes, there it was. Up ahead stood a walled building with people coming in and out through a large iron gate. For a moment, he stood and looked at the place and the people. He dropped the bag and frisked himself with his right hand, running over each piece of weaponry. Guns, knives, rope, tape. Everything not supporting a body part was accounted for and ready to be dispatched at will. His left hand and fingers were swollen and bulging between the strips of tape and knife splint. Still, very little pain. He slapped his belly, picked up his bag, and continued on the final leg of his premeditated journey. He hobbled faster, his arm swung quicker, and his head bobbed higher. But just as his momentum began to build, he slowed down to a stagger. He came to a grinding halt, and leaned against the wall to catch his breath. He forced puffs of air in and out, as his hand clutched at his chest. He labored for a moment then eased into nasal mode and looked ahead to see a tiny elderly woman struggle to push the gate open. He watched as she put her weight behind her bony arms. She stopped and looked at him, then backed away from the gate. He rolled his eyes, pushed himself forward, and waved her out of the way, then leaned against the gate until it opened, and held it for her. She waited until he motioned for her to go through and gave him an appreciative smile and nod. He held the gate for another woman, then let it swing shut and followed them up the path. He picked up his gimpy pace and approached the old woman as she struggled with the front door. Again, he pushed it open for her and allowed her to pass into the front room of the clinic.

It was filled with people. A young nurse in a blue smock stood at the entrance with a clipboard and pencil. She spoke quickly in Spanish to the woman who had just entered. The nurse jotted something on the clipboard and pointed to a wall. The woman ambled over to an empty seat. The nurse turned to Murdoch.

"¿*Como se llama?*"

"No speako Spanish."

"What is your name, Señor?"

"What do you need my name for?"

"For your appointment."

"I don't have an appointment."

"Sí, Señor. That is why I need your name."

"I want to see the person in charge."

"I need your name for that," she said tapping her pencil.

"I'm not givin' it to you."

"Then you will have to wait until the last appointment."

Murdoch rolled his eyes and heaved a breath. He dropped his bag and with his right hand he lifted up his left, so she could see his arm.

"*Oh! Señor! You cannot have a knife in here!*"

"No, not that." He began to unwrap the tape from the knives. "I hurt my arm." He took off a few more bands. Near the bend of the disfigured arm, the white bones glistened as they poked through the skin. He unwrapped it further. As the knives were unwrapped and no longer supported his arm, the rest of the hand bent and dangled toward the floor. He looked up at the people and returned their stares from around the room.

"*Oh,*" she gasped, dropping the clipboard and the pencil, "*Santa Maria!*" Her hands flew to her cheeks, and she ran to Juanita who was sitting comfortably at her station. The nurse shrieked and waved her hands toward Murdoch as she explained the emergency. Juanita poked her head around the nurse, and motioned a quick wave with a stiff hand for him to approach. Murdoch finished re-taping the knives back in place, picked up his bag, and limped toward her.

"Broken arm?"

"Yes, ma'am. Happened this morning or yesterday morning. Can't remember which."

"Well, you're just going to have to wait your turn. And you're going to have to put those knives away."

"I'm not waitin'."

"You're going to have to sit down and wait your turn. I'm sorry."

"Look," he said, as his right hand slipped inside his shirt. "I have an appointment—*right now!*" He wrapped his fingers around the knobby handle of the pistol. He lifted it out of the holster high enough for his index finger to curl around the trigger. Just as his hand exposed the butt, his finger twitched and the gun exploded. The bullet shredded his shirt and blasted into the thin floor. After his hand recoiled, he lifted the gun all the way out and waved it above his head. Shrieks and screams sounded throughout the room. He fired another shot at a vacant wall. Patients scrambled to the floor. Mothers covered their children.

Juanita rattled off orders in Spanish to the nurse, who whipped around and disappeared through the curtain. Murdoch tapped the nose of the gun on the knife laying his arm. He turned around to survey the room covered with crouching bodies.

"Señor, we get you right back. *Un momento*." Juanita looked nervously back at the curtain.

"*Gracias*." He smiled at her.

After a moment, the curtain flew open and Duane leaped into the room. The nurse followed close behind.

"Señor, please. No more! *Give me the gun!*" Duane grabbed it out of Murdoch's shaky hand. "Now, come with me." Duane took him by the right arm and pulled him past the curtain and into the hall. The third room had only two people in it, and they exited quickly as Duane hauled Murdoch inside and shoved him against the table. "Sit! Here!"

Murdoch tried to slow himself, but crashed into the crude examination table in the middle of the room.

Duane turned to the nurse. "Go get the plaster from the supply room. It's up on the top shelf." She hurried from the room.

Duane put the gun on the counter and began to prep. As he washed his hands, he turned to look at Murdoch over his shoulder. "Get up on the table. Here," he threw him a towel from a rack on the counter, "wipe that shit off your face."

Murdoch missed the towel and it fell to the floor. He bent down slowly, clawing at it with his stubby fingers. He slowly raised his wracked body to an upright posture, sat on top of the old exam table, and glanced up into the cracked mirror. He was an atrocious sight, not the noble, bold warrior he had started out as a few days ago. His face was a frightening smear. It was sweaty and grimy and had pieces of grass, dirt, and other muck stuck on it. He took the towel and rubbed it over his face. It smeared even more. He wiped it once again, not even bothering to look in the mirror, and let the towel drop to the floor.

The nurse ran into the room and set the rolls of plaster on the counter, glanced at Murdoch, then disappeared back into the hall. Duane took the strips of plaster and dipped them into the water in the sink. He turned to look at his new patient. The knives were barely hanging on by the tape.

"*This* is a medical clinic! Take those knives off and give 'em to me."

Murdoch daintily picked at the tape on his arm and tried to pull it. Duane set the wet plaster down on the table and with a disgusted look, grabbed the edge of the tape and gave it a yank. The two knives crashed to the floor and the broken arm flopped backwards at the break.

"Hey. Watch it, would ya? You pulled my skin."

Duane picked up the knives and tossed them into the sink. "What the hell are you doing with these? And the gun?"

"I was passing through."

"Well you're not getting them back, they're going to the police. Now, how did you do this?" Duane picked up the wet plaster and looked at Murdoch. It dripped on the floor in front of him.

"I fell."

"You *fell* on your arm?"

"Yeah, I tripped."

"Well, I'm going to have to reduce it and I'm out of anesthesia at the moment. Now, lie on your back."

Murdoch lifted up his heavy legs, turned ninety degrees, and lowered himself onto his back. He dropped his head down on the hard table. Duane laid the wet plaster across Murdoch's pants.

"And it's going to hurt."

"That's all right."

"I have to *pull* it." Duane watched his face as he spoke.

"I said *okay*," Murdoch said louder. "Go right ahead." He looked straight up at the ceiling.

Duane reached for a towel and wrapped it around the end of the broken arm like a crude traction device. He braced himself with his foot inside Murdoch's armpit, and locked both of his hands around the towel. He pulled carefully at first, watching his face for an expression. Murdoch didn't flinch. Duane pulled harder, this time getting his back into it. Murdoch lay on the table, as relaxed as if he were napping. Finally, Duane just yanked on the arm. Suddenly it cracked, and the crooked arm was made straight. Murdoch lay as comfortable as could be.

"You didn't *feel* that?" Duane leaned over and looked at him.

"I felt you tugging on my arm."

"But you didn't feel any pain?"

"Nah, just a little tug."

Duane shook his head. He grabbed a bottle of antiseptic and poured it out over the open wound. He reached to the counter again, grabbed a wad of gauze, and wiped the arm dry. Then he put a sock-like article over Murdoch's hand and pulled it over the arm. He took the wet plaster strip that he had laid across Murdoch's pant leg and placed it lengthwise over the sock. He continued wetting and placing the strips around the arm. The layers of plaster built and began to harden. Murdoch's fat, purple fingers dangled out, like bait for a deep-sea creature.

"That too tight? Can you move your fingers?"

"Yeah, it's all right."

Duane squeezed both of his hands tight around the new cast and wrung out the excess water. He turned, rinsed his plastered hands in the sink, and dried them with a towel. "You just stay here and rest. The plaster has to set."

"I'm not going anywhere."

Duane quickly left the room, slamming the door behind. He hurried down the busy hall, sticking his head inside the rooms as he passed by. "*Evacuate! We have to evacuate!*" The nurse poked her head into the hall after he passed.

"*¿Que, Señor?*" she called.

Duane turned around. "There is a *militant—VAMOS!*"

People flocked out of rooms and ran into each other as they all hurried to the exit. The nurse ran down the hall, directing the frenzied traffic, shouting orders. The clinic, which was not at all efficient in taking care of its patients, was remarkable at evacuation.

Duane ran back to his office and burst through the door.

"What was that?" Elliott, who was almost clobbered as Duane jetted past him, asked. "Sounded like firecrackers out there."

"It's *gunfire!* Some kind of lunatic was firing off shots in the waiting room." Duane hurried to his desk and reached for the telephone. "Go get your friend and tell him to contain room three, down the hall."

"What's going on?"

"We have a military problem."

"Antonio! What's he doing?"

"No, not him. Get him to guard the door to room three. There's a wild militant in there with a busted arm. He has to be guarded. But you get right back here—Hello . . . Dr. Duane Rice . . . yes . . . at the clinic near the park . . . we're under another attack . . . *RIGHT NOW!* Only one . . . appears to be alone. No, it's being evacuated. Well call them in! *AN HOUR!* No sooner? No, just forget it." He slammed the telephone down. "Damn city police. Have to do things myself around here." He turned and walked to the door. "Go tell Antonio to guard room three, and I'll meet him there in just a minute. Have him stay there. I have to evacuate this place." Duane pushed past Elliott and raced down the hall.

Elliott hurried down the hall and opened the door to the second equipment room. Antonio sat as if he hadn't moved for an hour. He held both briefcases tight.

"Let's go. We have a situation. Someone's attacking the clinic."

Antonio placed the briefcases on the counter, sprang to his feet, and marched quickly after Elliott.

"Room three," Elliott said as he hurried into the hall. Antonio reached for his gun as he took orders. "Go stand guard at room number three. Dr. Rice will meet you there in a few minutes."

Antonio lifted his gun and pointed it forward. "Sí, Señor." He hurried down the hall, turned the corner, and disappeared. Elliott quickly returned to Duane's office.

Antonio found room three. It was the only room with the door closed. Every other room was empty. He wrapped both hands around the grip of the gun, slowly nudged the door open with his shoulder, and quietly crept inside, low to the floor.

"Doctor? Is that you? Doctor?" Murdoch lay still, with one eye cracked open. "There's sure a lot of noise out there in the hall. Could you tell them to keep quiet? How's anyone supposed to rest around here?"

Antonio lurched closer with his gun poised.

"Doctor, do you wanna check the cast? I think it's dry now." Murdoch opened both eyes wider and saw his new caregiver pointing a gun at him.

Antonio moved closer.

"I think it's a little tight. My fingers feel hot and, they're throbbing. I'm starting to feel 'em get a little *too* hot now. That's not so good, is it?" Slowly he reached under his shirt and located his backup pistol. He moved it under his shirt into position. "If you could come and loosen it just a bit. I think my circulation's gettin' cut off."

Antonio swept his gun quickly over the table. Murdoch pulled his finger tighter around the trigger and raised the gun higher underneath his shirt. One shot fired, then another. Murdoch shrieked; Antonio flung against the wall and dropped to the floor. The other bullet had ripped through Murdoch's shirt. It split open and thousands of tiny particles flew up into the air, filling the room in a dense cloud. They floated like feathers in every direction.

Elliott jumped to his feet and rushed to room three, just as Duane pushed the door open. The storm of particles fluttered around the room. Murdoch slowly raised himself from the table and swung his feet around, letting them dangle to the floor.

"What the hell . . . " Duane said as he moved inside.

"*Murdoch! What are you doing?*" Elliott rushed in behind Duane.

"Some lunatic was gonna take me out." He looked at the crumpled heap on the floor. Blood bubbles formed on the man's lips and trickled down the side of his face.

"You know this guy?" Duane asked Elliott, pointing to Murdoch.

"Yeah, vaguely," Elliott said. "He's a Magalto driver."

Duane looked at Murdoch. "So you *shot* him?" He rushed to check the man's pulse.

"He had a gun pointed at me," Murdoch whined.

"He wasn't going to shoot you." Elliott said.

"He won't be doing much of anything now," Duane said looking up at them. "He's dead."

"Oh, jeez, Murdoch. What'd you have to go and shoot him for?"

"He was sneaking up on me. It was all in self-defense. I swear it."

Duane stood, his face flushed. "The FARC will be coming," he said flatly.

"The what?" Murdoch asked.

"I thought I heard two shots," Elliott said.

"There will probably be a battalion of them," Duane said in shock. He stared at the body.

"You did. He shot me here somewhere." Murdoch pointed to his own chest.

"So will the police. They'll kill each other," Duane continued.

"Where?" Elliott asked. "You don't look hurt. He probably missed." He looked around the room. "What the hell *is all this shit* floating in the air?"

Each of them looked in a different direction and watched the little pieces flutter lazily to the floor. Elliott reached out in mid air and let a clump gather in his hand. Duane rolled some between his fingers for a closer look.

"What is this? Looks like leaves." Duane turned to Murdoch then flicked the wad on the floor.

"Dunno," Murdoch said dusting himself off with his right hand. He brushed his arms and legs then lightly touched at his chest. He reached inside his mangled shirt and pulled out the rest of the brick Carlos had given him. He picked at the bullet lodged in the leaves, pulled it out, and held it in his hand. "Well, looky there."

"Where did you get this?" Duane asked sharply grabbing the half-shredded block of leaves out of his hand.

"Someone gave it to me."

"Who? Who gave this to you?" Duane shook the brick at him.

"Coupla of friends. You wouldn't know 'em."

"This came from the compound, didn't it?" Duane lifted the contraband to his nose and smelled it. He took a pinch, put it into his mouth, and chewed. He spat it out. "No taste, no smell."

"What is it?" Elliott asked, looking at the specimen in his hand.

"This is the mother load of cocaine," Duane said, holding it as a careful display.

Elliott looked at the leaves in his hand. *"Cocaine?"*

"Cocaine." Duane sniffed it again. He looked at Murdoch. "That's why you didn't feel pain from your fracture, isn't it? You've been *chewing* it!"

"Maybe a little," Murdoch said, as if he'd gotten caught reaching into his mother's cookie jar.

"It doesn't take much." Duane put the frayed brick on the counter near the sink.

"So this is a coca leaf." Elliott picked it up and inspected it closely.

"No. These are tomato leaves," Duane said, watching Elliott. "This cocaine comes from the common tomato plant."

"Tomato leaves? How?"

"Cocaine is a molecule extracted from the coca leaf. The genetic sequence has been coded and inserted it into the tomato leaf." Duane grabbed the brick out of Elliott's hand.

"Dr. Barringer," Elliott said nodding slowly. "Easy."

"Yeah, he calls it tomato-cocaine puree. Dammit! They're *still* engineering this." Duane slammed it on the counter. "They were supposed to stop six months ago."

"Where are they growing it?" Elliott raised his eyebrows.

"At the compound. They grow and harvest these plants in a corner of the farm."

"*They're all cocaine plants?*"

"No, no. Just the tomatoes."

"That's *perfect*! Growing cocaine in a tomato." Elliott laughed.

"Yeah, it's all Easy's idea."

"I'm impressed." Elliott smiled, eyeing the brick on the counter.

"This began as a joke. Easy just wanted to see if it worked. I helped him with the initial steps myself years ago, before we got so busy here at the clinic. But he kept tinkering with it until he was able to insert the gene into the tomato. So then Sloan finds out about it, and all of a sudden no one's talking. I just assumed they stopped doing it." Duane swallowed hard and had a far off look on his face. "The same drug they used to get *me* busted."

"But this is *incredible*! Putting cocaine in tomato leaves. So how do they get the cocaine out of it?"

"These leaves are taken to a big vat and washed in sulfuric acid and sodium nitrate, to remove any genetic contaminants. They do it up at Magalto."

"Contaminants like the Terminator?"

"The Terminator, as a contaminant?" Duane looked at him. "No, not necessarily. They just wash it to clear any kind of contamination. After the leaves are washed, you get very potent cocaine, but the molecule becomes very unstable, so it has to be converted to a salt called cocaine hydrochloride, right away. A solvent like alcohol extracts the cocaine molecule from the leaves, just like from a coca plant. Then it's heated, and kerosene is poured over it to treat the cocaine alkaloids that form. After the kerosene is extracted, you're left with salt crystals that dissolve in sulfuric acid."

"So it's like processing the coca leaf? We did a lab simulation with Dr. Kingsley."

"Yeah, after the contaminates are washed off. But the molecule is very unstable. You have to be very careful with it. Not long ago, Martino got a hold of the washed leaves and transported them to Columbia. It wasn't detected by the drug enforcements because it was still in the tomato leaf, and nobody thought to look. But when he tried to convert it to the freebase form, the potency dropped way off. The molecule just disintegrated. No more cocaine."

"Why does that happen?"

"I don't know why. Maybe it was the higher elevation. Solar radiation, X-rays. Could have been their laboratory. Whatever it was, the cocaine molecule was gone. All he had left after he processed it was a kind of tomato leaf salt."

"So this hasn't been washed?"

"No, but it's on its way."

"Smuggled into the U.S.?"

"Yep. Actually, it's walked in, usually in backpacks, right across the border. Nobody stops tomato leaves. They probably have stockpiles of these bricks at Magalto, waiting to be processed. If this brick was tested right now using color chromatography or even a simple drug kit, you could find the cocaine molecule. But who's going to test tomato leaves?"

"Well," Murdoch said wobbling off the table. "Looks to me like ya'll are right in the middle of a drug operation." He landed on his good ankle and hobbled a few steps. He patted his belly with his right hand. "So since you won't be needing me, I think I'll be going now." He pushed his way between Elliott and Duane.

"Oh no, you're not," Duane said, grabbing his shoulder. He pushed him back down hard against the table.

"What were you going to do here, anyway, Murdoch?" Elliott asked.

"Blow the place up," he said with a straight face.

"Blow the place up?" Elliott shot. "Why would you do that?"

"Sloan fired me so I was going to annihilate the computers and take out all the backup data storages that he keeps here. Except I bumped my arm a bit."

"You're not going to go through with it," Duane said. "Some of that data is irreplaceable. And the equipment . . . " Duane stepped and bumped something on the floor. "Oh, no," Duane wailed, "the body!"

At that moment, Juanita porpulated into the room. She held the door for balance and her head bobbed around like a wobble doll. She goggled at Duane. "Señor, a call for you." She looked around the room again, shaking her head. "You are always *so messy*," she scolded, then quickly left.

"Oh, *no!*" Duane said slapping his forehead. "Sloan."

"Or the police," Elliott said.

"Ohhh . . . " Duane rushed to the door then stopped. "You guys get this body to the back room. Cover him with some blankets from the bottom drawer." He glanced to the top of the counter, swiped the brick of leaves with a quick movement, and dropped it into the front pocket of his clinic jacket. "I'll take this call, then you're both going to have to get out of here."

"But what about Martino?" Elliott asked.

"Can't deal with him right now," Duane said as he whirled out of the room. "You'll think of something."

Duane ran down the hall, turned the corner, and went into his office. He stood over his desk and picked up the telephone. "Duane Rice speaking."

"Dr. Rice," said a soft voice with a Spanish accent. "This is Jorge Martino."

"Mr. Martino!"

"Yes. I have just spoken with Steven Sloan. He said you were under inspection, is that correct?"

Duane took a deep breath. "Well, no, actually the inspection has been completed. Now we are . . . under siege!" He raised his voice and spoke faster as he continued, "We are being attacked! There is a militant and he's shot one of the inspectors. He's dressed in Right National gear and on a rampage. We've had to evacuate the entire clinic!"

"Is the data secure?" Martino asked calmly.

"Data? You mean the computers? No," he said quickly. "They've been . . . uhm . . . hit."

"Is everything safe?"

"No, nothing's safe! I'm trying to keep him from destroying everything."

"I will send help."

"No, no. The city police will be here very soon, and they'll get everything under control."

Martino was silent.

"Look, Mr. Martino. I've got to get your man to the hospital, unless it's too late. I have to go." He hung up the phone before Martino could ask another question.

Elliott tossed the blanket on the body. "Come on, Murdoch, get over here and give me a hand." He bent over and reached for the shoulders. He looked up from a crouched position, holding the body. "You were going to blow up the place because Sloan *fired* you?"

Murdoch stepped to the feet of the body and bent forward. "Yeah. It's my only way to get revenge. I still can. I can blow up the computers. That would settle me with Sloan."

"Get a hold of his feet. We need to take care of this, so just let it go."

Murdoch made a feeble attempt to lift with his handicaps. "The FARC are comin'. They're going to blow the place up, anyway. I'll do it, then you could tell Sloan it was them."

"*Lift*, would ya? Use your good arm." Elliott looked up at him as he raised the body higher.

"Or you could tell them some militant broke in, blew the place up, and took off."

"They'd find you, then you'd sit in a Mexican jail the rest of your life. Why would you want to do that?"

"Jail wouldn't be so bad."

They bantered all the way to the back of the clinic, carrying the body between them. They lowered it to the floor in the computer room and pushed it against the wall. They spread the blanket out and covered the heap so that no clothing or body parts were visible. Elliott put an empty box and a wastebasket in front. Murdoch helped him finish by unfolding a corner of the blanket. A telephone rang. Elliott looked at Murdoch, then at the telephone on the desk that wasn't ringing. The phone rang again.

"I don't have a phone," Elliott said. "Must be yours."

"I don't have a phone."

Elliott looked at the crypt they had created. "It's on *him*!" He looked back at Murdoch. "*His* phone is ringing."

"Don't answer it," Murdoch said.

"It's *Martino*! I gotta answer it." Elliott looked at Murdoch as he bent down and began throwing the burial artifacts off the body. "Help me get these things off of him!"

They threw without caution. Elliott dug around and found the ringing telephone in the dead man's pocket. He reached inside and pulled it out.

"Hello," Elliott said awkwardly.

"Antonio?" an accented voice asked.

"No . . . this is Elliott Chapman." He said this slowly as he looked at Murdoch. "Mr. Martino?"

"Do you have the information?"

"Yes." Elliott looked at the body then up at Murdoch, who had begun wandering around the room. Suddenly a shot fired, and a loud boom echoed. A monitor exploded and a thousand shards of glass and plastic showered the room.

"Is everything satisfactory? What was that noise?"

"Someone smashed a monitor to pieces." Elliott cupped the mouthpiece and yelled, "Stop it, Murdoch!"

Murdoch turned around, his eyes wild. He held the gun waist high, so Elliott could see. He turned around to the second monitor. Another blast, and another monitor burst to pieces.

"Señor Chapman!"

"*STOP SHOOTING!*" Elliott yelled at Murdoch.

The door flew open and Duane rushed into the room. "What the hell's going on in here?" He looked at Murdoch. Murdoch fired another bullet. The third monitor exploded, blowing chunks of debris across the room, adding to the wreckage. Duane sprung at him, grabbed the gun, and tried to rip it away.

"Help me, Elliott!" Duane yelled.

"I gotta go, Mr. Martino," Elliott said quickly into the phone.

"Wait. Señor Chapman. Please, tell me what is going on!"

"I gotta go."

Duane struggled with Murdoch. Another shot was fired.

"*Help! Now!*" Duane shouted to Elliott. "Get the gun from this lunatic!"

"I'll talk to you later, Mr. Martino," Elliott said. He dropped the phone on the body.

Another shot resounded. Elliott grabbed Murdoch's fat finger. He pried the middle sausage backward, but Murdoch held the gun tight. Elliott bent it further until it cracked. The gun dropped to the floor.

"Sonafa*bitch*!" Murdoch screamed as he grabbed his latest injured appendage. "You broke my finger!" He held it in Elliott's face. The knuckle was disjointed; the end of the finger stuck out like a nub in his palm. "*Look* at it!"

"What the hell are you shooting the monitors for, anyway?" Duane asked. "The monitor is *not* the computer." He stooped down and picked up the gun. He walked to the first computer tower and fired. It exploded with a puff of smoke. He turned the gun on the second computer and fired. He shot the next and the next. He took aim at the briefcase lying on the table.

"*Nooo . . . !*" Elliott leapt across the room and swung the gun out of the way.

Duane raised the gun. "Take it and get out of here!" He looked around at the disaster then back to Elliott. "Sloan just called. He told Martino that we're under a military attack."

"And that was Martino on the phone," Elliott said. "He called Antonio and wanted to know about the Terminator."

"Oh, God," Duane moaned. "They're coming. Martino's sending his men over, he's got 'em all over the place, and they're coming after *you* and the Terminator."

"Wait!" Murdoch said. "What about my finger?" He held it up in front of Duane.

"Oh, give me your damn finger," Duane said angrily. He took the damaged finger with a firm grip, and gave a quick snap forward. It popped like a cork. "There. Now just leave things alone, would ya? Everything you touch becomes a disaster. You can't walk without tripping over your feet and breakin' your arm. You can't even shoot a computer right. Just stay away from things. This is all your fault. This whole mess is your fault. I oughta just shoot you right now." He pointed the gun at him, then tossed it on the body.

Murdoch rested the dislocated finger on his new cast and hung his head.

Elliott reached down and picked up the telephone. He brought it to his ear, listened to the vortex for a moment, then stuffed it into his pocket. "*Where* are we going to go?"

Duane whipped around and faced him. "You're going to have to get across the border tonight. You have to get out before the FARC get here."

"Wha . . . what the hell are we going to do?" Murdoch whimpered.

"They're going to break in and take everything, aren't they?" Elliott asked.

"The FARC won't. We just blew up everything. All the data transfers are out. You did this!" He pointed to Murdoch and kicked the body. "And you killed him. The FARC's going to take the body and both of you, if you're still here."

"But if we get back into Texas, Sloan will hunt us down," Elliot cried. "We *can't* go back."

"Not unless we hunt him down first," Murdoch said.

"Sloan doesn't know you're here," Duane said to Elliott. He turned to Murdoch. "What do you mean? You're gonna gun him down?"

Murdoch lifted his head and looked at Elliott.

"Forget it, Murdoch," Duane said. "This is enough for one day. You both need to get out of here. I called a cab and it should be here any minute." He turned to Elliott. "You're going to have to get across the border at Brownsville, then get back up to Portland. Get to Royce and blend in. No one there will know a thing."

"Kingsley will fail me. I won't graduate."

"No, you did your project. You just have to show up and graduate."

"Do'ya think I could take the rest of my leaves before we go?" Murdoch asked timidly. "I'd kinda like to keep it as a, ah, souvenir, or sumpthin'."

Duane shook his head. He reached into the front pocket of his clinic jacket and slammed the brick of leaves into the hand with the dislocated finger.

"Owww! Careful, will you? I felt that." He tried to comfort his finger by rubbing it with his broken arm. "I haven't had a cigarette in a coupla days. You oughta be a little nicer to someone who hasn't had a cigarette for a coupla days."

"That's just too bad," Duane said. "You should think about quitting."

"Besides, I can take this across the border easier than I can the cigarettes they sell around here. You can never be sure what's in 'em."

Elliott looked up quickly. His eyes widened and he grinned, first at Murdoch, then at Duane.

"What is it?" Duane asked, smiling with him. "You just figured it out, didn't you?"

Elliott nodded.

"There's the horn," Duane said as he turned and hurried to the door. "Your taxi's here. Meet me up front in just a second." He tore out of the room.

"Come on, Murdoch, let's go." Elliott grabbed his briefcase, stepped out of the room, and ran down the hall with Murdoch in tow. He pushed aside the curtain and approached Duane's nurse Juanita, still sitting squarely on her small chair in the empty waiting room.

"Here," Duane said, running up to Elliott with a stack of papers. "Take these."

"I can't take all these. Mail them to me."

"I'm not mailing them."

"Sure. Send them to Royce. I'll pick 'em up in a week."

Duane glared at him. "Take them with you!"

"What are they?"

"These are genetic reports I've been putting together. They're from my years of research. I don't want them around here. They'll be destroyed. Now, give me the Terminator discs you copied. It took three didn't it?"

"Yeah." Elliott reached down and opened up the briefcase. He took out the three discs and handed them to Duane.

"All right, now." Duane reached inside his lab jacket pocket, pulled out three discs, and held them up in front of Elliott. "These three are the neurotransmitter protocols Easy has been working on. Take the first two Terminator discs and these first two neurotransmitter discs." He did this as he spoke and held the four discs in front of Elliott. "This is what you are to give Martino. These two discs will give him enough Terminator protocol to be satisfied with, but not enough to decipher the code. And these two are the neurotransmitter protocols." He held the discs out for Elliott to take.

"Cocaine?" Elliott took the four discs and put them into a pocket inside the briefcase.

"Yeah, some of it is. But most of it is neurotransmitter sequences." Duane handed him the last two discs, one from each protocol. "Keep these last two discs in a safe place."

"All right." Elliott put them into a pocket on the other side of the briefcase.

"Martino is getting more than he bargained for, if anyone can figure it out for him." Duane turned to his nurse. "Juanita. Get me a handicap badge."

She tilted her head at him.

"They're behind you on the shelf," Duane directed. "I just used one last week."

She grumbled at him in Spanish then plopped both of her hands on the desk. Her bare upper arms shook like Jello. She flexed her pectorals, snapped her triceps, and boosted herself up to reach the shelf. She dug in a box, fished out a badge, and handed it to Duane.

"Thank you. Now, come here," he said to Murdoch. Murdoch held his bag tight.

"What's in there?" Duane asked. He reached for it.

Murdoch pulled it away. "Nothin'."

"What's in there? Open it up." Duane got a hold of the zipper and pulled it open before Murdoch could move away.

"You can't take this!" He looked at Elliott. "*Look* at this." He held the bag open.

Elliott looked inside. "What do you have in there, *bombs*?"

"Yeah, a few. It's a hobby of mine."

Duane pulled the bag out of his hand and placed it behind Juanita. She immediately grabbed it and walked it through the curtain and down the hall.

"Come here," Duane snapped at him.

Murdoch slowly approached.

"Come here," Duane said louder, holding up the badge. "You are handicapped." He stuck the pin of the badge deep into his chest.

"Ye-ow!" Murdoch backed away. "You trying to stick me?"

Duane stepped closer, pulled it out of his chest, and pinned it into his shirt. "Elliott is your escort across the border. Let him *escort* you. Act like your arm is broke and don't make a scene." He turned the badge over. "The number and address of the clinic are on the back, in case you need them."

Murdoch lifted it up and looked at it. "Okay."

Duane slapped him in his chest with an open hand. "There you go." He looked Elliott up and down. "You better take that FDA necklace off. That's going to be too conspicuous. No, actually, keep it on. It might help you get across." He stopped a moment and the taxi's horn blasted again. "The driver will drop you off at the pedestrian crossing right at the border. Now, get outta here, both of you."

CHAPTER 19

Steven Sloan waited impatiently, holding his overnight bag in the first class line at Kennedy International Airport. At his feet stood his large briefcase bulging with papers stuffed in the side pockets. He picked up both pieces, moved a few steps, and set his carry-on down again.

"No, Quinton!" he roared into his telephone. "Duane Rice called me from the clinic. I called Stu Bainsworth in Washington right away. He didn't know anything about an inspection. Then Duane calls me back, says it was a prank...*I don't know why*! No! That's why I'm going back. Now Bainsworth's sweating. I called Martino—he's always interested in the inspections, and he sounded very nervous on the phone this time. Sompthin's up, Quinton. No . . . the Terminator Protocol. Whadaya mean? No, that's where it's backed up, in the clinic with all the other . . . well, they'd have to know how to recognize the data and know the coding . . . *that's why I'm leaving*! Yes, I finalized the contract with Bard and Hegel. I didn't have time to do that . . . no . . . Europe. They're going to bring us out in the media, television first. Then print. No. We have to do it their way . . . BECAUSE! The Greens are making too many inroads with their damn coalitions. Even working the fruity health quacks . . . that's right. If they ever get a foothold, they'll make noise on a national level. Can't let that happen."

He banged his suitcase against the ticket counter. The agent waited patiently. Everyone else in line watched the loud, vulgar Texan talk on his phone. They were too entertained to be irritated.

" . . . well, I didn't even *finish* the damn conference, and I have to turn right around and find out what's going on. Yes, I told you I've already called Martino. As soon as your classes are over, I want you down in the lab. We have work to do. I'm going after Martino. I'm gonna get the DEQ and immigration after him. I'll get 'em records of our last coupla meetings. We'll see how far the little rebel gets. Look Quinton, I gotta go. I'm standing here holding up the line. I'll call again when I get to Brownsville."

"Well now, sir," said the agent with her fingers interlaced and resting on the counter. "Are you alone, or will you be traveling with everyone else in line who's been listening to you for the last five minutes?"

"I'm alone," he snapped without looking around. "Just give me a damn boarding pass."

CHAPTER 20

Duane Rice finished off the last computer. The data room was a complete disaster; it was littered with broken pieces of plastic from computer casings, shattered glass from the monitors, and a dead man buried off to the side. Duane walked quickly down the hall until he reached the curtain. He grabbed it in the middle, ripped it down, and tossed it to the side.

"Oh, Señor. The clinic is . . . such a mess!" Juanita said, turning to him.

"What are you still doing here? Why haven't you left?" He continued through the waiting room.

"You never told me."

"Well—*Go! Inmediatamente!*"

At that moment, three loud bangs sounded at the front door. It flew open and two Matamoros city police burst inside with their weapons drawn.

"Oh, amigos!" Duane cried, rushing up to them. "It's been horrible! The clinic has been in a horrible uproar. A man's been shot. I think he's dead." Four more police trampled inside.

"Where are the assailants?" asked the chief officer.

"They're gone."

"Where is this man?"

"He's in the back." Duane pointed and turned. "Come, I'll show you."

They followed Duane as he hurried down the hall, speaking as he trotted. "Officer, it was horrible, and it came without warning. They stormed in and started shooting up the place. We're just a small clinic, trying to help the community . . . " He pushed the door open and stood to the side. "Look, they blew up all my computers! The records are gone and the data is gone. These guys are maniacs on a shooting spree. They even shot one of their own." He pointed to the crypt.

One of the men lifted the blanket, looked at the body, and dropped it.

"How many?"

"I only saw two others, but I'm sure they're coming back, and bringing more with them. They'll look until they find what they want."

"Who are they?"

"Another militant group after drugs. That's why I always hide my narcotics and needles. They didn't find what they wanted, so they started blowing up the place. Here, look"— Duane reached for Murdoch's bag and held it open in front of the officers—"they left this bag of explosives. I know they're coming back!"

The chief turned and rattled off orders to his men. Two dashed down the hall.

"Do you have a back door and windows that are accessible?"

"The back door is around the corner and each room has a small window, but they're all barred."

The chief spoke again and one man darted to the back door and stood guard. The last two officers charged down the hall and positioned themselves. The chief pulled out his radio and spat orders into it. He dropped it back into its holster.

"You leave, *rapido*. And secretary to go."

Duane turned and tore down the hall. "*Vamos!*" He lifted Juanita up by her elbow and hoisted her to her feet. "Let's go!"

Juanita waddled quickly after him through the waiting room. The guards let them exit. Duane hurried her down the path. He stopped at the gate and let her pass through, then turned and gazed sorrowfully at the clinic he operated for so many years.

"Come, Señor," Juanita said, tugging on his white jacket, looking up at him. "We go."

He looked at her hand on his sleeve and leaned away. He took off the jacket, rolled it up, and tossed it inside the gate.

"Señor! *Vamos!*" She turned and he followed.

They walked down the road as fast as she could move. Just before they reached the city park, a group of four militants came running down the middle of the road. Duane grabbed Juanita and pulled her off to the side. They both ducked out of sight and watched their private parade.

The men were in complete combat gear and carrying a large arsenal. The one in front called a command to his men, pointed with his gun, and the three went on ahead. The leader slowed, yelled something into his radio, then ran after the others.

Duane hurried his nurse down the road.

After a moment, the guns went off.

CHAPTER 21

Elliott sunk into the seat and nervously watched the sights from the taxi window. The driver spoke excitedly in a heavy accent as he pointed to highlights along the road. Finally they approached the border. Vehicle and pedestrian traffic converged to a standstill, all waiting to cross into the United States of America.

The sun was setting by the time they got close enough to see the border entrance. The driver pulled into a turnout and slowed the car. Elliott jumped out with the briefcase in one hand, and the bag of reports Duane had given him hanging from his shoulder. Murdoch wobbled out from the back seat, mumbling something incoherent.

Elliott led Murdoch down the sidewalk next to the busy road, over-flowing with a crowd of tourists who were overloaded with bags of souvenirs and useless trinkets won proudly with their superb bargaining skills. American women were coaxing along both their children who were chewing Chiclets and clutching foreign coins they would never use, and their tired, grumpy men carrying heavy clay pots filled with overstuffed animals. They were all returning home with the stuff that, sooner or later, would end up in boxes in the attic or on shelves in their oversized garages; and when the garages could no longer house their cars, they would have yard sales.

"Come on, Murdoch. Would ya hurry?" Elliott stopped walking and looked behind. He waited for the handicapped man to catch up. Murdoch stood far behind, furiously sucking the innards from another cigarette, not allowing any smoke to escape. The glowing tip moved quickly toward his mouth. He finally exhaled, threw down the last of the burning nub, lit another, then slowly shuffled towards Elliott. He limped on his right leg now, and carried his broken arm with the cigarette hand instead of in the sling Duane was supposed to give him; Duane may not have remembered.

"I . . . um . . . comin' . . . as fast . . . as I . . . kin." He looked worse than he did during the siege. His sparse hair was frizzed in all directions, and his head was one big sweatshop, squeezing out tiny droplets from every pore. The dirty liquid dripped off his chin. His military fatigues were wet all over again. He stopped to catch his breath.

"You really need to quite smoking those things." Elliott shook his head at him.

"I gotta . . . stop awhile." He pulled the shirt up from the bottom and wiped his beaded head. "I gotta . . . rest."

"No. Come on, Murdoch, we have to get in line and get across before Martino's guys come looking for us."

Murdoch shook his head like a wet dog then looked at Elliott. "Follow someone who looks unnatural."

"*You* look unnatural."

"No. I mean . . . what I mean is . . . they'll draw attention away from us." He flicked the cigarette on the sidewalk.

"All right then, let's get up there and find somebody."

They walked another football-field length and approached the throng. Ahead, a couple was arguing loudly. Sometimes they stood in line and fought civilly, and other times they got out of line when one of them had to yell. Murdoch nodded to Elliott, and they hurried up in line behind them.

The man wore a big, floppy sombrero, a bright yellow shirt, and blue Bermuda shorts. His fingers were interlaced around a large pink pig, and he had to poke his head around the side to speak to his wife. She had on a strapless red dress that brushed her tan thighs way above her knees. She carried a small black handbag that bounced up and down when she spoke to him. The argument centered on their long weekend from hell. Murdoch winked at Elliott and they both listened to the rehashed vacation . . . their baggage was lost in Matamoros on the way back from Cancun . . . where *he* ran into an old flame from high school who *just happened* to be in the same hotel . . . no honey, she's a travel agent, who made us a great deal so you could spend the rest of our money at the most expensive store in Cancun buying the most expensive designer purse . . . well it's better than hanging out in sleazy bars all night, gambling for stuffed animals like that *stupid pig* you shoulda left behind with your girlfriend . . . *no* she's not my girlfriend, she's a travel agent who chartered this trip for us, so just drop it, and besides it's sure better than the *stupid* hat you got me to cover the bald spot you so kindly pointed out to the people at that party last night . . . no, it's a sombrero honey, and you should wear it, or get rid of it, and while you're at it, why don't you just forget about going away together *ever again*!

"Hey." The man turned to Elliott. He took off the sombrero and grimaced. "Would you like a hat? Take the damn hat." He held the pig with one hand and with the other, handed the sombrero to Elliott.

"Sure, if it wouldn't be a bother. It's a nice hat." Elliott took it and tried it on.

"It's a *sombrero—sheeze,*" the wife scowled, sighed loudly, then whipped herself around back in line.

"Looks good on you," the man said. He brushed his mussed hair over his bald spot and turned around. "*What?* You just said I should give it away . . . "

During this commotion, Murdoch had reached inside a pocket, taken out a pinch of leaves, and placed them inside his mouth. Elliott turned and saw a wide grin spread across his face.

"What'd you do? Did you take some of that?"

"Yep."

"Give that to me!"

Murdoch reached inside his pocket and pulled out the last of the brick, still wrapped in brown paper. "What're you going to do with it, turn it in? No one knows what it is, Duane said so."

Elliott took the brick and shook it at him. "Still, you don't play with things like this." He took off the sombrero, put the brick inside the crown, and placed it back on his head.

They walked in silence for the next several minutes, watching the people ahead answer questions or give up their possessions to be inspected.

"Where is your destination?" the officer asked sharply.

"Brownsville," said Elliott confidently.

"What did you put under your hat?"

"It's a sombrero. They're some leaves I bought down . . . "

"Step over to the side. You, come too," he said to Murdoch.

They both walked to the holding area as the crowd watched. Elliott nodded to the man who had given him such a nice, unexpected gift.

"What the hell did you do that for . . . put it under the hat?" Murdoch spoke from the side of his mouth.

Two senior security officers approached and quickly took over the interrogation.

"Take off your hat," snapped an officer.

Elliott slowly raised the sombrero and took the brick off his head. He looked closely and read the man's badge.

"*This*! Where did you get this?" The officer reached for the brick.

"In a clinic. Officer Doyle, is it?" Elliott offered it to him.

"A clinic?" Doyle glared at Elliott, then down at the brick in his hand.

"They gave it to me. I'm supposed to use it for medicinal purposes. It's for my attention problems . . . or something like that."

Officer Doyle looked at it carefully. He sniffed it. He rolled a few pieces between his fingers. "You wait right here." Doyle took the brick and disappeared through another door. His partner held them in check.

Elliott exchanged looks with the other tourists who were staring at them. Murdoch picked at his fresh cast, dropping flakes on the floor near the feet of the officer.

After a moment, Doyle returned with the leafy brick in a bag and another man, his superior.

"Where did you get this?" the senior officer asked.

"At a clinic."

"What kind of clinic?"

"A health clinic in Matamoros. It's a private clinic owned by Magalto from Brownsville. They manufacture this stuff in Matamoros, and stockpile it in their facility in Brownsville."

The officer looked at Murdoch flaking the plaster from his cast. "Were you at this clinic too?"

"Yeah. They fixed my arm."

"What's wrong with it?"

"It's broke. Don'tcha see the cast?"

"Take it off."

"I'm not takin' it off," Murdoch growled.

"Take it off," the chief said to the other officer. "Get the shears."

The officer reached down in the cabinet below and pulled out a pair of heavy-duty pruning shears.

"Oh no you're not." Murdoch backed away. "You're not using those on my arm. It's broke, I'm tellin' ya."

The officer approached with the shears pointed at Murdoch's arm. Murdoch backed away. "Hold it right there. Now, I'm warning ya. I'll sue all three of yous."

"Sue us," said the senior officer. He walked to Murdoch, took hold of his right arm, and held him tight.

"I'm handicapped! You can't do this to a handicap. Look at my badge." Murdoch pulled away from the officer and lifted it up from his shirt for them to see. "Right there it says Han-di-cap."

The chief officer reached up, grabbed the badge, and held it in his hand. He read the back and released it. "Cut it off."

The officers grabbed Murdoch. They pinned him against a counter and the officer wielding the blades began to cut. He started on the inside of his arm at his hand, passed near the wound site, and cut all the way to the end with surprising agility. The cast fell on the floor and revealed the puncture site and the discoloration of a broken arm. The chief officer picked up the cast from the floor and pealed away a layer of plaster. He took the shears and cut it in half, then cut it in half again. White pieces of plaster flaked all over the floor. Murdoch looked up helplessly, cradling his useless appendage.

"This isn't cocaine, officer," Elliott said, kicking a piece of plaster on the floor.

The officer looked up at him. "Don't get smart with me." He sniffed the plaster he held, tossed it on the pile, and turned to his assistant. "Get this mess cleaned up."

"What about my arm?" Murdoch lifted his arm up and it dangled down. It hung limp by the skin and the few muscles that escaped previous accidents. Officer Doyle looked away, holding his stomach.

"All right, someone get him a bandage," said the chief, looking at Doyle. He turned to Elliott. "I want to see a piece of ID."

"ID?"

"You have any ID?"

"Yes. As a matter of fact I do." Elliott reached into his pocket, took out the badge, and handed it to him. "Here. I'm with the FDA."

"The FDA?" The chief looked at him with a wary eye. "You're with the FDA?"

"Yes." He pointed to Murdoch. "He's my assistant. We just finished a job, and now we have to go report to Washington. I'm to describe anything that looks suspicious, especially here at the border."

The chief looked him over carefully and handed a small notepad and the FDA badge over to him. "I want your name and the phone number of your department. Next time you guys come through, let us know, and we'll let you pass without all this drama."

Elliott stuffed the badge into his pocket. "We've just finished a very difficult assignment, a crisis, really. We've been a little unnerved. I'm sorry if we caused you problems."

"Well, like I said. Next time show us your badges before we have to ask for them." The chief turned to leave.

"Somebody's got to help me wrap this thing," Murdoch whined.

"Help him, John," said the chief, nodding to the officer holding a flimsy bandage. "All right, the rest of you. Let's clear out of here." He turned back to Elliott and pointed. "Take your information to the desk over there. Then you're both free to proceed, but no more funny stuff." He looked closely at the bag of leaves as he handed it over to him. "What're you doing, some kind of agricultural testing on the leaves?"

"Yes. As a matter of fact, we are."

"We've sure had a lot of this coming through lately." The officer turned and walked away.

"Thank you officer," Elliott called after him. "There won't be any more problems with us." He began scribbling on the paper.

The officer assigned to Murdoch labored over the elastic wrap. He couldn't get it started. It kept falling off, and he had to try all over again. Murdoch stood still, watching the vehicles pass through checkpoint.

"Hey! *Carlos*!" Murdoch pointed to the window. "Elliott, there's our ride."

Elliott's head was buried in his work on the notepad. It read:

Steven Sloan
Magalto
Brownsville, TX
This brick of leaves is one of our finest products. It is a tomato plant engineered with cocaine. We transport this every day from our compound in Matamoros into America. Use your drug kit to test it. Call me and I'll send you a sample.

With love,
Steve
P.S. Check out the pink pig going down the sidewalk.

Elliott folded the note, stuffed it into the bag holding the brick of leaves, and twisted it shut. "Who?"

"He's stopped in line." Murdoch stared and pointed. "Come on, he can give us a ride." He pulled the bandage out of the officer's hand and moved as fast as he could across the room toward the exit.

Elliott walked up to the officer and handed him the bag with the note stuffed inside. "Hey, would you take this to officer Doyle? And make sure he reads the note right away. I gotta go. The pig just went through, and this hat belongs to the man holding it." He handed the sombrero to him.

The man shrugged his shoulders. "Okay."

"Thank you." Elliott smiled, picked up his bag and briefcase, and walked quickly toward the door. He stepped outside into the fumes and noise of vehicles stopped for detainment. Murdoch was three lanes away, and struggling trying to climb up into the cab of a truck. His rear end hung out of the door, and his upper body was somewhere inside. Elliott ran up and gave him a push from behind.

"It's good to see you again, Carlos," Murdoch said as he plopped mostly on the floorboard.

"Amigo!" Carlos smiled a toothy smile. "Come in."

"This here's Elliott. He's come along for the ride."

"Elliott! Come in Elliott." Carlos smiled at him and waved him inside. "You're not *muchacha*." Carlos looked at Murdoch. "Miguel stay and look for *muchacha*."

"I'm happy for him."

They both settled in the truck and finished the introductions. Carlos moved the vehicle to the next inspection station. The officer stopped the truck and asked Carlos a few questions about entering into the United States of America. The certificate from Magalto, still displayed on his windshield, reminded all federal employees who glanced at it that jobs were a commodity and easily replaced. The officer stiffly waved them on.

Carlos shifted gears, exchanged waves with his new friend the customs officer, and the truck slogged forward. They eased in line with the moving traffic and slowly made their way across the border. Pedestrians were in throngs on the sidewalk, making their way to the parking deck. But right in the middle, a group had stopped to watch a tantrum. An officer held back a woman in a short red dress who was kicking wildly at a giant pink pig that lay on the sidewalk. Another officer restrained a man in a bright yellow shirt, trying to keep him away from the woman. Two other officers pushed their way through the crowd. One went to help control the feisty woman. The other officer ran up to the pig, dropped on top of the beast, and with several swings of a long blade, gutted the animal. He ripped out the innards by the handfuls, and tossed the fluff high into the air. The vacation was officially over.

"Step on it, Carlos," Elliott said, watching the scene in the side mirror and sliding down in his seat.

"Where you want to go?" Carlos asked.

"The airport," Elliott said quickly.

"Airport?" Murdoch looked crooked at him. "What are you going to do at the airport?"

"I'm going to Portland."

"You can't leave. There are no more flights out tonight. Look at the time."

"What time is it?"

"I dunno," Murdoch said, looking at his multi-task watch which had died a day ago. "Carlos, what time is it?"

"Late."

Murdoch looked at Elliott. "Nothing leaves this late."

"It's an international airport. There's always a flight somewhere."

"Well, I'm goin' with you."

"To Portland? What do you want to do in Portland?"

"I'll get a job somewhere. I'll find something in security."

"Nobody will let you work in security."

"Well, I gotta go somewhere." He reached for Carlos. "You got an extra cigarette?"

"Yeah, amigo." Carlos handed him a pack.

Murdoch took a cigarette out and lit it. He blew the first puff toward Elliott and dropped the match on his arm.

"Ye-ow!" Elliott said, flicking the smoldering match on the floor, rubbing his arm. "You just burned me!"

Murdoch took another long drag and blew it toward the dashboard. "Sorry."

"I don't want you to come with me. You're going to burn something up and blame me for it. Your record today is very shitty." He grabbed the cigarette from Murdoch and tossed it out the window. He tossed the pack of cigarettes back to Carlos.

"Hey!" Murdoch said. "I wasn't done with that."

"Yes, you are. Just sit still and don't move, for once. You've caused enough trouble for a lifetime."

The three continued the drive into the United States of America. Murdoch tried to wrap his wrist with some bracings he found on the floorboard, and talked nonstop about his bravery and the heroic measures he had taken. Carlos, his captive driver, listened. Elliott fell asleep.

CHAPTER 22

Carlos dropped off his two passengers at the Brownsville International Airport and turned back to his duties at Magalto. Elliott, with his bag and briefcase, and Murdoch, with his mangled arm, lacerated thumb, dislocated middle finger, bruised ribs, sprained neck, wrists, and ankle, managed to get through the revolving door and into the ticket lobby. It was mostly deserted. A few cowboy hats bobbed up and down to the cadence of their stiff boots.

Only a few ticket agents worked behind the counters, clicking keys and looking at things undisclosed to the public. Elliott stopped and looked at the reader board. A few flights were arriving and departing within the hour, some coming from New York, others going to California.

Murdoch bumped up beside him.

"There's one to Portland at midnight," Elliott said. He puffed out a breath. "Always the late flights." He turned to Murdoch. "Where are you going? You're not really going to Portland, are you?"

"Hawaii, maybe. Not sure. Have to see what they got."

Elliott led the way to the nearest agent. She was busy clicking at a keyboard. "Yes," she said without looking up. "I'll be with you in a moment."

"There's no one here, ma'am," Elliott said leaning over the counter.

Her head stayed bent forward but her eyes rolled up and glared at him. "I said, I'll be with you in a moment." She went back to her clicking.

Murdoch stood with his back to the counter and watched a new pack of arrivals walk sleepy-eyed down the corridor. Exhausted parents carried sleeping kids. Tired business travelers holding crumpled newspapers were trying to scoot ahead of the slowpokes.

Elliott took the telephone from his pocket and looked at it. He thought about his options; there weren't many. But he had one detail he had to take care of. He dialed the last incoming number, held the telephone up to his ear, and waited as it rang.

"Antonio," Martino said in his soothing, familiar voice.

"No. This is Elliott Chapman."

"Oh, Señor Chapman. Yes. How is the operation?"

"It has been aborted," Elliott said slowly.

"Aborted? I do not understand."

"Antonio is dead. He was shot and killed in crossfire at the clinic."

Martino paused. "Did you retrieve the data?"

"Well . . . umm . . . most of it, I think. I managed to sneak it out before the place erupted. Your men and the police were in a standoff. It became very violent when we tried to leave. And Antonio. He was shot. I had to leave him. I knew I had to get out with the protocol. Isn't that what you wanted—the protocol?"

Martino was silent.

"I have most of the data, and I don't think any of it is damaged. I'd *never* be able to get it now. The place is a disaster." He waited for a response that didn't come. "I don't know how I made it out alive."

"Where are you?"

"Well, I'm trying to catch a flight, here at the airport."

"You cannot leave," Martino said quickly.

"Why not? I've finished the job." Elliott paused again. Martino didn't respond. "I have to get back to Portland."

"I need the protocol," Martino enunciated.

"I'll leave it here in an airport locker. You can mail me the rest of the money."

"No. We exchange goods."

"It's eleven o'clock at night!"

"Tomorrow. You will get the rest of the money tomorrow, and I will get the protocol."

Elliott waited.

"There is a café two blocks from Magalto, near the river, on Rio Grande Street. Outside is a burrito with a worm. Meet there. Nine, tomorrow morning."

"Nine o'clock? I have to be in Portland by then."

"Nine," Martino said clearly. "Then, you go to Portland. Señor Chapman, you are not in a position to argue. Do not make this difficult. You will not like the consequences if I have to send for you in Portland."

"All right," Elliott breathed out.

"Thank you, for your work in this matter. I know we can conclude this event without any more unpleasantness."

"*There's Sloan!*" Murdoch yelled, tapping Elliott on the arm.

Elliott craned his head to look.

"What was that?" Martino asked.

"There's a sad guy walking around, lost, and he's trying to find someone," Elliott said into the telephone, frowning at Murdoch as he put his finger to his lips.

"Sloan? Did someone say Sloan?"

Murdoch began walking. Elliott grabbed him by the shoulder and pulled him back.

"I gotta go," Elliott said quickly. "I'll be there at nine tomorrow." He hung up before Martino continued questioning.

"Where?" Elliott asked Murdoch, still holding him back.

"Over there, on the far edge."

"I don't see . . . oh, there he is."

Murdoch twisted away from Elliott and began walking against the stream of pedestrians. He walked without much of a limp, determined, like he wanted to have it out with Sloan right there on the spot. But the luggage-toting travelers didn't slow for him. After a few hits to the knees from the swinging suitcases, he stopped and waited.

"Yes, now," said the agent looking up with a smile, "what can I do for you?"

Elliott turned around. "I need a ticket to Portland, Oregon."

She turned to her keyboard and tapped away, and in a few seconds she confirmed his ticket for eleven-fifty the next morning. He paid for it with cash from the briefcase, turned around, and followed Murdoch.

"Hey, you sonafabitch!" Murdoch yelled, waking the tired crowd as he began walking crosscurrent again. Parents hurried their children along and people in business gear picked up their pace.

"*Hey, Sloan!*" he yelled louder, gimping faster toward him.

Steven Sloan stopped, slowly turned to the side, and lowered his glasses down on his nose. His hair was wisped from laying his head against the airplane seat. His suit hung rumpled off of his body. His shirt was wrinkled and his tie undone.

People tried not to look as they passed by.

"Yeah, *you!*"

Sloan shook his head with a smile and calmly said, "You're fired, Murdoch. Just a few days ago."

"You remember what you said when you *threw me out of the car?*"

"No, not exactly."

Murdoch walked right up to him. "You said I should mind my *own damn business.*" He jabbed his index finger into Sloan's chest on the last three words. Sloan backed away. "Well *this is* my business."

"Look, Murdoch." Sloan looked around at the crowd, too tired to be embarrassed. "I'm in no mood for this tonight. I just arrived from New York and—I'm tired." He turned to Murdoch. "Don't take it personally. You just didn't work out."

"Well, *I am* taking it personally."

"I'm sorry. I don't know what to tell you."

Elliott walked up behind Murdoch. "Is this how you treat your employees?"

Sloan narrowed his eyes as he looked at Elliott. "What are *you* doing here?"

"Right now, I'm helping Murdoch get his job back."

"Well," Sloan snorted, "he can't have it back." He looked at Murdoch. "He was fired for good reason. Maybe we can give him a recommendation somewhere." He stopped and waited for the last of the passengers to walk by. The three were left standing alone in the middle of the long hall. Sloan looked curiously at Elliott. "Is the squash project finished? I didn't get a call."

Elliott stood beside Murdoch. "Yes. Mr. Martino will call you tomorrow. But there really seems to be a problem with the tomatoes growing near the squash."

"What kind of problem? What's wrong with the tomatoes?"

"Something about their composition. Martino says they're affecting the other crops in the field. He wants to uproot the whole batch and dump 'em in the Andes somewhere."

"Is that what he said?" Sloan asked, his voice elevating. He cleared his throat and calmed himself. "Well. It's not for you to worry about. You went down to help with the problem, and I appreciate it. I'll call Dr. Kingsley tomorrow and send along a good report." He turned to Murdoch. "As for you. Come by in the morning and I'll have a decent job recommendation waiting for you. Now, if you both don't mind, I'm going home." He turned and walked away. His boots clomped loudly down the empty hall.

"The sonafabitch." Murdoch raised his right arm and his hand folded into a fist, all except the stiff, dislocated middle finger. "There he goes."

"What were you going to do?" Elliott looked from Sloan to Murdoch.

Murdoch stared after him with a clenched jaw. "I'm gonna get him."

Elliott picked up the bag and briefcase. "Well, I'm going to find a motel."

Murdoch stood a moment then walked to a bench and plopped down. "I'm gotta sit for awhile."

"Suit yourself." Elliott walked over to him and reached out his hand. "Been nice knowing ya. Good luck with . . . whatever."

"Yeah." Murdoch shook his hand.

Elliott walked down the hall and out of the terminal. He took the last shuttle of the night to the same hotel he stayed before, checked in, and paid cash for the room. He stripped off his small FDA suit, fell into bed, and slept the night through with barely a muscle twitch.

CHAPTER 23

The morning sun was Texas-bright and shone directly into the motel room. It moved up the floor, onto the bed, and roused Elliott. He rolled over, looked at the clock, and jumped out of bed. He took a quick shower and struggled into the tiny FDA suit. With his bag and briefcase, he hurried down to the lobby and almost bumped into the same two men he had met several mornings before, who were once again foraging at the breakfast buffet, as if they'd never left. Elliott snatched two large cinnamon rolls right off the closest man's heaping plate, ran outside, and waved down a taxi.

"Where to, Señor?" asked the taxi driver from his window.

"Do you know where a company named Magalto is?" Elliott asked, leaning down to speak.

"Sí."

"There's a café with a worm eating a burrito, or something like that, close by."

"Bassongs. Yes, come in. Few minutes, we go."

Elliott opened the back door, tossed his bags inside and jumped in. "Burrito and worm? Is that a delicacy around here?"

"Yes. They go together. If there is a worm in your burrito at Bassongs, it is a good burrito. If not, I wouldn't eat it. You can never know what's in it." He and smiled in the rearview mirror at Elliott.

"Who told you that?"

"Everybody knows, amigo."

Elliott told the driver he had to be at Bassongs at nine o'clock, so no touristy things. The driver said not to worry, but he did speed up a little. The taxi careened through the busy downtown. In and out of traffic the driver shuttled. They paralleled the Rio Grande and cut down a few side roads to the older, bohemian part of the city. They came to an industrial park. Large grounds—each with their own entrances, gates, and security stations—protected vast parking lots. The driver slowed as the traffic became congested. Several cars had stopped along the side of the road and people stood staring in the same direction.

"Hey, slow down a little." Elliott looked ahead and tried to see what was happening.

The huge sign on the landscaped grounds read 'MAGALTO.' The taxi stopped behind the last car on the street, just outside of the property.

Right at that moment, a police car with a screeching siren and red and blue spinning lights whizzed by and pulled into the drive, sped past the defunct security post, and joined the large rendezvous of government vehicles. They had all driven up to the building in a hurry, stopping at every angle. Their colored lights spun out of sync. City police, county sheriffs, Texas Rangers, the DEA, and the FBI were running in and out of the building. A SWAT team spilled out of two large vans and bounded after the others into the building. Several officers were talking into radios; others were directing their hurried teams. A large television news truck rolled to a stop near the entrance, and a news crew rushed out with their equipment.

Then, from out of the building, came a man dressed in a dark suit with his arms handcuffed behind his back. Several more suits were escorted after him. A man with a television camera perched on his shoulder rushed from the truck with a cable bearer in tow, and began filming the incident. An interviewer ran past him and stuck a microphone in the face of the accused. The man promptly dropped his head and continued with his escort. The media quickly passed him and converged on the next suspect, who offered the same response.

The next captive to emerge was striking. A long, colorful lab jacket flapped briskly as a man with a ponytail was hurriedly guided along. He stopped and tried to speak into the microphone, but was pulled ahead by his two escorts. The cameraman and the interviewer followed him to the back of the police van. All the suspects were helped up and put inside. The van was filled and its doors were slammed shut. The media hurried to a second van as it was opened and ready to be filled. Reporters tried to record every piece of the fast-breaking story.

Elliott stuck his head out the window and yelled to a man standing with his arms crossed, leaning against the car ahead. "What's happening?"

"Something to do with the border. The Mexican police are here with a truck that was seized about a half hour ago. They towed it in with an FBI parade."

"Smuggling?"

"I guess. It'll be on the news tonight. That's a big TV crew they got over there."

"It'll probably be on after the garden show. I heard tomatoes are the bomb this season."

The man looked at him screwy-eyed, then smiled, and shrugged his shoulders.

A fire truck blasting a loud siren suddenly whizzed by, screeched around the corner, and sped into the property. Another followed. They continued through the parking lot, off to the right side of the building. There, from the third story, a large ball of fire and a plume of dark black smoke billowed from the two windows on the corner of the marble building. The trucks approached the blaze and the firemen jumped out and began their work. Elliott looked, and, away from the commotion, saw a short, portly man lighting a cigarette with a gimp left hand. The man took a long puff, threw his match down, and hobbled away as fast as he could manage.

Elliott brought his head back in the car. "Okay," he said to the driver. "Let's go."

The driver carefully pulled out into the street just as another government vehicle screeched into the compound from the other direction. A line of onlookers leaned against their cars, watching the event unfold.

The taxi continued two more blocks and approached the café. The neon worm stood as tall as the neon beer bottle. It had a patch over one eye and pointed with a cane to the neon burrito that lay on a plate. The burrito was cut open, and most of the insides spilt out. Neon flames rose from it up to the BASSONGS sign.

"Here you are, Señor." The driver turned around with a smile.

Elliott opened the briefcase and pulled out a $100 bill. He hesitated then handed it to the wide-eyed taxi driver, who watched the bill slide into his hand.

The driver looked up with a smile. "Sorry. No change, amigo."

"Sure." Elliott grabbed his gear and got out.

"Do you need a ride back?" The driver continued smiling as he leaned out the window after him. "I be happy to take you, amigo."

"I'll call you," Elliott said as he kicked the door shut, holding his baggage.

The exterior of Bassongs had more neon decorations. There were cacti in the sunset, a couple of coyotes howling at a moon, and a large "Open" sign next to the entrance. Elliott slowly pushed on the door, jingling the cowbells attached to it. He stepped inside the dark room and blinked a few times, as if he could adjust his pupil size any faster. Up ahead to the left, the worn wooden bar hosted three patrons an early drink. The bartender tipped his head at Elliott as he wiped a glass clean. A waitress in a white peasant blouse with frills on the shoulders approached with a smile and a menu.

"Señor, will there be one?"

"No, I'm waiting for someone."

"Are you Elliott Chapman?"

"Yes," he said importantly.

"This way, please." She turned and walked down through the center, tapping her hand with the edge of the menu. Most of the tables were filled with diners eating a late breakfast. Elliott looked around, hoping to find someone familiar. His hostess cut over to another row and walked closer to the booths. She stopped and held her hand open.

"Your seat. I'll be back for your order." She smiled, dropped the menu on the table, and spun away.

"*Rina Das!*" Elliott stopped cold.

"Hello, Elliott," she said in a soft voice.

He dropped the bag and briefcase, and fell into the booth.

She blinked her dark eyes slowly.

He stared at her. "What . . . are . . . "

"Let me explain, Elliott."

"Ex-*plain*?" He let out a puff of breath.

"Are you okay? I've been worried about you. Ever since you left." She reached across the table for his hand.

He let her touch it then pulled away. "Barely. Do you know what's happened to me?"

She took her hand back and lowered her head. "I'm sorry, Elliott."

"You knew everything, didn't you? Magalto . . . the compound . . . the clinic . . . "

"I was going to tell you."

Elliott waited, staring at her.

"Remember in Dr. Kingsley's class, when he made you that deal? Then the three of us were there together after class?"

"Yeah."

"The last argument you had with him, he said you could take his pretest in place of the final."

"Yeah . . . "

"Well, he switched it on you. He made you go to Texas to do the project instead."

"Yeah."

"I tried to get you to talk when I took you to the airport, but you didn't know anything about it, so I dropped it."

"Know anything about what?"

"I thought you knew what Kingsley was up to."

"He consults for Magalto."

"Yes. And when I heard he wanted you to do a project for the South American client, I called my uncle and told him you were coming. Oh, Elliott, I've been telling him about you for years! When he heard you were coming, he immediately changed his plans to have you get the Terminator protocol."

Elliott stared at her.

"The Terminator," she said. "He sent you to get the Terminator."

Elliott didn't move.

"Jorge Martino is my uncle."

"Your *uncle*? Martino is your uncle?" His eyes widened as he looked at her.

"Elliott. Let me explain."

"What's to explain?" He slid to the edge of the bench, ready to bolt.

"Just wait. You need to hear me."

He relaxed and looked at her, shaking his head. "Four years. You had four years to tell me."

"Please. Sit." She lowered her head but kept her eyes on him.

He moved slowly into the seat, reached down, and pulled his luggage closer to his feet. "What?"

"Elliott, I know you don't understand this right now, but please listen to me."

He looked away then back to her.

She lifted her head and opened her brown eyes wide as she spoke. "My parents were killed in the revolution when I was a child. I was without parents, just like you. I lived most of my childhood in a shack in a poor village outside of Bogotá. You can't even imagine, Elliott."

The waitress returned, ready to take orders. Rina ordered another iced tea. Elliott ordered a tea and a burrito like the one on the sign, without the worm. The waitress whirled away.

He looked at her.

"There were many days we went hungry, and I'd go to sleep the nights wondering if I'd be able to find food in the morning. We wore our clothes until they fell off as rags. Most of the money we made selling goods at the market went to pay taxes to a corrupt government. And if we didn't pay, they would threaten to flatten the shell of a house we lived in. Five of us, all living in a two-room shack!"

The waitress returned with the drinks and said the burrito would be right up. Rina stirred her drink with a straw and watched Elliott take a sip. The conversation over at the bar turned pathetic; the early morning drinkers were slipping well into their premature stupor. Elliott took another sip and swallowed slowly.

"The government wanted more and filched from us, taking more taxes than was reasonable. My papa didn't want to contribute anymore. He protested louder, and others joined with him. The government took notice of the crowd he drew, and began harassing him day and night. They tore our house down more times than I can remember. They bulldozed through our small plot of land, and they turned over his stands at the market every week. Finally, he turned to the Armed Forces of Columbia for support."

"Why? They smuggle drugs, they kidnap and murder."

"What's the difference who does it?"

"What do you mean, what's the difference? It's criminal."

"That's what the American corporations are doing."

"They're not murdering."

"Does murder have to mean killing? Does murder have to be so obvious?"

"What's that supposed to mean?"

"For decades, American corporations have been destroying our country and fostering corruption. Every international law supports them! Your government makes endless statements about the wonderful cooperation it has from submissive governments like ours, while huge corporations with unlimited power play their own game made by their own rules. There is no democratic process. I've been saying all along, it's altruistic domination—the worst kind of corruption."

"That's not true. Without the United States fighting for countries like your Columbia, there would be fewer human rights, more corruption, and more dictatorships spreading throughout the world! The United States fights for global democracy."

"No, Elliott. The democracy of the United States is not made for the people; it is made for the corporations. Who elects your politicians—people or money? Corporate money buys power, to make sure that developing countries cannot protect even their own services and industry. They help the developing countries, all right. Help convince them to participate in trade agreements that they scheme up. They want to spread their own policy on human rights. They want to protect and promote their own style of democracy."

"And what's wrong with that? It works, doesn't it?"

"It works for Americans. The laws are written to protect self-interests, but it's creating chaos throughout the world. Why is there never an end to the war on drugs in both of our countries? Because corporations and drug enforcement agencies would lose money! It's not in the government's interest, nor is it in corporate interest to win that war. All the money is in fighting."

"That's not true."

The waitress brought the burrito and extra napkins. It was split open in the middle and piping hot. Elliott picked off a two-inch long worm, dropped it on the side of his plate, and dug in.

"Sure it is," she said. "The United States depends on drugs just as much as Columbia does. It's the locals who get the bad end of the deal. Our people have nothing. If each of our small communities could own some kind of capital, we may be able to change the economical crisis we're in. Then we wouldn't have to rely on your government to protect us and purchase our drugs. As it is, we have no choice. Just like you. You have no choice."

"What do you mean?"

"With Kingsley. You've been submissive to him for four years, playing all his stupid games and doing things to get on his good side. I've seen you. And when you finally realized he doesn't have a good side, you did anything just to get a rise out of him; because that's the kind of game you play. Now all of a sudden your life is wrapped around him. You can't get away, and that's why you're here."

"No way. I decided to do this."

She smiled at him and shook her head slowly. "No you didn't. He threatened you—I was there. If you didn't do what he wanted, he was going to sanction you. You would have failed his course and your project."

"That's not true."

"Yes it is, Elliott. He is more educated and has more resources. And he's been using both to get what he wants. He couldn't care less about you. That's exactly what's happened, and I've been trying to tell you that for four years. You can't stand up on your own two feet without looking around to see if Kingsley's there watching you!"

He looked at her then down at his plate. He dug a prong of his fork into the bloated worm. The worm rolled underneath until it burst open and spewed hot entrails onto the plate. He glanced up at the bar. The middle head was facedown, and the other two talked over him.

"Democracy is about you and I deciding what we think is best, not what an idolized professor or handful of wealthy people decide for us. You should have figured that out a long time ago. You're into all these moral and ethical issues. This should be your personal issue, but you can't even see it."

Elliott looked at her. "So what are you going to do?"

"I'm soliciting for a position on the World Trade Organization. I'm going to rewrite international rules as they apply to Columbia. That's what my senior project is all about, how to play international politics. Then, I'm going to motivate my people to participate in the events that are happening to them."

"World Trade? *You're* the delegate?"

"I will be. I've been preparing my entire education to make public policy for my country."

"That sounds noble."

"It's what I have to do. I'm going to free my people from altruistic tyranny."

"How are you going to do that?"

"I'm going to work the basics back into the country. First, we have to take care of our land and maintain basic life support for it. Then, we have to protect the welfare of people and all living things. We need economic rules that are equal to all parties. And to accomplish this, we need ethical rules to guide appropriate human behaviour. That's where you come in, Elliott. You know this stuff, you can do something about it!"

"Now you sound like Kelly."

Rina forced a smile then took a lingering sip of tea. "My uncle took care of us after they killed my papa. He gained favor with the FARC and became a strong leader with the people. He fought for them, because they made a difference for the common person. Now he is about to lead the country, but he fights a global war. The government has fallen under the grip of this American altruistic domination, like so many others have. Everyone else is too blind to see it. It's the same fight as it's always been, but today the weapons have changed. *You* can do something to help because you understand the new weapons."

"Genetic engineering."

"Laboratory biology. Whoever owns it will control races, religions, and nations, and the hope and future of the world."

"And you came to Royce to learn about it."

"The best—with an unlimited supply of money from Magalto. They fund the entire science program: all the equipment, supplies, and breakthrough technology. Quinton Kingsley is a very well paid consultant, and the major link between academics and business. He's the one who's made the connection strong between the two. I don't think anyone else at Royce knows about all of his activities. Kingsley chooses who will go to work for the company. It was you this year."

"*He* chose me?"

"He's known about me from the beginning of school. He knows my uncle and all about the FARC. He's never liked me for that reason. Now the FARC have got Magalto running scared."

"What would happen if Magalto wasn't in the picture?"

"Well, in a year it won't matter. Right now, they're a vital link. They're still supplying us with the bioengineering protocols."

"Like the Terminator?"

"Yes. The Terminator."

"What do you want it for?"

"Some time ago, one of their researchers engineered the cocaine molecule."

"Easy."

"Easy . . . I doubt it was easy."

"No. Dr. Barringer. The researcher. The guy with the ponytail and wild lab jacket. They call him Easy."

"Oh," she nodded and smiled. "My uncle always calls him Dr. Ponytail. I've never seen him."

"Same guy."

"Well, he inserted the cocaine gene into a tomato plant and had us grow it on a small side plot of land. It grew for a long time, without anyone knowing what it was. When my uncle found out about it, he was willing to pay five times the price he was paying for any other crop he purchased from Magalto. Magalto agreed because they wanted the money. But my uncle wanted to copy the gene and put it into all the crops that we grow at the compound. When Mr. Sloan figured this out, he had Dr. Barringer—Easy—put the Terminator sequence in it. The Terminator locks the cocaine in the tomato DNA, and we couldn't get it out to release the cocaine. The Terminator is what's been contaminating the surrounding crops. It causes genetic drift that has affected everything around it. It's been those tomatoes that have been skewing your data."

"You knew all along!"

"I didn't know until you went down to get the protocol. I didn't put it together until now. Kingsley wants you to get the data in, so they can submit the project to get the patent on it. My uncle knew they were working on the Terminator patents. Once Magalto gets the patents filed, we'll be finished because Mr. Sloan won't need our money, and he won't need us to grow the crops."

"So you don't need the Terminator. You need the sequence to unlock the cocaine gene."

"I need the protocol, Elliott. Where is it?"

"I have it."

She moved her opened hand across the table.

"It's over, Rina. Magalto is history. You're finished growing their crops and getting their technology." Elliott reached for his bag and took out the four discs Duane had put together for him.

"How can you say that?" She pulled her hand back.

"They just got busted. There's a ton of agents at their compound right now, hauling them all away. Probably be charged with illegal drug manufacturing and international drug trafficking. The Feds have been onto them for months, but had no idea that the tomato leaves were transporting the drug."

She stared at him.

"I spelled it out for them."

"*You*? You told them?"

"Last night, when we crossed the border. I gave them a brick of leaves with a note explaining what was in it. They must've tested it right away. Do you know what that means?"

"Civil forfeiture," she said calmly.

"Everything becomes federal property. All land, equipment, and even intellectual property, that is, if there's anything left. A fire was raging on the other side of the building as they were hauling everyone away. I watched it happen on my way over this morning. They're finished, Rina."

Rina stared at him and twisted the straw in her drink. She submerged an ice cube a few times. "Do you have the protocol?" She looked up at him with her big brown eyes.

"Right here." He handed over the discs. "Don't do this, Rina."

"I have to." She put the discs inside her purse then reached under the table, lifted up a bag, and opened it in front of him. "My job is to liberate my people. No one else is going to do this for them." She pared a few crisp bills. "Here's the rest of your money, fifty thousand dollars."

He stared at all the green money. She zipped the bag shut and moved it across the table. "Now, take it."

He looked at her without moving.

"Take it." She narrowed her eyes at him. "Take the money, Elliott."

He didn't move.

"Look, we both have different ways of wanting the same thing," she said. "This is the only way I can make the changes that we desperately need."

"But what you're doing is illegal. You're preying on the weaknesses of other people. That's exactly what you've been talking about. It's drug money, Rina. You're selling drugs to create social change. How can you do that?"

"It's the means to an end. Once we gain power in the country, we will use it to do good. We will create a social condition that is self-sustaining. Our people will be free from democratic tyranny. The fall of Magalto may slow us down, but it won't stop us. When we get the appointment to the World Trade Organization, we will submit the laws that will eventually protect us in our movement. It's only a matter of months. If you don't like this, you should have done something when your conscience had wings. Now it's too late for you to give lip-service to your version of morality." She slid the bag against his plate. "Here, now take it and use it for whatever you think is good."

He reached across the table for the bag then slid out to the edge of the bench. "You're doing this all wrong. The means to the end defines your way of life. You can't expect to change the things you're talking about. It just won't work." He stood and reached down for the briefcase and the bag Duane had given him. "I'll take this. I'll use it for good."

"I'm sure you will." She smiled at him and shook her head. "You're doing just what you said was wrong."

"Yeah, but *I'll* do what's right."

"You're just like the immoral people you're always talking about."

"Yeah, but *I know* what's immoral."

"Goodbye, Elliott."

Elliott turned with his luggage and walked away.

Chapter 24

Elliott arrived in Portland, took a taxi to his grandparents' home, and stashed the bags and briefcase in his room. He then drove his old car to Royce, traipsed across the manicured grounds, and rushed to Rothman Science Center. He pulled the door open and hurried down the hall to the auditorium. Out of breath, he leaned against the door.

The door vibrated against his shoulder. He leaned his head closer and heard the sound of rock and roll music pounding from inside the room. It was a Kingsley inspiration. During every examination he played some type of music. He'd played classical compositions earlier in the year, when he wanted to impress upon his fresh disciples how refined and in control he was. He would tell them, "the chemicals in that equation sound like Mozart's piano Concerto Number 21, and when it's not balanced, it sounds like one of those startup grunge bands from Seattle." The classical symphonies during an exam helped to refresh the memories of such astounding chemical balances.

Then, as the course stress and his obnoxiousness increased, the music during the exams changed. He said it helped sharpen their concentration levels and it wasn't so much the chemicals anymore, so much as how *you* reacted: "the more irritating the music, the better your response, if you know the material." So, he'd turn up the country and western, and let the drawls about some sad truck driver coming home late one night getting a frying-pan-greeting in the chops, stimulate some kind of reaction from his test takers.

But what he liked most of all was the pounding beat of a rock and roll group. Didn't matter how good the group sang, as how well the drum and bass played against the guitars. No band sounded bad with the music turned up so loud. "When the beat cycles synchronize with the brain wave patterns, the molecules of memory are dislodged. They flood your nerve system, rush down your arm, and squeeze out through the lead in your pencil." Uh-huh. What it really did was mess with your mind and paralyze your ability to think. It was a cruel and unusual form of teaching sadism. There were rumors that the European, blue-eyed, blond girl, with a touch of Mediterranean pigment examples had come from actual students taking his final exams.

The volume was up very loud today.

Elliott pulled the pulsating door open and snuck into the room during a screaming guitar lick in one of Kingsley's 1970's favorites, 'Hotel California': "*you can check out anytime you like, but you can never leave . . .* " His classmates were all too busy writing, thinking, or wondering how they were going to get through the test to notice his entrance. Kingsley spotted him immediately and watched his every move. Elliott continued walking slowly down the main aisle, looking on either side for an empty seat. The professor quickly moved to the sound control and turned off the music. Everyone looked to the front, to see what could possibly have caused the horrible interruption.

"Well, *Mister* Chapman." Kingsley walked to his power zone on the very edge of the platform. He clasped his hands in front and rolled his thumbs around each other.

All heads spun around to the back of the room to look at the intruder. Elliott smiled and nodded back to those who greeted him. He continued walking down the aisle.

Kelly Landis sitting next to the aisle, bumped his leg as he walked by and whispered, "What's going on?"

"Not much, really," he said back to her.

Kingsley looked around the room at his students. "You all just go about your business and finish your exams." Most of them quickly dropped their heads, but they all kept their ears open. Kingsley looked at Elliott, now standing in front of him. "I got a call from Mr. Sloan this morning."

"You did?"

"Yeah. He said you finished the project just fine."

"He did? When did he call?"

"Right after I got here. Must've been about six-thirty or so."

"Eight-thirty, in Texas."

"That's right, two hour time difference. I guess you should know." Kingsley walked to his podium and took the only report setting on top. "Now all I need is your signature, and you'll be finished with this." He smiled at Elliott as he handed it to him.

"I'm not signing it."

Kingsley laughed. "What do you mean, you're not signing it? Right here"—he pointed to the bottom of the report—"I want you to sign this, right here. You're finished with your senior project."

"But I'm not signing it."

The intellectuals sitting in the first three rows all suddenly had to stretch or yawn or do something to find an excuse to look up at the unbelievable event taking place in front of them.

"Elliott. I'm asking you to sign your project." Kingsley's voice elevated. The room was quiet and his voice carried to the back of the room. Everyone was watching.

"I'm not signing it. I'm going to take my exam, just like everybody else."

"Oh, no, you're not! You are not taking the exam. You're not like everybody else." Kingsley's brow furrowed, his face turned red and sweaty, and his hands shook as he spoke with strained control. "You might as well turn right around and get out of my class, then."

Elliott stood three feet away from Kingsley, below the stage, looking up at him. "Do you know what happened at Magalto, after Mr. Sloan called you this morning?"

Kingsley held the report tight; it shook in his hands.

"They got busted. The police, the FBI . . . probably every drug agent in Texas was there. Sloan and all his executive goons were hauled away. What a cover you've had here, in the nice cozy confines of Royce. You did all your work up here, and they're getting busted for it."

"*Get out of my class*!" Kingsley leaned forward and pointed to the door. His face became brighter red under the sweat, and the veins bulged on his neck. His brow furrowed deeper.

"Cocaine. It was your idea all along, wasn't it?"

"*YOU FAIL! GET THE HELL OUT OF MY CLASS!*"

Elliott stepped back. "You thought it up and had Easy Barringer put it together. He couldn't have done it without you."

Kingsley hopped off the stage.

Elliott moved another step backward. "That's where Royce gets its money. From your cocaine tomatoes the Columbians grow and traffic for you."

"I'm *warn*ing you . . . " Kingsley stepped toward him.

Elliott turned and walked up the aisle. "It's over, Dr. Kingsley. Now the Columbians have the cocaine protocol. When Martino gets elected, they're going to own the patents too. My report is useless. Magalto is history."

"Your report is going to the Patent Office, and Magalto will own those patents. It doesn't take a building to own patents."

"Not if the Columbians get there first."

Kingsley stopped in the middle of the aisle. Every eye in the auditorium was on him. "How did they get the cocaine protocols?"

Elliott turned around. "I found them and gave 'em to one of your students."

"You *what*? Gave it—to *who*?"

"Remember Rina Das?"

Kingsley looked grimly at her empty seat. "*That* was her so-called emergency."

"The job Sloan sent me to do was a job for Martino. All he wanted was your cocaine. And for shame, somehow the cocaine leaked out at the border and got pinned on your company."

"You sonafabitch! I'll make you pay for this."

Elliott turned and strolled up the aisle.

"*You've failed my class and anything that's left of your damn project! I'll make sure of it!*"

Elliott pulled the door open so hard on his way out that it slammed back against the wall.

"What's going on, Dr. Kingsley?" Kelly bravely asked in the quiet room.

Kingsley shot her a dangerous look then turned and walked down the aisle. "Elliott Chapman just got expelled. *That's* what's going on." He reached the stage and turned around sharply. "*Time's up!* Bring your exams to the front, whether you are *finished* or not!"

The entire class gasped. "It's not time! . . . I'm not done! . . . we have ten minutes left!" The intellectuals almost fainted.

"That's too bad. *You're finished!*"

Everyone quickly put their pencils in their backpacks, walked their exams down front, and dropped them on the stage at Kingsley's feet. Kelly was the last to finish. She walked slowly and shook her incomplete exam at him.

"You are the worst professor I have ever had! You shouldn't even be allowed to teach. You oughta be fired right here on the spot."

"Fired?" He laughed. "*Au contraire.* Who would ever replace me?"

"*Anyone's* better than you. You're so full of yourself. You can't even teach for one second without talking about how important you are all the time."

"Are you taking issue with me?"

"Yes, I am! I'm going to see Dr. Whitman right now, and tell him how you screwed Elliott and the rest of us. I'll tell him everything that happened here in class, and see that you get your ass fired!"

"Go ahead." He grabbed the exam out of her hand. "I just failed *your* project too."

"You can't fail me. I already turned it in to the critique board."

"*I'm* the chair of the critique board and apparently, I never saw your project. Don't mess with me, Kelly Landis. As far as I'm concerned, you can join Elliott and the two of you can repeat another year. Or, drop out—I really don't care."

Kelly gasped, turned, and ran up the aisle.

CHAPTER 25

Elliott sat in President Whitman's office, telling him everything that had happened over the last few days. Dr. Whitman was a polite listener, and one who liked to maintain his objectivity about a story. He didn't say a thing, the entire time Elliott rambled on about Brownsville, and Matamoros, and the Columbian connection. He let out a few grunts and nodded appropriately, but he never interrupted. He seemed to understand, in almost a grandfatherly way, what happened. Elliott didn't leave out much. He was just beginning to tell him what had happened in class a few moments ago, when the secretary opened the door and let another student barge into their meeting.

Elliott turned.

Kelly stormed inside and flipped her hands up in the air. "Ohhh, I can't *stand* him! He's such a conceited SOB."

"What happened?" Elliott asked, watching her as she plopped down next to him.

She looked straight at Whitman. "He's the worst teacher I've ever had in my life. I want him fired, Dr. Whitman. He didn't let us finish the final, and we had ten minutes left in class. Then when I said I was going to talk to you about it, he says he's going to fail my project! He didn't even *look* at it. He can't *do* that!"

"Dr. Kingsley has been under a lot of stress lately. Finals, senior projects are due . . . I'm sure it was just a miscommunication."

"No—he said that." She turned to Elliott. "Right after he said he was going expel you."

"Expel me?" Elliott looked at Whitman. "He can't expel me."

"No, he can't expel you," Whitman said quickly, shaking his head. "It takes an indictment and a vote from the faculty council. The dean has to approve it. No one's going to expel you, Elliott." He turned to Kelly. "And he can't fail your project either, Kelly, if you have done a decent job on it, and I'm sure you have. It's for your critique board to decide." Whitman pushed himself away from his desk. "Look. Everyone is on edge this time of year, especially you seniors. You have finals to take and projects to finish up before you graduate. Dr. Kingsley and all the other professors are just as testy. It always happens and there's nothing you can do but just get through it."

"What about *my* project?" Elliott asked.

"What about your project?"

"He said I failed too."

Whitman leaned forward. "Yours is finished. All you have to do is sign it."

Elliott sat and stared at him. "I'm not signing it."

Whitman cocked his head. "What do you mean, you're not signing it? That's what we agreed on before you left. You were to go to work on a company project as a favor for Dr. Kingsley, and when you returned you were to sign your project."

"I know we agreed, but I'm not going to sign it. I'm the one who should decide what happens to it. It's my intellectual property. Maybe I don't want it going to the *Cambridge Science Review*."

Whitman smiled, his jaw clenched.

"Elliott," Kelly said, shaking her head at him. "Sign it. Don't start this all over again."

Elliott looked at her then at Whitman. "No, I'm not going to. My project was to help Magalto get the Terminator patented. They're going to get it patented along with their drugs, and anything else they can throw in. That's how Royce gets all the money, isn't it? Dr. Kingsley gets paid for doing all the statistics they need. He uses Royce as an independent institution to confirm data, so they can get their patents approved, and to do that, it has to be in a peer-reviewed journal like the *Cambridge Science Review*, which Dr. Kingsley tells us to submit to all the time. And the journal requires students to do their own research in order for Royce to qualify for the National Scientific Merit Scholarship. So I do the project and everything falls into place."

"What?" Whitman looked hard at him.

"That's what I've been trying to tell you! My project! Those statistics are going into Magalto's final report, to be reviewed by the Patent and Trademark Office."

"I heard what you said—and that is *not* true. Based on the abstract that Dr. Kingsley wrote at the beginning of the year, your project is about genetically engineered food, and has been elected to win the spot in The *Cambridge Science Review*. That's the second time in ten years someone from our university will win that honor. Your project is expected to win the highest award from the Federal Academy of Science and Industry, the agency that grants the National Scientific Merit Scholarships. It will be a boon to our science department and bring even more prestige to our university. No, our money comes from tuition and alumni support. It comes from exceptional projects like yours that find their way into the business world each year. That's how both of you can attend Royce. Your educations are paid for by the projects you come up with while you are still in school. We train you from day one to begin using your skills to help pay off your education as well as lay the foundation for your future."

Elliott shook his head as he looked at him. "You don't believe a word I said, do you? Your money comes from Magalto. Millions, every year. You'll take the chump change from us and from your alumni. You'll take it from federal awards. But Dr. Kingsley funnels in your big money. Drug money from the Columbians, because Magalto hasn't hit the patent jackpot yet. They're waiting for my project. That's why Dr. Kingsley is in a bind—because my project isn't finished."

"That is absolutely preposterous. You have no idea what you're talking about."

"Ask him if I'm right."

"I don't have to ask him."

"No you don't have to ask him, because you know all about this—you're the president! And like a good president, you'll never fire him as long as he's bringing in the money."

Whitman narrowed his eyes and stared at Elliott. "Dr. Kingsley prepares day and night to train you to be the best-educated scientists in the country. He has no time, interest, or ability, to even conceive of hatching a plan like you have made up here today, and if you continue with your accusations, I will see to it that your expulsion gets high priority. *Do I make myself clear?*"

Elliott stared at him.

"If you are not going to sign over your project, then I have no choice but to require that you complete another."

"*What*? How am I supposed to do a project before graduation?"

"That's your problem now, isn't it? I want an outline of it on my desk tomorrow morning."

"*Tomorrow*?"

"Yes. It can be on any subject you want—except this one. And I want the project finished before graduation ceremonies begin." Whitman paused and looked hard at both students. "If either one of you so much as mention this conversation to *any*one, I will call an emergency board meeting and have Dr. Kingsley state his case against both of you, and you'll both be expelled. Am I crystal clear? This discussion is over."

Exasperated, Kelly looked at Elliott. She stood, and he followed her out of Whitman's office.

As soon as the door closed, Whitman had Kingsley on the phone, ordering him to his office, and telling him to bring Elliott's unfinished project.

"What the hell's going on, Quinton?" Whitman said as Kingsley burst inside.

"He turned the shit over at the border." Kingsley tossed Elliott's report on the desk and stood in front of Whitman with both hands on his hips. "I've just been on the phone with Brownsville. The place is under an international drug lockdown, and what hasn't been damaged by arson fire is under federal containment. Elliott Chapman did this."

"What was he doing at the border?"

"I don't know. I found out he was helping the Columbians. He must've gotten a hold of it somehow."

"Our funding . . . " Whitman said softly, looking at Kingsley with dazed eyes. "What's going to happen to our funding?"

Kingsley pointed to the report. "We're going to have to get this in somehow. We still have time to get the patents approved."

"The sonafabitch didn't sign it."

"No—he wouldn't," Kingsley said.

"Then I'll forge his signature myself and have it expressed to the journal right away. I'll include a personal letter, explaining our circumstances. That should work, don't you think?"

"Let's hope it'll work." Kingsley shook his head and looked down at Whitman's desk. "Let's hope." He looked up at Whitman. "I failed him because he's not cooperating with us, David. I failed him in class, and I failed his project. Didn't even faze him. Do you see what I've been dealing with? The hope of an Elliott Chapman indolent has turned into a lethal infection. I want him expelled."

"Quinton, I can't do that. We don't have probable cause. Besides, we need this paper published. If we expel him, he'll turn right around and testify against the signature. No. We can't even think about it."

"Well, we have to do something."

"I told him he had to submit another project, and I'll give him the satisfaction of completing it. I want him busy and out of the way."

"You can't just let him walk out of here!"

"Yes. Let him go, Quinton. We'll give him his diploma and let him graduate. Just let him go. If you try to do anything to him, the infection will spread. We can't allow it."

Kingsley tightened his jaw. "All right. I'll let him graduate. But after he gets his diploma, he's all mine."

Whitman nodded then slid Elliott's report closer and looked at it. "Fine. Now, I'll get this fixed up and expressed out today."

Kingsley turned and stormed out of the room.

President Whitman went through Elliott's final report. Everything looked first rate, for a senior project. Even the conclusion fit the hypothesis. It hadn't earlier. That's what Elliott was supposed to have changed weeks ago. But Dr. Kingsley went over it earlier this morning. He found a few data points that needed to be manipulated, otherwise the report would not be printed in the peer-reviewed journal.

Under no other circumstance would Whitman have forged a student's signature. This circumstance, however, was greatly mutated.

CHAPTER 26

Leo's pub wasn't busy on the Tuesday afternoon of finals week. A few locals enjoying an early dinner out occupied two tables near the door. College students were smattered throughout the place studying, eating, and talking. Several played pinball and video games in the corner. Leo had to work the tables himself with two other full-timers. He got nervous every year, around the end of school. Most of the students at Royce went back home and never had another thought of Leo again. He took it personal.

"He ain't comin', is he?" Leo spat at Kelly. "People come, people go. They eat here. They eat there. That's what people do. Ya can't ever rely on 'em."

Kelly glanced at the front door. "He'll be here. But maybe he wanted to meet at a place that serves real food."

"Don't botha me a bit."

"No, he said Leo's. He wanted the liver. You still have liver, don't you?"

"It's been a specialty. Never thought of blendin' it like that."

Kelly made a disgusted face and looked at her plate. She shifted in her seat then turned to the door, taking another sip from the straw. "There he is now," she said, gulping down the drink.

Elliott rushed through the doorway carrying a bag.

"Well, well, well, whadaya' know. He's back, lookin' to cause more trouble. You gonna pack some food in your bag there, to take on the road somewhere?"

"Hello, Leo." Elliott slid into the booth across from Kelly. "Yeah, I'm stocking up. I haven't been here for awhile and I missed your place."

"Now, that's what I like to hear." He turned to Kelly with an approving nod.

"We have work to do now, Leo," Kelly said as she turned to Elliott. "Don't we?"

"We're fresh out of liva' shakes," Leo said to Elliott. "What else do ya want?"

"Liver shakes?" Elliott turned to Kelly.

"Yeah, it's been a big hit since you were in the kitchen," Kelly said.

Leo grinned.

"Glad to see I made such an impression on your menu. No, I'm good," Elliott said to Leo, who shrugged his shoulders and sauntered away. Elliott reached for the bag, took out a stack of papers, put them on the table, then slammed his hand on top. "Here's what I was talking about. This is all the stuff I brought back from the clinic in Matamoros."

"Okay." Kelly blinked her eyes.

"I scanned through them on the plane this morning. They're all about GMO's."

"GMO's?

"Genetically modified organisms."

"Yeah, I know what it means. But what can we put together tonight about GMO's?"

"Listen to this." He flipped through the pages and read the titles. "New toxins and allergens in foods." "The creation of herbicide-resistant weeds." "The spread of diseases across species barriers." "Gene pollution." "The disturbance of ecological balance." "Unpredictable health damaging effects." "Inadequate government regulation." "Ethical concerns." "Inadequate safety at research facilities." "Global threat to humanity's food supply . . . " He looked up at her. "You following this?"

"Yeah," she said, wide-eyed.

"There's more," he said paging through trying to find his markers. "The artificially-induced characteristics and inevitable imperfections will be passed on to all future generations, and to other related and unrelated organisms. GMO's can never be recalled or contained. The consequences of GMO's are incalculable. Unnatural gene transfers from one species to another are dangerous. Health-damaging effects caused by genetic engineering will continue forever. Genetic transfer across species lines upsets natural balance. Competition from new species damages the environment. Ninety percent of consumers want clear labeling of all genetically engineered foods. Terminator patents." He looked up at Kelly with a scowl. "And I gave Rina all that information."

"Just forget about her. Don't even get started."

Elliott reached for her drink and took a sip. "Well, I came out ahead on the deal." He set the drink down and looked at her. "You don't like talking about Rina, do you? Are you a little jealous?"

"NO. I'm not jealous." Kelly flicked back her hair that had fallen across her face.

"You're jealous because I had breakfast with her at an exotic restaurant."

"A baked worm on a burrito does not sound exotic." She glared at him. "Come on, would you? We have a project to do here. I suggest we get moving on it." She slid the top page off the stack, picked it up, and tried to concentrate. "Now what do you want to do?"

"I want to avenge the evildoers," he said, smiling at her.

"And *you're* going to decide who they are?" She put the paper down and thumbed through more, scanning the article headlines as she went. And after a moment of watching her, Elliott felt compelled to join her in her work on his project.

For another hour, the two razed through the entire stack of material. Kelly made notes as Elliott read the topics he had outlined earlier, and when Leo interrupted them with a fresh batch of liver shake, it was more than she could take. If she was going to help him with his project, she demanded that they take it up somewhere else, free from any more biological disturbances. And not her apartment—it was a mess. It would have to be at Elliott's grandparents. They packed the bag, took their notes, and left the place.

Leo stood in his near-empty diner with a forlorn expression on his face as he watched them leave. He took it personal.

CHAPTER 27

This was meant to be Rina Das's last return to Bogotá. She had enough university credits to graduate, even if she didn't walk down the aisle to receive her diploma in person. She could wait three months and receive it through the slow Columbian mail. Pre-election activities were heating up, and her job was to get the Terminator decoded and the cocaine gene inserted into another type of plant, so that the hundreds of thousands of farmers remembered who to vote for.

She had two rooms in Martino's villa. One room was her bedroom, which overlooked the snowcapped Andes. No one else entered this room except the cleaners, twice a week. The other room was her workroom, and she allowed officers to enter if they needed. It had all the modern electronic necessities: four computers, wireless networking, and satellite transmission and receiving dishes. Anything she wanted, she purchased in the United States and had shipped to the villa.

She sat at a computer and Martino watching over her shoulder, not understanding a thing she was doing. She pointed to icons and descriptions on the monitor. He smiled and nodded and tried to seem interested in something he would never comprehend. But this was her job. His was to win the election and control the vast amounts of the new produce throughout the world. He had no time to see how a computer operated, or learn the biology of this new technology. After a few moments of trying to understand her explanations, he left her alone to whiz through the discs she brought back from the American in Texas.

Rina worked all morning, trying to read the format that cataloged the Terminator protocol. Through some ingenuity and mostly persistence, she finally managed to unlock the code that opened the new world.

The very first sentence in bold letters explained a United States Patent Pending on file, registered number 5,723,765 as Terminator Plant Technology.

History: The Terminator Technology came from plant hybridization. A farmer crossing two distinct plant relatives could improve the yield, but the tradeoff caused the plants to become sterile. Sterility happened via a gene turn-off mechanism. This process is the platform for which other companies will pay royalties to the patent holder if they want certain genetic traits spliced into the Terminator Plant Technology. Anyone purchasing these seed traits will do so every year, so that distribution is adequately controlled. The efforts of the company, Magalto, will be directed toward inadequate economic countries, beginning in South America.

The next few pages described the genetic procedure and mechanism of the suicide system:

Three new genes are inserted into the plant. The first, a Promoter gene, turns pre-selected genes on and off like a switch. Next, a gene, Recombinase, acts like molecular scissors and cuts a space in the DNA sequence. Then the third gene is inserted. This gene is engineered to produce a Repressor to keep the Recombinase gene dormant until the plant is exposed to a specific outside stimulus. The choice of stimulus is based entirely on preference. It could be shock, temperature, or sunlight. It could even be based on lunar cycles, so the process could be timed precisely. The stimulus is applied to the seed before sale. Once the stimulus is initiated, the production of the preferred genes used in the suicide mission are activated, and the seeds will self-destruct by increasing the hydrogen potential: acidic poisoning and the application of the following:

1. R.I.P. Ribosomal Inhibitor Protein can be any protein susceptible to gene insertion.

2. For Recombinase gene, use the CRE/LOX system from a bacteriophage; viruses that attack bacteria.

3. For Repressor gene, tetracycline repressor system, Tn10 tet.

The two discs described in detail the genetic procedure and how the Terminator system operated. Rina continued to the third disc. Suddenly, she was amid a bizarre arrangement, spelling out an entirely different sequence. But it looked very familiar to anyone who was fortunate enough to experience a biochemistry course taught by Dr. Quinton Kingsley. For the toxin gene, instead of the ribosomal inhibitor protein (R.I.P.), the application of 2-beta-carbomethoxy-3-beta-benzoxytropane was to be used. $C_{17}H_{21}NO_4$! She recognized this molecule immediately.

The rest of the document went on and on about nitric oxide, and introduced an entire new class of neuropeptides. There were descriptions about engineering these chemicals into all kinds of host DNA. She put the fourth disc in, scrolled through it, and watched as a strange kind of neurotransmitter engineering protocol appeared. Her fingers flew over the keyboard as she tried to find the completion of the Terminator protocol. It wasn't anywhere.

"Uncle," she said slowly, staring at the monitor. "We have a problem."

He hurried into the room. "What is it?"

Her eyes darted across the screen. "It's . . . not here."

"What is not here?"

She looked up at him. "The Terminator. The Terminator isn't here. There seem to be two different types of protocol. The beginning of the Terminator is here, and then there's a kind of neurotransmitter protocol. But there is no application of the Terminator anywhere."

"Where is Terminator?" he asked quickly.

"I don't know." She waved to the screen. "But this is cocaine synthesis. I've seen this before. This molecule, C-seventeen, H-twenty one, N-O-four, is cocaine." She looked up at him. "And these others all look like neurotransmitters. Why would they be here?"

"Then, we need the rest of it."

"But this," she looked back at the screen, "is a neurotransmitter application. This is a protocol for neurotransmitter insertion. It's a model for inserting other substances into host DNA."

"Well you will have to get these, what you call neuro-trans-mutations, out of here."

"They're called neurotransmitters." Rina kept her eyes on the monitor. She scrolled down the document.

"You will go and exchange this disc for the rest of the Terminator." He looked at her as she sat, staring.

She wasn't ignoring him. She was searching her years of education, trying to make sense of what was dancing before her. There was a Terminator synthesis, but no application. There was a cocaine synthesis, but no application. The only application was that of a neurotransmitter, and with it was its entire synthesis from molecular structure to chromosomal placement.

"These are chemicals that activate certain parts of the brain and nervous system."

"It is not what we want. You will return to Ore*gon* immediately and get the correct protocol."

"No." She turned and looked at him with a smile. "This is much better than cocaine. And the entire protocol is here. We can manufacture these powerful nerve system stimulants in our laboratory and transfer the gene into the number three chromosome of anything we want. The way the molecular structure is arranged, and as large as it is, the reuptake of the release in the nerve system will be very slow. The effects will last a long time. Much longer than cocaine."

Martino nodded, still not understanding a word she said. "I don't understand."

She turned her chair to look at him as she spoke. "Cocaine is synthesized from a plant, the coca plant, by using chemical formulas in a lab. But it takes a lot of work to purify it. Magalto has put the gene into the tomato plant and improved its effects moderately, but it still needs to be processed and sometimes when it is, the cocaine molecule disintegrates.

"With this *new* protocol, neurotransmitters are made inside the body and are released in very small amounts, with very powerful stimulating effects. There is nothing in nature that compares. If a neurotransmitter is inserted the same way into a tomato, or squash, or whatever, its effects will be unlike anything the world has ever seen! We don't need Magalto. We don't need to decipher the Terminator. We have it all right here." She pointed to the screen. "Everything is right here."

Martino nodded slowly.

"We can do this right here in the lab," Rina said, smiling. "This is a gift."

"Yes. We do this, but we must hurry. The people are growing uneasy and the government is becoming hostile to our activities. How long will this take?"

"Maybe a week to work through the sequencing. It may take less. But I'm going to need help around the clock."

"In five days, the vote will be cast for the new President of Columbia, and I will win in a civil, bloodless election. You have four days, Katrina Maria, to complete this new procedure."

Chapter 28

Elliott drove Kelly from Leo's to his grandparent's house. For the second time, he explained to her what happened on his trip. He did this because she kept asking him about what else happened in Whitman's office. A new project outline due tomorrow? How could that happen?

But with all the information Duane had given him from the clinic in Matamoros, his research was finished. All he had to do now was put it on paper. Kelly said this whole thing was related to Procrustes. Cutting off appendages or stretching his victims to fit the bed he prepared just for them was Procrustean. These projects were Procrustean. He agreed. Procrustes made his bed fit everyone.

"No," Kelly said. "He made everyone fit his bed. That's what you mean." She bumped into him as he turned the key to the front door of his grandparent's home.

"That's what I said." He opened it and let her walk through.

"No, you didn't. You said he made his bed fit everyone. That's not what he did—don't you remember? What he did was make everyone fit his bed." She walked inside the small living room. Elliott shut the door and followed. She continued, "That was his problem. He slaughtered people so they would fit his bed. He made them *conform* to it. He forced conformity. No one wants to be forced into conformity, Elliott. It would have been totally different if he made his *bed* fit everyone."

"Elliott," his grandmother called in a delicate voice from the kitchen. "Is that you, Elliott?"

"Yes, Grandma!" he yelled back. He turned to Kelly. "Whatever. It's an ethical riddle. Don't get so excited about it." He went to the old coffee table, spread the papers across the top, then turned on his laptop computer. He sat on the couch. "You always do that."

"No." She walked over to him, looked at him with a smile, and waved her hand as she spoke. "Don't you get it? That's what we're going to do."

He turned and looked up at her. "What?"

"If the travelers knew they were going to be stretched on his bed, they never would have gone with him, never would've feasted with him, or even had a conversation with him."

"Yeah."

His grandmother walked into the living room, wiping her hands on a flowered hand towel.

"Hi Grandma," Kelly said, sitting down beside Elliott.

"Oh, hello, Kelly," she greeted her sweetly. "I didn't know you were here."

"She's helping me with some school work," Elliott said.

"Well, that's nice of you. I haven't been able to help much since last year." She smiled at her then looked at Elliott.

Kelly gaped at him. *She does your homework?*

He shrugged his shoulders. "Yeah, a little. I was always too busy."

"Busy with *what?*" Kelly shook her head.

"Will you both be here for dinner?" Grandma asked.

Elliott turned to Kelly with a smile. "Wanna stay for dinner?"

"Sure, Mrs. Chapman. I'd love to stay for dinner. Is there anything I can do to help?"

"No, you just stay put and help Elliott. Dinner will be ready about half past."

"All right," Kelly said.

Grandmother stayed a moment and watched Kelly sitting beside Elliott. They began sorting through their papers on the table. "I'll let you two get to work," she said as she turned and walked back to the kitchen.

"Now what were you saying?" Elliott asked. "Something about the travelers?"

"Yeah, the travelers. The only reason they went home with Procrustes was because he offered to help them. He welcomed the aimless, wandering travelers. But they didn't know *anything* about him. They thought he was another nice guy helping them out along the journey. Quinton Kingsley is your Procrustes."

"No, he's not," Elliott said quickly.

"Oh yes he is. You were the aimless freshman, wandering around here four years ago looking to find yourself, looking for someone to point you the way down the road. Then Your Obnoxiousness comes along and says, 'I'm your advisor, listen to me.' And you fell head over heels, because the most popular professor took you under his wing and gave you all kinds of privileges."

"I deserved every single one of 'em!"

"No, you didn't. He gave them to you, and they were all teasers."

"That's not true."

"Yes it is, Elliott. You want his approval so bad; you've been looking for it ever since you started school. You try to get close to him in a dismal attempt to get his attention and win his affection. You play and joke around with him, because you want that kind of relationship with him. But he doesn't like you—he'll *never* like you. He doesn't like anybody."

"No. He does like me. He let me teach any course I wanted. He got me accepted into four med schools. He assigned me to work on his own project."

"You're blind, Elliott. He did all that to keep you away from him. Closeness isn't his greatest asset. But you figured out another way. You challenged his intelligence, and he just digs that. He challenged you right back. Then it escalated until you find yourself competing with him on his stage. So he gives you a senior project and tells you, 'It's the project of the decade, Elliott. Your name will be emblazed in the annals of science.' And you say, 'Okay, I'll do it for you, O Great One.' Then you go blindly into the thing. Your emotions are stronger than your common sense."

"No. He recom*mended* it to me. He never forced me to do it."

"Like you're going to argue with him about it."

"I could have done anything I wanted."

"So why didn't you? You didn't really have a choice, that's why. You thought you'd just breeze right through it and go sit on his lap, or something. But you couldn't finish it, so you got on another one of your educational ethical tirades about how these illegitimate projects are completely senseless; a total waste of time. You argue about it all the way down into the bowels of a Columbian drug operation in Mexico, of all places."

"I uncovered that drug operation and helped put those guys behind bars. I stopped Rina and her uncle from legitimizing their guerilla government and taking over Columbia."

"Oh, really? You think what you did is going to stop anyone? You're so naïve, Elliott. You don't know how anything works. You may have masqueraded as an ethical bystander, a real slacktivist for sure, but you didn't do yourself any favors. Kingsley's out to get you."

"He won't do anything to me. He's not that courageous."

Kelly shook her head at him. "I can't be*lieve* you! You're about to wander into the same mess as your friend Duane you babbled on about, and you sit there innocent as a blade of grass. No, once Kingsley finds out you were involved, he'll be a crazed psycho hot on your trail and he'll flatten you!"

"You're wrong. My project turned out to be a project for the CEO of Magalto, which turned out to be a project for the FARC, Rina's uncle. I never told Kingsley that I gave the Terminator to Rina. I told him that I gave Rina the cocaine protocols. And for all he knows, Rina's uncle turned the cocaine over at the border. Kingsley won't find out I gave them the Terminator. Besides, what would he do, shoot me?

You think he'd go to jail for the rest of his life, just to kill me? He's all blabber."

"No. He won't do that. But he'll find out and go after you somehow, and you're not even concerned."

"Why should I be?"

"Because you threaten him, Elliott! You've risen above his challenges and he doesn't know what to do with you. On his stage, there's only room for one, and he's about ready to knock you flat off of it. He's taken swings at you that you don't even see coming. He's out to get you. This is totally Procrustes! You've gotten into his house, you've been at his table, and you've finished his meal. And you play around with him like it's all some big joke, taunting him along the way. He knows that, and that's what makes him so set on getting you. Once he gets you into his bed, he'll hack you to pieces. You can't play his game and win because he's made all the rules! No one gets help from Procrustes, and you're certainly not going to get his approval for anything you do. You gotta take him out. Yeah, the only thing you can do now, is get him before he gets you."

"No, the only thing I can do is graduate. I don't care about him, besides you're not even right. I don't look for his approval. I couldn't care less about it."

"Yes, you do. You care about it all the way to accepting your expulsion. If it wasn't for Whitman, you'd be gone. You don't even see it. And you know, the really sad thing is, you like it. I don't know why, but you do. You like the sadistic way he treats you. But take him away from Royce, and he's nothing. A nobody. He's nothing without an audience to parade in front of."

"What are you saying?"

"Let's take him out. Let's take one of these topics and write a position paper. We'll write up an environmental statement and pin him to some kind of genetic engineered environmental pollutant, or something. We'll have the EPA on Royce's back before tomorrow. They'll get him fired if he doesn't quit from the pressure."

"Look, shrink Kelly. I don't have time for this. Maybe Kingsley has it in for me, as you say. But Whitman has given me a chance to get another project finished so I can graduate, and that's exactly what I'm going to do. I'm not going after Kingsley. I'm not messing around trying to be one of your Kingsley-raging activists. It would kill him if he couldn't teach. That's not what I'm about."

"Well then, *what*, Elliott? What are you going to do?"

Elliott stared down at the mess. "I don't know."

Kelly shifted on the couch. She sat on her leg and it touched Elliott's. "Explain to me again how that Terminator stuff related to your project."

He moved so they weren't touching and looked over at her. "It was part of the data I've been working with since the beginning of the school year. Kingsley had me collect the data they were keeping on all Magalto's produce, but it never did turn out right, because the tomato data was way off the charts. They were waiting for it to go down, but it never did, because the Terminator sequences were combined with the cocaine. It had to be."

"Why would Kingsley want that data? I mean, him and Whitman were so concerned you get it finished, and then it's like, they both gave up on you doing it."

"It has to do with the Terminator protocol. That's what Steven Sloan was pushing for. He needed those health statistics to send in to the U.S. Patent Office. But the data will be rejected because it's so far off the scale. They won't get patents issued if there's a health risk."

Kelly quickly thumbed through the papers. Halfway through the stack she pulled out two pages that had the corners folded over. She held them up. "They're trying to get the Terminator patented, right? That's why they needed your project."

"Yeah. But a patent won't be issued unless all the data are in synch."

"And Rina's uncle, why did he want it?"

"Jorge Martino. He wanted the Terminator sequences so he could get the cocaine gene out from the tomatoes. All he wanted was the cocaine. But he won't be able to decode it, because the discs I gave Rina don't have all the information for them to do it. It's the Terminator that has to be stopped, if you want to go after something."

"All right." She smiled wide at him. "Then that's our Procrustes. The Terminator will be our Procrustes."

"What?"

"We're going to expose our friend, Procrustes."

"How?" He grabbed the papers out of her hand and looked at them. "Labeling?" He looked at her, waving the papers. "How's this going to stop them?"

"Okay, listen." She grabbed the papers out of his hand and spread them on her lap. "Here is your new project. You're going to call it the Procrustes Project. This is going to stop the Terminator cold in its tracks."

"How are you going to do that?"

"Yeah, this'll be great." She patted his arm and smiled. "Okay, listen. This is really like finishing your old project, but it's better."

"I'm listening."

"All right. We're going to protest."

"No, you're the activist. I'm the slacktivist. I don't protest."

"Wait—we're going to do this differently." She picked up two papers and read the title. "'Ninety percent of the public want labeling on Genetically Modified Organisms in the food market'." She looked up at him. "True?"

"Yeah."

"That means any organism that's genetically engineered, whether it's in cereal, bread, coffee, or tacos, should be labeled as being genetically modified so the people can decide for themselves if they want to eat it."

"Uh-huh."

"Well, what we're going to do is send emails out to listserve groups and ask them two questions. The first question is about the labeling. We'll ask, 'Do you want labels on genetically modified food?' Ninety percent of the population will answer this question, 'yes.' We already know this. Are you with me?"

"Uh-huh."

"Now, the second question is, 'Do you think it's a good idea to patent life forms?' If we get these people to answer the first question, they'll probably answer the second one. We'll just ask those two questions. And then we'll have them send a hardcopy response to President Whitman at Royce University. We'll email it to everybody who might be concerned. I have a huge list of them: Nrage, Gene-Watch, The Campaign, Union of Concerned Scientists, Greenpeace, Earth First!, The Sierra Club, Green Acres, The American Organic Society, and even Amnesty International. I can get a huge list of student activist groups from the College and University directory. I'll get as many groups as I can. Then I'll send everything to MoveOn.org. They'll take care of worldwide distribution."

"No. I don't want to do that. I'm not using science to make some kind of political statement when all *you* really want to do is attack Kingsley and Whitman. I'm just not doing it."

"Then why don't you use your stupid philosophy for something? You're always talking about how your moral opinion is going to save the world. Go ahead. Make up your own moral-ass theoretical project, then. You'll be having an ethical discussion with unreasonable people."

"Maybe I will. But right now, I'm having an unreasonable conversation with you and not getting anywhere."

Elliott shook his head away and watched as his grandmother ambled into the room. She stood, rubbing her hands on the towel. "Sorry to bother you both, but dinner's ready." She smiled and looked at their mess on the coffee table. "Are you able to come anytime soon?"

"Yeah, we'll be right there, Grandma."

"Good. Elliott, would you wake your Grandpa? He's sleeping in his chair."

"Sure." He turned to Kelly. "Let's go eat. We both need a break."

Kelly followed Grandma into the kitchen and Elliott went to wake Grandpa.

"Well, well," Mr. Chapman said, combing his gray hair, walking behind Elliott. "It's nice of you to join us for dinner."

"Thank you, Mr. Chapman." Kelly smiled at him as she set the last plate.

Mr. Chapman walked to his chair and sat. "It's not very often Elliott brings a girl home like this."

"Well, it's nice to be here again." Kelly sat next to Elliott.

"That last girl he brought home, boy oh boy," he shook his head as he smiled, "she was a fanatic. Didn't eat meat because of some kooky idea about animal rights, or something. Wore those darn baggy clothes with slogans written all over herself. I think most of our conversation was her talking about all the problems she was going to fix when she graduated."

"Grandpa," Elliott said softly. "This is Kelly."

"Ohhh, Kelly. I must be thinking of someone else."

"No, this is her."

"That's okay," Kelly said, smiling at him. "I'm glad you remember me and I'm sorry I'm not wearing those clothes. They're in the laundry."

Mrs. Chapman was rummaging around inside the refrigerator. She finally brought out three salad dressings.

"This looks very good, Mrs. Chapman," Kelly said, looking at the food on the table. "Is it some kind of bean casserole?"

"No, it's beef," said Mrs. Chapman quickly. She set the dressings on the table and picked up the salad bowl. "Here, please. Have some salad." She handed the bowl to Kelly with all three dressings.

"Thank you," Kelly answered cheerfully.

Mr. Chapman said a prayer and everyone ate for a few minutes, chatting about weather-kinds-of-things people talk about at dinner.

"Yeah, now I remember what it was," Mr. Chapman said, wiping the corners of his mouth. "You didn't eat the shrimp because you said they're full of mercury. Wasn't that it?" He looked at her as she tonged more salad onto her plate.

"Yes," Kelly said looking up at him as she spoke. "Mercury is a poison. All those old thermometers were taken off the market because they had mercury in them, you know." She put the tongs back in the bowl and picked up her fork.

"Open your mouth," he said to her.

"What?"

"Not now, Bernie," said Mrs. Chapman looking at him crossly.

"No," he said to Kelly. "It's all right. Open your mouth. I want to check something."

She opened her mouth and tipped her head back.

Mr. Chapman stood up, leaned across the table and peeked inside her mouth. "One, two, three, four . . . "

"What?" She closed her mouth. "What are you looking at?"

"Mercury. Every one of those fillings has mercury in 'em. You have a lot of it in your mouth for one being so concerned about eating shrimp. You know, there's probably enough mercury in one tooth to poison a lake. Seems like they oughta take those fillings out, just like they took those thermometers off the market." Mr. Chapman sat back down and looked at Elliott. "Don't you think, Elliott? I had all mine taken out." He reached inside his mouth and took out his dentures. "See these?" he gummed.

Elliott helplessly looked at Kelly. "I'm sorry. This is our usual dinner conversation."

"No," she said. "Don't be." She turned to Mr. Chapman. "How much mercury is in there?"

He maneuvered his teeth back inside his mouth and chewed on his lips a few times. "I don't know really, but they've been putting that stuff in teeth for years. The dentists call it silver, so they can get it by their regulations. That's what I thought was so funny after you left, that last time you were here. You being concerned about mercury in them tiny shrimp, and all. Seems to me it's the same thing."

"It is. I had no idea."

"You'd have to ask an honest dentist who could tell you. Seems like you'd be knowing these things, as well informed as you are."

"Well I'm going to check on it." She turned to Elliott with her palms up. "That's Procrustes, again!"

"What, the dentist?"

"Yes! If they're putting mercury in teeth when it's a poison, and not telling you about it, that's Procrustes."

"Wha'da you calling that, Pro—what?" Mr. Chapman looked at her with a wrinkled forehead.

"Procrustes. The Greek myth." She said and turned back to Elliott. "The people have a right to know. Then, they can decide for themselves if they want to go lay on his bed, or have mercury in their teeth, or eat genetically altered food."

"Mary," Mr. Chapman said to his wife. "You ever heard of Pro"—he turned to Kelly for help with pronunciation—"Pro . . . ."

"Procrustes. It's Elliott's story."

"It's an old myth about forcing things on others," Elliott said to his grandfather. "No big deal."

"Well, how come you never tell me about things like this?"

"Bernie," Mrs. Chapman scolded. "If you'd helped him with his homework every once in a while, like he's asked, you'd be knowing some of these things. As it is, you probably wouldn't understand if he told you."

"Yes, I would. I've been around a few years, you know." He turned to Kelly, raised his eyebrows up and down and said, "It sounds dirty."

"Yes," Elliott said to Kelly, ignoring his grandfather. "You might be right." He looked at his grandmother. "Thanks for dinner, Grandma. We have to get back to work." He pushed himself away from the table and carried his plate to the sink.

"Don't you want some dessert? I cut up an apple pie I baked this morning."

"You eat pie now, don't you?" Mr. Chapman asked Kelly. "Or are you afraid of biting into a baked worm?"

"No, actually I like apple worms. I don't eat sugar." Kelly pushed her chair in and picked up her plate.

"Not right now, Grandma," Elliott said walking to the doorway. "Kelly has a lot of work to do."

Elliott and Kelly moved back into the living room. The room became a torrent of papers as the two outlined the project. Elliott took ownership of his new project and directed Kelly to keep notes on his computer as he scanned through the sheaves of research material.

Thirty minutes later, his grandmother entered the room and asked Elliott about the two computer discs he had in the pants she was about to wash. He took them from her. She asked if they needed anything, like a nice cold drink. Kelly, needing a break, followed her into the kitchen.

Elliott put a disc in his computer and scanned the document, working uninterrupted for a few minutes. Kelly returned, carrying two cans of soda; one of them diet. Elliott stopped what he was doing and went into deliberation about what she was about to give him. Based on the information from the disc, this drink began as a great social experiment in the form of elixirs, tonics, and wines. Scientists, clergy, and even great writers drank the soothing refreshment. It was the coca plant that stimulated Jules Verne, H.G. Wells, and Lewis Carroll's brilliant book, *Alice in Wonderland*. The name of the world's most popular soft drink comes from the coca plant and they call it the Real Thing, Always. The great social experiment has turned into a legal multi-billion dollar sugar-water industry. Diet soda's even worse: made of aspartame, it is a powerful neurotoxin developed by one of those other genetic engineering companies. It's Procrustes all over again. Kelly set the cans down on a cabinet just inside the room, walked to the couch, and pretended to be busy.

For the next few hours they worked. Elliott framed the skeleton of Procrustes and it was an ethical treatise about how senior projects at Royce were turned into stolen intellectual property. He explained how companies like Magalto paid big money for research data done by students who didn't know any better. They, in turn, won big patents on products like the Terminator Technology. People like Dr. Quinton Kingsley, President Whitman, and even Mr. Steven Sloan, got involved with these projects. Money was exchanged when it shouldn't, and the University was a front to these activities. The system was flawed. No one was really responsible.

Elliott continued writing and Kelly tried to stay awake.

CHAPTER 29

Elliott rubbed his sleepy eyes, stretched, and looked across the heaps of papers at Kelly buried in the middle of them, asleep on the couch. Books and pamphlets were stacked on the floor, and some teetered on the coffee table next to her. Her hand rested on her flat belly, over a paper Elliott had given her to read, about the effects of genetically engineered weed spray. It rose and fell as she breathed.

"Kelly." He reached over and nudged her.

She moaned and stretched, knocking two books to the floor.

"Wake up, genetic princess."

"What time is it?" she asked with her eyes closed.

"Late." He piled a few books and crumpled up some scrap paper.

"*One-thirty?*" She looked at the clock on the wall and sat up quickly. "How long have I been sleeping?"

"You've been incoherent for at least an hour."

"Oh, I'm sorry." She rubbed her eyes. "How far did you get?"

He smiled at her and held up his new project. "I'm finished."

"You're finished? With *everything*?"

"The whole thing. It's seventeen pages, including references."

"Wow!" She reached for it. "Let me see."

Elliott gave it to her then began straightening up the coffee table. He put the books in a pile and gathered up the loose papers.

Kelly scanned through the first page, then the second, then the third. She held the pages up and let out a huff. "You did exactly what I told you to do. You're so original." She leafed through the pages as she spoke. "Labeling on genetically modified food . . . patent life forms . . . yeah, this is good." She continued reading then stopped. She pulled out the last several pages and looked up at him with a smile. "But you can't do this."

"Why not?"

She stopped smiling and shook the pages at him. "Because here you get into your stupid opinion, and you don't have any references to back up what you say."

"It's an ethical discourse. I'm assuming the reader has a little background in basic science, and doesn't need any references."

"But this is just your opinion. You need references to differentiate your opinion from real science. As it is, most of this has nothing to do with science." She leafed through and pulled out a page. "You can't write whatever falls out of your head. It's unethical."

"No it's not. Don't confuse yourself."

She leafed through the rest. "In the first half of this report you talk about the dangers of genetic engineering, and you have decent references, I'll give you that. But then you go completely insane, and talk about Royce students being forced to do senior projects that you say are stolen by the conglomerates. You actually *name* Whitman and Kingsley, and describe how they accept money in order to compete with other institutions. You talk about Magalto and the investment they have made in Royce, in exchange for independent research to get patents like the Terminator." She looked up and dropped the pile on the table. The papers flew across it; some fell to the floor. "You're framing everybody—then calling them victims of the system."

"We're all victims."

"Victims?"

"Yeah, victims."

"But most of this has nothing to do with engineering or biology. You have minimal scientific references. It's mostly your dumb opinion."

"It's bioethics, for your information, something we had to figure out for ourselves. That's why you don't recognize it. I put those two questions in it."

She shook her head. "You can't give this to Whitman."

"He said I could do it on anything."

"Yeah I know he did, but he'll fail you. He's not going to like this at all."

"He won't even read it. Look, maybe I wrote this up for myself. Maybe I wrote it because this is the first time I've done something that I wanted to do. I don't know. But my project is finished. I'm turning it in tomorrow, and I'm going to graduate. So I really don't care what you think."

"So why don't you send it to the *Cambridge Science Review* while you're at it, and see what they think about it."

"Maybe I will."

"Well, I'd be embarrassed."

"I don't care if you'd be embarrassed." He smiled at her and shrugged his shoulders.

"Do whatever makes you happy."

"Thank you, I will."

She reached down and began gathering up the papers that had fallen near her. "What time did you say it was?"

"Late."

"Late is not a time. Ohhh, I gotta go home." She reached for her shoes and tried to put one on as she balanced on the other leg. She hopped on one leg a few times, and sat on the floor to put the shoe on.

Elliott scooped up the papers and put them into a folder.

She tied her second shoe and stood.

"Kelly, thanks for your help." Elliott stood in front of her. "Even though you really don't care what I've done."

The top of her head, when she tipped it up, was level with his nose. She smiled into his tired eyes. "You know, I really don't care. You finally got your project done. That's what matters. And, it makes you happy." She stepped away as she tapped him lightly on his face. "You get some rest."

"I will. I'll need it when I deliver this, the Procrustes Project."

She left and he finished cleaning up the room.

CHAPTER 30

Rina Das and her Columbian researchers worked day and night in their laboratory. The Terminator sequencing was aborted. The cocaine synthesis was aborted. The only project the team focused on was the neurotransmitter protocol found in the discs given to them by the American.

They finished developing the dopamine-like substance and found the gene on number three chromosome of the tomato, squash, and lettuce plants for insertion. This neurotransmitter would be activated when exposed to *salivary amylase*, an enzyme found in human saliva. She programmed the gene and coded it to be that specific.

Word about the new product spread quickly throughout the country. Farmers traveled from the hillsides and byways. They began lining up at the FARC compound, anxious to receive the new plant seeds, which would be ready in one or two more days.

Martino wasn't in the laboratory all week. He was in his Office of Strategy, deploying his militia into position for his upcoming election. There was to be no bloodshed during this campaign, he fervently reminded his groups.

He warned each of his generals about the Columbian government and their opposition to the FARC. This was the first time that an outsider to the government was making a serious run at this high office, and they should tread lightly. Even if threatened to resign from the race? Yes, even if threatened. Peaceful conduct will be this campaign's operation.

The tension and unrest mounted throughout the country.

But privately, Martino realized that his group could no longer hide behind a small profile any longer. They were a large target now, and growing. Hundreds of thousands called themselves allies of the FARC. Hundreds of thousands were armed and trained in paramilitary techniques. Still, there was no way Martino could compete with the Columbian Army and the backing they had from international companies and the government of United States. He had neither men, money, nor weapons to stage a traditional coup.

Martino didn't want a coup. He wanted to win the election through a confident vote of the people. If the elections were held tomorrow, he would win. The existing President lived low in the bowels of public opinion. The established government parties had no one of Martino's stature or popularity. Martino knew this, but acted on his fears. He canvassed his friends in the southern countries and solicited their help. He made a respectable attempt to add to his armamentarium by tapping them for support. Still, he felt inferior. He needed one more infusion of money to buy more weapons and the men to use them.

So, he did what any reasonable politician would do. He called an acquaintance in Brownsville, Texas.

Outside of Brownsville, in a remote part of the desert, was a large building that housed a certain group of people from society waiting to be convicted of their crimes. It was called the Brownsville Minimum Security Facility. No one called it a jail. It was like a camp for adults. The people who stayed at this camp were taken from society for offenses they may or may not have committed. They remained there until the charges were dropped or until the camp counselors had enough outside pressure to release them. Dr. John Barringer and the rest of the researchers were already gone. They had rented laboratory space at the University of Texas and were continuing their work of securing the patents, as if nothing happened.

Steven Sloan had a nice enough room at camp BMSF. He was using it as an office when he wasn't in the weight room or hot tub. He had been haggling with the insurance company about the Magalto building for two straight days. At first, they weren't going to cover the damage caused by the Federal raid and they weren't going to cover the damage of the arson fire. But Sloan threatened to spend every day for weeks, if that's what it took, to gather enough information to sue the company for triple damages because of some-sort-or-other government contracts they were working on—and look for another insurer. The insurance company countered, offering complete coverage and another million to cover those expensive laboratory crops damaged by the fire.

He was packing his clothes into his last suitcase when his private telephone rang.

"Mr. Sloan. This is Jorge Martino."

Sloan laughed into the phone. "Mr. Martino. What a pleasant surprise. I trust the work we did has been completed to your satisfaction."

"Yes. The work is done. Your researcher helped with the problem."

"Good, good. I did speak to him about it. I'm always happy to be of assistance to you. So, what can I do for you? I know you're not calling to exchange pleasantries."

"Mr. Sloan. I do apologize about your unfortunate disaster in Brownsville."

"Well, thank you for being concerned. It'll just be a matter of time until we get back on our feet again. I have parts of the lab up and running right now, but I do appreciate your concern in the matter."

"Was it drug charges, as they say?"

Sloan laughed. "Drug charges? No, no. There were no drugs. It was just a simple misunderstanding. I had the whole thing cleared up. No, there were no drugs. A raging fire damaged about half the building. That's what all the excitement was about."

"Oh. I see. It will be repaired?"

"*Repaired*? Hell, no! We're going to build a new one. Three times the size!" Sloan paused. "There something I can help you with, Jorge?"

"Yes. You seem to have another building problem."

"Problem? What other building problem? No one's said anything to me about another building."

"Your clinic in Matamoros."

"Clinic? What happened to the clinic?"

"It seems that after your researcher finished with our project, he went to your clinic and destroyed all your computers, everything."

"Oh, now. No one's said anything to me about the clinic. Besides, why would he want to do something like that?"

"He took the Terminator protocol before he destroyed everything."

"*HE WHAT?* Took the *Terminator*?"

"Yes. I have it. He sold it to me."

"*That's bullshit*! He has no idea about the Terminator! You have no proof."

"Oh, Señor Sloan. It is right here in my laboratory."

"How the hell did you get it?"

"That is my business. But as it is, I have no need for it. It is waiting to be returned."

"What do you want, Martino? I'm in no mood for your antics."

"I want two million American dollars for the Terminator."

"*Two million?*"

"Oh, yes. Is a very good buy for someone interested in this protocol. Anyone in this business will appreciate its value."

Sloan sat on his bed and dropped his folded shirt inside his suitcase. "This is extortion, Jorge."

"You are in no position to argue. We take the Terminator out that has been causing so many problems. We are finished and now, sell it back to you for a fair price."

"It's *my Terminator*! You stole it from me—damn you, Jorge!"

"No, your researcher stole it. I am here to give it back to you. I want to make things right between us. We have been in business together for too long, Mr. Sloan, to let a simple engineering problem come between us. I no longer need it, so I return it to you."

"Then give it back to me."

"Oh, I cannot *give* it to you. There is a price. That is how we do business. I have always paid you for things. This time it is your turn to pay me."

"I'm not paying you two million dollars!"

"Then I make you a business proposal. You will like."

"What?"

"I give you Terminator and you pay me two million. Then, after I become President of Columbia, I pay you back. All of it."

Sloan paused.

"I am being very reasonable," Martino said. "Presidents can be reasonable when they need to be."

"You're asking for a loan?"

"Yes. And, I give you Terminator. A good deal for you."

"You'll pay it all back?"

"Six months. I pay it back."

"And the Terminator? When do I get the Terminator?"

"You get Terminator in one week. Can we have a deal?"

Sloan shook his head slowly and spoke into the phone, "You sonafabitch. This is extortion, Jorge."

"No? Then I sell to someone else. You do not have to buy it. I am sure I will find another customer."

"You can't do this to me! *We* designed it. *We* developed it and made it work. It is *mine*!"

"But, it has been my problem. So I take it out, and our plants work. Now, you can have it back."

"Dammit, Jorge!" Sloan paused a long moment. "All right, I'll wire half of it today. After I get the Terminator, I'll send the other half."

"Yes. That is good. I take care of you. You take care of me. *Simpatico*."

The last phone call Steven Sloan made from camp BMSF was to Portland, Oregon. It went directly to Dr. Quinton Kingsley's secretary. He sat on the bed waiting for Kingsley to get out of class and answer.

"What's going on, Steve?" Kingsley said breathing hard. "I can't keep leaving in the middle of my lectures. I'm giving term reviews."

"They're not *that* good, Quinton. Just sit down and listen a minute."

Kingsley kicked the door shut and sat at his desk holding the telephone. "What is it?"

"Martino called me. Seems that your little shit of a student knocked off the clinic."

"He what?" Kingsley leaned into his desk, propping his head up with his elbows. "What'd he do?"

"*He stole the damn Terminator! That's what he did!*"

"Oh . . . my . . . God."

"*AND GAVE IT TO MARTINO!*"

Kingsley pulled the phone away from his ear then slowly put it back.

"Martino's holding it for ransom. He wants two million dollars for it!"

"*Two million?*"

"He wants a loan for his campaign, I'm sure. But he won't pay it back. I know he won't. He's trying to be diplomatic."

"We've gotta have it, Steve. The Terminator is everything we've been working toward. I fixed all the numbers. We just sent in the final report for publication to the *Journal* and to the Patent Office. In a year we'll own the patents. You're going to have to get it—pay him."

"I am. I'm sending half of the money this afternoon. He'll get the Terminator to me in a week. When I get it, I'll send him the other half."

"Well, under the circumstances, that's all we can do."

"Quinton, I want Elliott Chapman. I want that sonafabitch plugged."

"No, we can't do that. Besides, it doesn't sound like Martino's going to help us out anymore, does it?"

"I have connections."

"Forget it, Steve."

"Well, I want him stopped before he causes us any more problems that you don't know about."

"We can't stop him until the *Journal* publishes the project. We had to forge his signature, so we have to keep cool until it's published."

"You had to forge his signature? He wouldn't *sign* it?"

"No. That's the only way we could send it off."

"Well, he can still deny it, even after it's published. He can still screw the project. Did you think about that?"

"What choice did we have?"

"Ah, Quinton—dammit. Then I want him silenced. We're going to have to get him locked up and put away until we get those patents. Then, I'm going after Martino. He's the one who started this whole thing in the first place."

Kingsley drummed his fingers on his desk and looked at the stack of papers he planned to look over tonight. Each senior project represented a promising career somewhere in the biology field. Some of his students would do well; others wouldn't. The working copy of Elliott Chapman's project lay on top. It was certain to bring a windfall to Royce University from many sources, but Elliott didn't have much to do with it. All he did was transcribe a few numbers and plot a simple graph. He was supposed to offer a conclusion. He was supposed to give his projection and summary comments. At least he was supposed to sign it. In the end, he had done nothing. Instead, he had become a heavy liability. Kingsley had been restrained by Whitman, and had given his word that nothing would happen to their student. But now, Sloan was pushing to do something severe.

Kingsley smiled into the phone and said, "Do you remember what we did to Duane Rice at Royce a few years ago?"

"Oh yeah, I remember."

"We'll do the same thing to Chapman. But this time, we'll plant so much on him, they'll lock him up for twenty years. No one will believe a word the little shit will say for two decades. By then, it will be a bad memory."

"That's brilliant, Quinton, brilliant."

"But I've got kids running around here trying to finish things up. I've got projects to look at and finals to grade. I have a few more lectures to give."

"You don't have time to do this?"

"No. Someone's always looking for me."

"Don't flatter yourself."

"Besides, I'm not supplied, and I'm certainly not going risk doing it myself."

"You don't have *any*?"

"Not *that* much."

"Well, I'll tell you what. I'll send John. He'll bring a package and mix it up there in your lab. He'll give it to Chapman as a graduation present. All you have to do is call Narcotics and report the biggest drug deal of the century, right after the ceremony. The biggest. John walks away, and the cops nab the sonafabitch. Whadaya think?"

"Yeah, that'll work."

"Sure it'll work. You just hold tight. When's graduation?"

"Saturday."

"Saturday? That's three days."

"That's what I'm saying. I don't have time to put it together."

"I'll have John up there Friday. Can he use your lab?"

"Yeah. No one will be in the labs on Friday. If he brings the leaves, I'll have everything else set up for him."

"Good. Let's put this kid away."

"Yeah, I'm with you. This will be a nice graduation present for him. A rigid cell is the perfect place for a defective biology major."

Dr. Quinton Kingsley hung up the telephone and quickly returned to his anxious freshman class. He finished his lecture, took one question, and dismissed the students. The back two rows tore out of the room, but several in the front approached him as he stacked his notes and stuffed them into his briefcase.

"Dr. Kingsley," a bespectacled female ventured in a nasal tone, "I don't understand. You said last week that if you give an infinite number of monkeys an infinite number of typewriters, one day they would eventually reproduce the works of Shakespeare, thereby proving Darwin's theory of evolution."

"Yes—I said that." He jammed the last of his notes inside a pocket without looking up.

"And you also said that everything that happens is built into the Schrödinger equation, and will someday prove Darwin correct."

"Yes."

She pushed her glasses up on the bridge of her nose. "Well, today you said that Schrödinger's equation is good for understanding the hydrogen atom, and is pretty much useless for everything else."

He stopped packing and looked at her with his head cocked to the side. "Sometimes scientists disagree with each other, and sometimes people talk about things they don't understand."

"So, what should we do if this comes up on the test? I don't want to get the question wrong."

"It's not about the test!" He slammed his briefcase shut. "Haven't you learned anything all year? It's all about how you interpret things. Darwin's theory of evolution doesn't need to be proved."

"But it's just a theory. That's how I interpret it." She looked at him with concern on her face.

"It's not a theory in my class! You should be careful where you get your interpretations." He picked up his briefcase and stormed out of the room before anyone else could ask another stupid question.

CHAPTER 31

At six o'clock Friday morning, Elliott was the only one awake in the house. He put the last page of the Procrustes Project in the binder and secured it with fasteners. His final copy spanned nineteen pages, including references. President Whitman would be so proud.

His grandmother shuffled in her slippers into the kitchen to see what all the noise was about. Elliott tried to explain what he had accomplished as she pursued her morning breakfast ritual of making stovetop oatmeal. She had done pretty well keeping up with him and his work, up until this year, but as he tried to explain where he had been and what he had done, she just stared at him like he was speaking a foreign language, as she stood holding a large stirring spoon in her hand. She nodded her uh-huhs until her oatmeal boiled over on the stove, and hurried to save it.

Elliott finished his dissertation as his grandfather wandered into the room in his raggedy pajamas. Of course, now he wanted to hear all about it. He sat down and pulled a chair right up next to Elliott, and waited for his personal discourse as Elliott finished eating. But before Elliott started into his new favorite subject, his grandmother reminded him that if he was going to turn his project in before his first class, he would have to leave immediately. Under his grandfather's protests, Elliott cleared his dishes, rushed from the room, and hurried to Royce with the project in hand.

President Whitman was unavailable, the secretary told him, and said there were problems with the graduation speaker from Texas. The big corporate man had an emergency that needed his immediate attention, and now President Whitman had to scramble to find the backup speaker.

Elliott told her it was a matter of life or death, this project, and would she make sure he got it right away? A diploma was riding on it.

"Sure thing," she said. "President Whitman is very busy but should have a moment when he checks in later today. Graduation is a big event around here, one sometimes filled with unexpected surprises." She took it from him and told him it was safe with her. "And by the way, did you notice the ficus tree looking a little better? It's not dropping the leaves, like it was last week."

"Why, yes it does," Elliott agreed.

CHAPTER 32

Dr. John Barringer stumbled onto the Royce campus on a rainy Friday afternoon, dressed in his favorite tie-dyed lab jacket. He wandered around the wet grounds, stopping to admire the newest shrubbery near the administration building. He trampled the brilliant ground cover on his way to smell the roses, the prize-winning hybrids. When he had inhaled enough of the vibrant fragrances, he sauntered to the bed of pansies. One by one, he popped off the blossoms that had been growing all spring for the festive graduation event, and stuffed them into his deep pockets.

"Ex—*cuuuse* me," Kelly Landis said, approaching him from behind, holding a dripping umbrella. "Are you picking those flowers?"

Barringer plucked another.

"Hey, I'm talking to you."

Barringer whipped around with a big grin. "Well, yes, I am." He held up a small bouquet.

"You're not to be taking those." She threw her hand on a hip. "We've been taking care of these flower beds all year and I'm not going to have someone like you walk up and destroy them."

"Oh, I'm very sorry." He looked at his bouquet, shaking his head, rainwater dripping off his nose. "I've never seen anything so beautiful as this. We just grow tumbleweeds, where I come from."

Kelly reached over and took the bouquet out of his hand. "Well, you're not taking these."

He stepped back.

"Did I see you put some into your pocket?"

"Yeah, a few." He grinned sheepishly, reached into his pocket, and pulled out a handful. Petals fluttered to the ground. "Here, want 'em?"

She looked him up and down. "Are you supposed to be here?"

He stuffed the flowers back into his pocket and leaned toward her. "Why, do they know I'm here?"

"Who?" she asked.

He turned his head from side to side; his ponytail whipped rainwater both ways. "Who?"

"That's what I'm asking—*who?*"

He crinkled up his face. "I thought you knew who."

Kelly stepped back and said angrily, "Who *are* you and what are you *doing* here?"

Barringer broke into a big grin; his mustache lifted on both sides and he offered his hand. "You can call me Easy Barring. I'm an old friend of Quintie's."

Kelly shook his hand and dropped it quickly. "Quintie?"

"Dr. Kingsley. I call him Quintie when he isn't lookin' and he *hates* it. That's why I do it all the time. Every chance I get."

"I didn't know Dr. Kingsley had any friends."

"Just me. We go way back. Went to school together here, years ago. I got out, but he's still here." He let out a belly laugh then composed himself. He looked at her with his eyes narrowed and leaned toward her. "He's a little whacko, lemme tell ya."

She looked at his jacket. "It looks to me like you're a little . . . well . . . "

"Off my rocker? Yeah. I am. I'm guilty of havin' obscure shades of genius. But the people—well, the people just see me as a curiosity on special occasions." Easy laughed. "Where can I find Ol' Quintie? Is he around here somewhere?"

"Over there, in Rothman." Kelly pointed to the building. "I'm heading that way now, if you want to follow me. Besides you should get out of this rain. You don't even have an umbrella."

"It's raining?" He looked up at the sky and blinked between the raindrops as they splattered on his face. "Well, looky there. Raining like a cow urinatin' on a flat rock."

Kelly shook her head and turned toward Rothman. Easy caught up and they walked across campus amidst the stares of a few students who were milling about. Easy's ponytail and colored lab jacket flapped as he strutted. He tried to describe, with great enthusiasm, what kinds of things he was working on in the temporary laboratory at the University of Texas. He moved his hands in all directions as he detailed his plans and ideas. Kelly had to jog to keep up with him. They reached Rothman and trotted through the halls. She left him at Kingsley's office and continued on her way. Easy knocked a nursery school rhythm on the door.

"Quintie. Are you in there, Quintie?" He banged louder. "Oh, *Quintie.*"

The door opened. "Well, look who's here. Easy B. Come in." Kingsley looked both directions down the hall and followed him inside. "I've told you not to call me that."

"I'm doing fine, just fine." Easy walked to the desk and picked up a paper. "Whatcha doin'?"

Kingsley shut the door. "Careful with those! You're getting everything all wet." Kingsley grabbed the paper out of Easy's hand and set it back on the stack. "I'm grading finals."

"Need any help?"

"No. I don't need any help." Kingsley looked him up and down. "Why are you so wet?"

"Because it's raining."

"Because it's raining isn't why you're wet." Kingsley shook his head. "Did you bring the leaves?"

"Yeah." Easy slapped his pocket. "Right here." He reached inside and pulled out a handful of the wet petals. "Oh, no! Must've traded them for these flowers, somewhere along the way." He pulled out a few more and let them drop on the desk. "No, wait. They must be in the other pocket. Yeah, here . . . " He smiled as he took out a large package of leaves.

"You carried it up here in your pocket?"

"No. I carried it in the duffle bag I've had since college. You remember the one. It's got those big flowers all over the sides. Everybody looks at it so funny. You should've seen 'em at the airport lookin' it over. They must've run it through X-ray a million times!"

Kingsley shook his head as he took the package from him. "Well, at least it's in one piece. I have a lab set up next door for you. Let's go and I'll get you started. Then I want you out of here, before you go and make a fool out of yourself."

Kingsley led the way down the hall. He opened the door to the main auditorium where half of his freshman class sat making up the final they had failed a few days earlier. He put his finger over his lips for Easy to keep quiet. They proceeded down the aisle, as the test-takers looked up at the intrusion. Easy stopped, stood over a female student, and looked at her test.

He snickered and pointed. "That's a dominant trait. Do ya see the letters? You got big X and little x. The big ones always win."

Kingsley whipped around and looked back up the aisle. "Easy, dammit! She's taking a test!"

"Oh, I'm sorry," he said to her, and whispered, "It's the dominance thing showin' up again. You can never get away from it."

"Thank you," she mouthed to him. The rest of the class took note of what he said and went back to check an answer or two.

Kingsley waited with his hand on his hip and his head cocked to the side for Easy to continue walking without bothering anyone else. Kingsley then turned and walked through the door, and the entire class waved to Easy as he bowed out of the room. The two continued to the lab without another word. Once inside, Kingsley gathered the flasks, beakers, and solvents Easy would need for the synthesis. He rechecked the small distillation system, the tubes and hoses, and fired up the Bunsen burners. Once he was sure Easy was operating the Rothman equipment properly, he went back to his office and continued grading final examinations.

Easy had free reign in the laboratory.

CHAPTER 33

Graduation at Royce was held outside on the well-manicured lawn, when it wasn't raining. At nine-thirty Saturday morning, it still hadn't rained, a great relief to the custodians who had worked most of the night setting up the place. The area was bordered by large leafy oak trees and landscaped with the school's own engineered tulips, iris, and azaleas. They blossomed in surprisingly lavish color for this late in the season. A sea of chairs stood in the freshly cut grass, facing the staged gazebo. The stage had a knee-high white thatched fence on three sides, and opened to the audience. A large trellis, decorated with flowering clematis, made an arch over the five important cushioned chairs. These were placed in a semi-circle on the stage and faced the audience. Huge speakers surrounded the seats, the wires were covered by green carpet.

Pairs of security people strolled the perimeter of the grounds, looking for anything suspect. Their trigger fingers rested on cans of mace, or on transmitters dialed to the city police. Once in awhile, one would speak to another from the talkie on his shoulder, while his partner scanned the surroundings with bare eyes, reporting nothing unusual. Guests began arriving for the occasion.

At ten o'clock, graduation was about to commence. Several hundred happy and excited spectators filled the place. At ten-fifteen, the school's conductor roused the alumni jazz band stationed near the stage. They began by playing a squeaky first tune, as guests laid claim to the prime seats. Proud parents tried to corral their children, who had been lost for four years, into just one more photo. Grandparents, who had begun this whole thing, waited patiently for their turn to get in the frame and stand right beside their graduating grandbabies. Siblings rolled their eyes at having to stand up straight, keep the hair out of their eyes, and please tuck that shirt in, for crying out loud!

The graduates, dressed in blue gowns and blue hats with white tassels, were told to quickly get in the rehearsal room and wait for the cue. Everything was ready but the sound system. The speakers cackled a few times as the harried audio people rushed around, unplugging and reconnecting cords and wires. Finally, after a few tap-taps on the microphone by the chief sound engineer, the system blasted to life. The anxious administrators breathed a concerted sigh of relief. The guests, standing around jabbering, took the clue and promptly filled the empty seats.

The promenade began with the musical number "Hoedown" instead of "Pomp and Circumstance," for the third year in a row. It was a Kingsley inspiration, which had begun when he challenged a student to prove that "Pomp and Circumstance" was an American original. It wasn't; it came from the old country. So he, a western American renaissance educator, came up with the idea to graduate his students to "Hoedown". No one complained. No one cared.

Elliott's grandparents sat right next to the aisle, in seats he had saved for them. They wore big smiles, the proudest grandparents in the audience. Then the graduates came. They paraded down the aisle smiling, waving, and nodding to those earthly saints who made this all possible. Some wore sneakers without socks under their robes. Someone rode in on a mountain bike. One guy was butt-naked, seen as clear as day from the back of his gown. Mrs. Chapman quickly turned her head away, but Mr. Chapman pointed with a laugh and slap on his knee.

The graduates took their seats in the front. The vice president welcomed the guests, made a few lousy jokes, and introduced the dean of the university, a bespectacled scholar who was never seen without a bowtie and a brown tweed coat with matching patches at the elbows. The man stood tall and smiled blandly.

Then President Whitman took over the podium and burst into a short liturgy. In a transformed, deep baritone voice, he acknowledged the difficulties each student had had at Royce, and reminded them of their duties now that they were the educated elite, which Cliff-Noted to one sentence: support your alma mater. He introduced one of their products, an alumnus who had made a real difference in the world. Ladies and gentlemen, the commencement speaker. This man, an Oregon State congressman now, walked importantly to the microphone. He said a few kind words to the dean and to the school he had graduated from—with honors, by the way—and went on and on about his own humble accomplishments. Sometime later, he dipped back into the present and offered some sage words to the new graduates: keep the faith, aim your hopes high, give generously to the school, blah, blah, blah.

President Whitman stood and roused the crowd to an ovation, directing it to the congressman whose message no one would ever remember. He thanked all the parents a third time for giving him their kids for four years, and reminded them, once again, that more than ninety percent would have outstanding jobs in whichever kind of field of industry they chose. A select few would even come back one day and teach the next generation at Royce University. He rambled on for another fifteen minutes then instructed the band to play the school chorus again.

When the band finished, President Whitman approached the podium again. He hung his head as he prepared to speak. "Ladies and gentlemen, I come to you with very difficult news." He looked up at the crowd who had become silent, then read from a note he had scribbled: "I have just received word earlier this morning that our valedictorian, Katrina Maria Das, was tragically killed in Bogotá, Columbia. She and her uncle were assassinated last night in their home, which was completely demolished during a raid. This attack was unprovoked, and comes during the tumultuous Columbian elections, which were held yesterday. Thousands of people are mourning their deaths today." He paused and looked up. He took his glasses off and scanned the crowd. "As many of you students know, Ms. Das was preparing to become a diplomat in international affairs. She wanted to work within her country to improve the lives of her people. She was a fine woman with such a promising future. She lived her life at Royce to better the world around her. Let us share our grief in a moment of silence." He closed his eyes. The audience bowed their heads. Elliott looked back and caught Kelly's eye. They both shook their heads in disbelief.

President Whitman coughed away from the microphone a few times, visibly moved. "In her place, we have asked another valedictorian, Dillon Bennett, to represent her and the graduating students on this memorable day."

Dillon sauntered to the podium, completely unaware of the art of stage striding. But he sailed through the first few sentences of his well-planned speech, his demeanor gaining excitement as he offered his colleagues a dull and unrealistic view of the world into which they would each be thrown. He spoke convincingly to those who didn't know him. When he finished, he nodded to President Whitman, who jumped to his feet, clearly impressed by his student's words.

President Whitman led the audience in another round of applause. As they quieted, he lowered the crowd to their chairs like a herd of puppets on strings. He directed his next few words to the group of graduates, venturing a few jokes and giving some very last admonitions before he called them each by name to receive their diploma. One by one, they made their way to the platform amid whoops and sobs from friends and relatives in the audience. President Whitman shook hands, said a nice word or two about how he enjoyed having them in school, and handed the million-dollar parchment to each excited graduate.

"You didn't read it, did you?" Elliott asked him as he shook his hand.

"*Sure* I did," Whitman said through smiling teeth.

"No, you didn't. Otherwise you wouldn't be handing this to me."

All President Whitman could do was smile back and nod.

Elliott took his diploma, opened it right on the stage, and read his name imprinted in gold leaf. He looked up and smiled at Whitman, then walked off, waving his education receipt to his grandparents.

Whitman stared after him for a moment as a line of graduates formed, waiting anxiously for their due reward. He called more names and they proceeded to the podium.

President Whitman continued through the alphabet. More hoots and hollers came from pockets in the crowd. Occasionally, a new grad showed the crowd something funny printed on his cap. But the bicycle never made it on stage, and the ass had to be covered.

After the Z's were called, the band played the school song for the last time. Everyone was invited for hors d'oeuvres and a fine selection of wine from the valley, donated by an alumnus' sumptuous vineyard. Immediately a line formed at the table, and the guests stacked their plates high. Small groups of well-groomed alumni began to cluster and chat about the old days, as they nibbled food they never would have bought with their own money. Parents talked among themselves until they got bored listening to each other brag about their child's tenure at Royce. Then they'd offer each their congratulations, and hurry off to tell a new group how much they enjoyed the food, but it wasn't anything like the party last week, Oh My Gosh.

President Whitman stood near the podium and shook hands with some alumni who were exaggerating how great their lives were. He listened and nodded, but his eyes were searching the crowd. The line grew and he couldn't get away. Parents, former faculty, and business partners joined in the schmoozing.

CHAPTER 34

Quinton Kingsley had made a call to the drug enforcement agency two hours ago. He reiterated to the chief narcotics officer that a known drug dealer was graduating and going to be carrying several kilos of ninety-nine percent pure cocaine. He told him this criminal had been heavily into drugs and had masterminded an elaborate methamphetamine lab at the Rothman Science Center earlier in the year. Of course the student vehemently denied it, saying he was crystallizing ascorbic acid. He denies everything. But this brilliant student can manufacture every kind of illegal drug imaginable. He knows how to do almost anything in the lab. He has to be stopped! He has to be apprehended. The largest drug deal in the Pacific Northwest was going down sometime during graduation!

The officer thanked Professor Kingsley for being such a willing informant, and promised a small battalion to be on guard before, during, and after the ceremony. All they needed was a signal and the identity of the perpetrator, and they would seize the criminal on the spot.

Kingsley dashed away from the herd of faculty, slipped into the graduation crowd, and went looking for Dr. Easy Barring.

Kelly Landis was well into an unbelievable tale about Rina Das. She had it going on. Her audience gathered in a wide-eyed semi-circle around her. It turned out that Rina worked for a dangerous rebel force in Columbia! They kidnap dignitaries, murder innocent civilians, and smuggle drugs all over the world. She was their secretary or something. The group probably manufactures drugs and sells contraband to the CIA, in exchange for the release of political prisoners. Can you *even* believe it? Some friend she turned out to be. Didn't tell anyone! For four *years* she never told anyone. She never even *planned* to finish school. They're criminals, all of 'em. Her death had been inevitable.

Elliott had his own group mesmerized as he tried to explain where he had been two weeks ago. He was simply working on his senior project for a company in Texas. " . . . okay. It wasn't Texas; it was Matamoros, Mexico, and the project was really for the rebels of Columbia. I'm not kidding. Turns out that Rina was the niece of the FARC general who was running for president of Columbia, and he had been waiting *years* to steal a plant terminator protocol, hidden away in a clinic in Mexico. For years, this clinic has been treating locals for deadly toxins that flaked off genetic foods; it was across the border, away from U.S. government detection and regulation. No one knew a thing about it except this cool red-haired guy who ran the clinic, an undercover doctor. Well, he wasn't a real doctor, but he went to Royce. That's right, Royce. He knows all about senior projects. So we make copies of the Terminator when this fat, ex-employee from the company that owned the clinic barges in and shoots the FARC dude who came to assist me. *Big* mistake. We had to get out, fast! So while we're trying to leave, the fat guy pulls out some tomato leaves that have been engineered into cocaine and starts chewing on 'em. Cocaine! Cocaine the Columbians were smuggling into the United States. So we get the hell out of there, because the FARC rebels and the Mexico City police are converging on the clinic. Then I come up with this idea of leaving the cocaine and a note at the border, with the names of a coupla guys from the company."

"You're so full of shit, Elliott," said Dillon, the newly appointed class representative. "You just have to come up with one more story, don't you? You're always trying to do pretend you're doing something worthwhile." He stood holding a plastic cup of punch, looking around for agreement. "You're pathetic."

"What part didn't you understand?" Elliott asked.

"None of it. You're making the whole thing up."

"Sounds pretty wild, Elliott. You gotta admit," said a Dillon-sider.

"That's what happened. What's your problem?"

"Tomato cocaine? Come on," said another.

"Don't believe me, then. It doesn't matter."

"I might believe you if it sounded close to reality. But it doesn't."

They all looked at him, shaking their heads.

"Well, congratulations, *Mister* Chapman!" crowed President Whitman, approaching him with his hand extended. He had finally broken away from his admirers but they were not far behind him, the pied piper. Elliott's friends dispersed when they saw the entourage coming.

"I didn't catch what you said to me on the platform. Something about your project."

"I said you must not have had time to read it, as busy as you are."

"Of course I did. I think your project is very honorable, but you make some pretty serious accusations."

"It's all referenced."

"That's a matter of opinion."

"You said I could do it on anything. It was an essay."

"Your opinion doesn't make a senior science project." He took his glasses off and narrowed his eyes. "Why'd you do it, Elliott?"

"So I could graduate."

Whitman studied his face. "That all? You're not going to do anything else with it?"

"Oh, Dr. Whitman . . . " called an admirer.

Whitman leaned close to him and said, "I don't want this going anywhere. Understand? You met all your requirements and graduated today. Let's call it even."

"I sent it to the *Cambridge Review* yesterday."

"Dr. Whitman, I want you to meet my darling mother." A graduate pulled her excited mother by the arm into his presence.

"What a very touching speech, Dr. Whitman . . . "

Whitman shot Elliott a furious look before he put his glasses on, then turned to greet the students as they approached with their parents. He put on his President's smile and posture, and appeared to be genuinely interested in meeting some for the very first time. He shook their hands and they burst into pleasantries. Others came and joined the group. Elliott was drawn into conversation about President Whitman's moving speech. And Dillon Bennett—can you believe he gave that wonderful oration, with only three hours to prepare? Leave it to Dillon to pull off something so amazing, just amazing. A few more students and guests joined the group.

Easy was jabbering with a large group of students he had befriended. He had on a suit that Kingsley made him wear, which he agreed to put on only if he could wear his sandals with it. Used to do that all the time in Oregon. It's what they do.

"*There* you are!" Kingsley approached Easy and his new group of admirers.

" . . . and so he says, 'I'll take it. I'll take the buefie, but put the worm on the side.'"

The entire group erupted in loud laughter. Easy bent forward and slapped his knees a few times, laughing like it was the funniest thing in the world.

"What's so funny? What'd I miss?" Kingsley asked Easy. He turned to the happy group to be let in on the punch line.

"Ohhh," Easy said as he stood straight, "it was *so funny.*" He wiped his eyes. "You should have seen the look on his face!"

"Go *away*," Kingsley said to everyone, flapping his hands at them. "Go find your parents, or something." He shooed them off and turned to Easy. "I've been looking all over for you. What're you *doing*, talking to these students?"

Easy finished laughing. "I was just telling them some Texas jokes. You know, they all seem so uptight and everything, and well, they just graduated! Had 'em bustin' seams."

"Well *stop* it!"

Easy let out a sigh and tried to contain himself.

"Do you *have* it? *The package?*"

"Yeah. Right here." Easy reached to the ground and picked up the bright yellow box. It was decorated with flower petals taped haphazardly on top.

"Good. Now he's right over there . . . " Kingsley pointed, looking at Elliott. "Go congratulate him and give it to him. *Then walk away!* Don't stay and talk, and don't ask him any questions. You got that?" He jabbed Easy in the chest.

"Yep." Easy finally found where Kingsley was pointing, and saw Elliott talking with a female.

"I'm going to make the call ten seconds after you leave— and you better have cleared out."

"Consider it done."

Easy weaved his way through the crowd, holding the graduation present with the afterglow of a smile on his face.

CHAPTER 35

Elliott and Kelly were talking about Rina's tragic death. She was to graduate today, four years after they had all met in freshman biology. It just didn't seem possible. Gone were the classroom debates with the professors she usually bested. Gone was the laughter at Leo's pub, eating food that had landed on the wrong plate. Gone were all the discussions about third world politics, and her ideas about how to change them. Gone were the genetic protocols that were to change her country and its position in the world.

"Hello there, Elliott." Easy waltzed up to them. "Congratulations on your graduation, and all."

Elliott looked at him, shocked. "Dr. Barringer! What're you doing here?"

"Thought I'd come up to watch you graduate."

"Me? Why would you do that?"

"Cause I like ya, that's why." He smiled and held out the package. "I got ya a little something. Here, take it."

Elliott took the package from him. "What is it?" He looked up at him.

"Just a little something. Thought you might enjoy it." Easy stuck his hands in his pants pockets, turned with a smile, and nodded at Kingsley.

Kelly reached over and picked at the flower petals. "Oh, these are pretty . . . " She stopped and looked up quickly. "Where'd you get these?"

"This is Kelly Landis," Elliott introduced. "Kelly, this is Dr. John Barringer."

"Easy, please." Easy reached out and shook her hand. "Have we met? You look familiar, like someone I'd see in a parade."

Kelly smiled. "Yeah, we met earlier. The flower destroyer. Nice to meet you again, Easy."

"Oh yeah, we were talkin' about your flowers, and then you showed me to Quintie's office."

"Quintie?" Elliott squinted at Kelly. "Quinton?"

"Yeah," she said, laughing. "We call him Quintie now. It beats Old Furrowed Brow, doesn't it? A little more personal."

"Old Furrowed Brow? Ha—that's radiant." Easy burst out laughing. Elliott joined in. Finally, after Easy settled down, he launched into a barrage of stories about old Quintie when they were roommates at Royce, about a hundred years ago. He wasn't the freakin tight-shirt conservative he is nowadays. Now he wants to impregnate the minds of his students with his ideas, like that's gonna help anyone. They're just opinions and nobody cares about 'em. He's turned into such a bore.

During a breath, Easy looked up at Kingsley standing thirty feet away with crossed arms, looking furious. He made a graphic motion with his hand across his throat a few times. Easy nodded.

"Okay," Easy said, looking around. "I gotta go." He turned and walked away.

"That was strange," Kelly said, smiling as she watched him cut through the crowd. "What a strange, strange man."

Elliott looked at the package. He shook it near his ear. "I wonder what this is."

"Open it," Kelly said, reaching for it.

He pulled it back from her. "I will, just give me a second." Elliott began to unwrap the paper. He peeled off a corner and let it fall to the ground. He peeled off another. Kelly grabbed the rest of it and ripped it all the way off. Elliott lifted the flap of cardboard and looked inside.

Kingsley didn't respond to Easy, who was standing beside him. He whispered loudly into his phone, "He's off to the North side. The one holding the box. He's going to give it to the girl. There, down at his feet, is a pile of yellow paper."

Suddenly a whistle sounded and the three closest officers rushed from all directions to surround them. The drug-sniffing dog barked wildly as the rest of the police hurried to the scene. One officer grabbed the box. Another pulled Elliott's arms behind his back, cuffing his wrists.

"What's going on?" Elliott yelled.

"You have the right to remain silent . . . " The officer read him his rights.

Everyone in the audience stopped their chatter and turned to watch. Elliott's grandmother dropped into the nearest chair. Friends and classmates pushed closer, shaking their heads, gawking. Kelly stepped back as more officers converged. The dog barked at the suspect.

"Well, Elliott," Kingsley said with a toothy smile, walking tall in his new dark suit. "Looks like it's finally over for you."

"Finally over," Easy repeated, following close behind.

"What? What's this all about?" Elliott looked up at his professor, dumbfounded.

"The drugs!" Kingsley said, laughing. "You've been manufacturing drugs in the laboratory. You didn't think I'd find out about it, but I know. I know everything. That's pure cocaine in the box, isn't it?"

"I don't know what you're talking about." Elliott looked at the box the officer held.

"This," the officer said, dipping his hand into the box. He let the white powder run between his fingers. "Looks like the purest cocaine I've ever seen."

"*You!*" Elliott yelled at Easy. "*You* gave that box to me!" He turned and looked helplessly to Kingsley.

"You can't do this!" Kelly screamed, pointing to Easy. She turned to an officer. "That man gave it to him just a minute ago. I saw the whole thing." An officer grabbed her arms and held her back.

"What's going on here?" President Whitman asked as he broke through the crowd. "Elliott—" He looked at him, then at Kingsley. "Drugs," he said quietly. He turned back to Elliott, shaking his head. "You were carrying drugs."

"No, Dr. Whitman. I *wasn't*. You gotta believe me!"

"I am so ashamed of you," Whitman said, still shaking his head.

"It's very ingenious, really," Easy said. "I had no idea that you could make cocaine out of tomato leaves. What would ya call it, ah, tomato surprise, or something like that?" He looked at Kingsley for agreement.

"No," Kingsley said, cackling now. "I'd call it a tomato-cocaine puree—which translates into a one-way ticket to the slammer for a long, long time." He looked back and laughed at Easy.

The officers gathered their suspect and began walking him to the van.

Suddenly Elliott stopped and pulled away from the officer holding him. "Just a minute," he said to him. He turned around and looked at the shocked crowd. Kingsley and Easy were smirking at each other.

"What did you say, Quintie? Tomato-cocaine puree?"

"Yeah," Kingsley laughed, then stopped. "And don't you call me that again. You made it out of tomato leaves."

"But that's not possible."

"It sure *is* possible. You isolated the cocaine molecule and jammed the sequence into the DNA of the tomato plant. Then you converted it into a cocaine hydrochloride salt. Isn't that correct, Dr. Barringer?"

"That's correct." Easy smiled, nodding his head.

"I read all your instructions. I'm giving you an 'A' on them, by the way." Kingsley laughed loudly for the first time anyone had ever witnessed.

"You *just* converted it into the hydrochloride?" Elliott tried to pull away from the officers, only to be held tighter.

Kingsley contained himself enough to answer, "No, *you* did. It was probably three hours ago that I saw you sneaking around in the lab. You just had to make one more batch before you left for good." He shook his head. "Such a shame . . . "

"So if I just made it this morning, where did I get the leaves?"

"Beats the shit outta me. Probably had them flown up in a cheap tin airplane by your ol' buddy, Martino." Kingsley wiped his eyes and said, "It's perfect. No one's going to suspect a drug deal at graduation"—he wagged his finger at him—"but I had you figured out. It took me awhile, you sneaky little bastard, but you're finished now."

"Let's go," the chief narcotics officer said. "Take him away."

The entourage whisked Elliott toward the police van. The crowd watched in silence. Elliott's grandfather tried to go after them, but a crowd control officer held him back.

"Hold it. Just a minute." Elliott resisted the officers again. "Just a minute. I need to ask Dr. Kingsley one more thing."

The officers stopped with him but held him tight.

"Really, just one more question."

The chief nodded to the officers and they let him turn around. Elliott walked toward Whitman, Kingsley, and Easy, who were talking among themselves with the smear of relief spread across their faces. As they saw him coming toward them, they stopped abruptly and watched him approach.

Elliott stepped in front of them with an officer at each side. "Easy brought the leaves up here. He made the final synthesis in the lab, so the cocaine wouldn't be detected."

"No, I didn't," Easy said with a forced grin. "I flew up here to see you graduate."

"No, you didn't. You flew up here with the tomato leaves right after they were washed—didn't you?"

"No. *You did*," Kingsley yelled.

"All right, say I did."

"You *did*! You brought the leaves up from Texas. Go look. Your drug apparatus is set up, and the lab is still a mess."

"Oh yeah, now I remember. I brought the leaves up in my carry-on. Then I went to the lab and synthesized the cocaine earlier this morning."

"Of course you did." Kingsley said with a laugh. "You are the bright one, Elliott Chapman."

Elliott looked at the officer holding the box. "That's not cocaine. Those are processed tomato leaves that *used* to be cocaine. But it's not cocaine." He looked up at Kingsley.

The officer looked at the box.

"Test it," Elliott said. "Have your dog sniff it."

The officers looked at each other. The chief narcotics officer stepped forward. "Get the dog over here. Let her have a sniff."

The officer walked his dog to the box. The dog stopped and dropped her nose inside. She sniffed a few times then looked up at her master, wagging her tail.

"What's wrong, Lady?" He patted her head.

"Bring the kit!" the chief yelled. "Let's run it through."

"It's not cocaine." Elliott said again, looking at the disbelieving trio.

Two officers rushed to the van and grabbed the toolbox of a test kit. The chief dumped a cupful of the powder into the small funnel. The white powder disappeared and everyone watched.

Elliott smiled at Kingsley. "Quintie, the cocaine molecule disintegrated. Now all that's left is the white powder of the hydrochloride salt."

"There's nothing here," said the chief, dropping the box on the ground. The white powder spilled out and made a white patch on the lawn. He turned to the officer holding Elliott. "There's nothing here to investigate. Dog's not responding to it. It's not converting the tester. It's just a mineral of some sort. This was a false alarm. Let him go."

The officer released Elliott.

"But there's *got* to be!" Kingsley cried as he ran up, dropped to his knees, and tried to salvage the rest of the powder spilt on the grass. He scooped it up with the box flap. "It's got to be here."

Elliott stood over his professor. "Easy brought the leaves up here right after they were washed, so that the cocaine wouldn't be detected. But the molecule is too unstable. It disintegrated when his bag went through X-ray security at the airport. You have to turn it into a cocaine hydrochloride salt right after it's washed. If you don't do it right away, the molecule disintegrates."

"What . . . ?" Kingsley sifted through the powder, looking at Easy.

Elliott rubbed his wrists. "You should have known that, Quintie. It's not always chemistry and mathematics. You forgot about physics. Physics, Quintie, is the application of mathematics. You said so yourself. I was there for that lecture."

Kingsley turned angrily to Easy, his brow deeply furrowed, the surface veins in his neck and face swelled. Easy turned quickly, excused himself, and pushed his way through the crowd. "Easy! *Dammit!*" Kingsley tore after him. The officers retreated and the crowd dissipated.

Kelly walked up to Elliott and wrapped her arms around him. "How did you *ever* do that?"

"Do what?"

"How did you know about all that?"

"I went to Royce University. Even graduated. I spent a lot of time in Dr. Quinton Kingsley's class."

"Yeah, I was in his class, too. But what he said was that chemistry and math were the only pure sciences. That's what he said. He didn't say anything about physics."

"He didn't?"

She smiled at him, looking up into his eyes.

His grandparents hurried over to them, Mr. Chapman ahead of his wife. He demanded to know what the heck kind of projects they were doing at this here, doggone school. Mrs. Chapman calmly told her husband things had changed since they'd gone to school fifty years ago, and if he'd have kept up with Elliott's homework once in awhile, he would know what was going on. And if the school required projects like these, well then, he should just go ahead and do them. Stop asking all kinds of questions, for goodness sakes, unless you're going to help.

The four walked across the lawn together. There were several groups of graduates chatting among themselves, oblivious to the action. Another student called out to President Whitman, interrupting his sorrowful contemplation. It was the senator's son, and he wanted President Whitman's expert opinion on something, as did a number of new alumni who were fast forming another throng of admiration.

Whitman was going to be wrapped up for a long time. Kingsley was last seen running to the Rothman Science Center, yelling for someone named Easy Dammit.

CHAPTER 36

Kelly held the door open to President Whitman's waiting room, and in walked Elliott, carrying a bushy, potted ficus tree. He set it down next to the leafless tree and stepped away. Kelly quickly went to her knees and began coddling their intertwined branches with her fingers, talking to them like an overprotective parent plotting for a budding relationship.

Not fully understanding husbandry or codependency issues, Elliott continued on his way past Whitman's busy secretary. He pointed as he walked by. "I brought you a new tree for your waiting room."

She looked up. "Oh, well, thank you." She saw Kelly digging in the pot.

"Now you can get that old diseased thing out of there."

"Yes. No one seems to know what's wrong with it."

"Probably been trimmed once too many times."

"Yes, probably." She smiled. "Well, this may be the last time I see you in here. I've gotten used to you being here every week or two."

"Yeah, I've gotten used to seeing you, too." Elliott smiled and walked inside Whitman's office.

Whitman looked over his glasses and maneuvered them off his face. "Come in, Elliott, and have a seat. Did you have a nice vacation?"

Elliott made his way through the room and sat in front of Whitman. "Yeah, it was all right. A week wasn't near long

enough, especially with my grandfolks. I can't keep up with
'em."

"Well, I'm glad you were able to get away. We all need
time away." Whitman sported a smile for a moment, then
made it disappear.

"I got your message as soon as I got back, Dr. Whitman. Is
there something else I need to do? I thought I finished
everything." Elliott sat upright in the chair.

Whitman glared at him. "*Cambridge Review* called me last
week."

"They called?"

"They received your little report. The one you turned in as
your project."

Elliott stared back.

"Problem is, Elliott, they can't print it without the
oversight of a faculty member from the university. You don't
have one—and you won't be getting one. They're sending it
back."

Elliott sat motionless.

Whitman leaned forward. "That report would have caused
a very serious setback to this institution, and probably cost the
school thousands. Do you realize that? Did you think for a
moment what kind of accusations you made?"

"Well, actually—"

"Personal accusations and your ethical opinions don't
belong in a professional journal."

"No, well, first I developed a moral case, then I made some
ethical statements—"

"It was neither. Your morals or ethics—whatever you call
them—are not mature enough for you to display them
publicly, and besides, no one cares what you think. You're a
new graduate with no real life experiences, and you won't be
taken seriously for a number of years. You remember that.
We're all just lucky this thing didn't get published."

"You asked for a report on anything."

"Not one that could put Royce University in jeopardy! You
don't realize. I would've been in a hot room all summer,

trying to explain your little tirade to the Board of Trustees."
Whitman spoke the last three words with strong diction and
they resonated throughout the room.

Upon hearing it, Elliott slowly nodded his head as he
looked at Whitman, and all he could do was agree with the
man, the president of Royce University, like he always did. He
had nothing to say.

Watching Elliott cower in his chair, Whitman relaxed his
expression and drew in a long breath. He had learned that
when he spoke with intensity and followed with a relaxed
statement, his words had more impact. He glanced down at his
desk then back up with a smile for Elliott. "I want you to get
rid of any evidence of that report that you have. Am I clear?"

"Yes sir."

"And there will be no mention of this to anyone. No one
knows anything about this, and I want to make sure it stays
that way. Are you reading me?"

"No one knows?"

"Nobody." Whitman shifted in his chair. "Now, about your
project . . . I've been arguing with myself about what to do.
What do you think, Elliott? Theoretically, you should have to
repay your scholarship money. That was in your admissions
contract. But I don't know . . . you seem to understand what
I'm saying." He stopped abruptly and Elliott responded with a
slow nod. "Good. And since you're going to keep your word
about this"—Whitman went into relaxed mode again and
mustered up a prophetic smile—"I'm not going to make you
repay the money, any money. I believe I'm giving you a
significant break here, Elliott, and I know you realize it."
Whitman looked to him for recognition.

"Yes. I do."

"Good. I want you to leave Royce on good terms, Elliott.
Everyone leaves here on good terms."

"Of course." Elliott thought for a moment. "Does Dr.
Kingsley know anything about this?"

"No," Whitman said quickly.

"But he's on the scholarship committee. He agreed to this?"

Whitman tapped his glasses on his desk and glanced up at Elliott. "Dr. Kingsley had to leave Royce. He doesn't serve on any committees here, anymore."

"You fired him?"

"No. It was more of a mutual agreement that he leave."

"You're kidding."

"No. I'm not. He outgrew his position here, so we both decided it was best for him to move on. In fact, he just finished up yesterday. He's been in and out all week, clearing his things. Was even in here a few times, asking about you."

"He was?"

"Yeah." Whitman chuckled.

"Why? Was he mad?"

"Oh, no, Quinton never stays mad. But he's been through a lot the last couple of weeks. I don't believe I need to tell you. Anyway, he wanted to know what you've decided to do next year. That's Dr. Kingsley for you; always got to know about his students."

"Really."

"Well," Whitman's smile faded as he pushed himself away from his desk and stood, "I've got some work to do before my four o'clock tee time."

Elliott stood in response.

Whitman reached out his hand and Elliott shook it. "It's been nice having you here as a student, Elliott. I'm happy things turned out the way they have, and I wish you the best in your future."

Elliott dropped his hand. "Thanks." He turned and quickly walked into the waiting room.

Kelly clipped the last lower branch on the old tree and placed it on the pile without turning to look at him. "What'd he say?"

"He said we should go to Leo's and grab a sandwich."

"No, really." She turned and looked up at him.

"Really. It was nothing."

Kelly stood and put her small pruning shears in a large pocket and admired her work. "See? Doesn't that look better? They're going to get along just fine." She turned to him with a questioning look. "When you said this tree had *leavious bottomous* disease, I didn't know what you meant, 'cause I never heard the term before. But now it makes sense."

"I know. Some things just make sense." He smiled feebly and taking her by the arm, led her through the room.

Elliott opened the door of Leo's Pub and let Kelly walk in first. He reached for her hand and they stopped and surveyed the room together.

"Be with ya in a minute," said the waitress, cracking her gum.

"Where's Leo?" Elliott asked her. "He's not on his perch."

The waitress reached under the counter and picked up two menus. "Where *you* been? He hasn't been here for last two weeks." She chewed her gum a few times. "He's been on vacation ever since school ended."

"Vacation? *Leo?*"

"Yeah, I'm running the place till he gets back. *If* he ever comes back."

"Where'd he go?"

"Said he was going fishing somewhere down on the Mexican Sea." She wrinkled her forehead. "Never heard of a Mexican Sea."

"Gulf of Mexico."

"Whatever. Says his brother runs a fishing charter down there, somewhere. Called his boat *Easy Pickins*, is what I remember. Guess he just started the thing and didn't have any customers, so he called Leo to come down and be one of 'em." She shrugged her shoulders and tapped the menus in her hand.

"Barring," Elliott said to her.

"No, tuna I think," said the waitress. "Do you wanna eat, or talk about fishing?"

Elliott looked and smiled at Kelly.

"Come on, follow me," the waitress said as she turned. "Let's find you two lovebirds a table." She walked past a few patrons then stopped and tapped the menus on a table. "This be all right?"

"Yes, this is fine," Kelly said as she slid into the bench.

"You both want the special?"

"Yeah," Elliott said.

"All right. Be right back." She turned and walked to the kitchen.

Elliott sat into the bench and looked at Kelly, who was looking past him to the next table. "Who is that?" Kelly whispered and pointed discreetly. "Right behind you."

Elliott slowly turned around and looked. The man's elbows were propped on the table and his hands held his head up. Off to the side sat a half bottle of beer, horseshoed by a pair of square-framed eyeglasses.

"It's Kingsley," she whispered eagerly.

Elliott turned around quickly and looked at her. "It is."

"I've never seen him here. I wonder what he's doing."

Elliott turned and faced the man directly. "Dr. Kingsley?"

The professor slowly raised his head, revealing a tattered Royce University T-shirt, which read 'ACADEMICS' in large block letters. His disheveled black hair covered his dark eyebrows and his face sported several days' of whisker stubble. "What . . . ?" He put on his glasses and looked at Elliott.

"What are you doing?" Elliott asked.

"I just ate lunch," Kingsley said slowly.

"No, I mean . . . you look like you've been sitting there all week."

"I have. I'm on *vacation*." He squinted at Elliott.

Kingsley said this so challengingly that Elliott turned around rather quickly and fixed his eyes on Kelly. He was visibly moved, and realized at that moment that he was not under the auspices of Royce University any longer. He couldn't even claim a seat in the back row. He just looked forward and waited.

Kingsley didn't say anything, and after a time he took his glasses off and rubbed his bloodshot eyes. Taking this as a harmless gesture, Kelly stood, walked up to his table, and slid into the bench across from him.

Elliott stayed facing the front of the pub, hoping for someone to come in and rescue him.

Kingsley attempted a smile as he looked at Kelly. "Took me a whole day to get those worms cleaned out of my office. Pretty good project you had there."

"Thank you." Kelly looked away, embarrassed. "It was all I could do."

"You went beyond my requirements." Kingsley looked around at Elliott, sitting behind her. "Well . . . Elliott, Elliott. My wonder student, Elliott. I've been looking for you."

"I heard," Elliott said without turning. "Whitman told me."

"Oh he did? Good old Whitman. Likes to talk about people. First he fires me, then—"

"Fires you!" Kelly interrupted. "Whitman fired you? When?"

"Oh, last week. I don't really remember, exactly."

Elliott turned around quickly. "He said you agreed to leave."

"Yeah, he'd say that, wouldn't he? That's what old Whitman would say. That's the way it goes in academics. You can say what ever you want, as long as you don't step on administration toes. Doesn't matter if you can deliver brilliant lectures . . . " Kingsley's voice cracked with despair. "I always held 'em spellbound, didn't I? And I know they were all impressed with my humor."

Elliott stood and sat next to Kelly, and they both watched Kingsley.

"I spoon-fed the fledglings! From beginning to end, I helped 'em understand biology so they could go on and make something of themselves." Kingsley rolled the edge of his bottle around the table and stared at it. He kept his head down and muttered, "I don't have any students. Never *been* without students."

"You'll get another job," Kelly said and quickly added, "What about all of your consulting jobs? You're paid well for your consulting."

"I don't consult anymore." He stopped the bottle and looked at Elliott. "It's all over. The biggest biological venture of the century."

"What?" Elliott looked at him quizzically.

"Steven Sloan was killed, shot dead two weeks ago."

"He *what*?" Elliott's mouth sprung open.

"Martino's men finally caught up with him. Yeah, that's right, Martino's band of thugs. They followed him home one night and gunned him down, right there in his long driveway."

"What are you talking about?" Elliott shook his head slowly.

Kingsley looked at him with an obtuse smile. "It was Steve who had Martino killed. He hired some of his own contractors to invade Martino's Columbian compound because the little man wouldn't give back the Terminator after he'd paid him for it. You gave the Terminator to Martino, didn't you? Steve told me you did."

"I was threatened!" Elliott protested.

"Understandable. That's how Martino worked. That's how all those guys work. Always making deals and reneging on 'em. Well, Martino asks Steve for a few million dollars, and promises to give back the Terminator. Steve sends the first installment, but Martino doesn't give it to him. Instead, Martino says he wants another five million. So Steve gets irate and calls his contractors down, to steal the thing back. Made a mess of the place and they didn't even find it. Ha!"

"So how did you know all this?" Elliott asked. "You weren't even down there."

"Easy told me. He overheard Steve talking about it, got all nervous, and calls me up, wanting to know what he should do. He thought they were after him. They weren't after him. They were after Steve. Well, you know Easy . . . old Dr. Paranoid." Kingsley paused for a moment in thought. He looked at

Elliott. "You know, he was the one that planted the snow on you at graduation. I hoped he wouldn't do it."

Elliott nodded.

Kingsley quickly continued, "Well, he up and left . . . everything. He's delusional, fishing for sea catfish in his very own Mexican Sea. Ha! I guess he gets the last laugh. Figures." He smiled at Elliott and let out a laugh. "You too . . . the last laugh."

"No." Elliott shook his head. "I wouldn't actually say that."

Kingsley peered into him. "What are you going to do? You've got everything going for you. Med school? A Doctorate somewhere? What, Elliott? What are you going to do with yourself?"

Without thinking, Elliott said, "I'm going to get your job back. I can get it back for you."

Kingsley's mouth dropped open. "What? How you gonna do that?"

"Well, there's this little project that old Whitman made me do, but it's not exactly done yet. I call it the Procrustes Project. It was *accep*ted for publication."

"Procrustes?"

"Yeah. Go to his office and tell him that we've just been talking about stretching appendages or lopping them off, and he'll probably flush bright red. No . . . just mention Procrustes. Wait for him to stammer around a little—he will. Then tell him that you're going to take the project over un*less* a professorship is available. Go tell him that right now while it's still fresh in his memory."

Kingsley stared at him a moment. He broke out in a big stubbly grin. "You can't think beyond the present, can you? You're always stuck on the moment. You always gotta figure out the moment."

Elliott smiled back. "You know, actually that's funny. I had a professor I'd listen to once in awhile, whenever I was in his class. He used to say there were gaps in time that lead to events in life."

"That's asinine."

"That's what a professor said once, in a lecture a long time ago. So what I figured was, I'd spend more time in the gaps than I ever would in the events. And if I could just get through the gaps, well, then, I'd get through the events."

"Really."

"Yeah," Elliott said.

Dr. Kingsley raised his eyebrows. "You must have been a good student to believe things like that."

"I was all right."

"Yeah, you were. You'll do all right." Kingsley slid to the side of the bench.

"You want to know something, Dr. Kingsley?"

Kingsley stood, itching to leave. "What? I gotta go." He hesitated, then turned.

Elliott called after him, "I was just going to say something brilliant about you."

"I know you were." Kingsley said over his shoulder. "And you would've been right!"

The waitress brought their food, which matched exactly what they had ordered, and had actually ever since Leo took his vacation. Kelly and Elliott sat on the same side of the bench and watched Dr. Quinton Kingsley hurry out of the eatery.

AUTHOR'S NOTE

I have used the genetic ideas of David Pearce and BLTC Research and referenced "The Golden Age of Cocaine Wine" by John Groff. Most GMO information was gleaned from The Ecologist and Townsend Newsletter for Doctors and Patients.

Dr. Jim Warner, my chiropractor, adjusted the manuscript and me many times, and made us both better.

Gina Ochsner taught me in gracious terms, how to think and write about the people in this story.

Thanks to Charity Heller-Hogge for her editing.

I am grateful to my wife for her ability to put up with this writing absurdness and I thank my three brilliant kids for listening at my knee in rapt attention and not rolling their eyes in my view.

If you are interested in my next project, please visit me at plind.com

Thank you for your interest.

Peter Lind was born in Jerusalem, Jordon to missionary parents. After completing his undergraduate studies in Virginia, he graduated with a bachelor's degree in biology. A few years later at a Los Angeles, California University, he earned a Doctorate of Chiropractic. Knowing the beauty and natural wonders of the Pacific Northwest, Dr. Lind opened a chiropractic practice in the Mid-Willamette Valley of Oregon. This is where he still maintains an active practice enjoying the life built with his wife

Photography by Palmer's Studio • Keizer, Oregon

Dr. Peter Lind

and three children. Over the years of serving the needs of his patients, Dr. Lind developed a diverse interest in health and wellness issues. His extensive study of nutrition opened the "Pandora's Box" of genetic engineering. Study of reliable well documented information has led Dr. Lind to come to a single conclusion; the most profound challenge to our health is already well in-grained into our every day lives. When it comes to genetic engineering, we may only be able to see the tip of an tremendously dangerous iceberg on the hazy horizon of our future. "Improvements" to our food supply, once thought of as miracles, have already begun to effect lives around the globe. *Baron Harvest* was written to shine light on a dark subject. This work of fiction begins to pry open the very real and grim workings of a baron establishment: Government agencies, medical professionals, diverse corporations and individuals profit on a carefully planned misleading of a trusting public. A well-financed effort is sustained everyday, desperately trying to keep the lid on a pot of an explosive conspiracy, which has made mankind the ultimate Guinea Pig.